The Chancellor and the Citadel

Maria Capelle Frantz

strange and amazing
inquiry@ironcircus.com   www.ironcircus.com

Publisher
C. Spike Trotman

Editor
C. Spike Trotman

Print Technician
Rhiannon Rasmussen-Silverstein

Published by
Iron Circus Comics
329 W. 18th Street Suite 604
Chicago, IL 60616
IronCircusComics.com

First edition: November 2018

Print Book ISBN: 978-1-945820-26-7

10 9 8 7 6 5 4 3 2 1

Printed in China

THE CHANCELLOR AND THE CITADEL

Names: Frantz, Maria, author.
Title: The Chancellor and the Citadel / Maria Capelle Frantz.
Description: [Chicago, Illinois] : Iron Circus Comics, [2018] | Interest age level: 008-012. | Summary: "In a dystopian magical world, a community's sworn protector struggles to keep a fracture in the populace from breaking out into violence."--Provided by publisher.
Identifiers: ISBN 9781945820267
Subjects: LCSH: Insurgency--Comic books, strips, etc. | Women heads of state--Comic books, strips, etc. | Peace officers--Comic books, strips, etc. | CYAC: Insurgency--Cartoons and comics. | Kings, queens, rulers, etc.--Cartoons and comics. | Peace officers--Cartoons and comics. | LCGFT: Dystopian comics. | Fantasy fiction. | Graphic novels.
Classification: LCC PZ7.7.F7254 Cl 2018 | DDC [Fic]--dc23

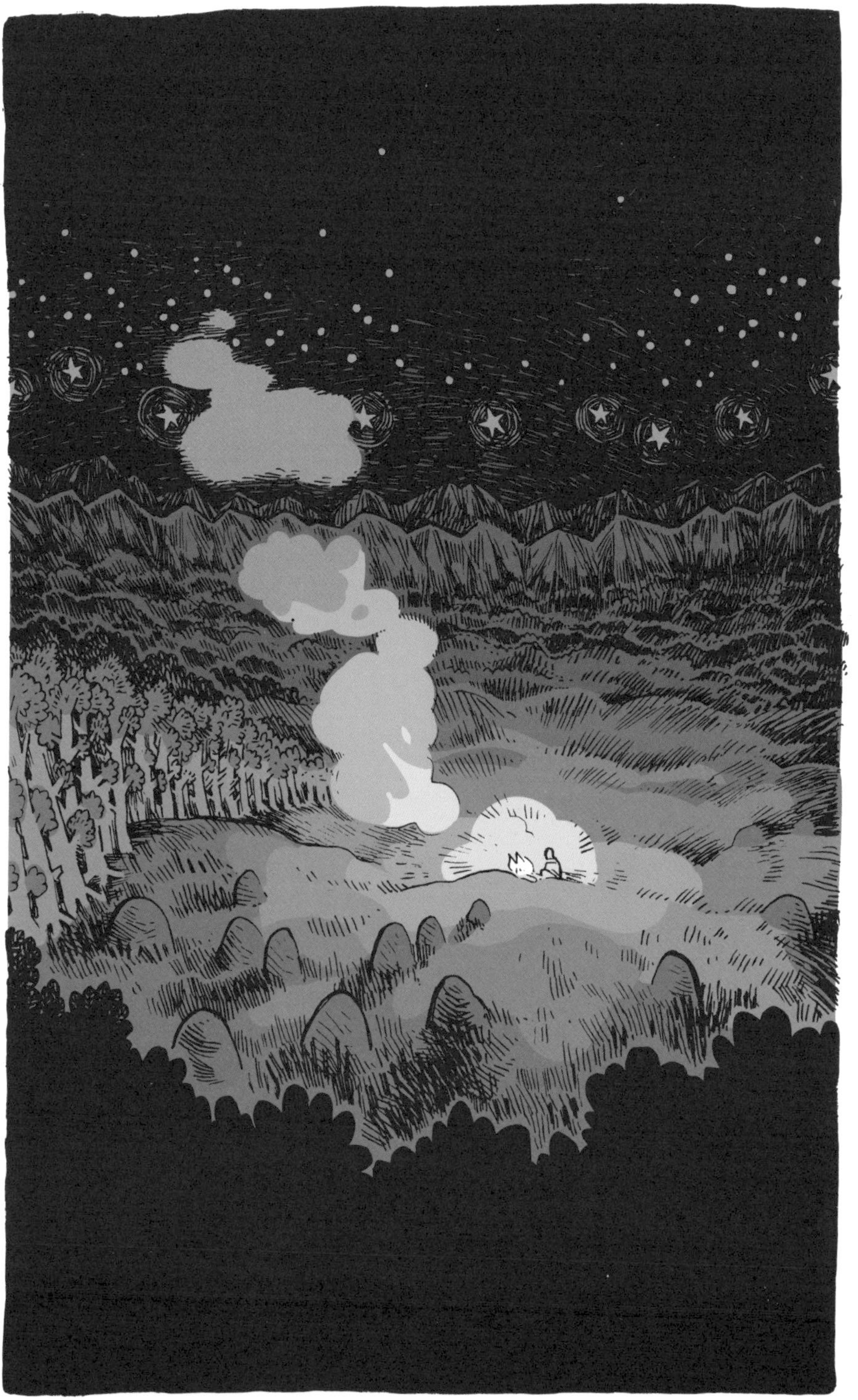

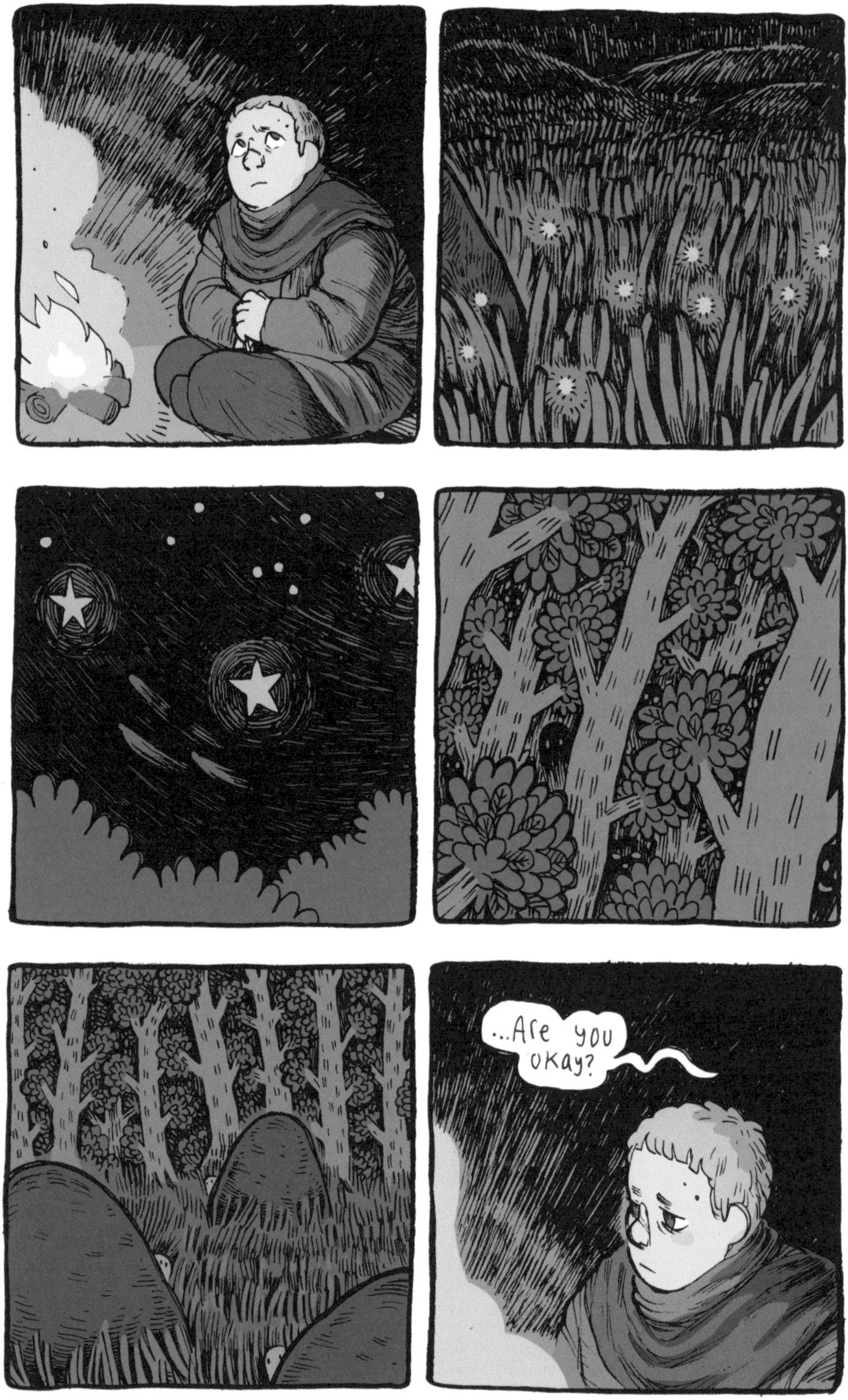
...Are you okay?

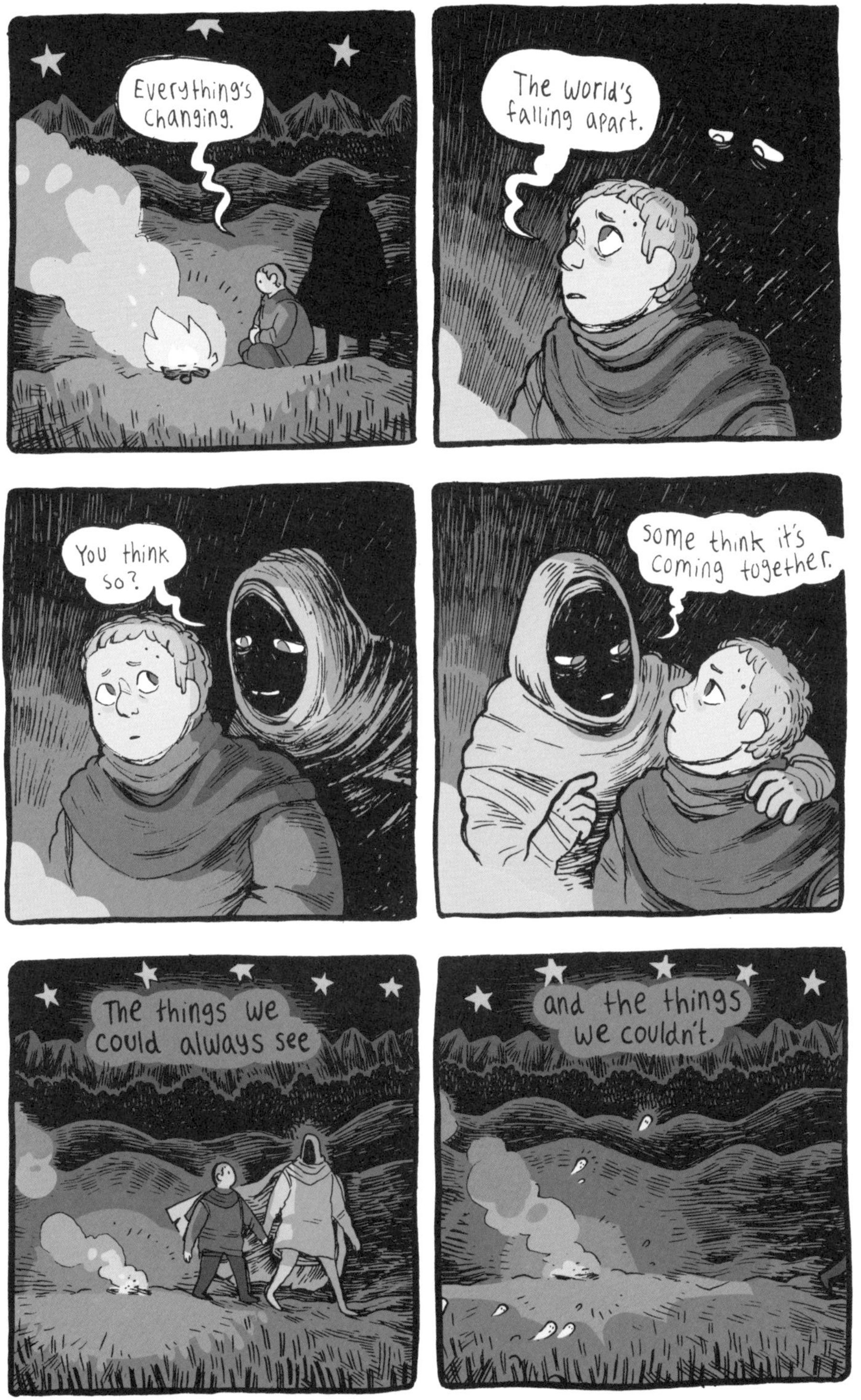
Everything's Changing.
The world's falling apart.
You think so?
Some think it's coming together.
The things we could always see
and the things we couldn't.

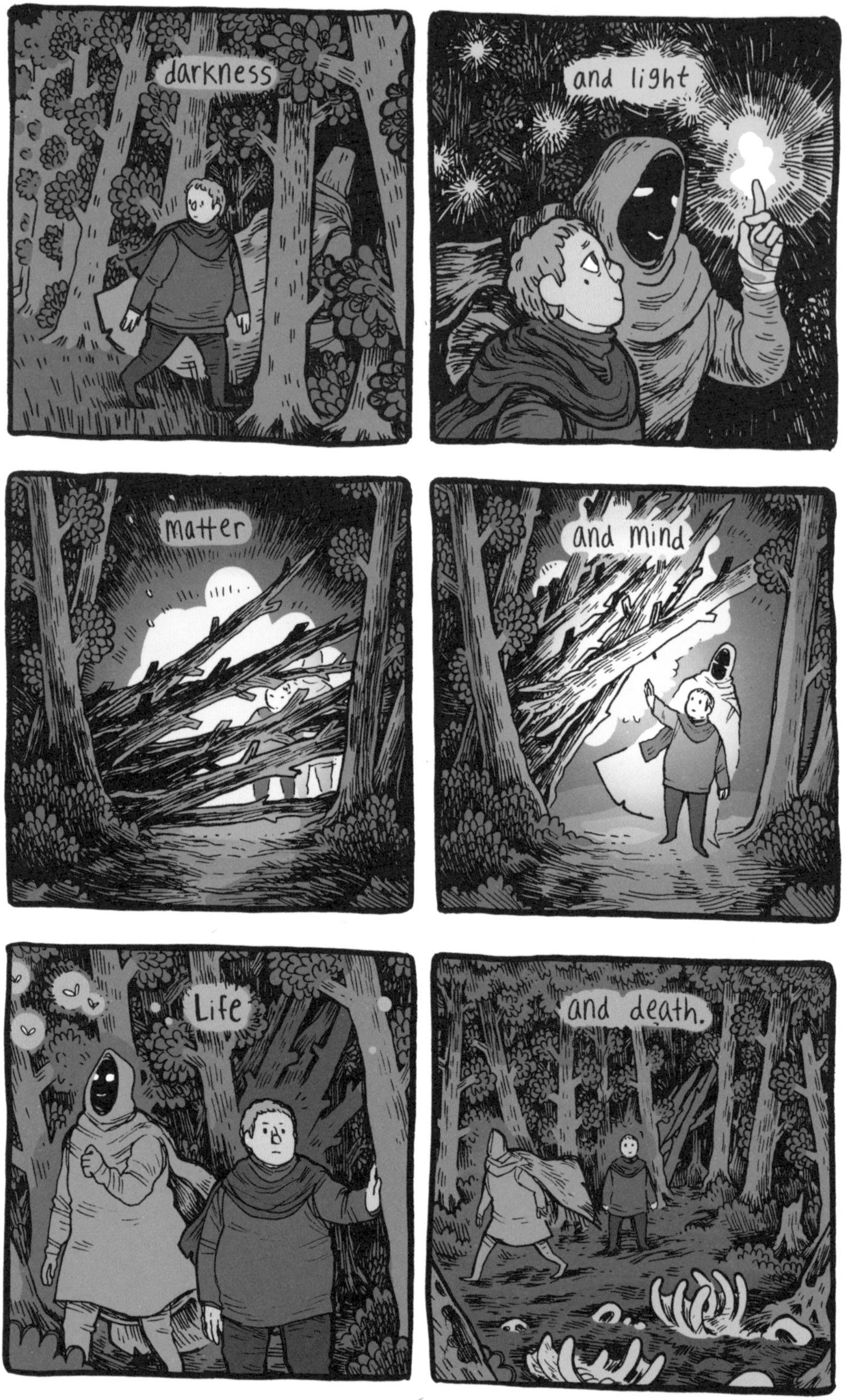
darkness
and light
matter
and mind
Life
and death.

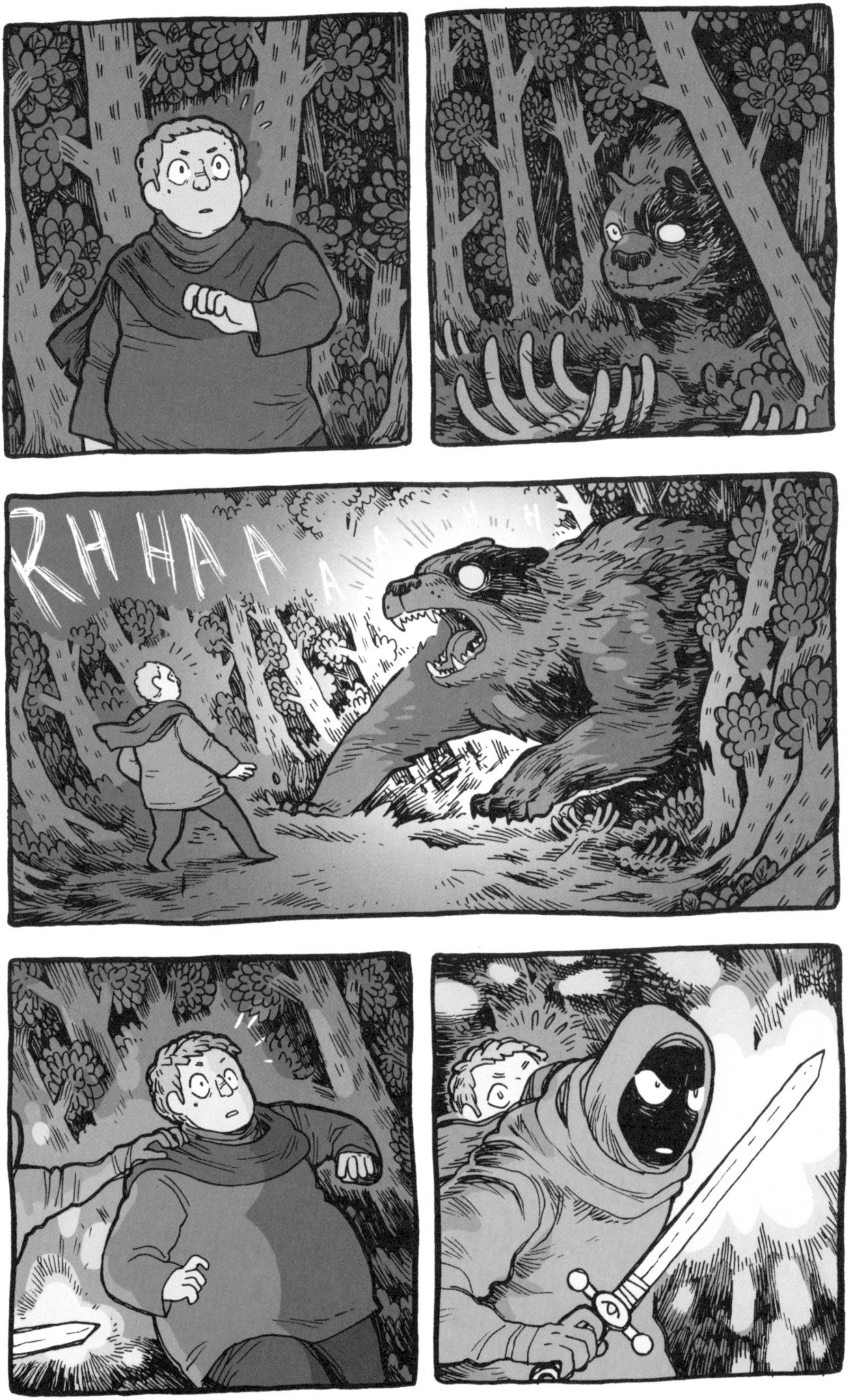
RHHAAAAHH

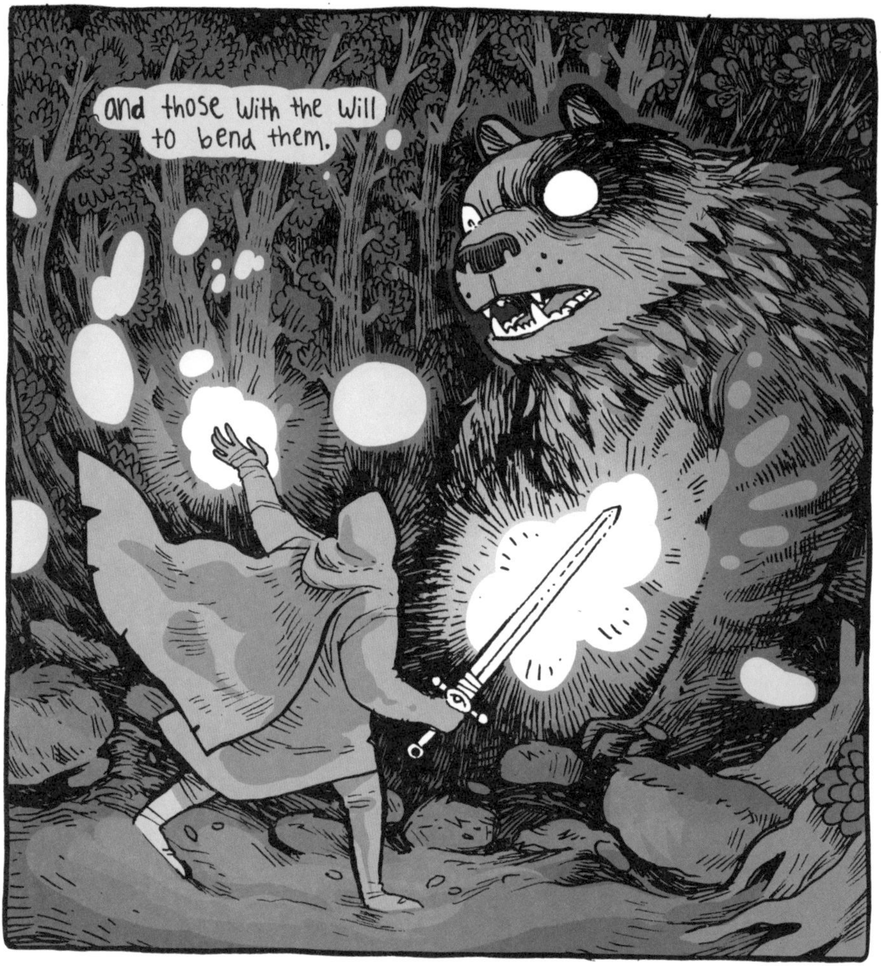
and those with the will to bend them.
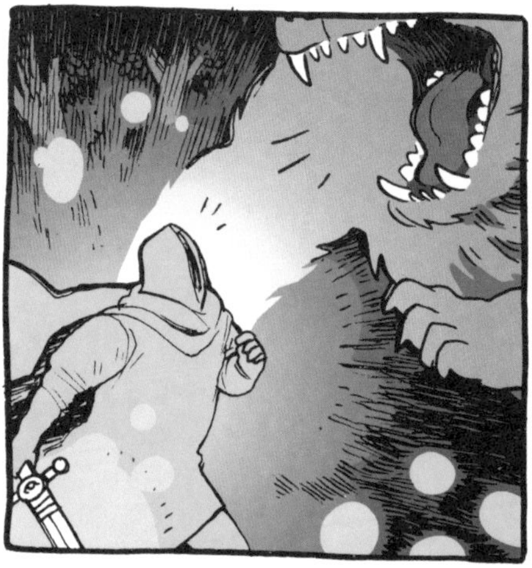
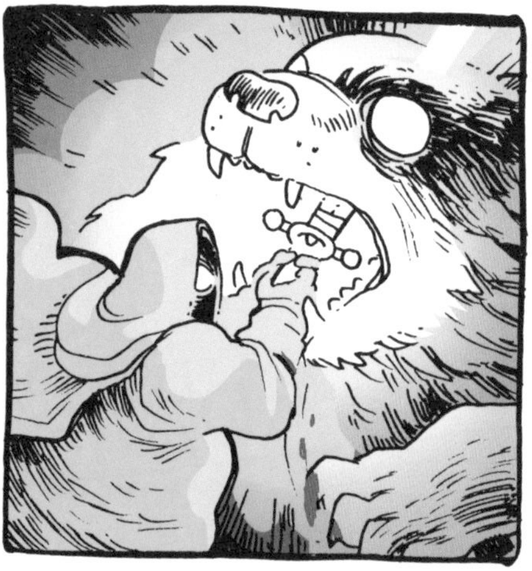

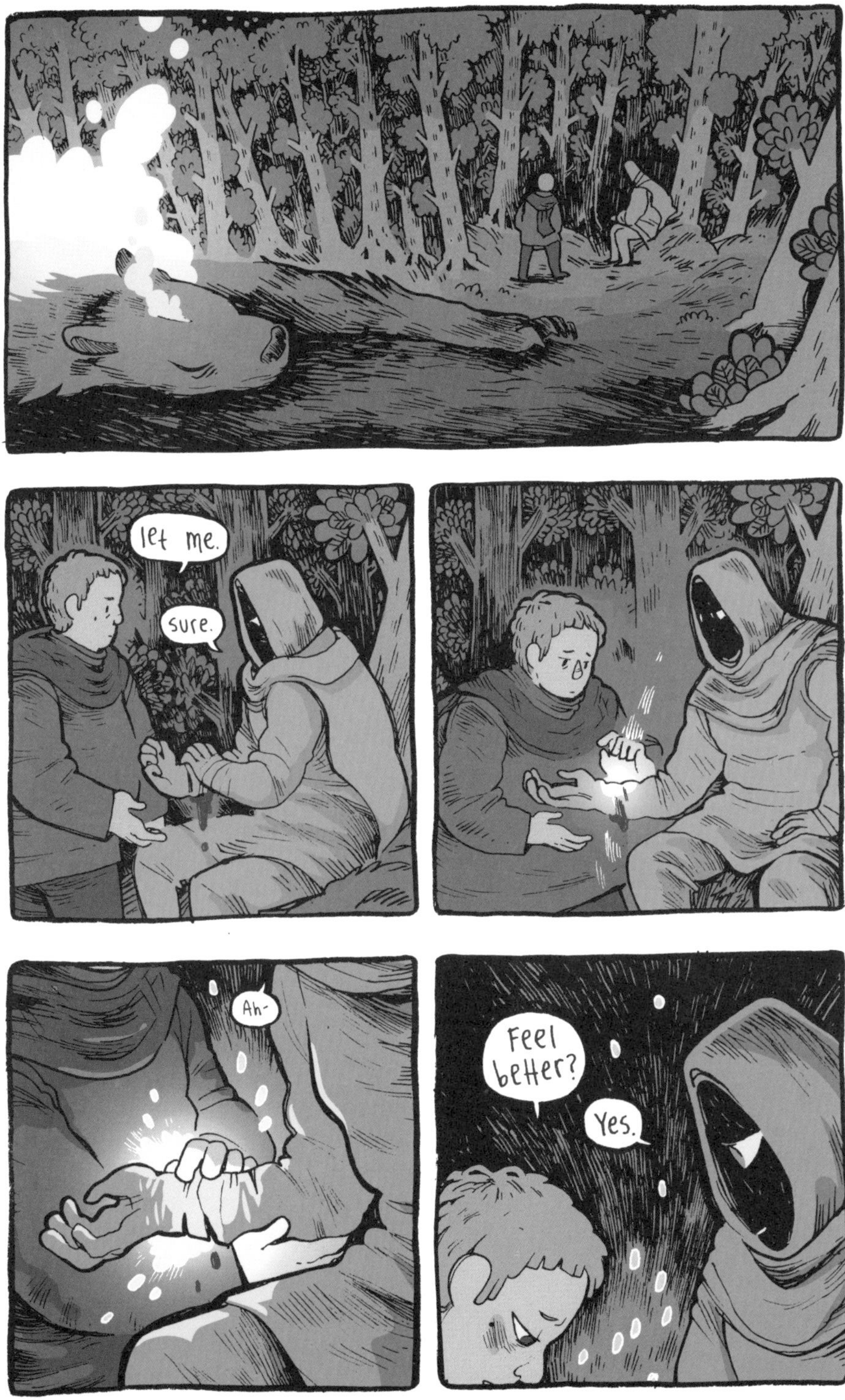
let me.
sure.
Ah-
Feel better?
Yes.

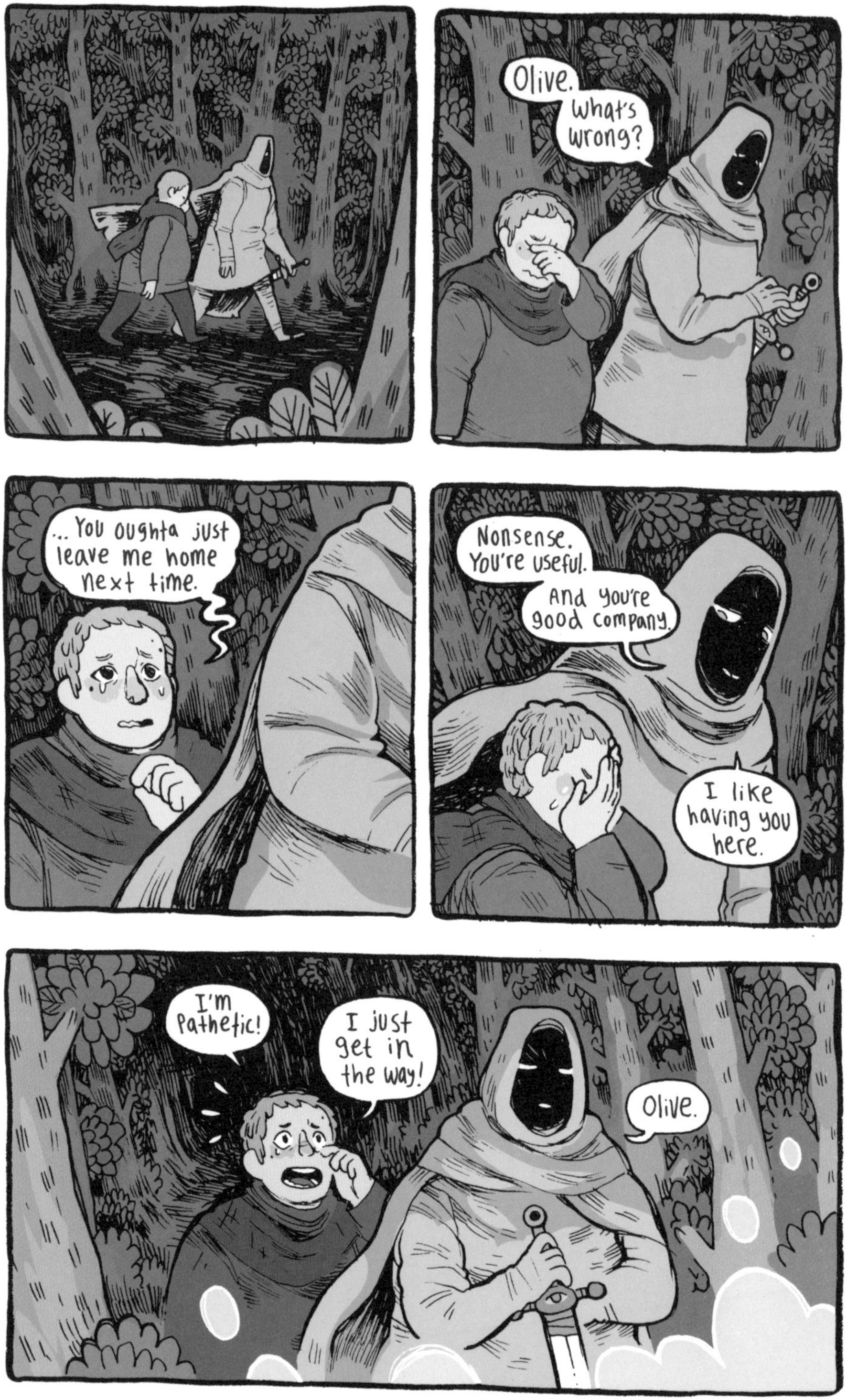
Olive. What's wrong?
... You oughta just leave me home next time.
Nonsense. You're useful.
And you're good company.
I like having you here.
I'm Pathetic!
I just get in the way!
Olive.

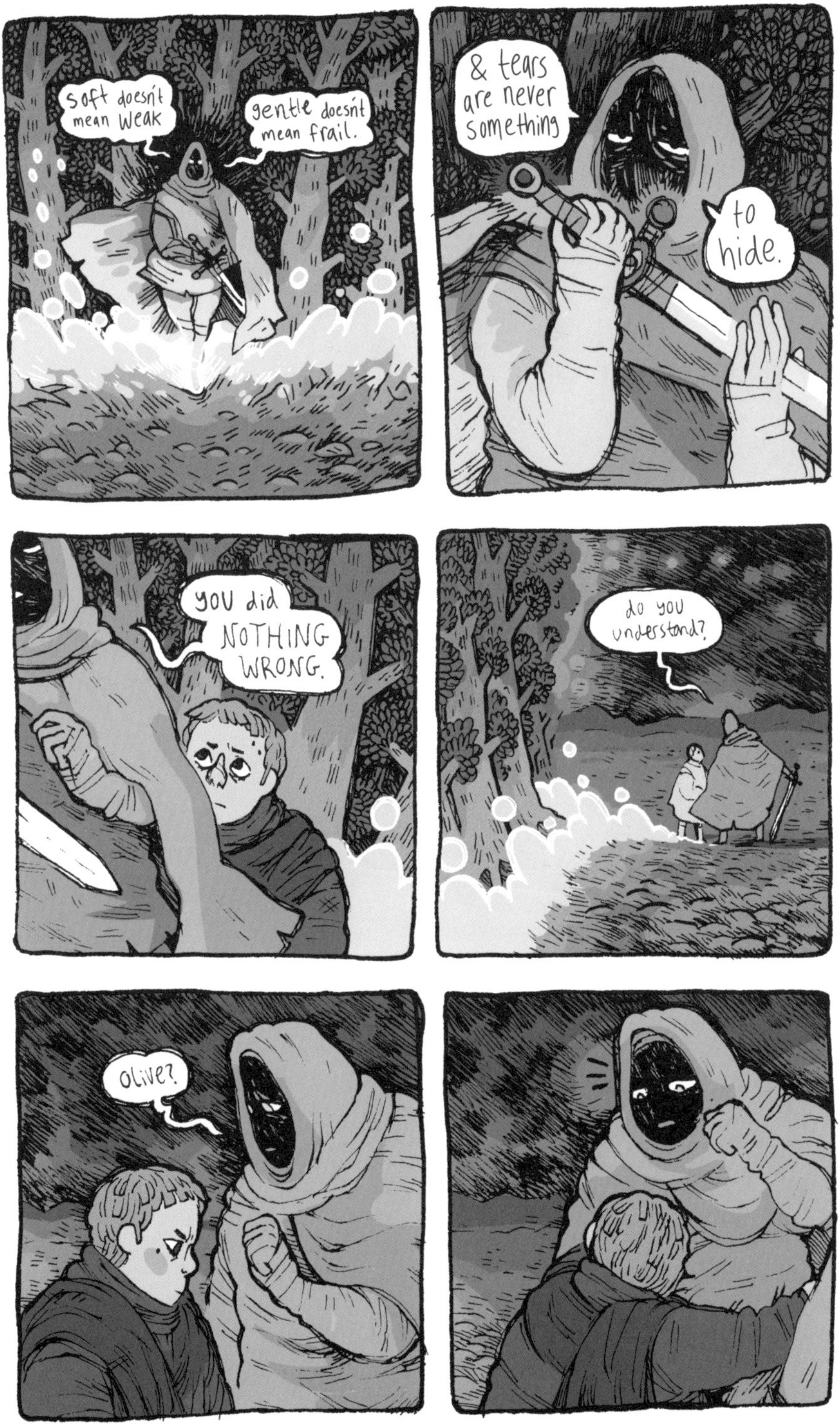
soft doesn't mean weak
gentle doesn't mean frail.
& tears are never something
to hide.
you did NOTHING WRONG.
do you understand?
Olive?

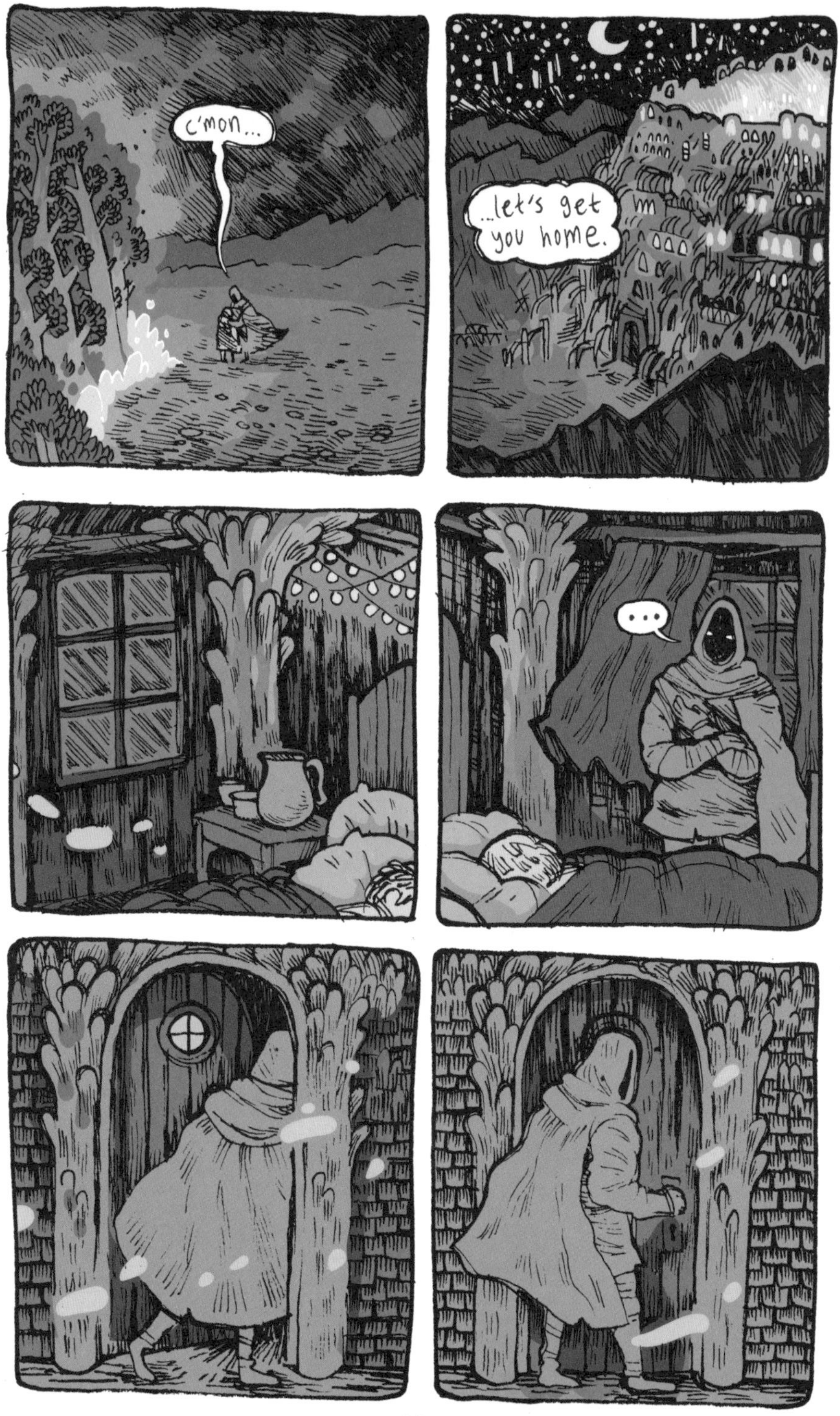
c'mon...
...let's get you home.
...

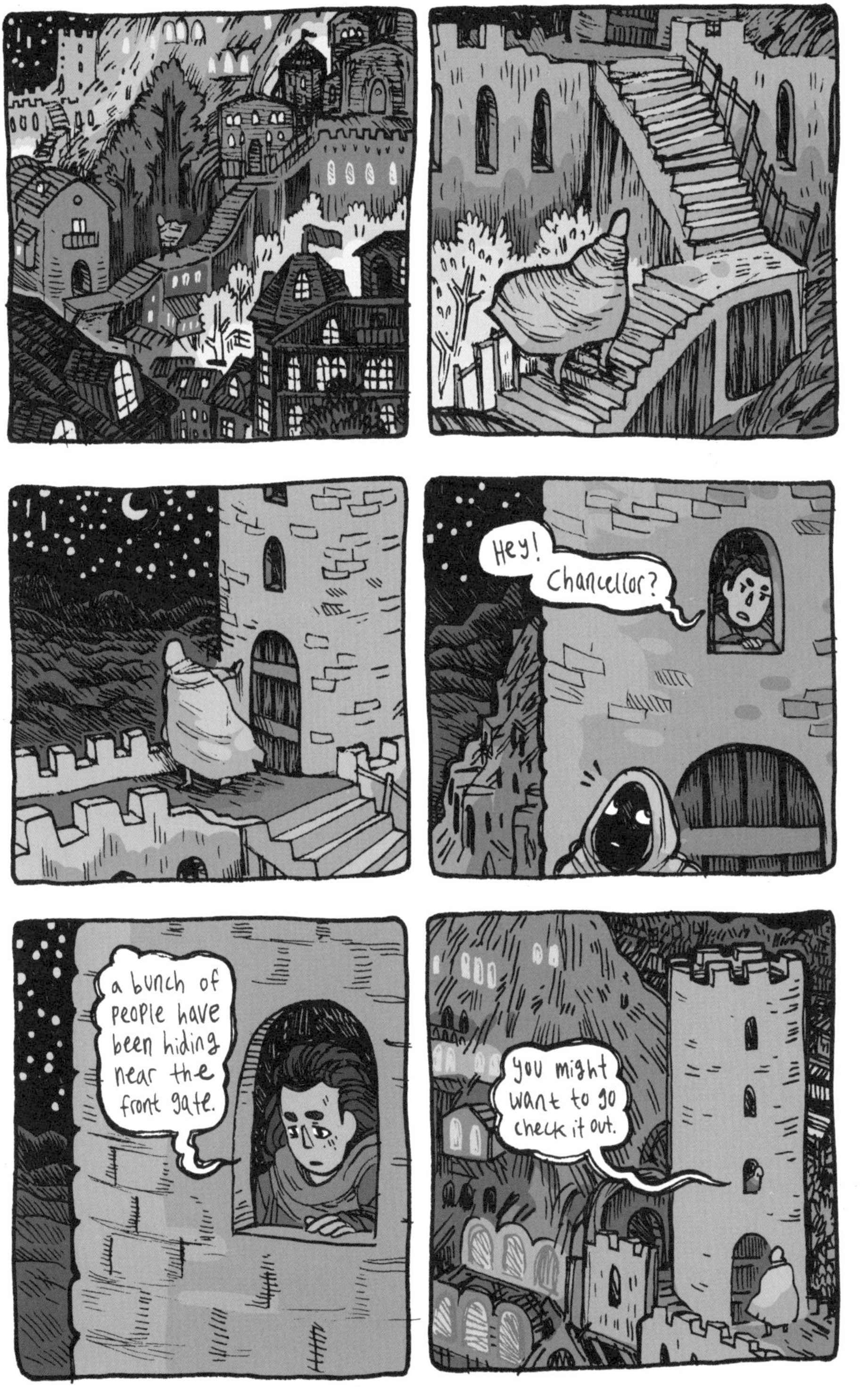
Hey!
Chancellor?
a bunch of people have been hiding near the front gate.
you might want to go check it out.

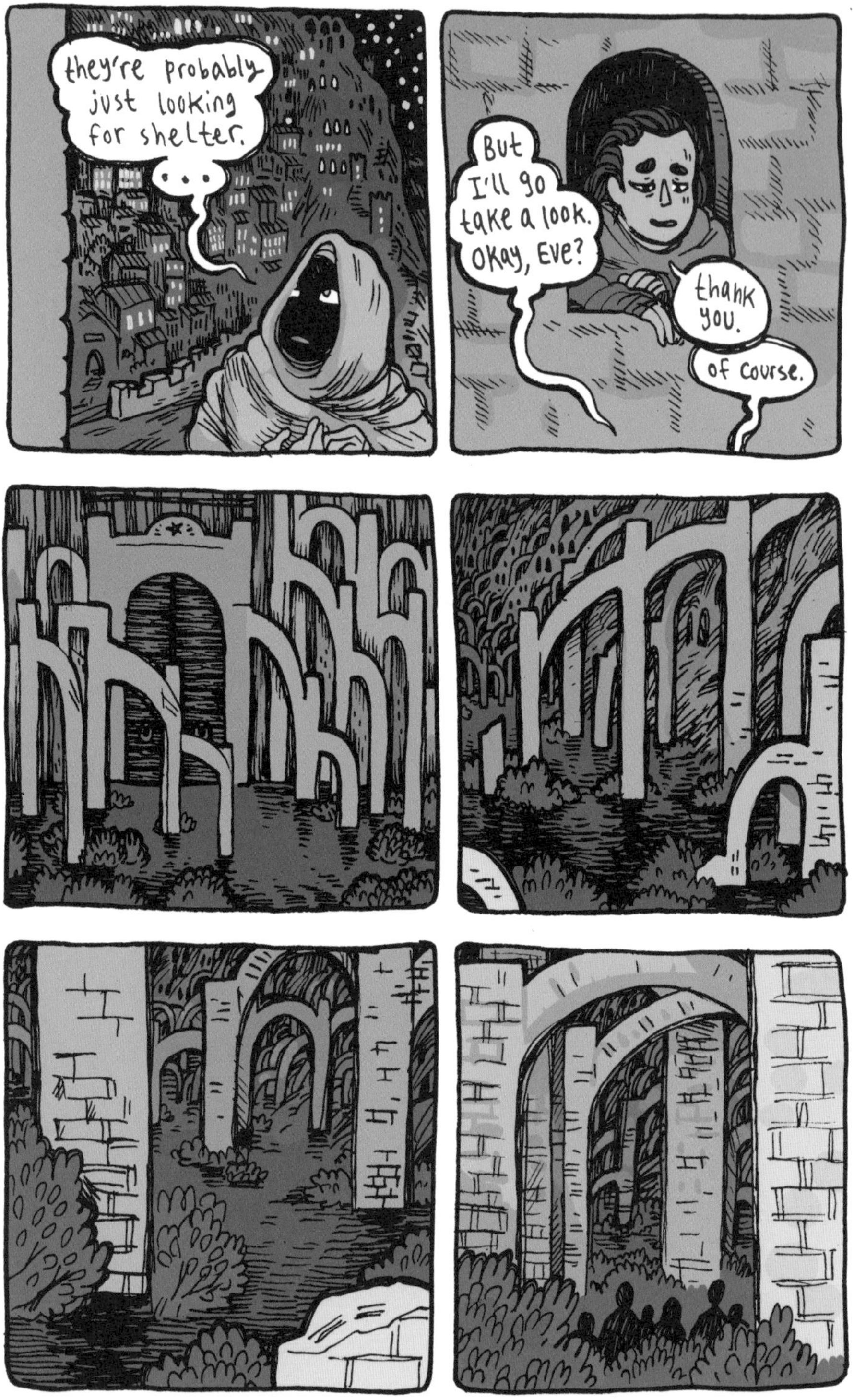
they're probably just looking for shelter.
. . .
But I'll go take a look. Okay, Eve?
thank you.
of course.

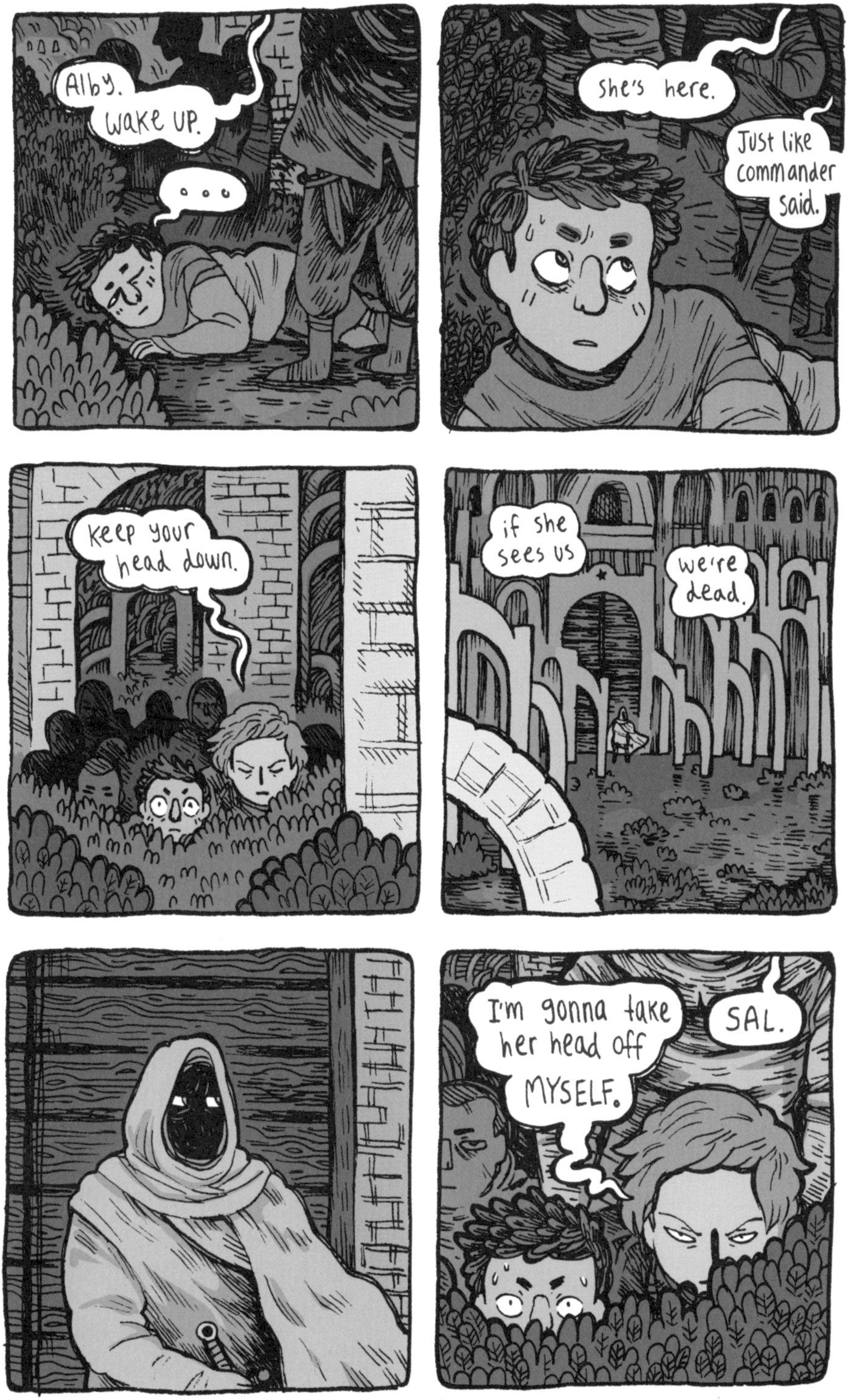
Alby.
WAKE UP.
...
She's here.
Just like commander said.
Keep your head down.
if she sees us
we're dead.
I'm gonna take her head off MYSELF.
SAL.

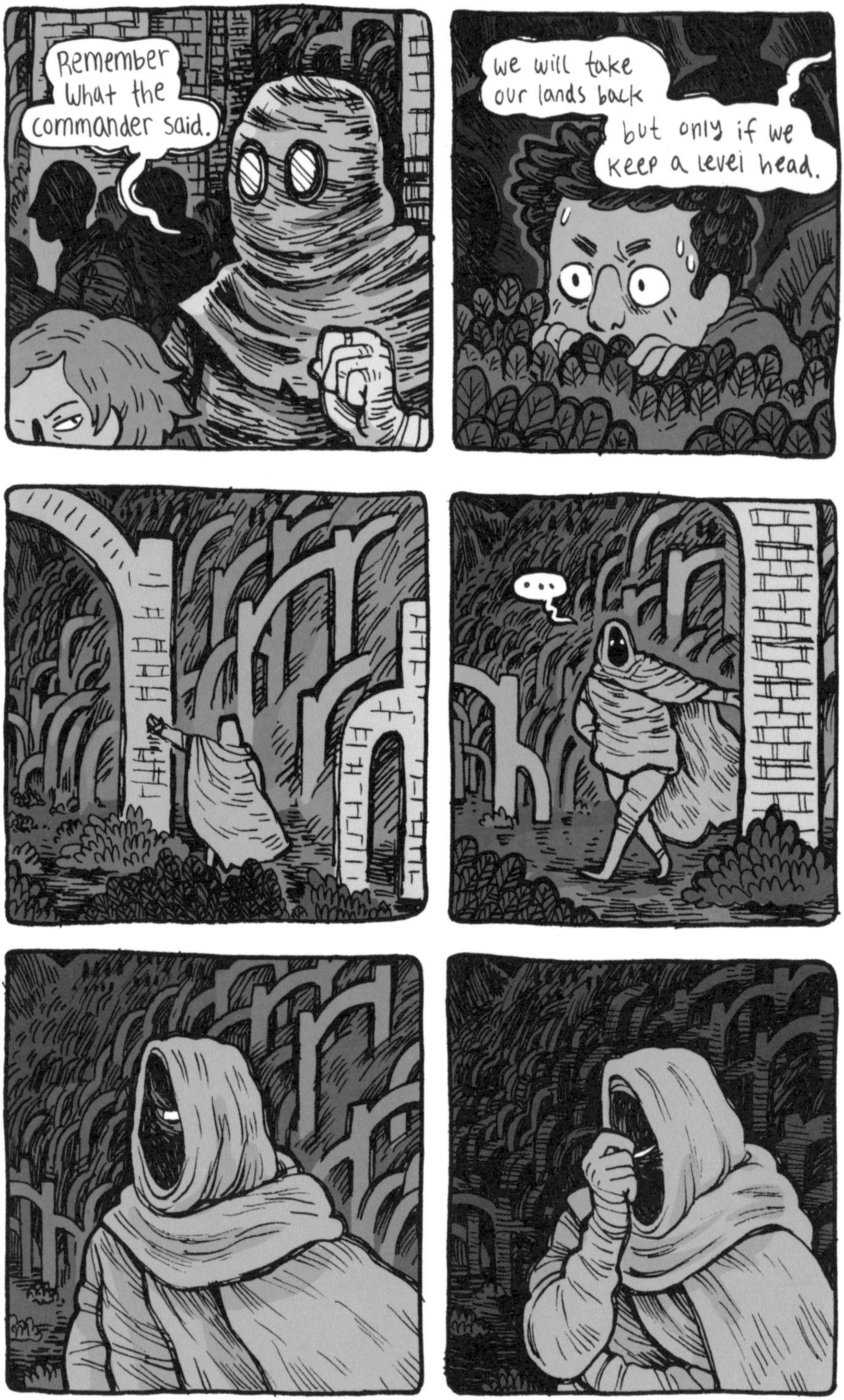
Remember what the commander said.
we will take our lands back
but only if we keep a level head.
...

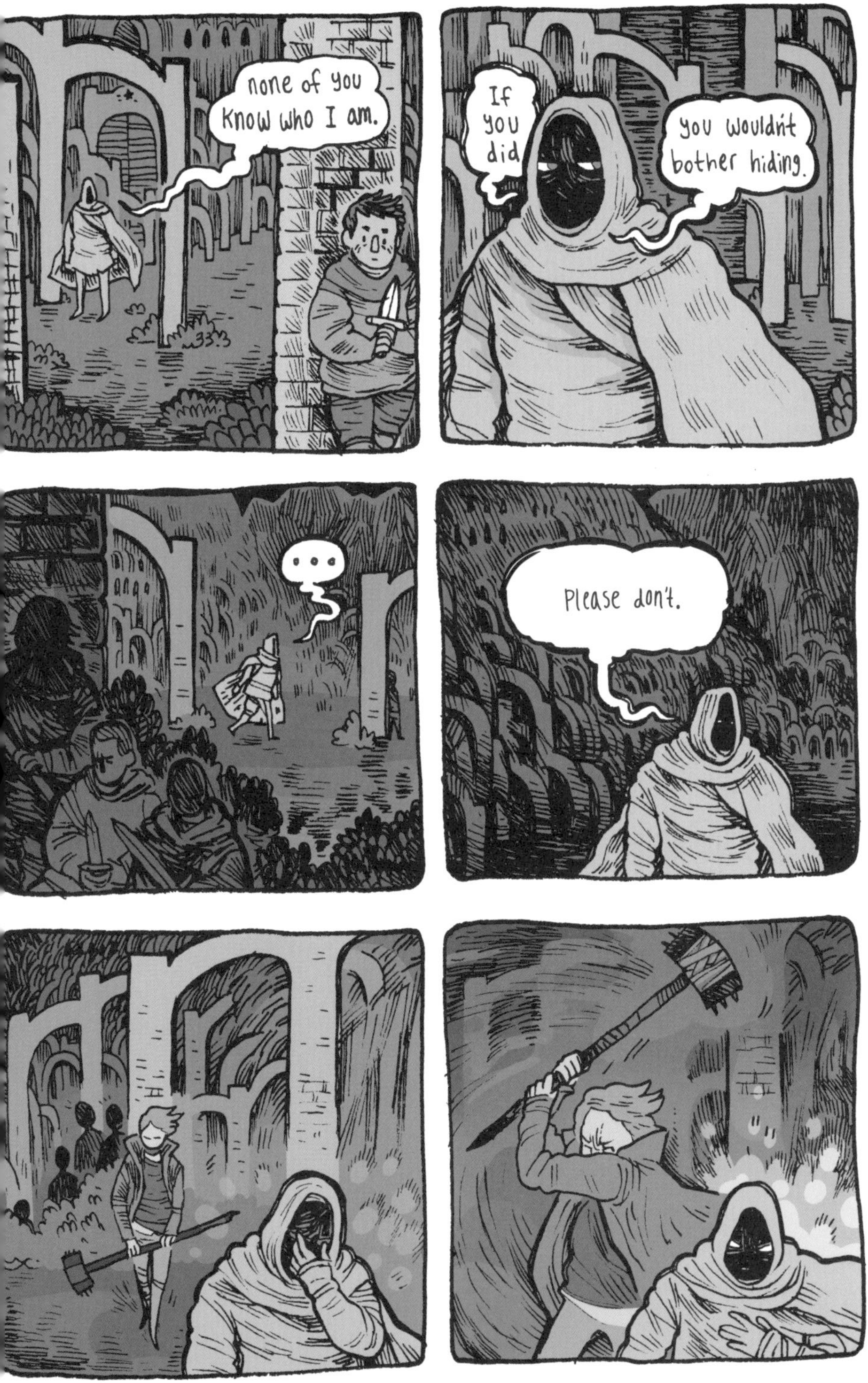
none of you know who I am.
If you did
you wouldn't bother hiding.
...
Please don't.

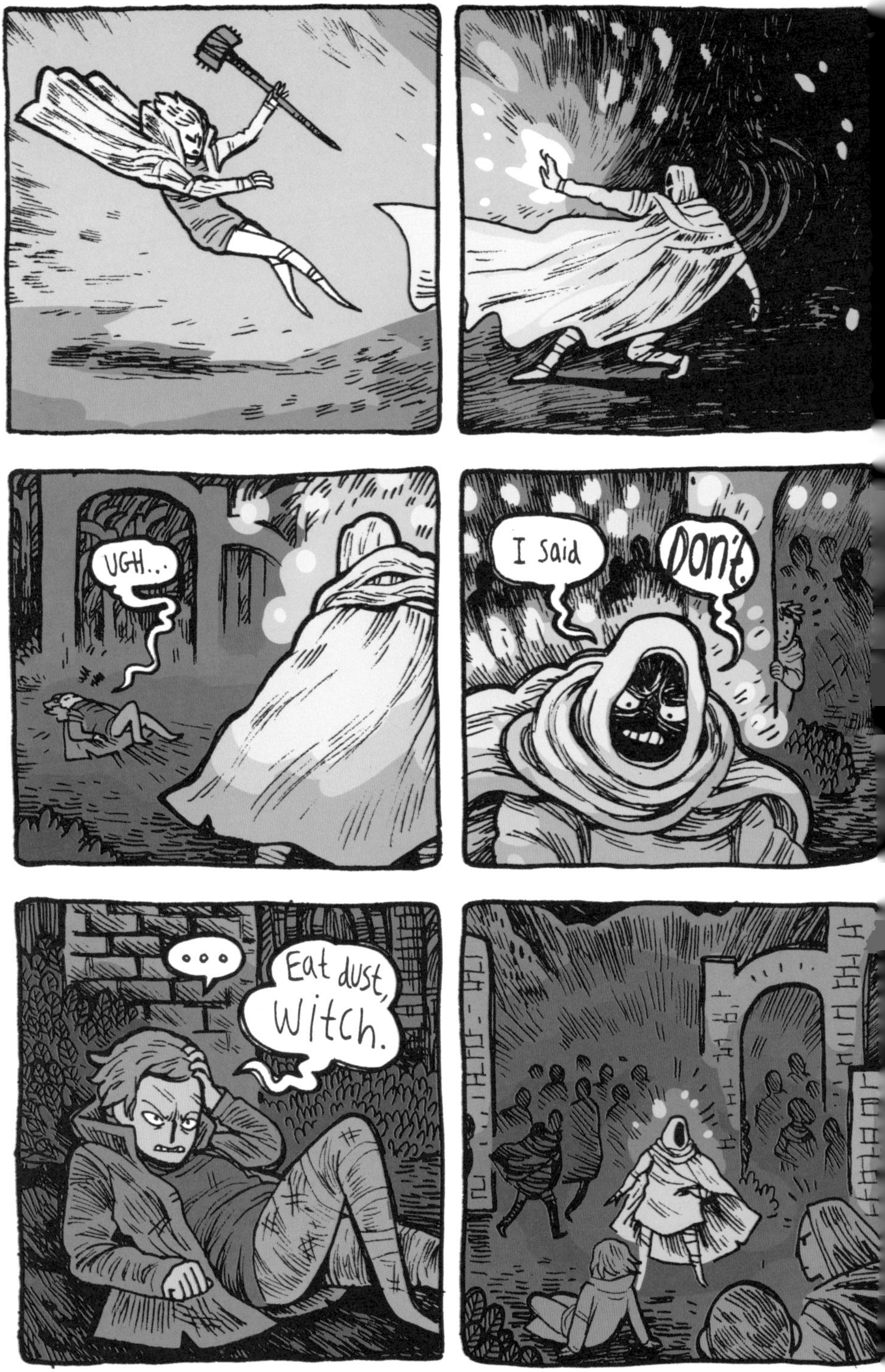
UGH...
I said
Don't.
...
Eat dust, witch.

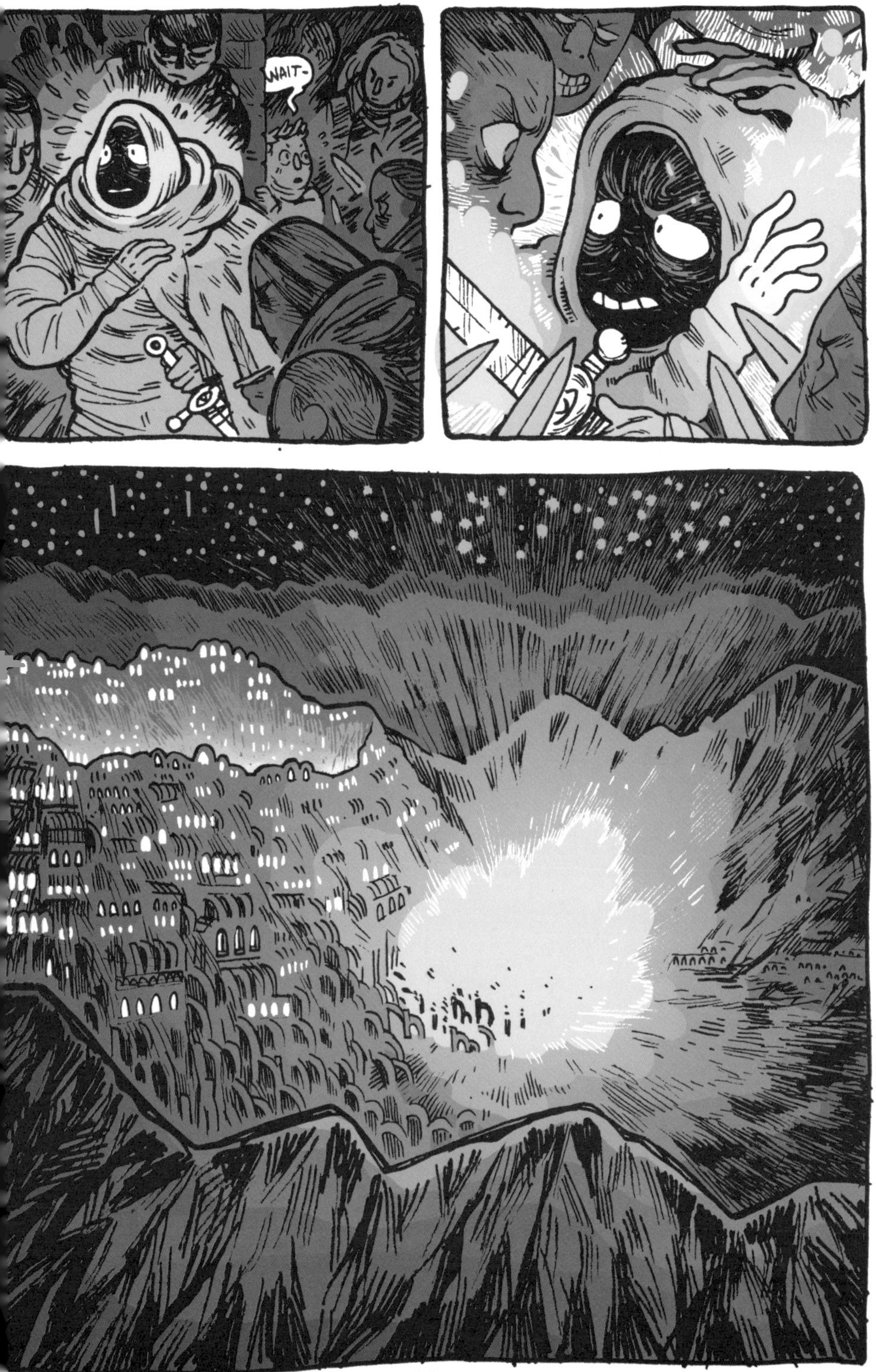
WAIT-

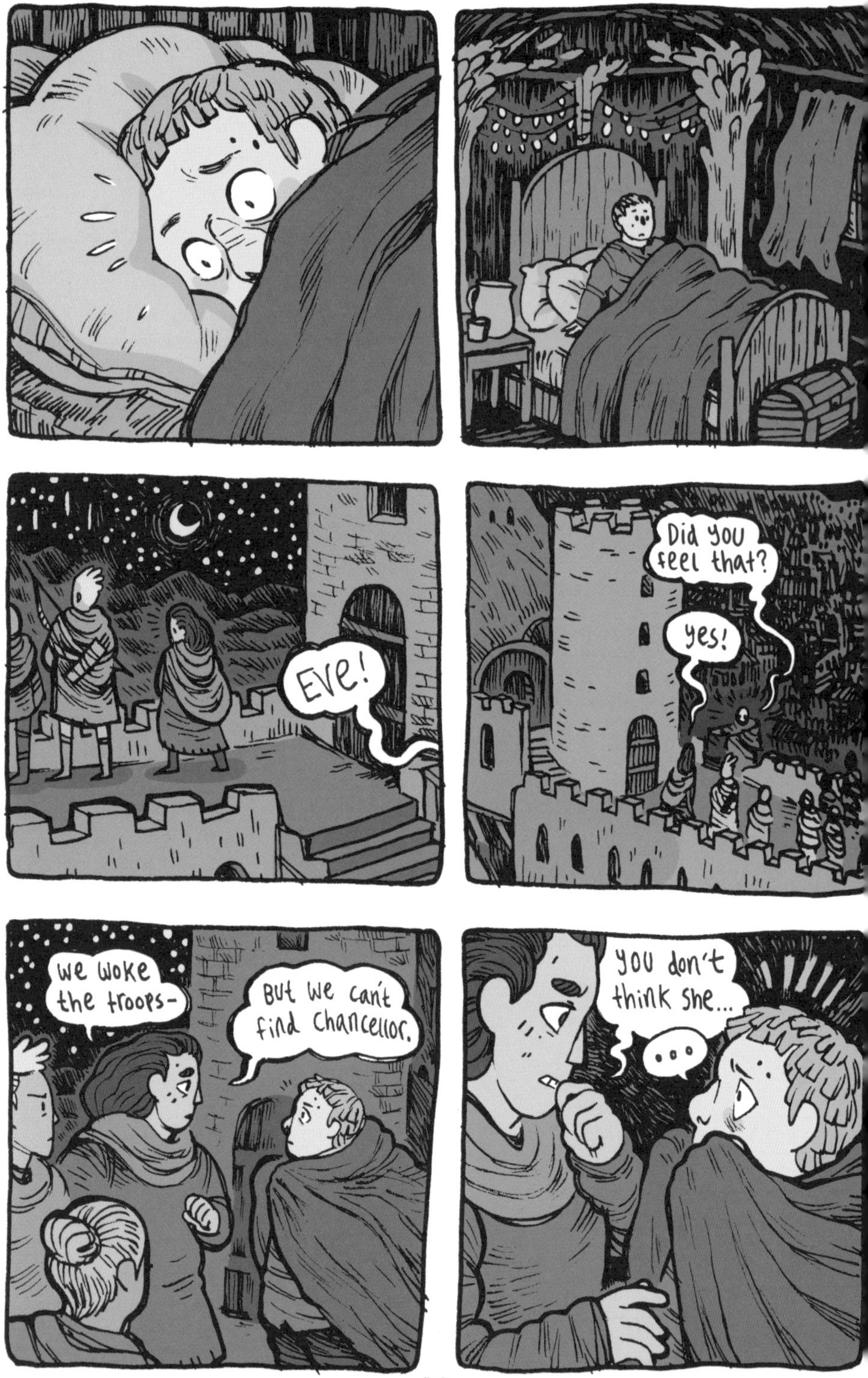
Eve!
Did you feel that?
yes!
we woke the troops-
But we can't find Chancellor.
you don't think she...
...

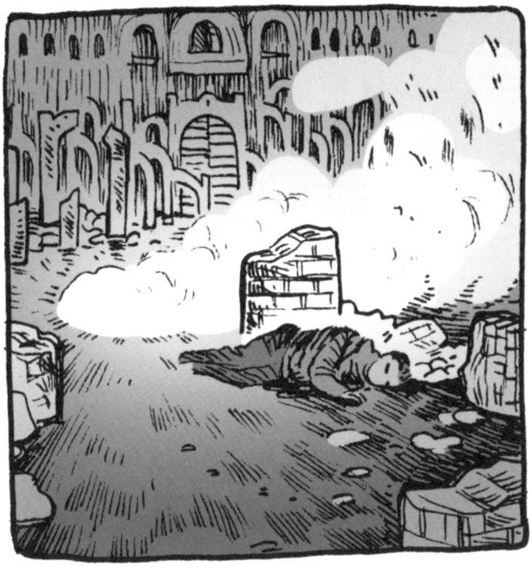
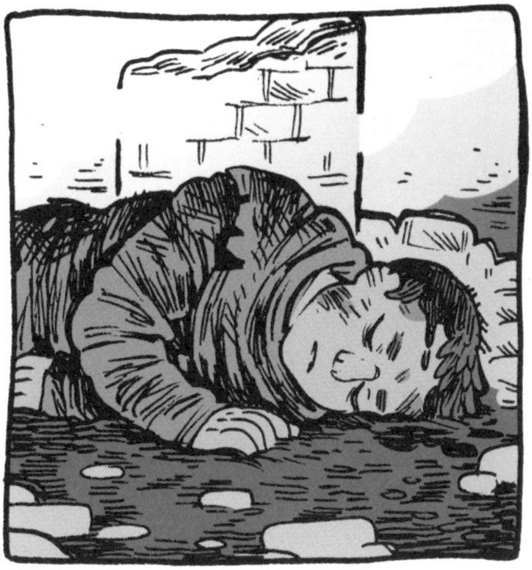
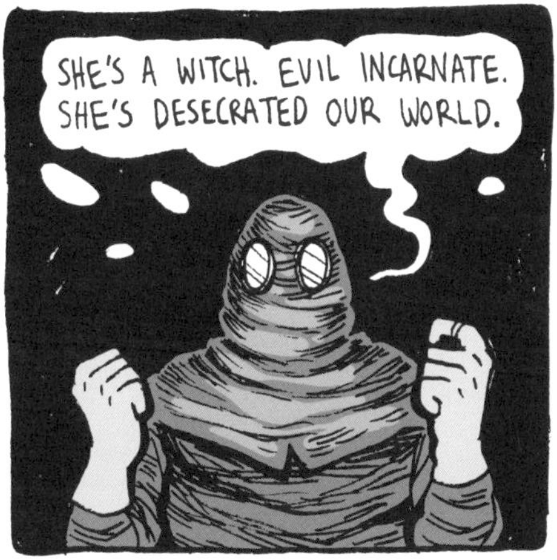
SHE'S A WITCH. EVIL INCARNATE. SHE'S DESECRATED OUR WORLD.
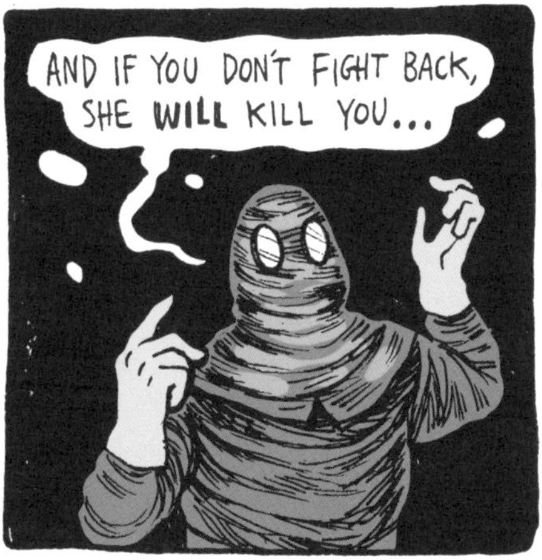
AND IF YOU DON'T FIGHT BACK, SHE **WILL** KILL YOU...
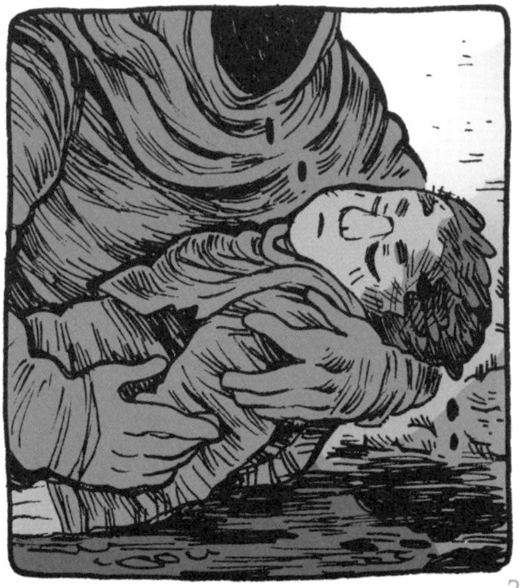
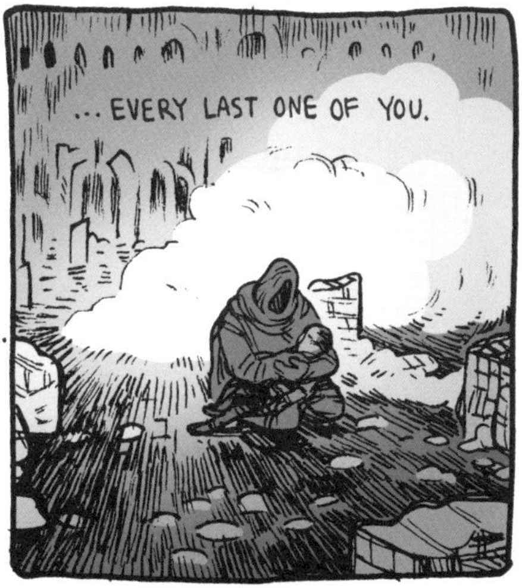
...EVERY LAST ONE OF YOU.

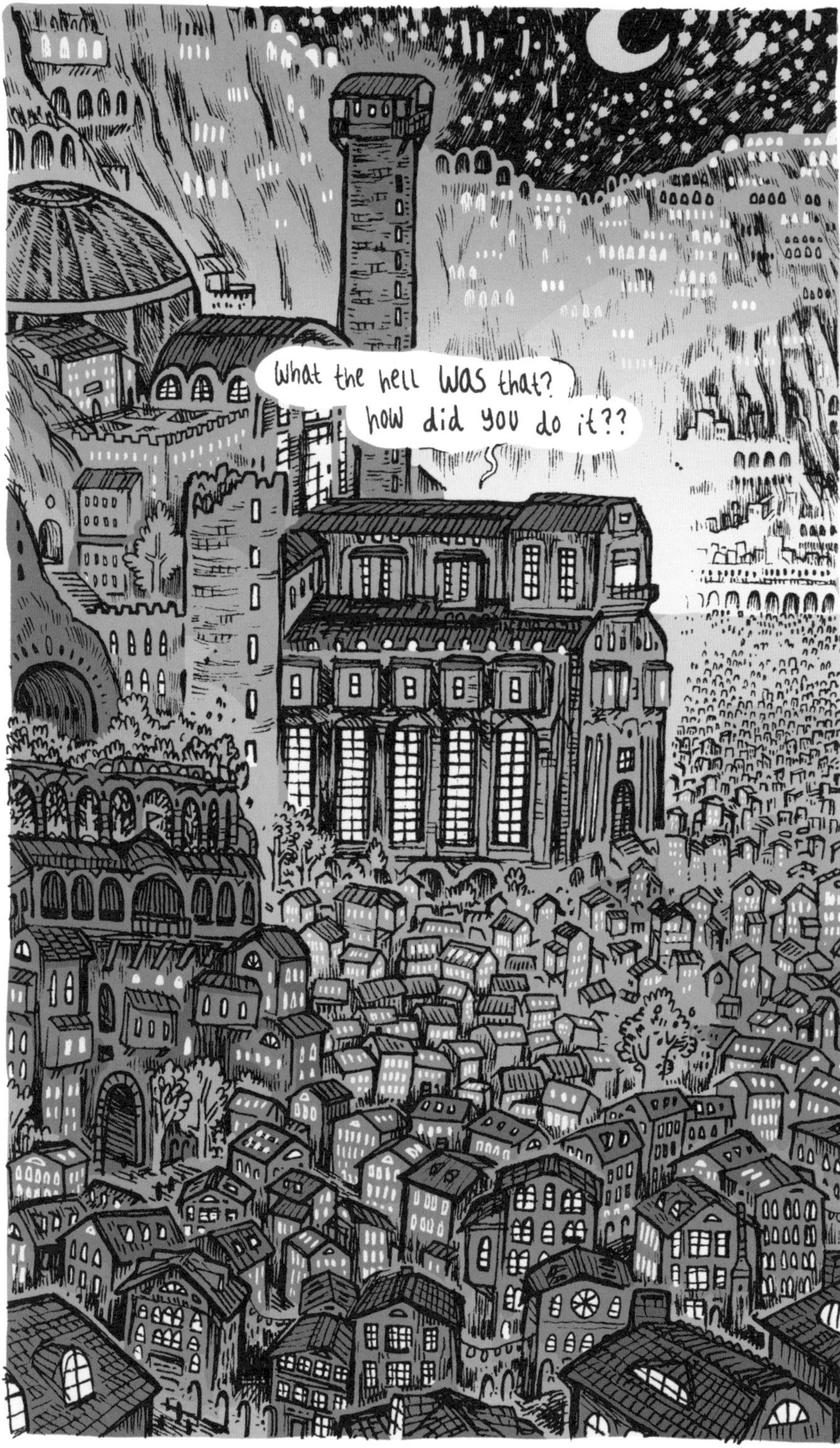
What the hell WAS that?
how did you do it??

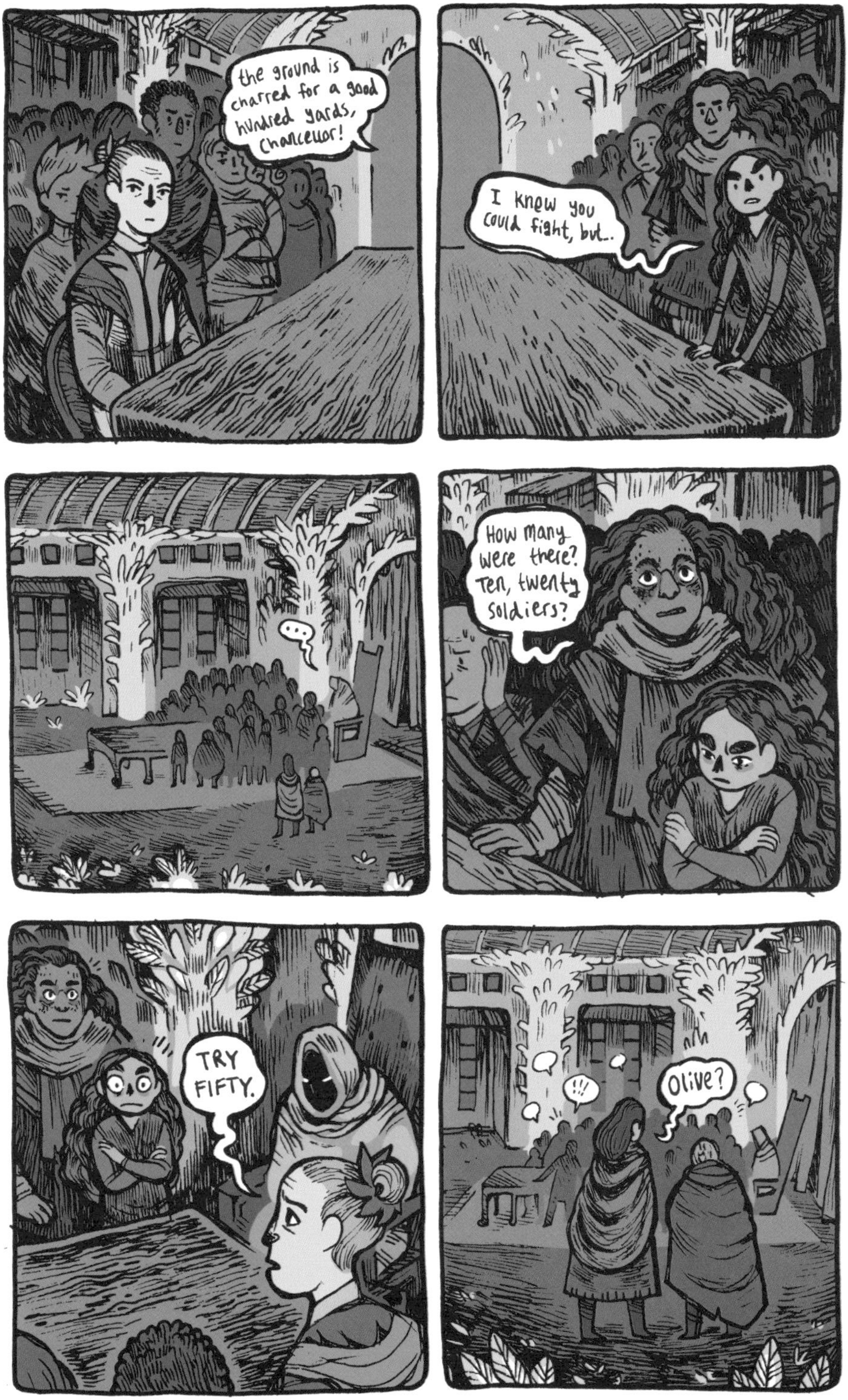
the ground is charred for a good hundred yards, Chancellor!
I knew you could fight, but...
...
How many were there? Ten, twenty soldiers?
TRY FIFTY.
!!!
Olive?

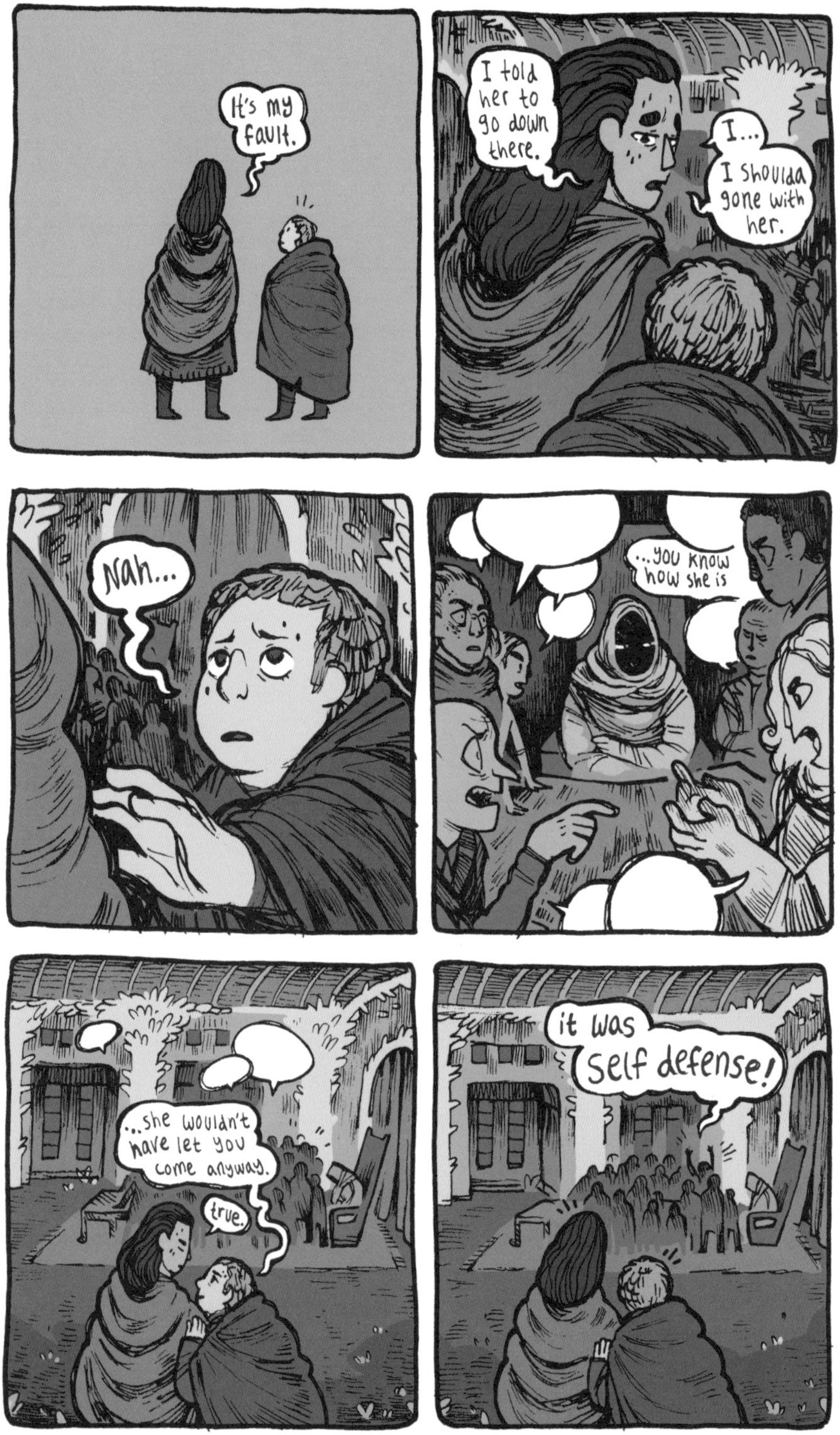
It's my fault.
I told her to go down there.
I...
I shoulda gone with her.
Nah...
...you know how she is
...she wouldn't have let you come anyway.
true.
it was self defense!

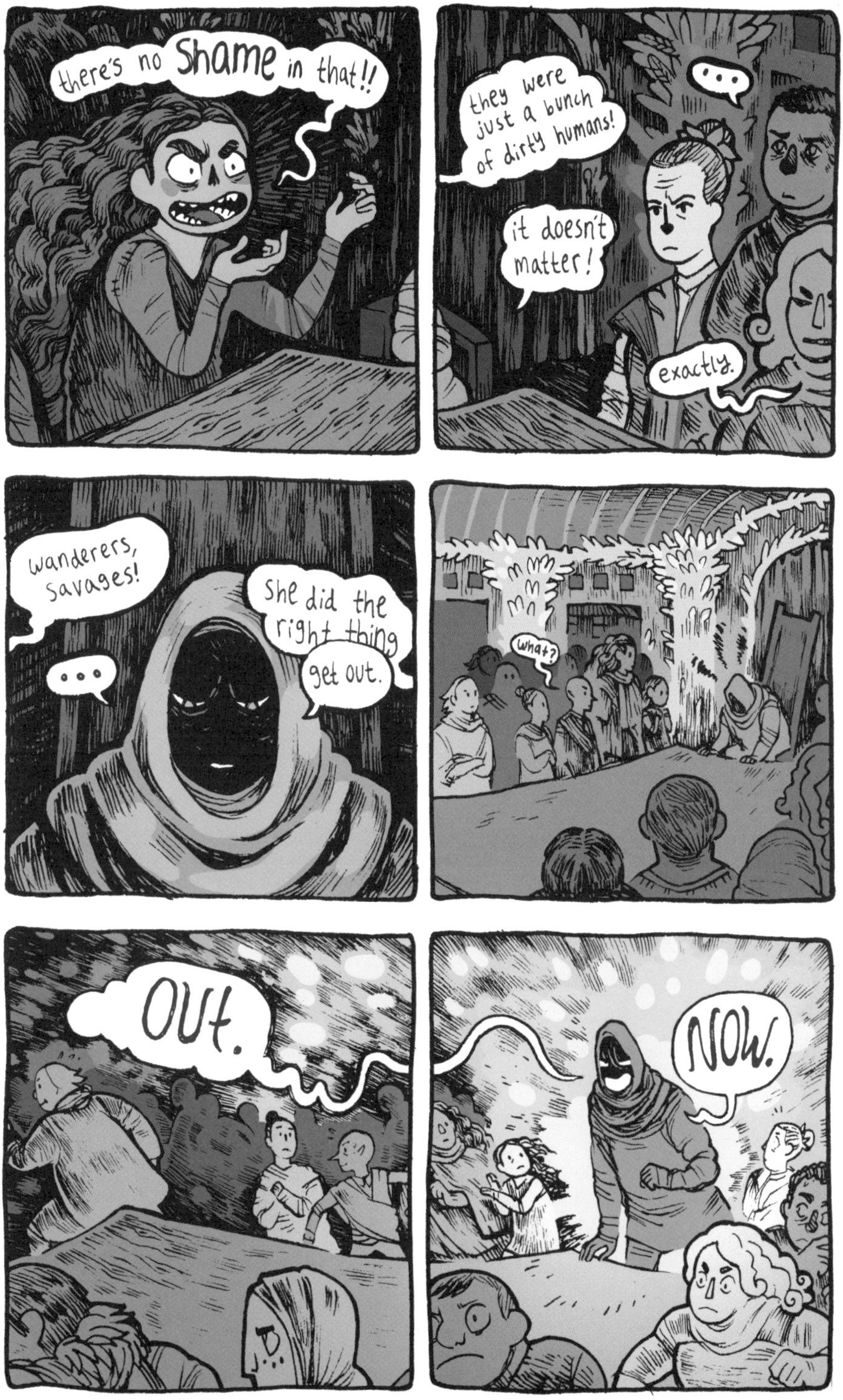
there's no Shame in that!!
they were just a bunch of dirty humans!
...
it doesn't matter!
exactly.
wanderers, savages!
She did the right thing
...
get out.
what?
OUt.
NOW.

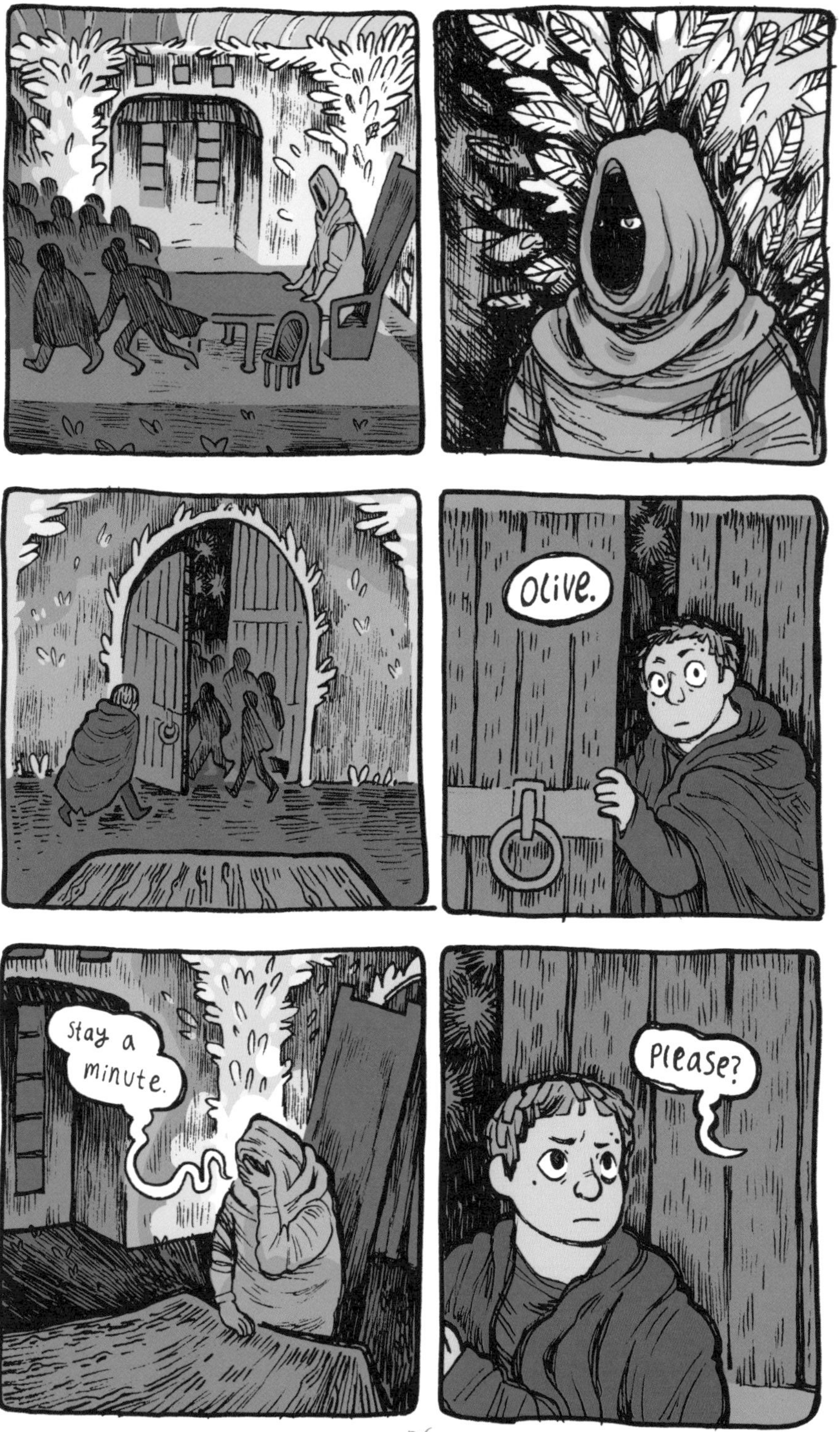
Olive.
Stay a minute.
Please?

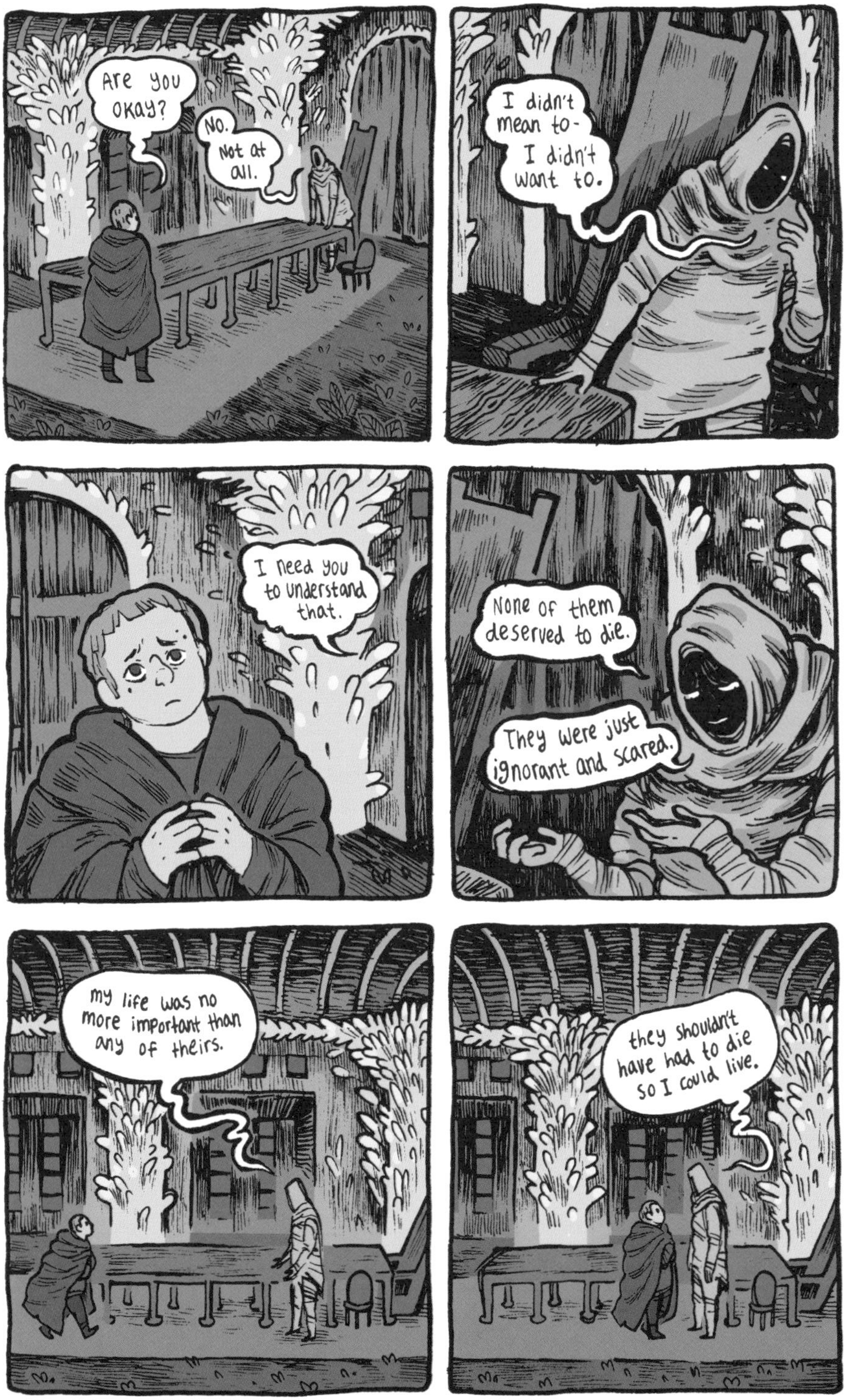
Are you okay?
No. Not at all.
I didn't mean to- I didn't want to.
I need you to understand that.
None of them deserved to die.
They were just ignorant and scared.
my life was no more important than any of theirs.
they shouldn't have had to die so I could live.

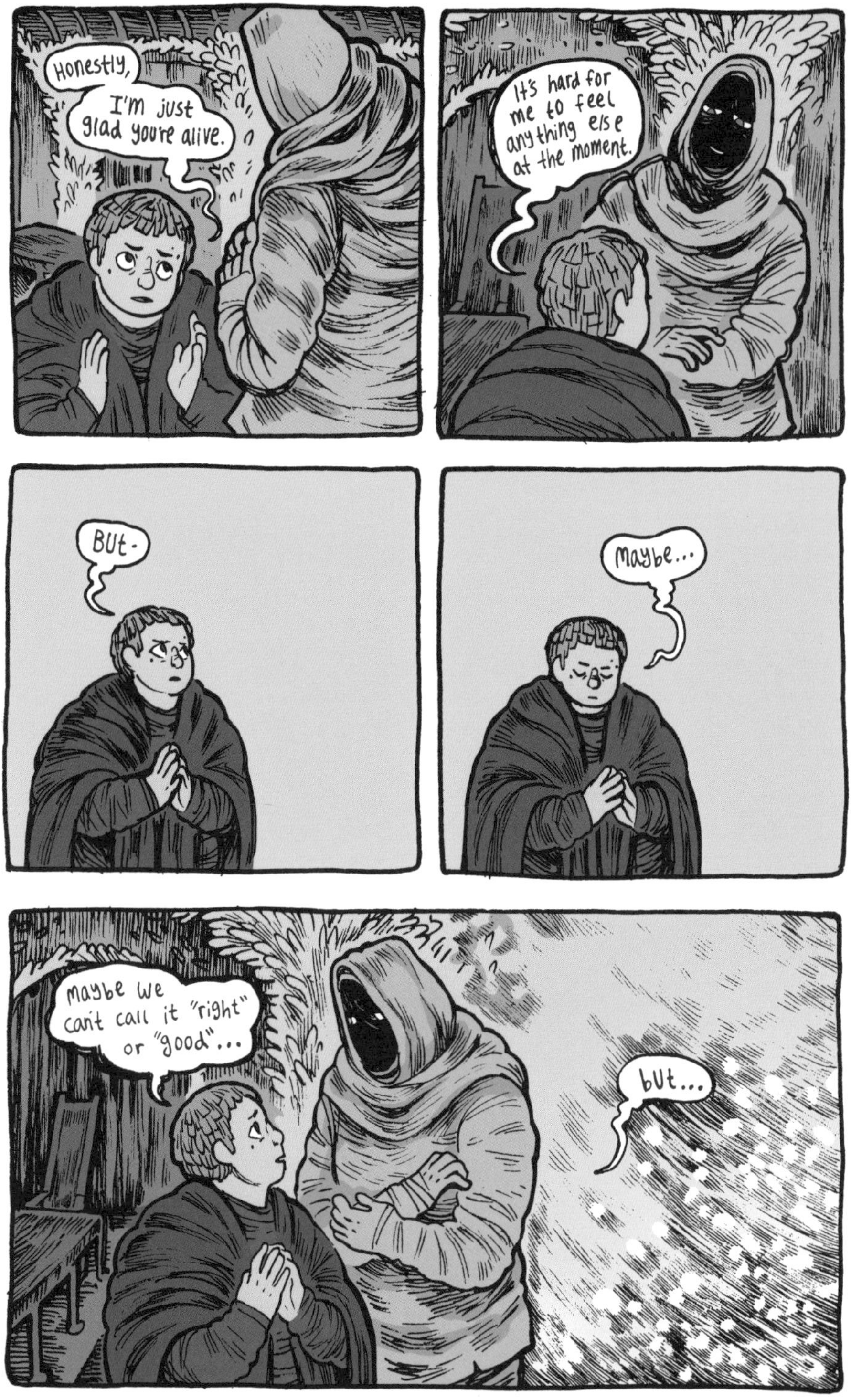
Honestly,
I'm just glad you're alive.
It's hard for me to feel anything else at the moment.
But-
Maybe...
Maybe we can't call it "right" or "good"...
but...

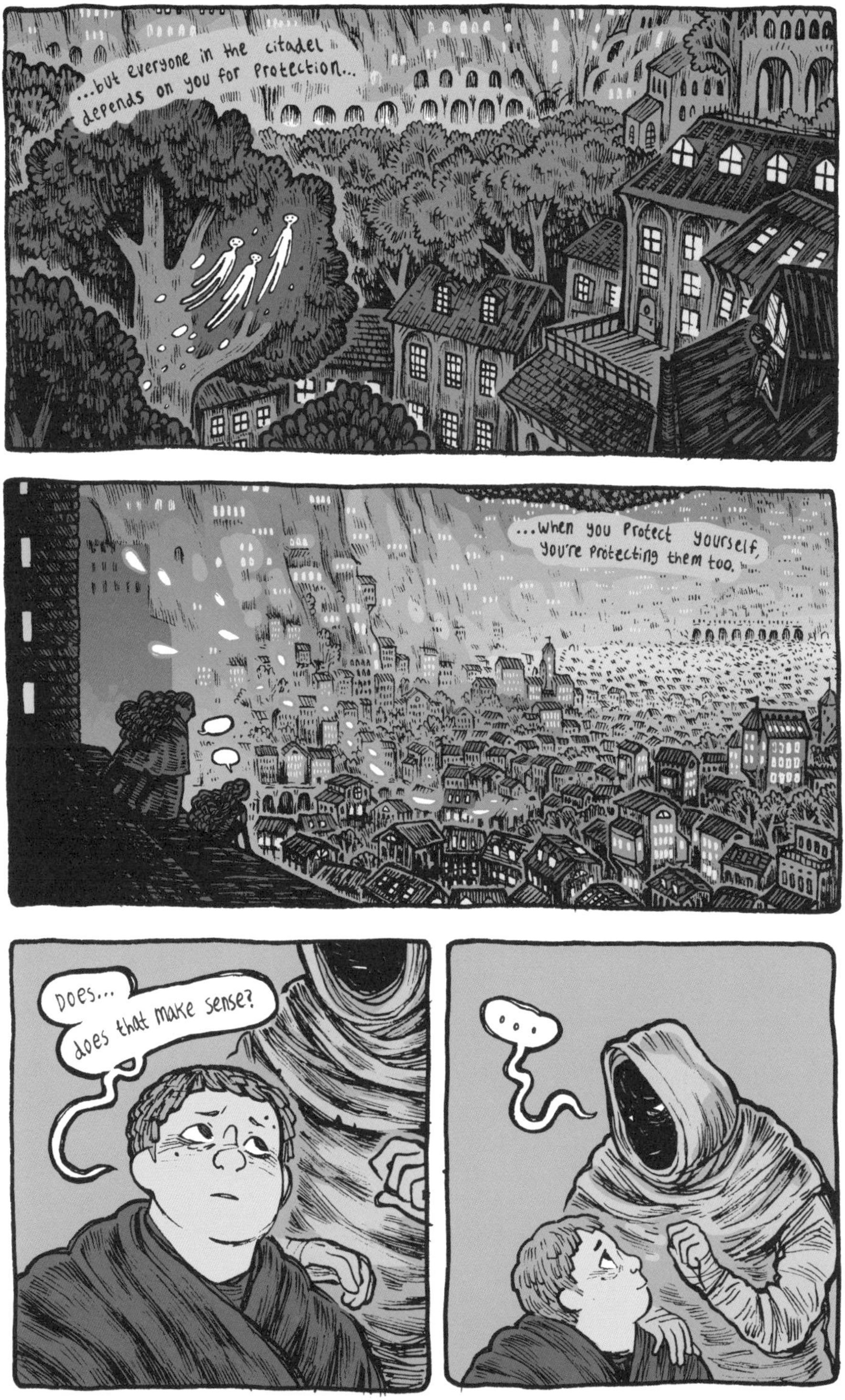
...but everyone in the citadel depends on you for protection...
...when you protect yourself, you're protecting them too.
Does... does that make sense?
...

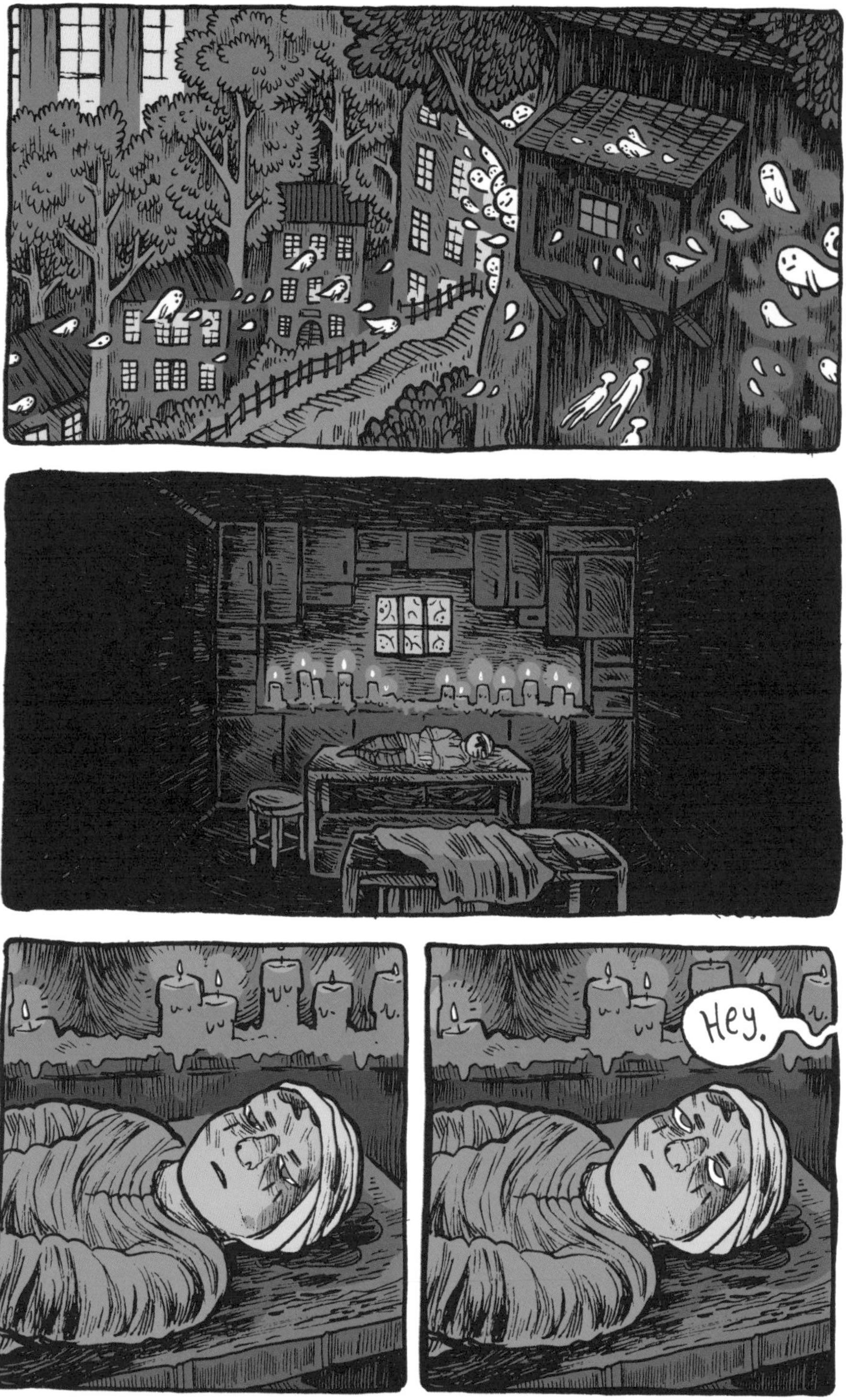
Hey.

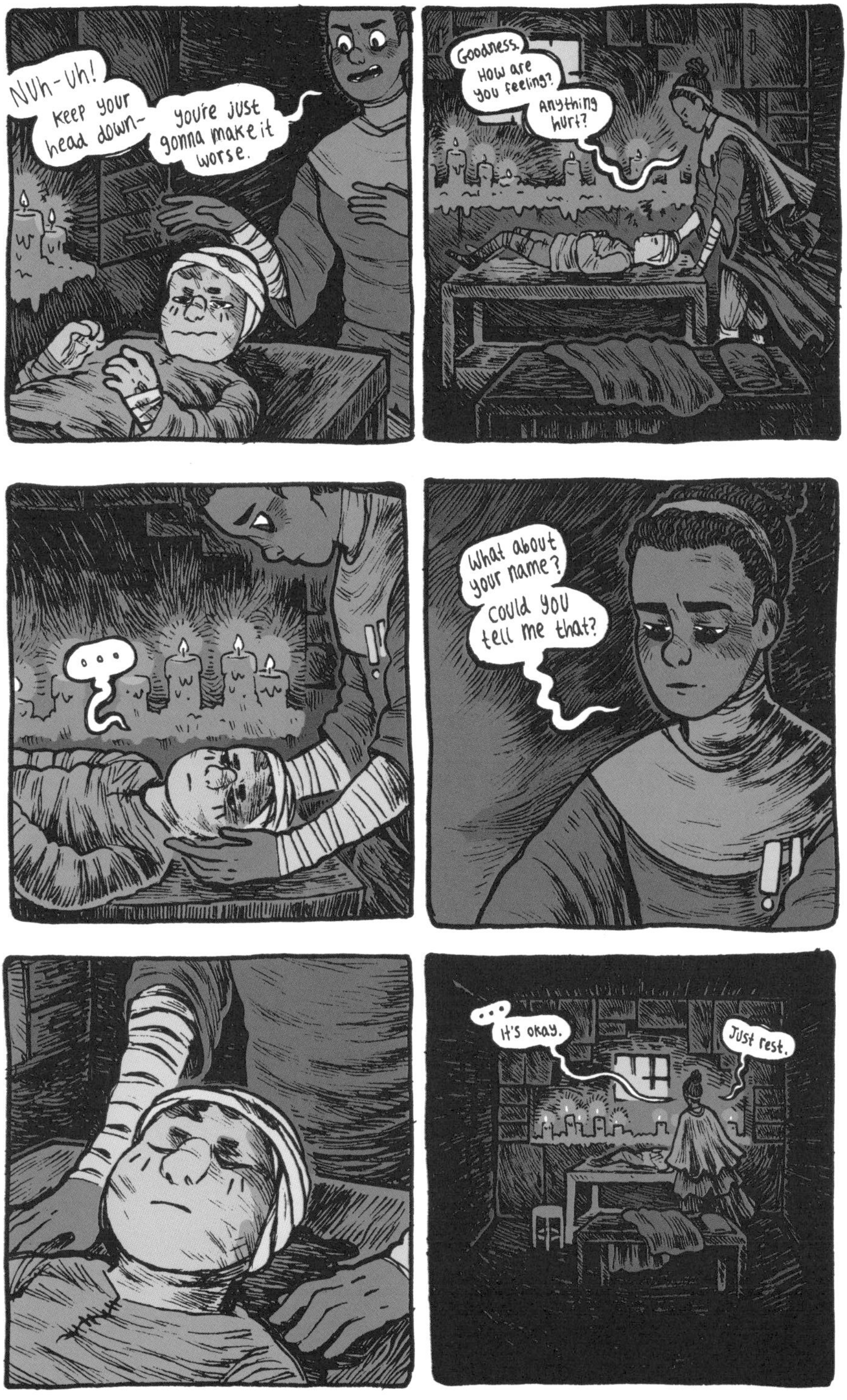
NUh-Uh!
Keep your head down-
You're just gonna make it worse.
Goodness.
How are you feeling?
Anything hurt?
...
What about your name?
Could you tell me that?
...
It's okay.
Just rest.

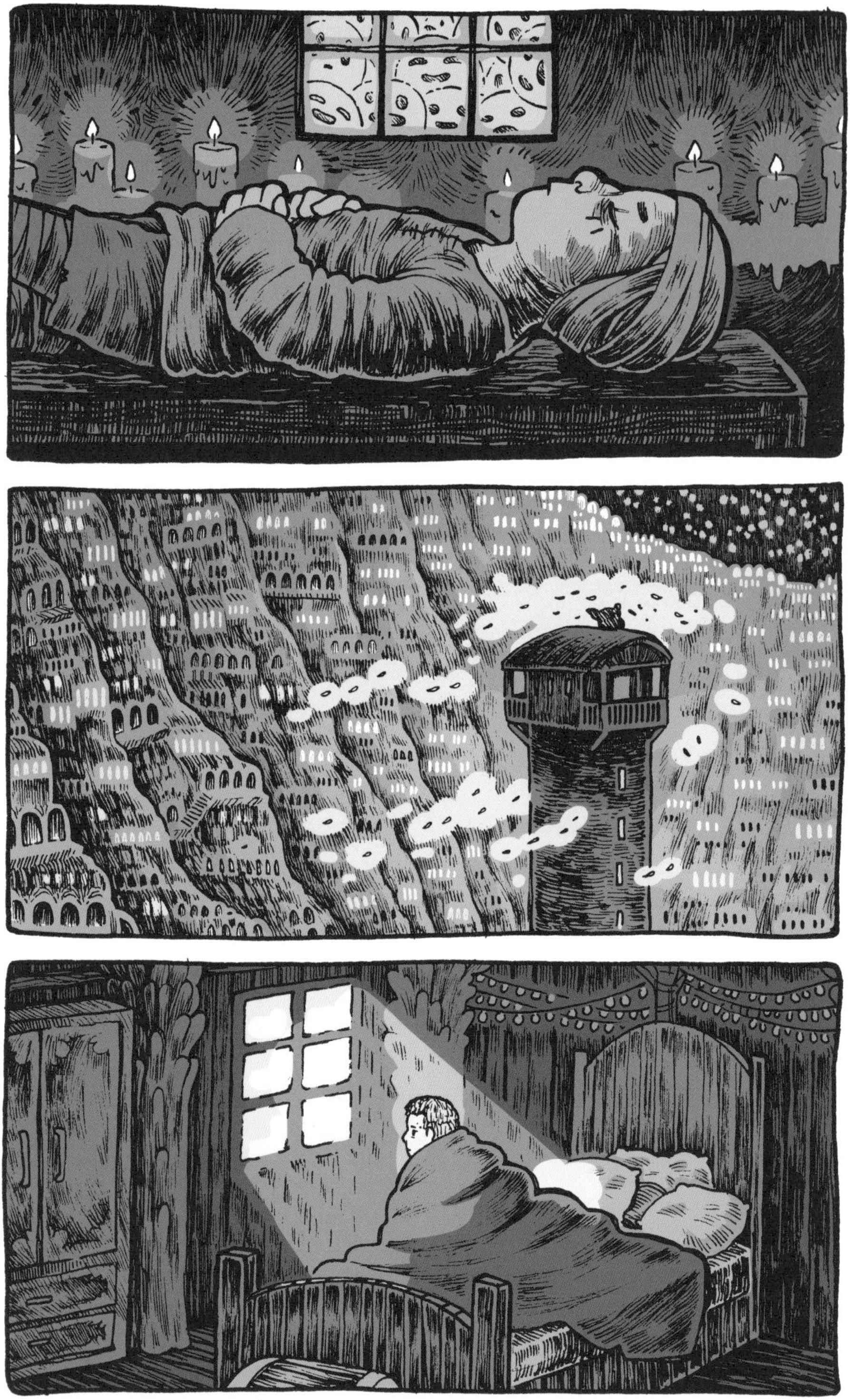

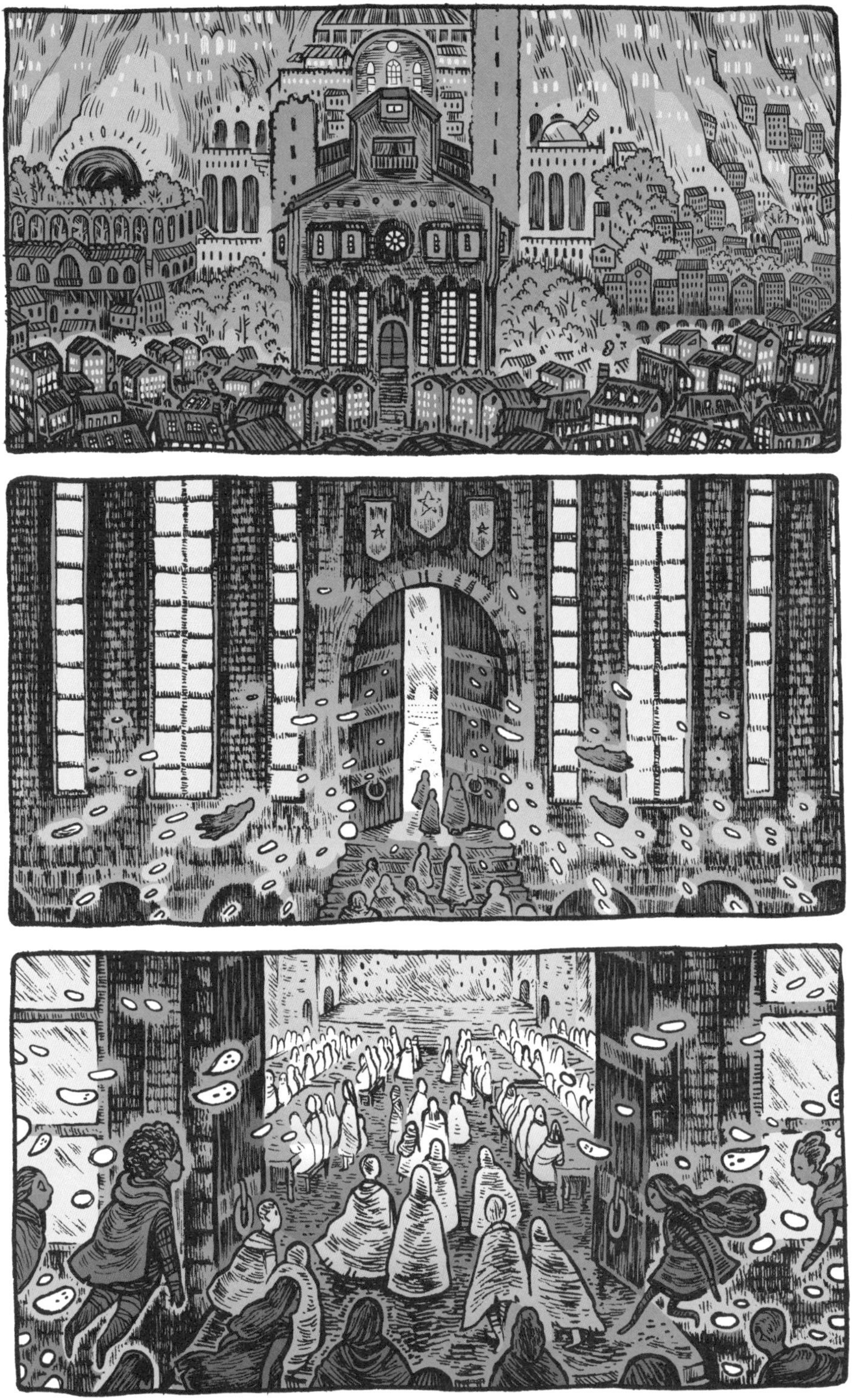

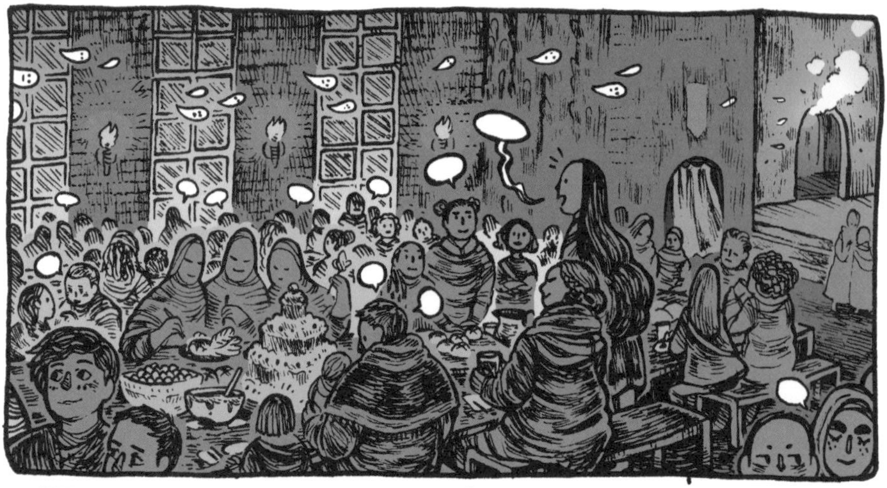
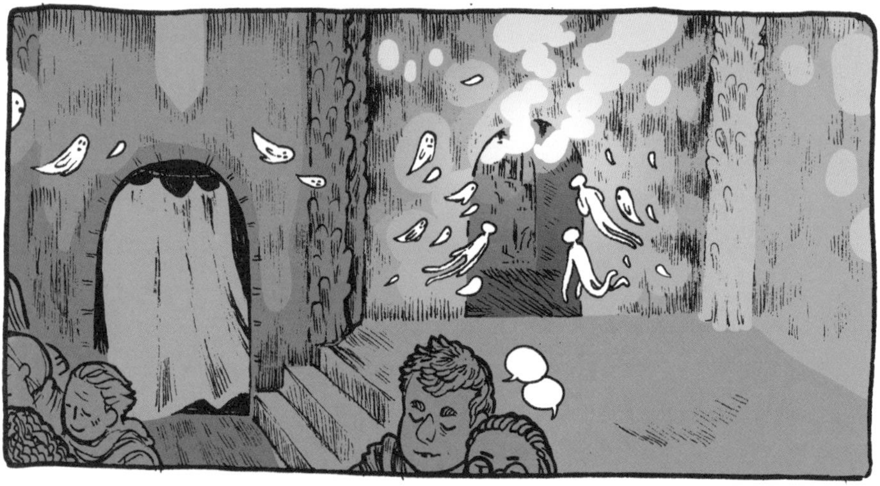
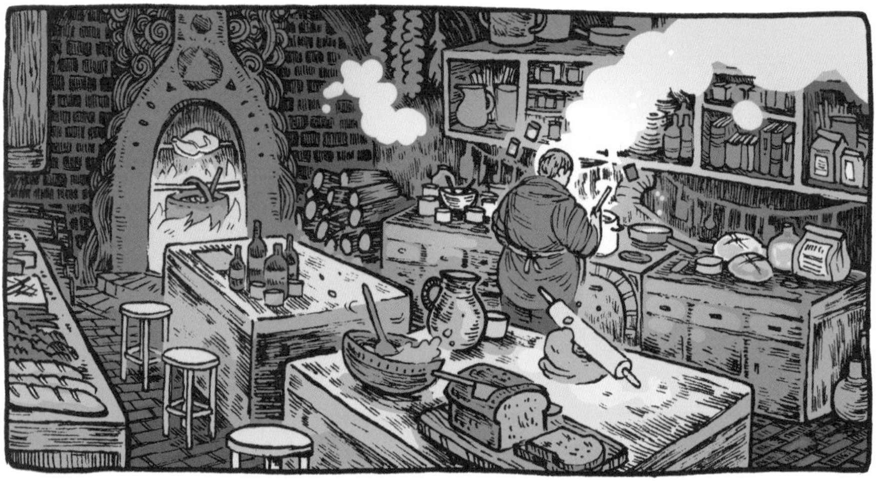

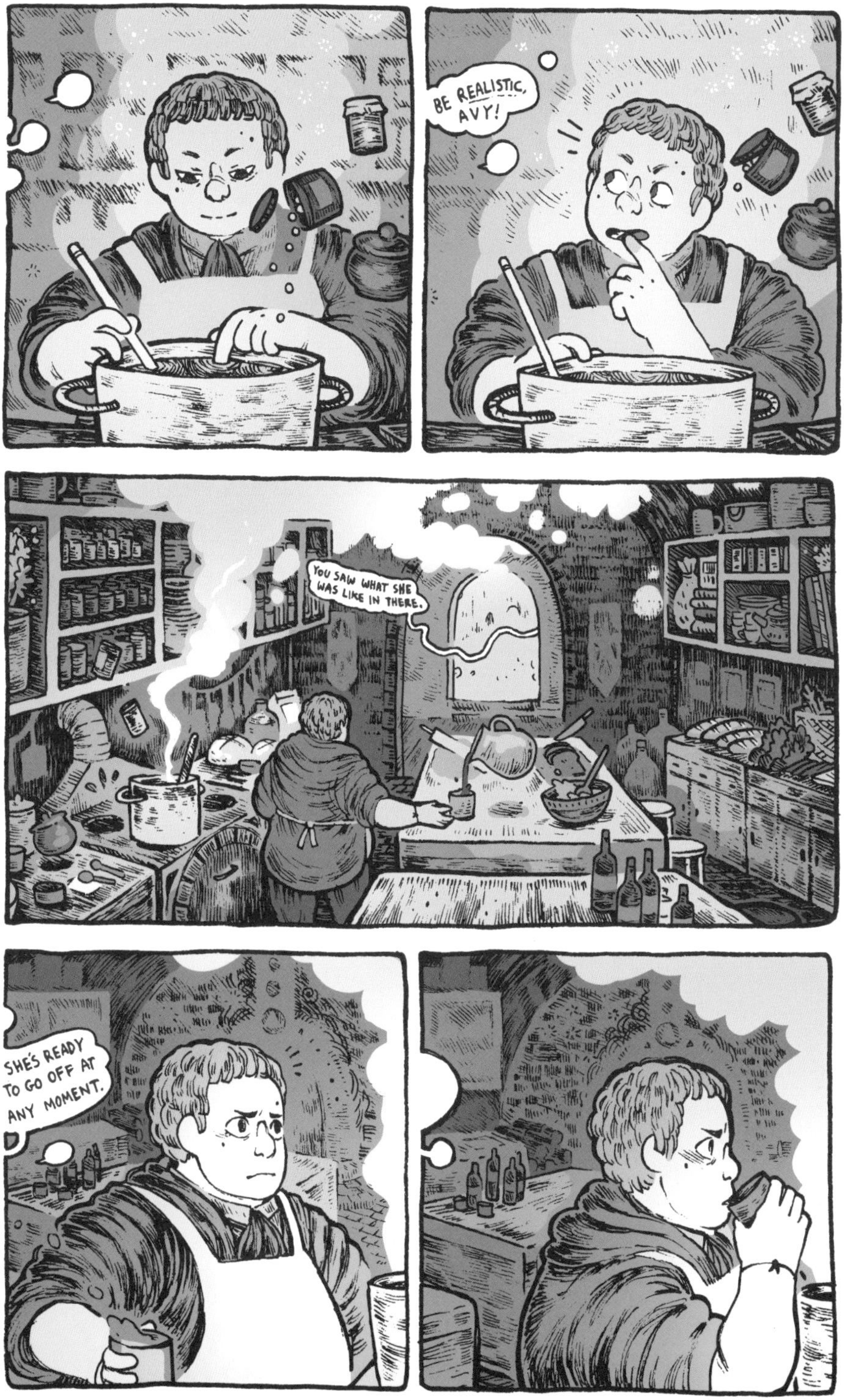
BE REALISTIC, AVY!
YOU SAW WHAT SHE WAS LIKE IN THERE.
SHE'S READY TO GO OFF AT ANY MOMENT.

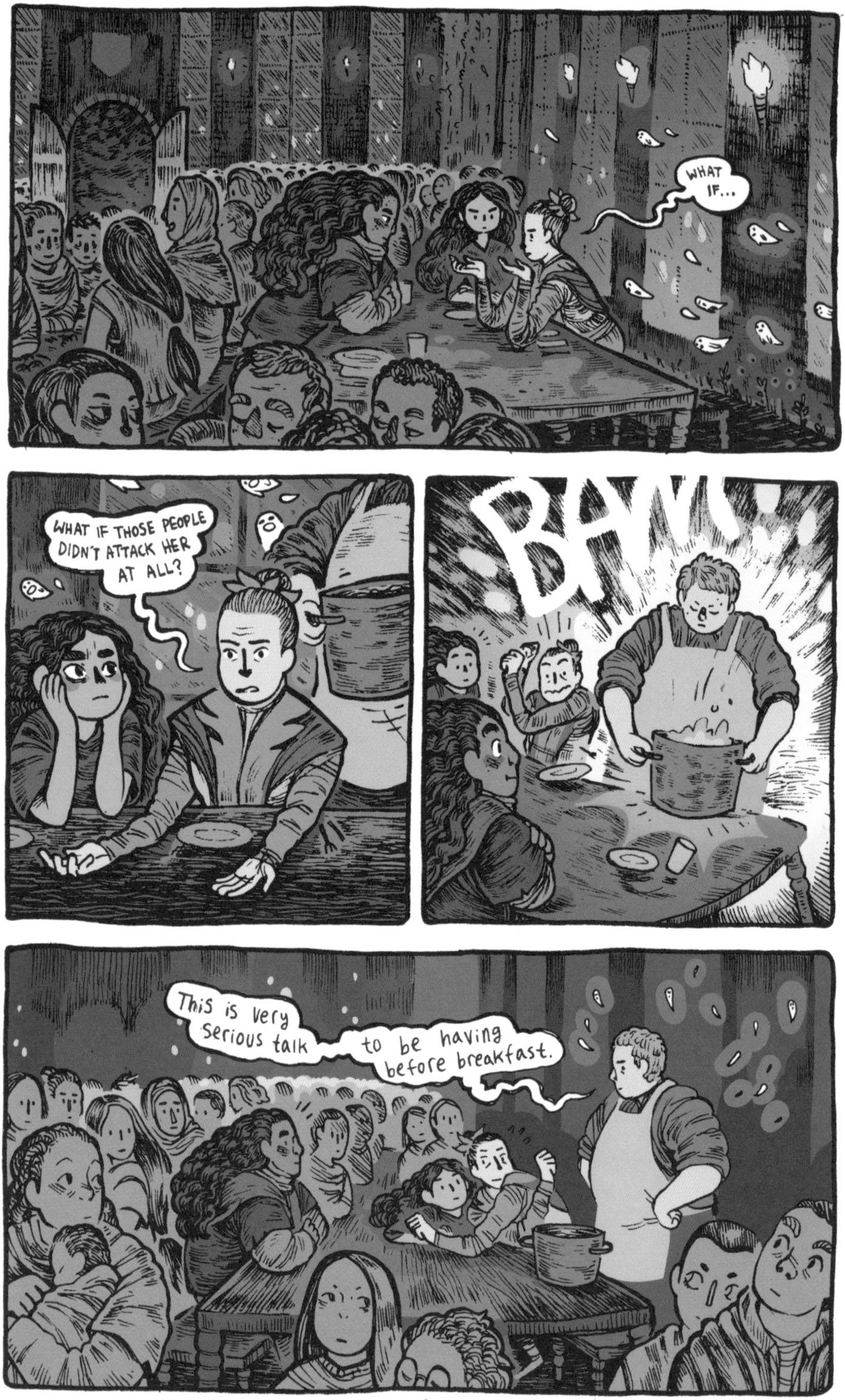
WHAT IF...
WHAT IF THOSE PEOPLE DIDN'T ATTACK HER AT ALL?
This is very serious talk
to be having before breakfast.

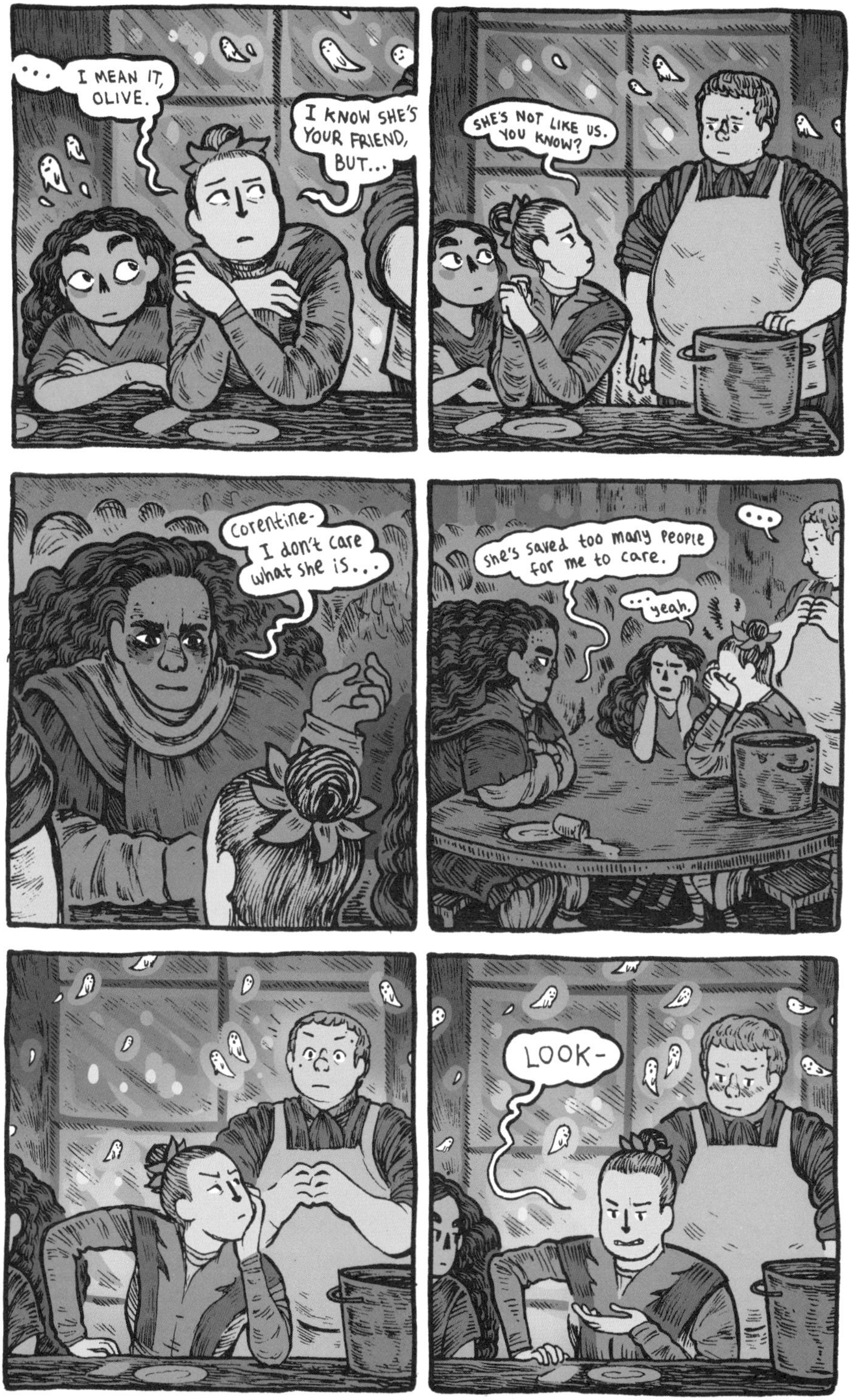
...
I MEAN IT, OLIVE.
I KNOW SHE'S YOUR FRIEND, BUT...
SHE'S NOT LIKE US. YOU KNOW?
Corentine- I don't care what she is...
She's saved too many people for me to care.
...
...yeah.
LOOK-

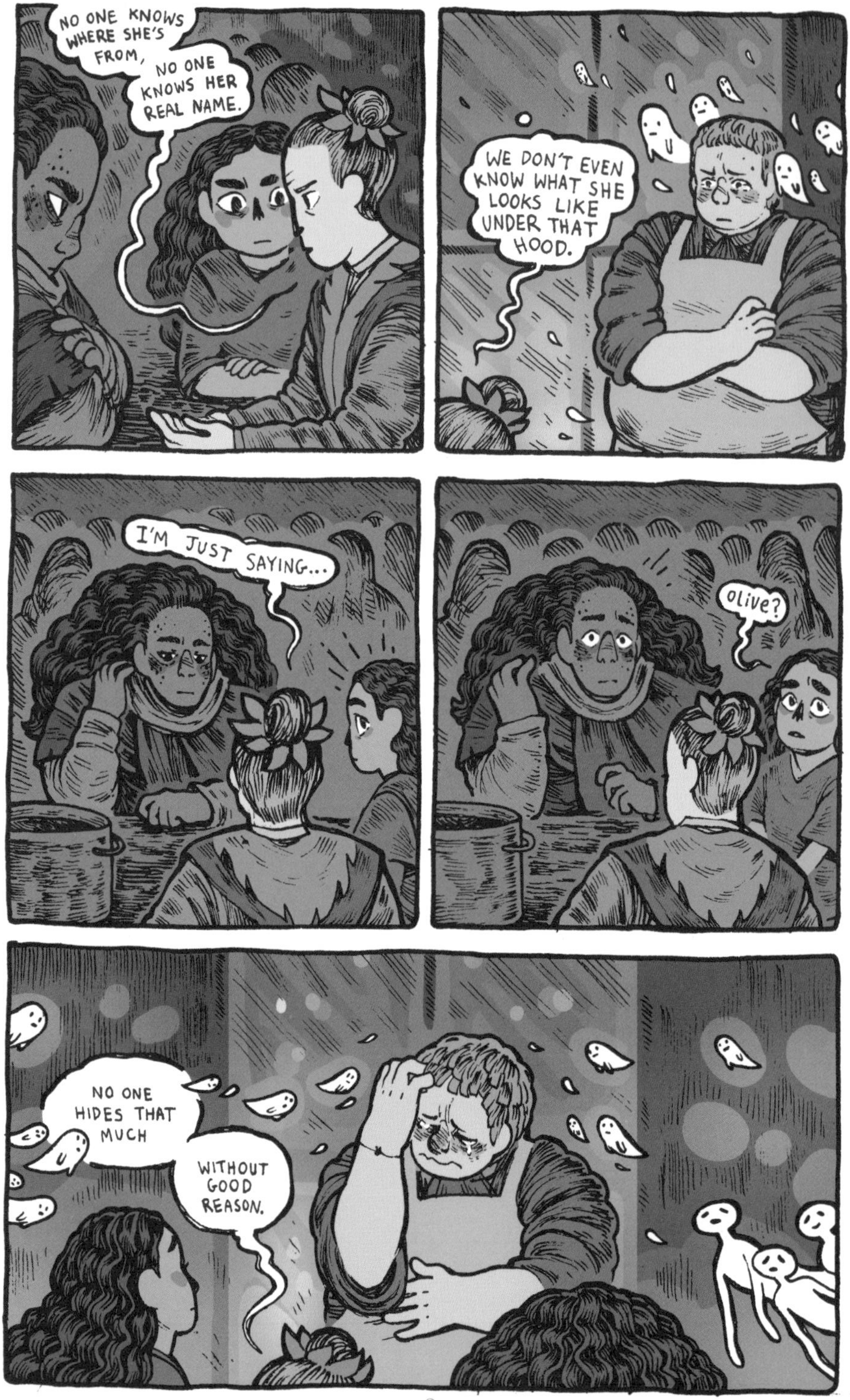
NO ONE KNOWS WHERE SHE'S FROM,
NO ONE KNOWS HER REAL NAME.
WE DON'T EVEN KNOW WHAT SHE LOOKS LIKE UNDER THAT HOOD.
I'M JUST SAYING...
olive?
NO ONE HIDES THAT MUCH
WITHOUT GOOD REASON.

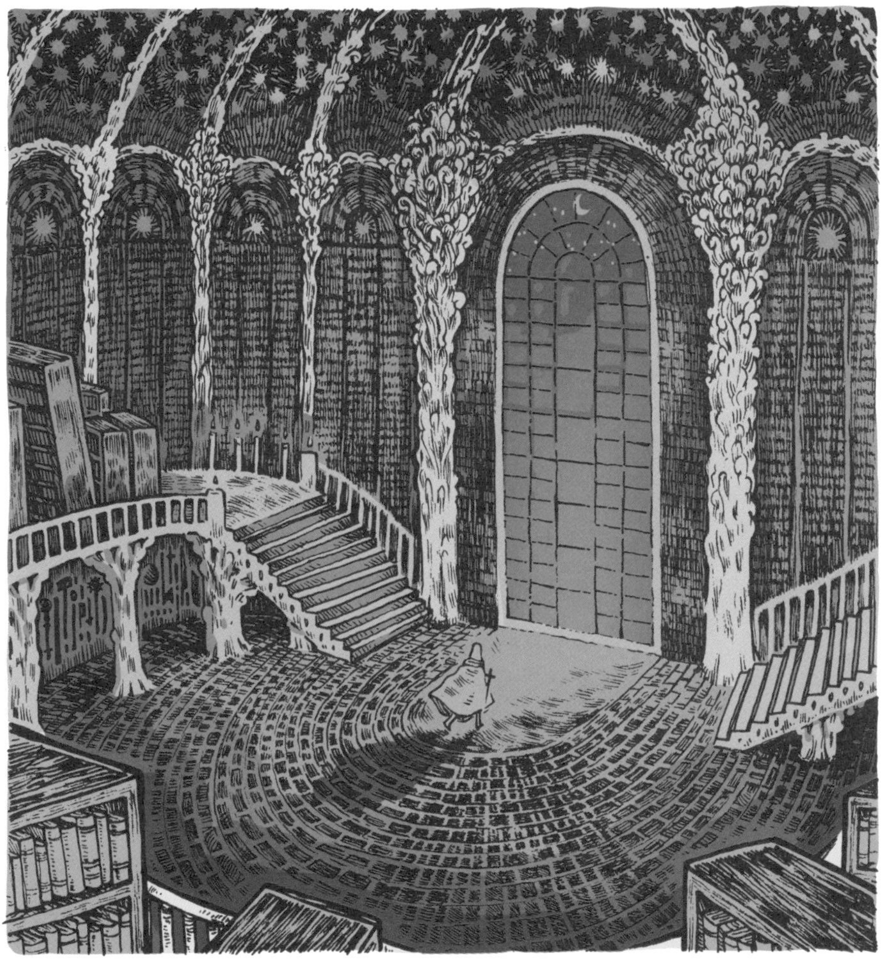

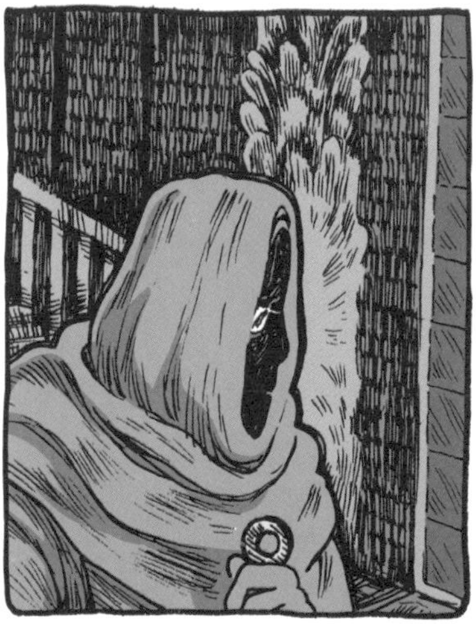

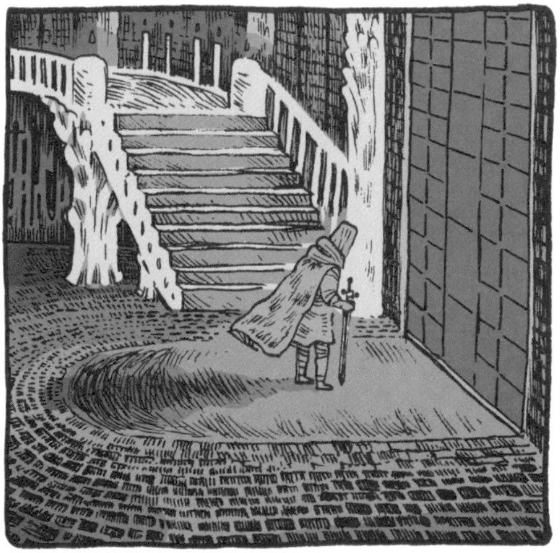

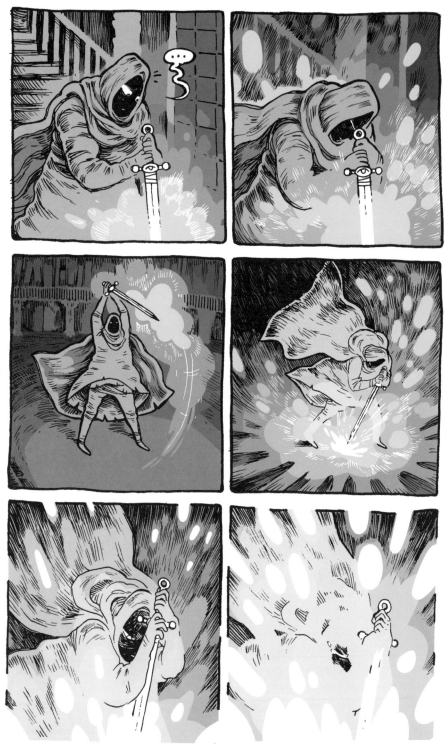

40

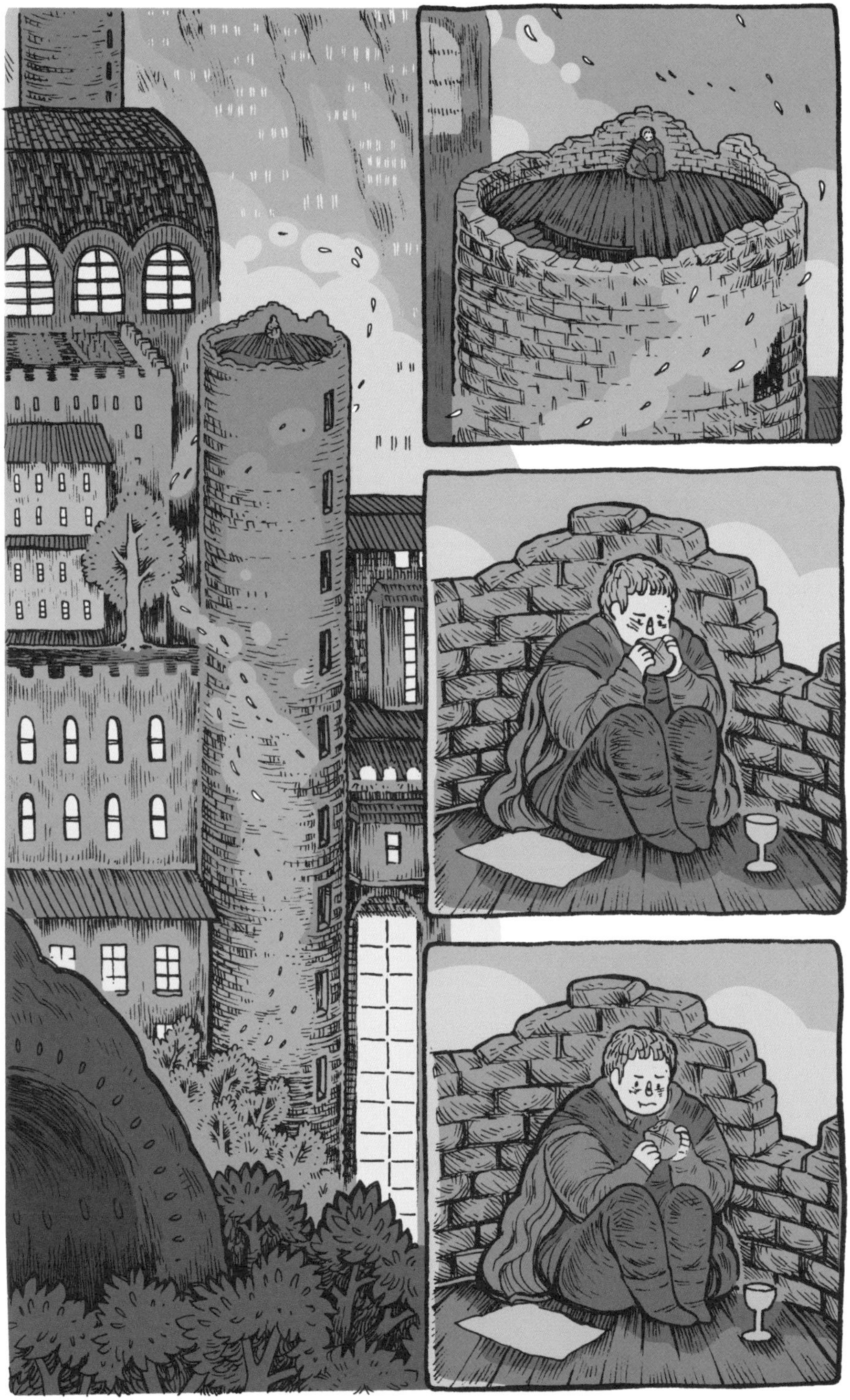

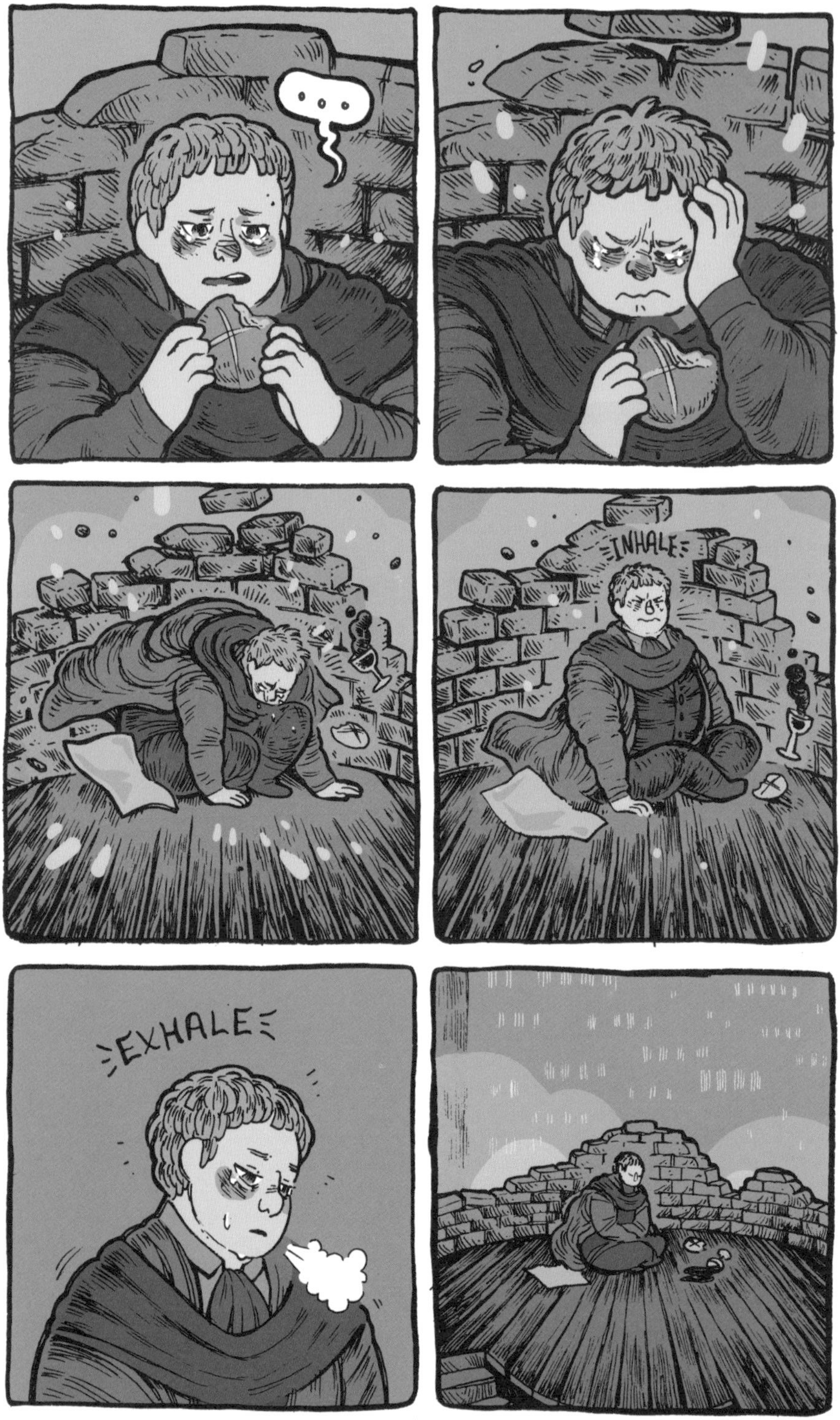
...
INHALE
EXHALE

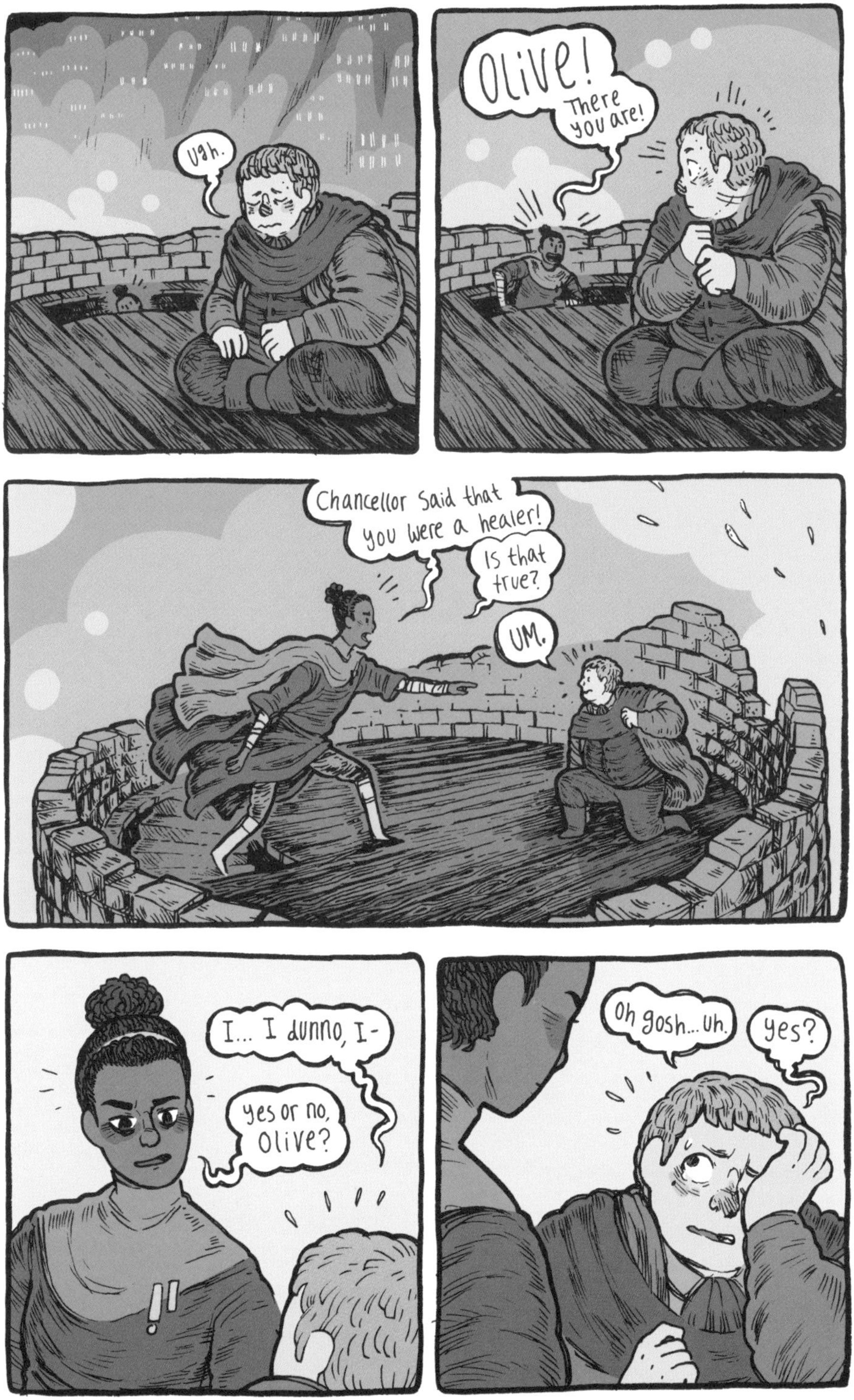
Ugh.
Olive! There you are!
Chancellor said that you were a healer!
Is that true?
UM.
I... I dunno, I-
yes or no, Olive?
Oh gosh...uh.
yes?

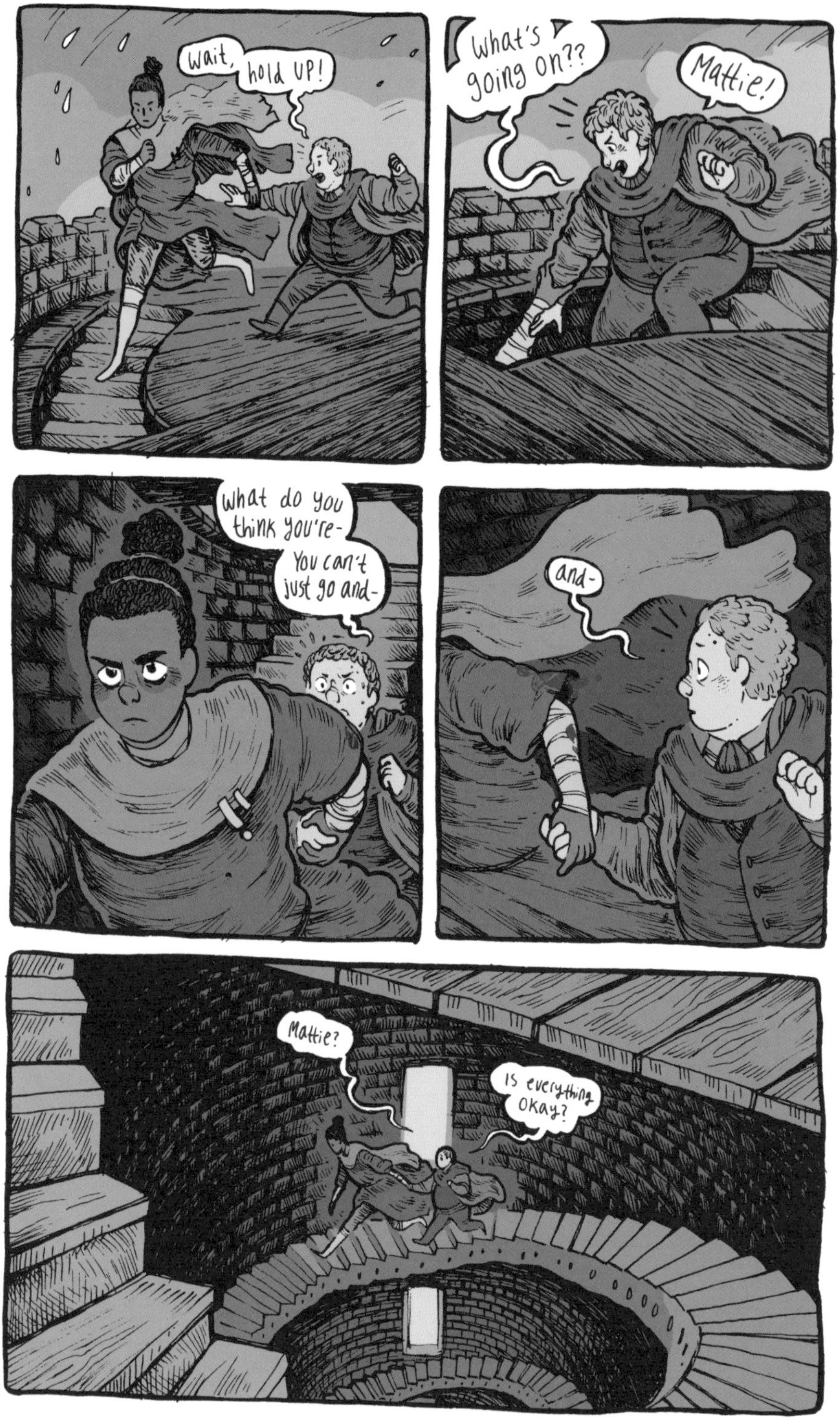
Wait,
hold up!
What's going on??
Mattie!
What do you think you're-
You can't just go and-
and-
Mattie?
Is everything okay?

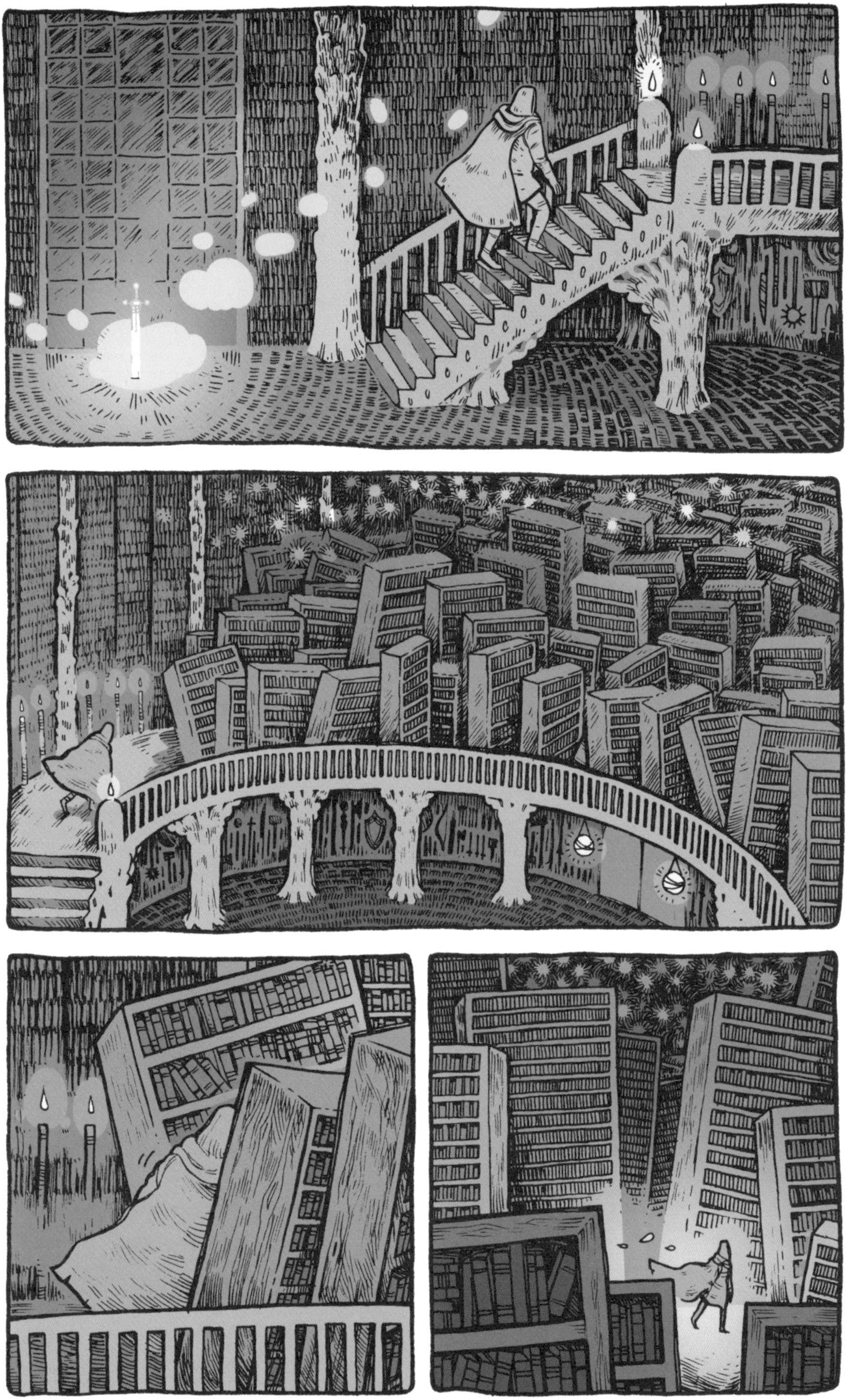

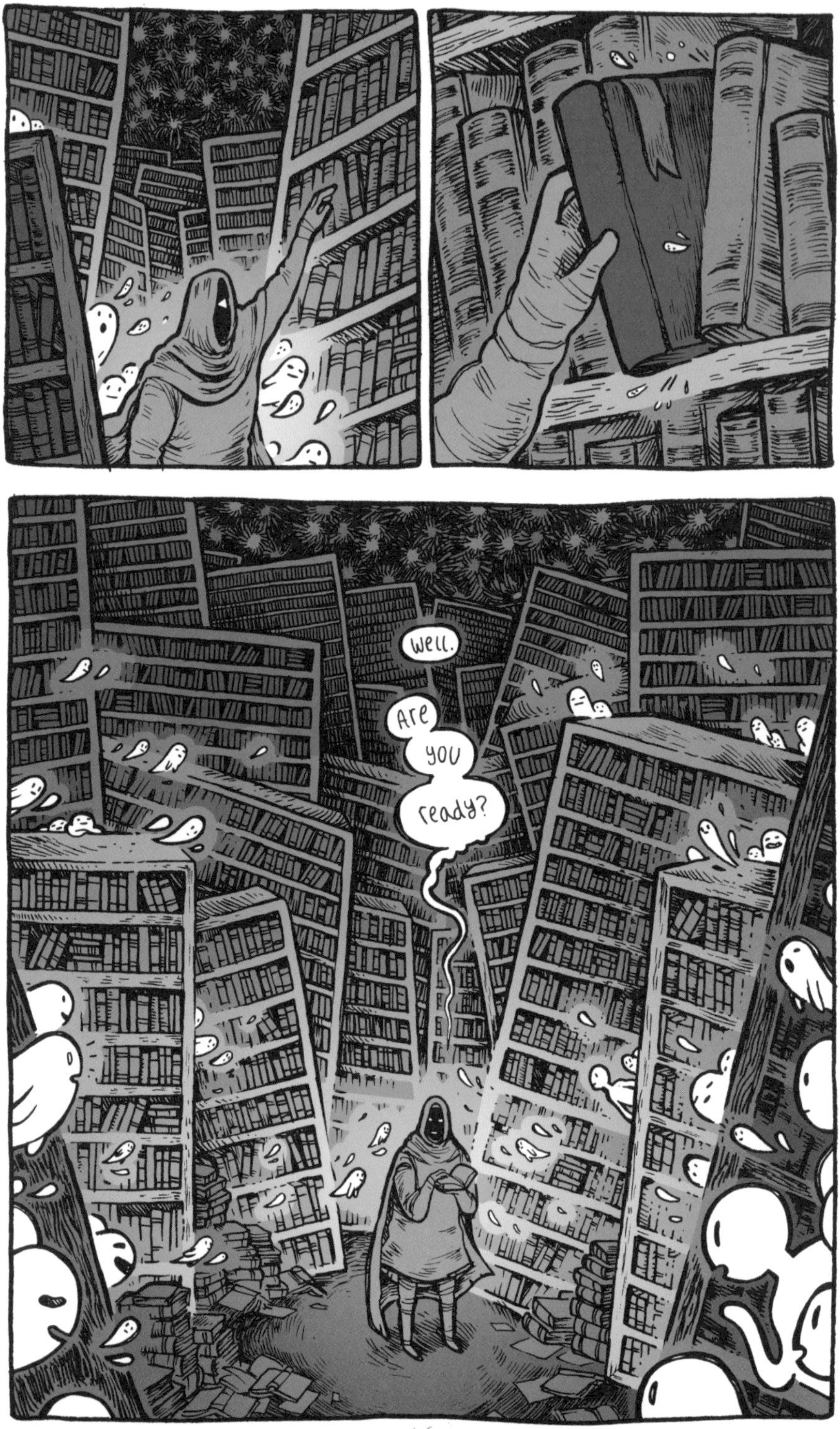
Well.
Are you ready?

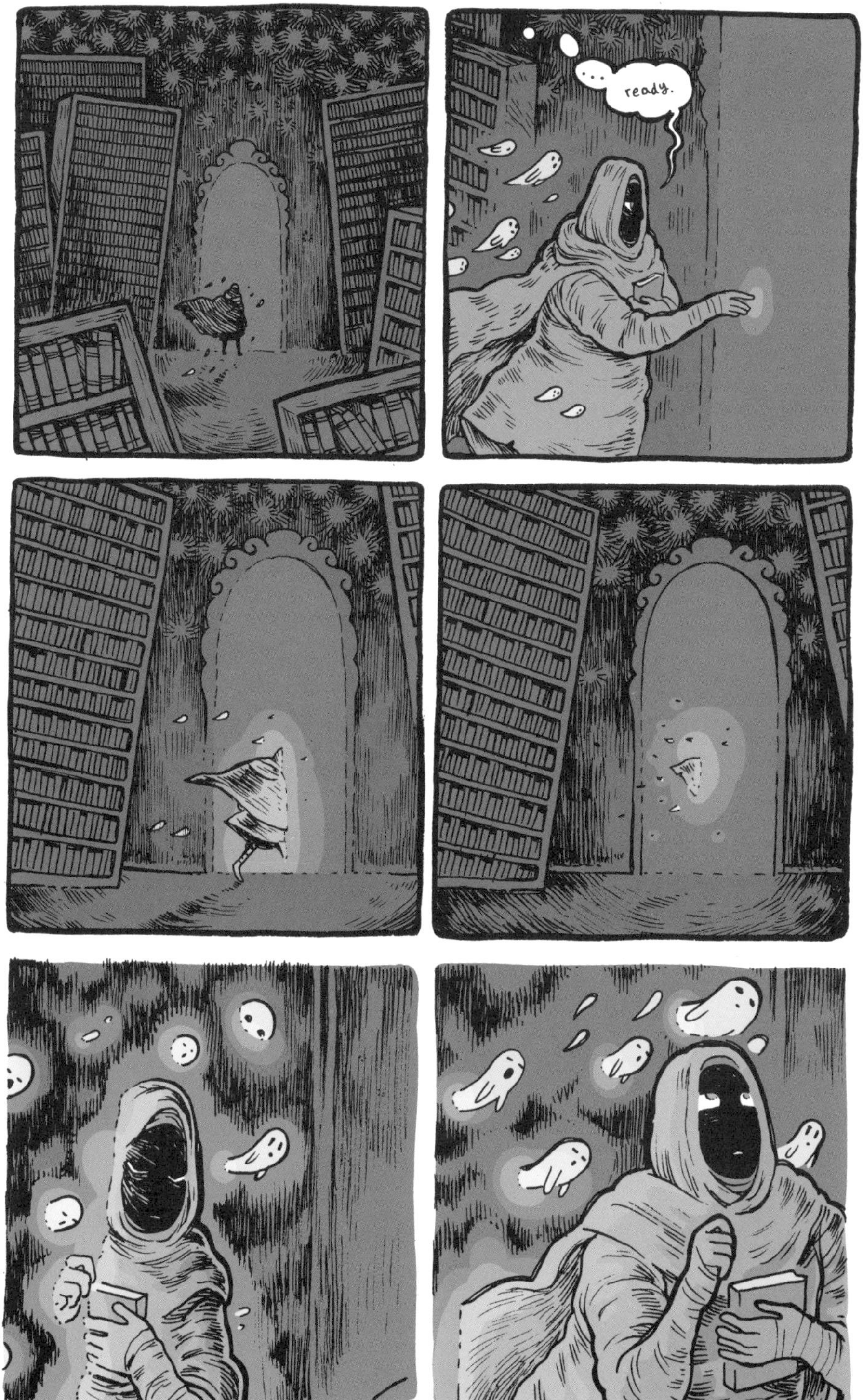
...
ready.

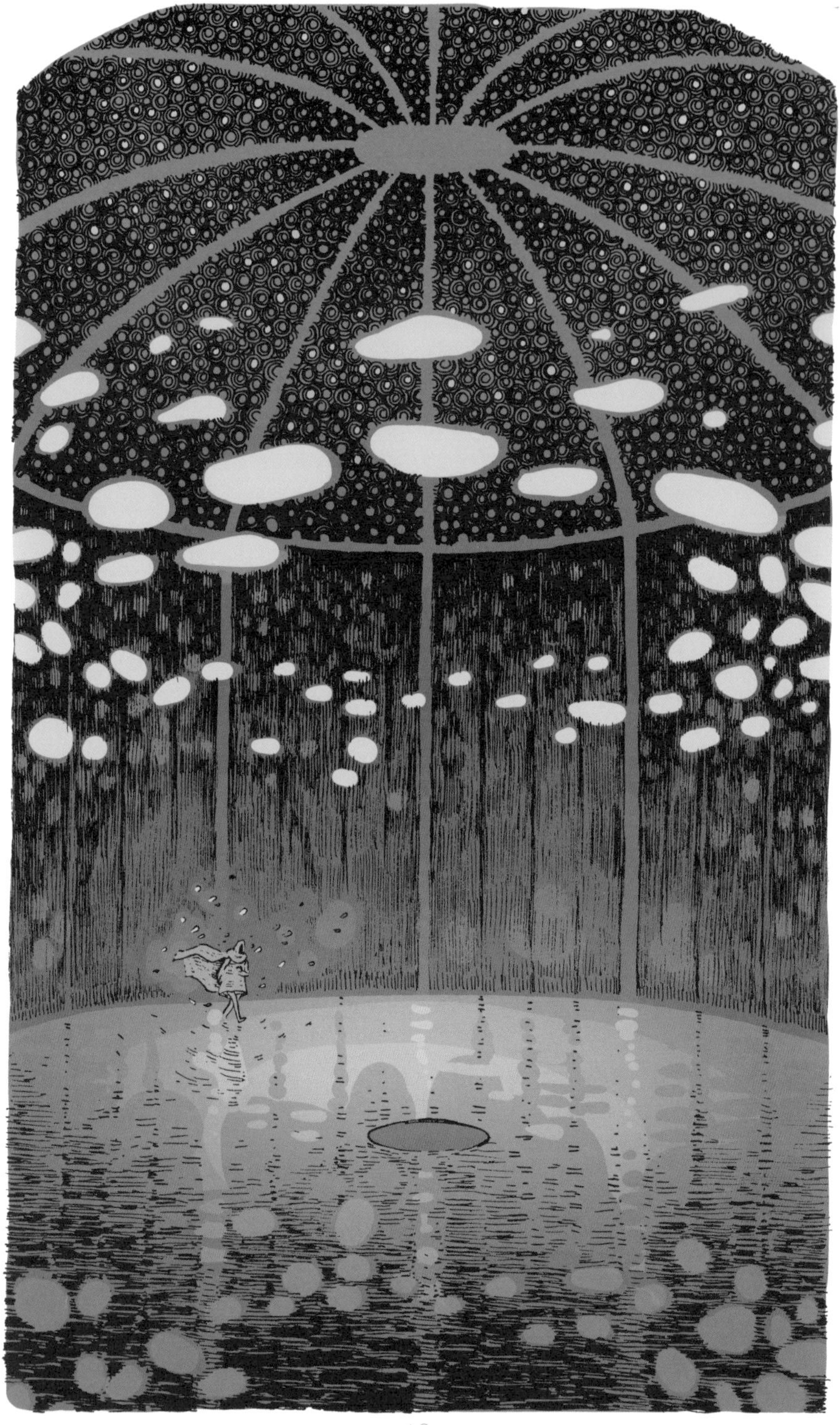

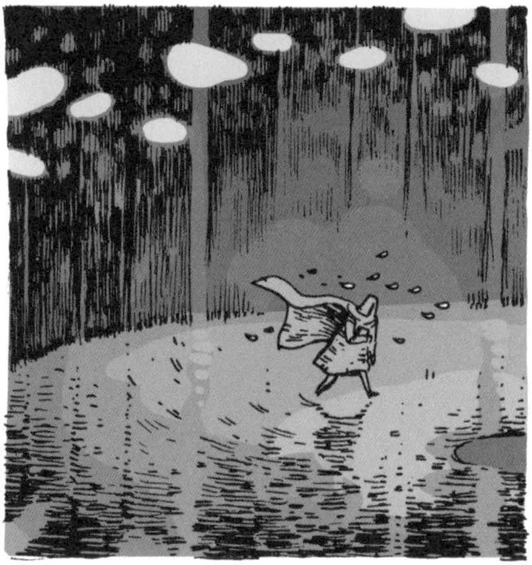
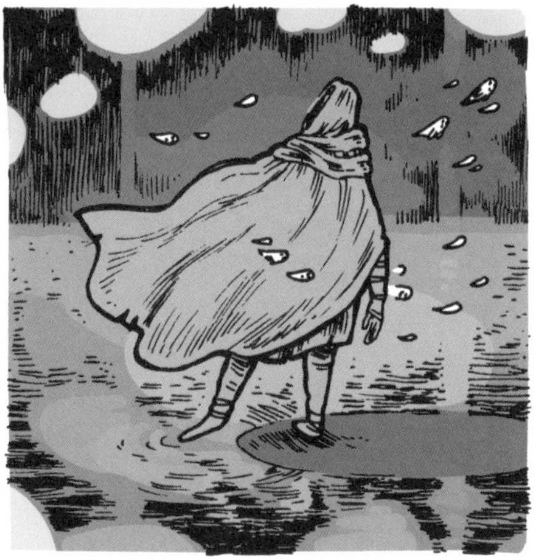
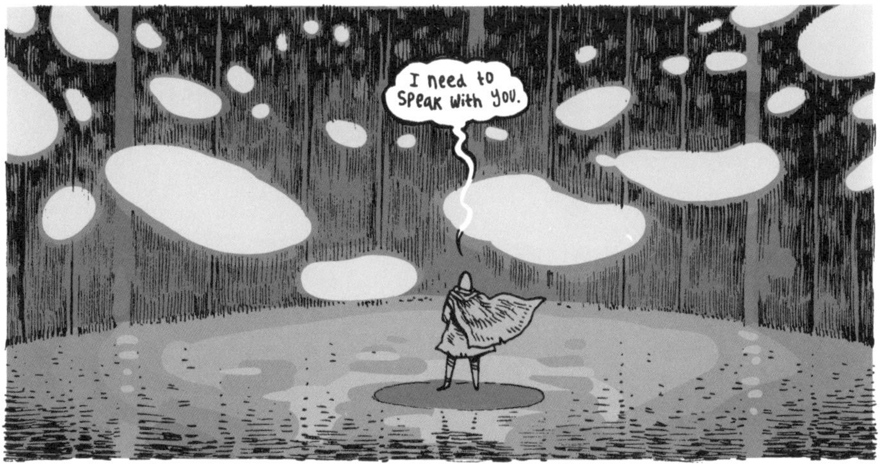
I need to speak with you.
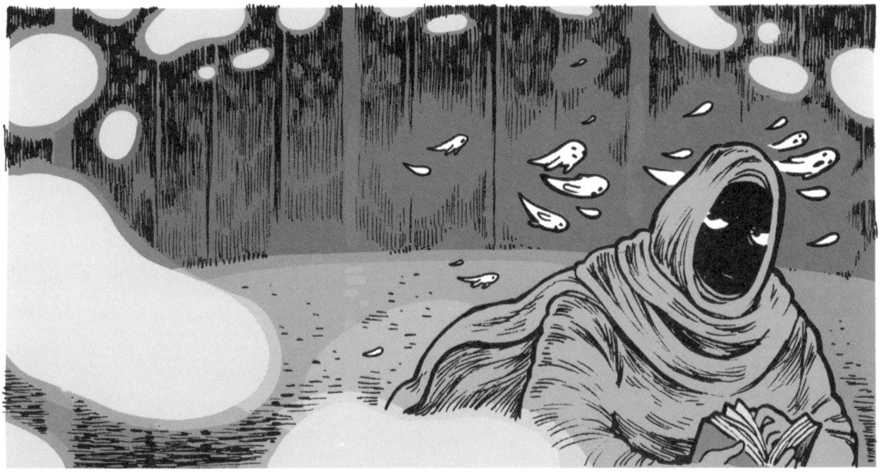

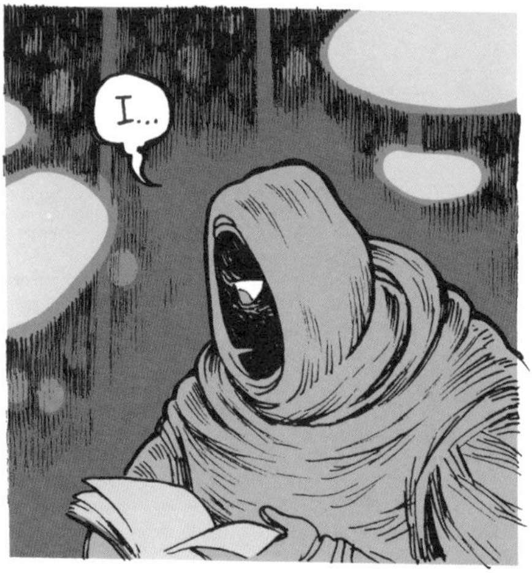
I...
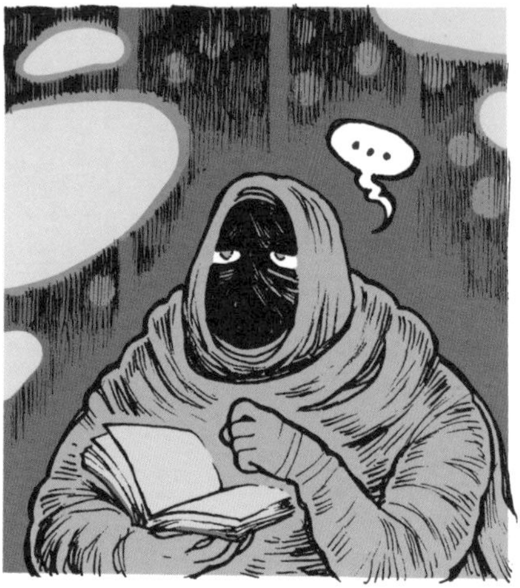
...
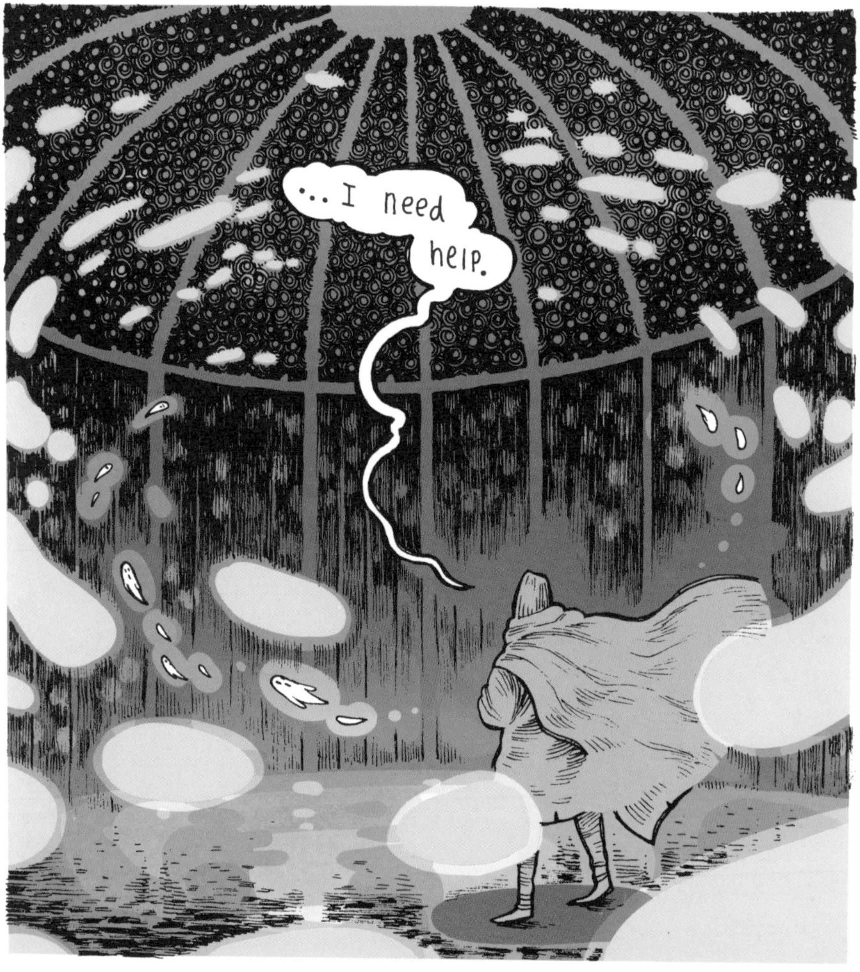
...I need help.

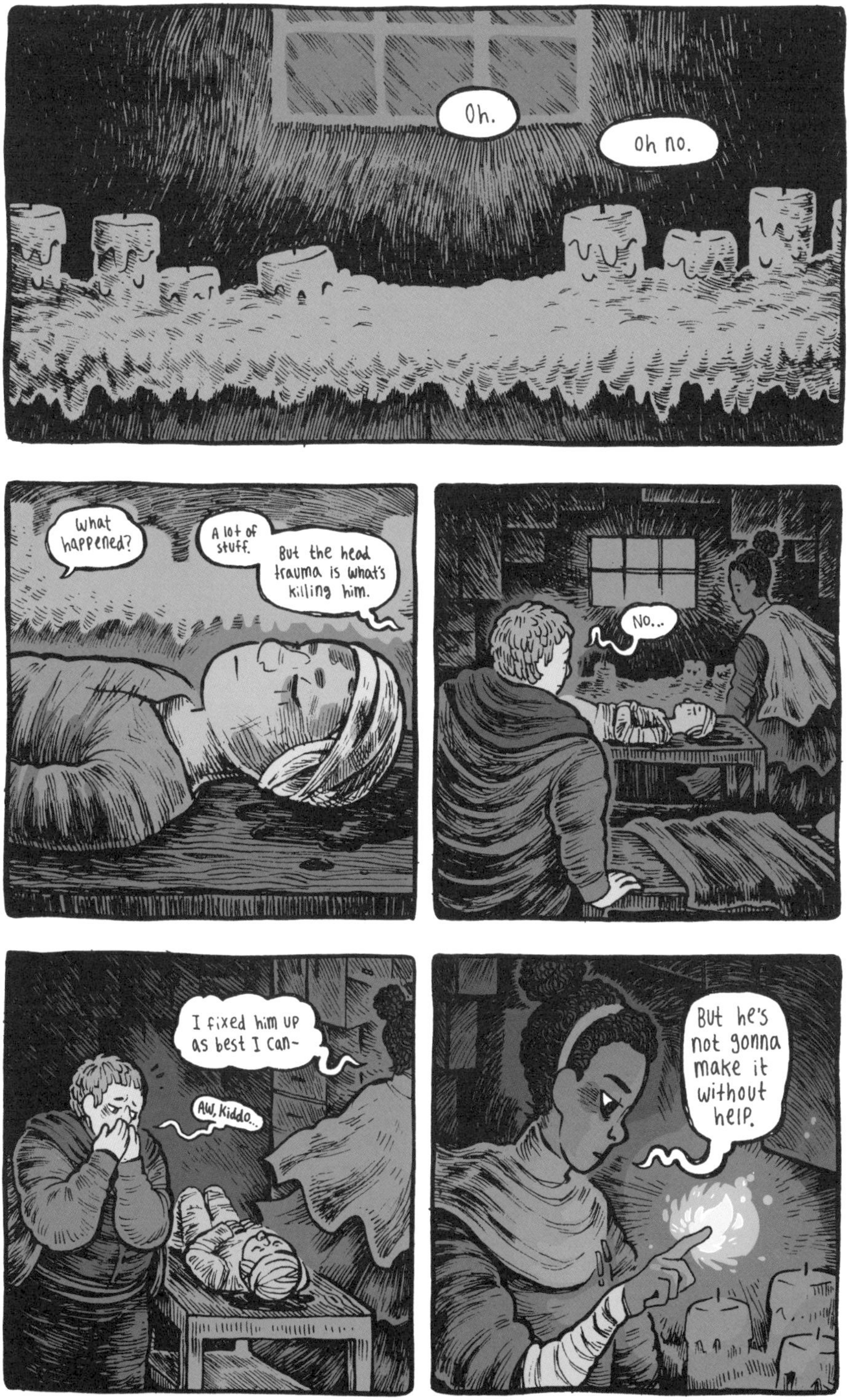
Oh.
Oh no.
What happened?
A lot of stuff.
But the head trauma is what's killing him.
No...
I fixed him up as best I can-
AW, Kiddo...
But he's not gonna make it without help.

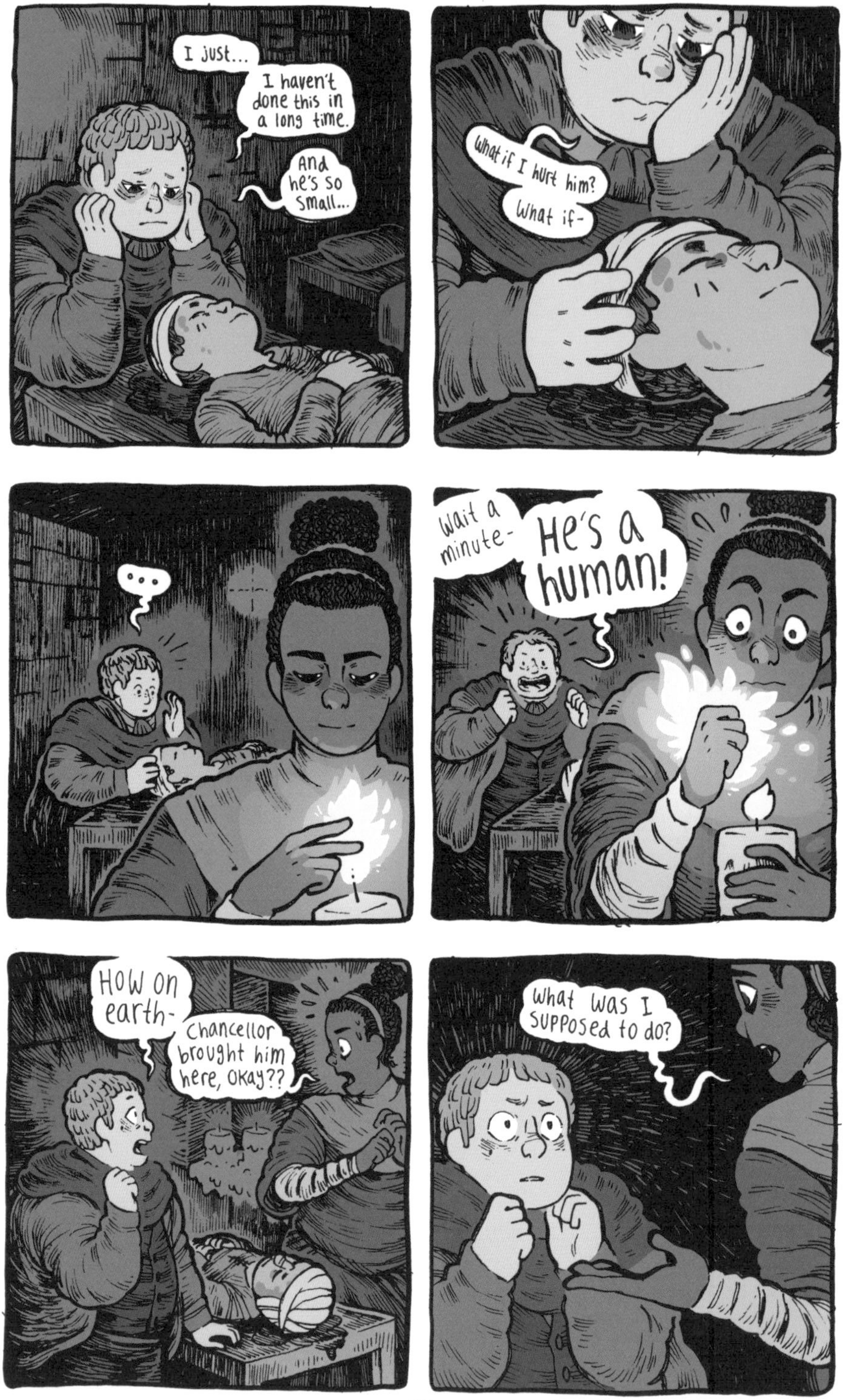
I just...
I haven't done this in a long time.
And he's so small...
What if I hurt him?
What if-
...
Wait a minute-
He's a human!
How on earth-
Chancellor brought him here, okay??
What was I supposed to do?

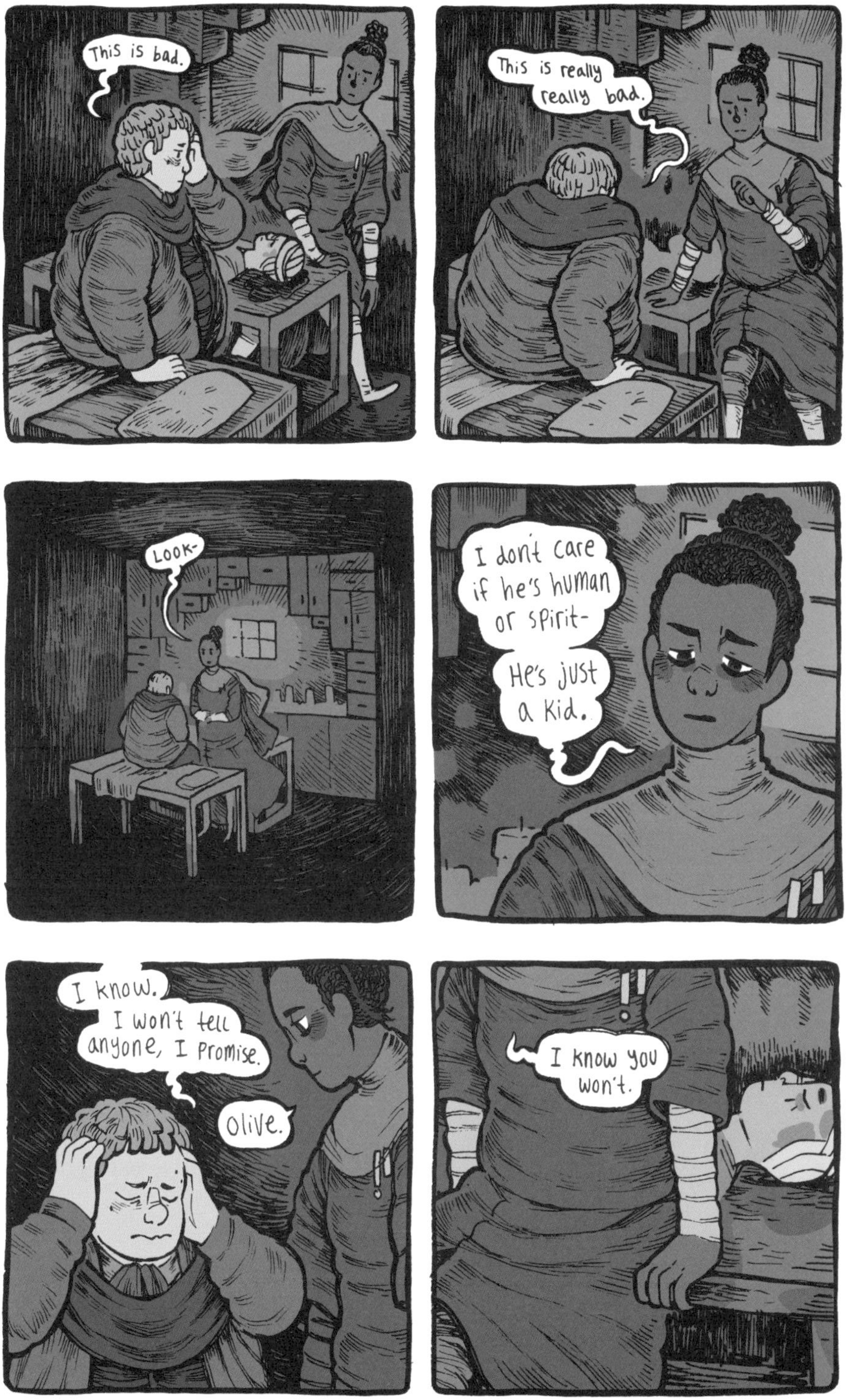
This is bad.
This is really really bad.
Look-
I don't care if he's human or spirit-
He's just a kid.
I know. I won't tell anyone, I promise.
Olive.
I know you won't.

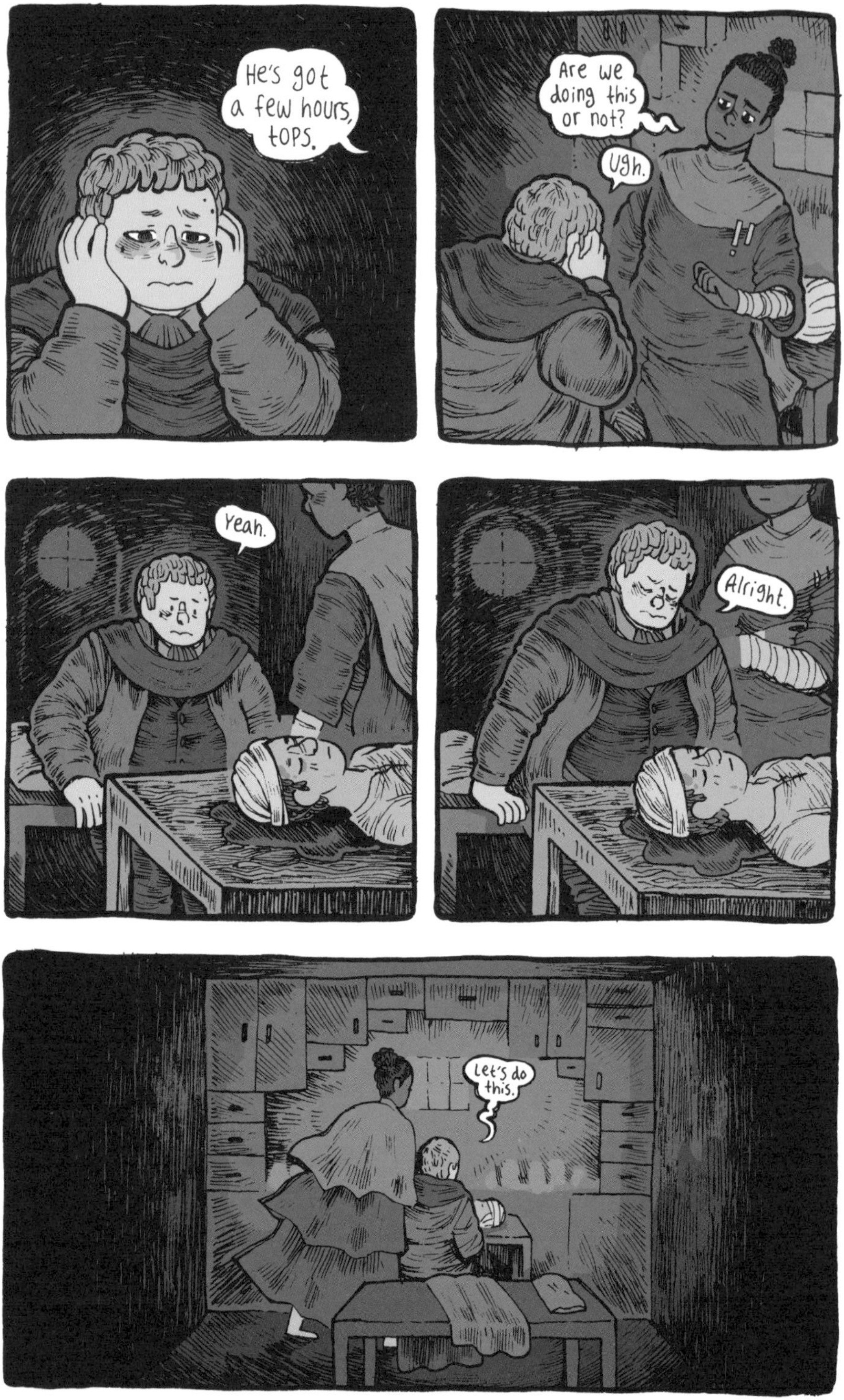
He's got a few hours, tops.
Are we doing this or not?
Ugh.
Yeah.
Alright.
Let's do this.

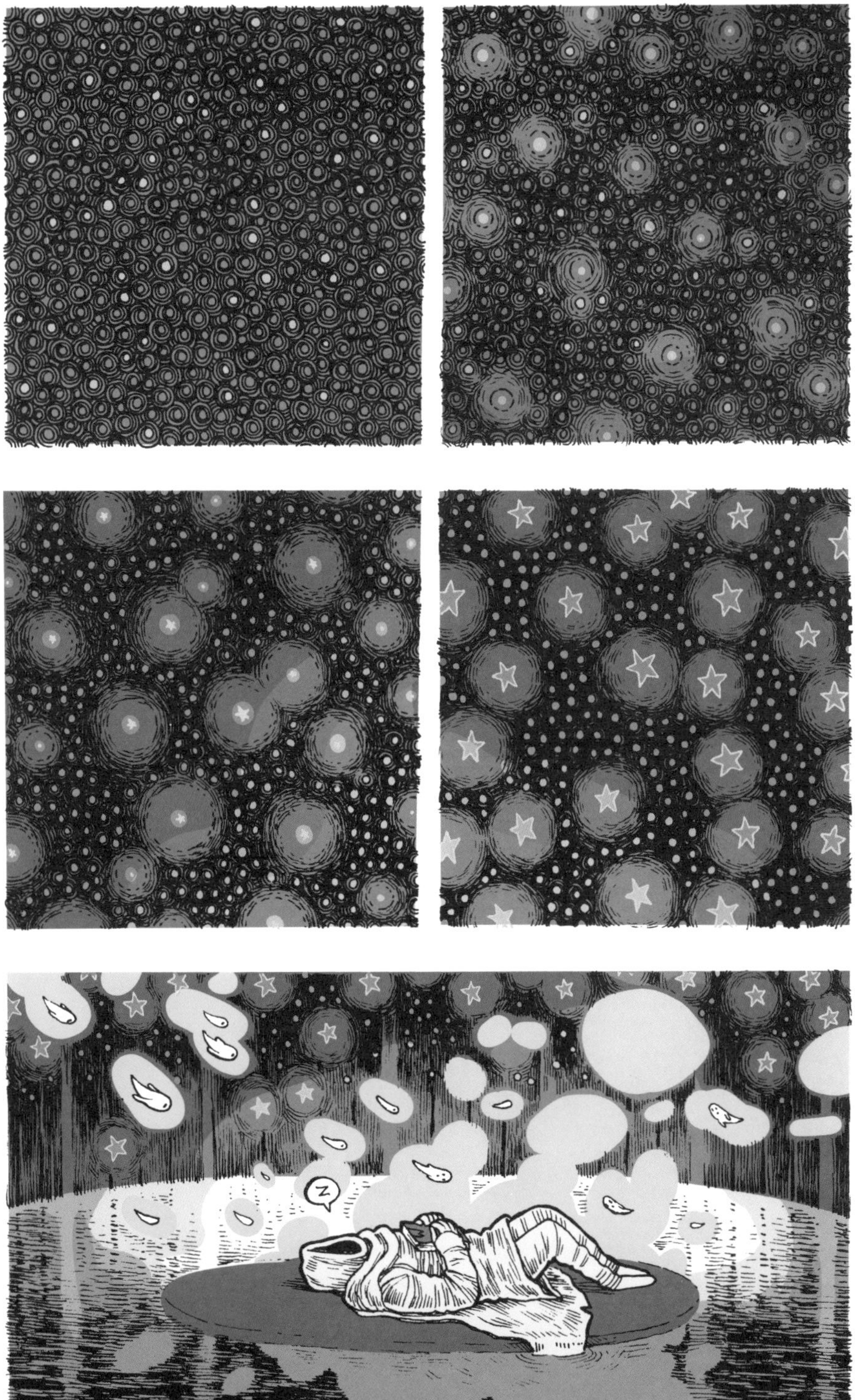
Z

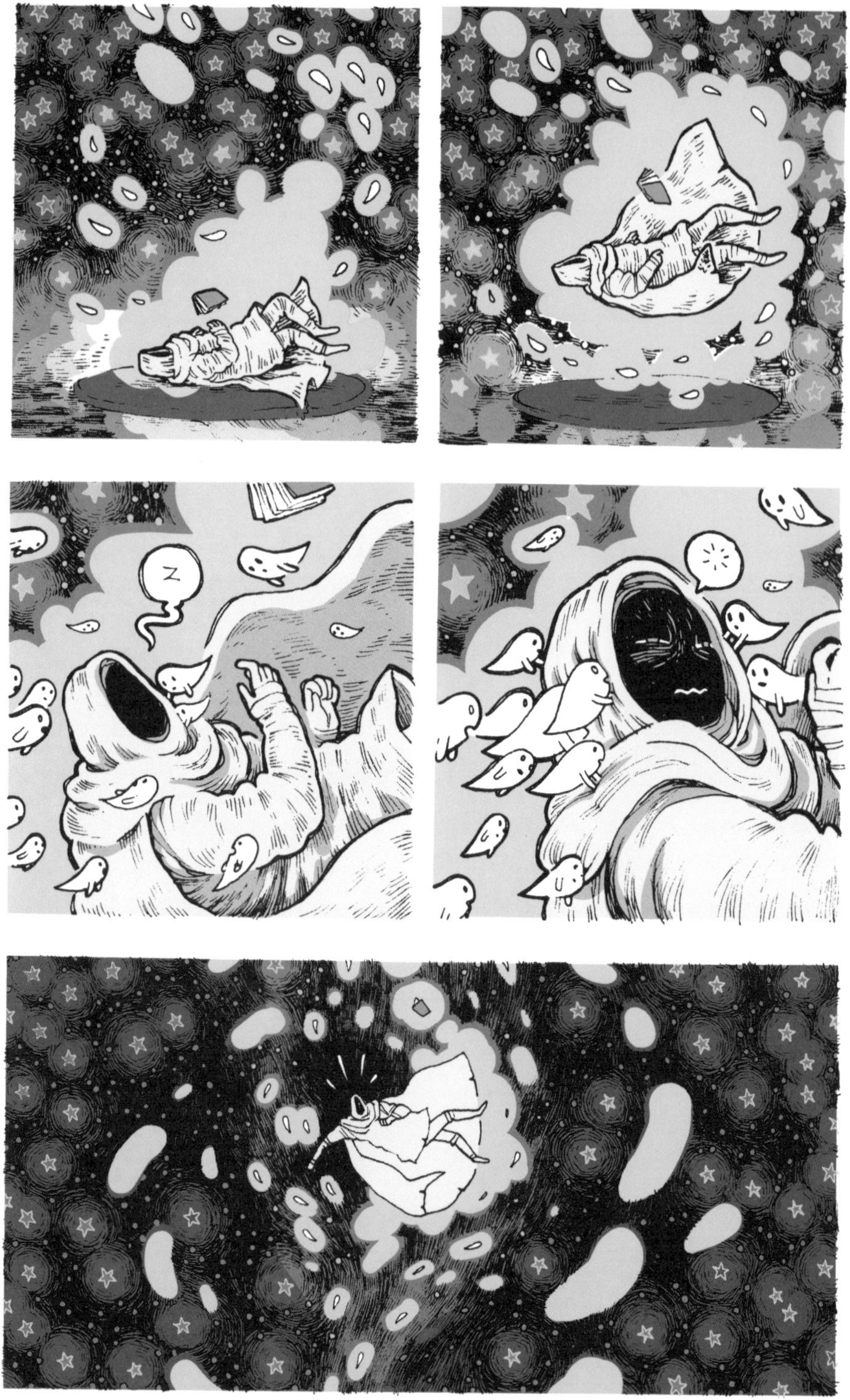
Z

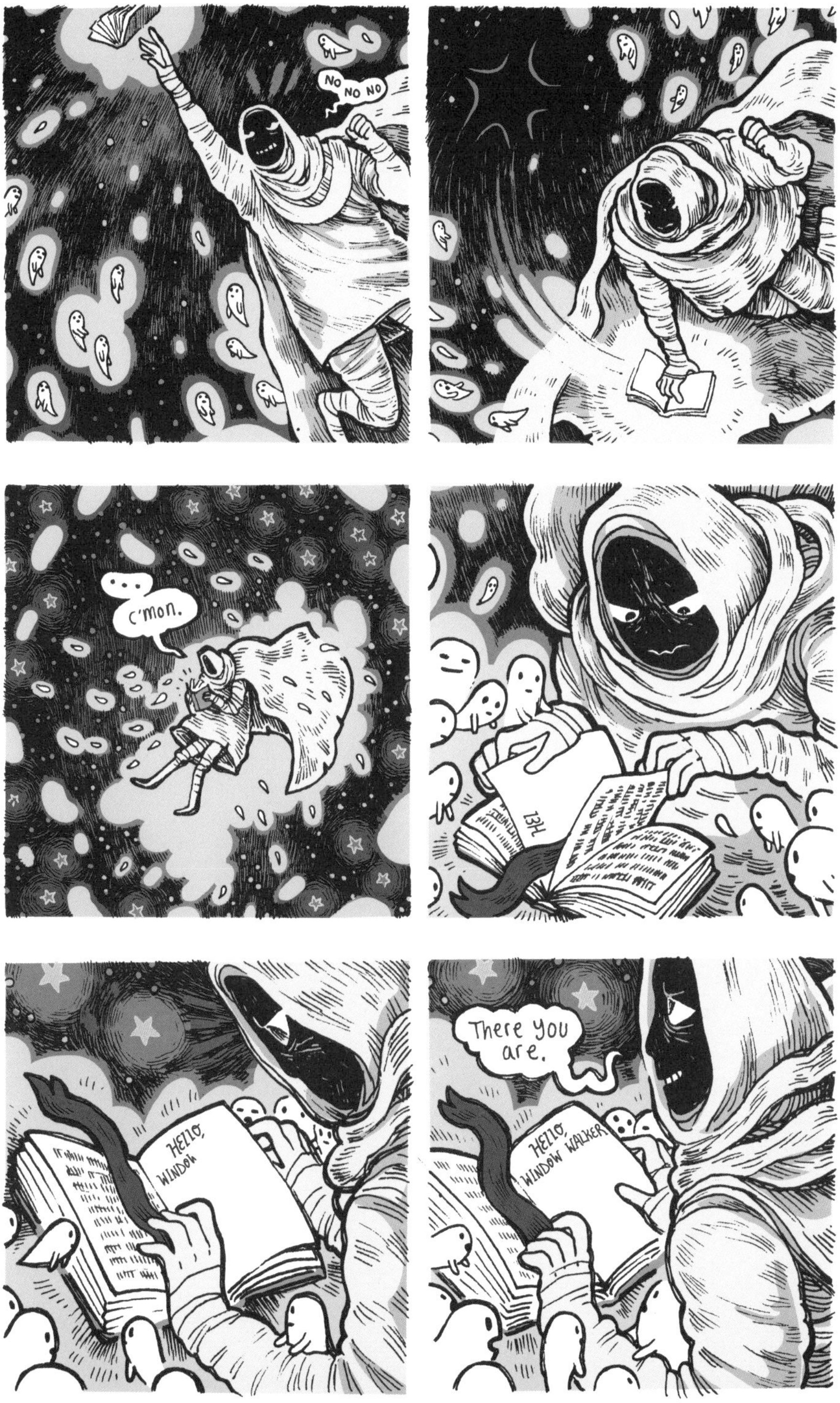
NO NO NO
C'mon.
HELLO, WINDOW
There you are.
HELLO, WINDOW WALKER

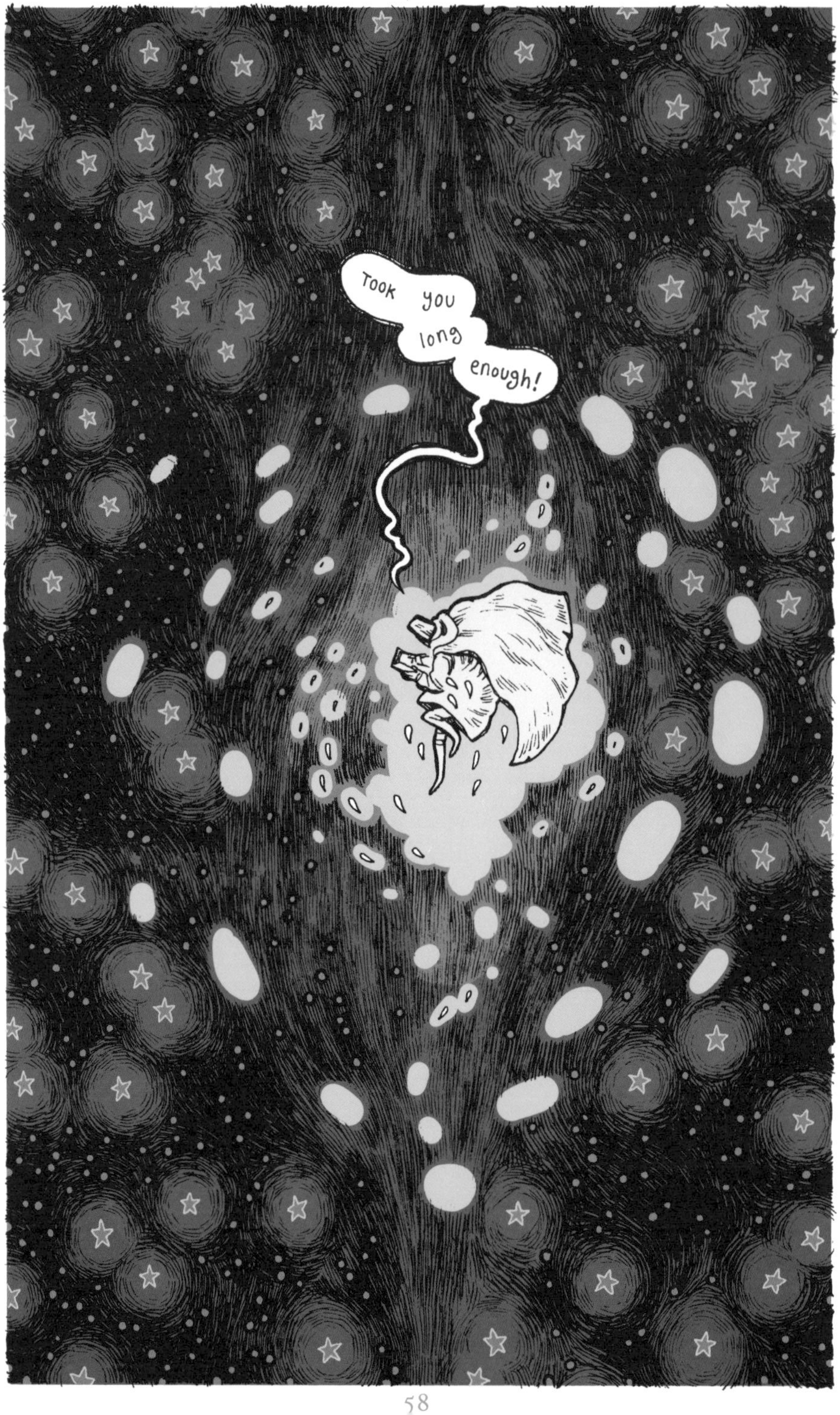
Took you long enough!

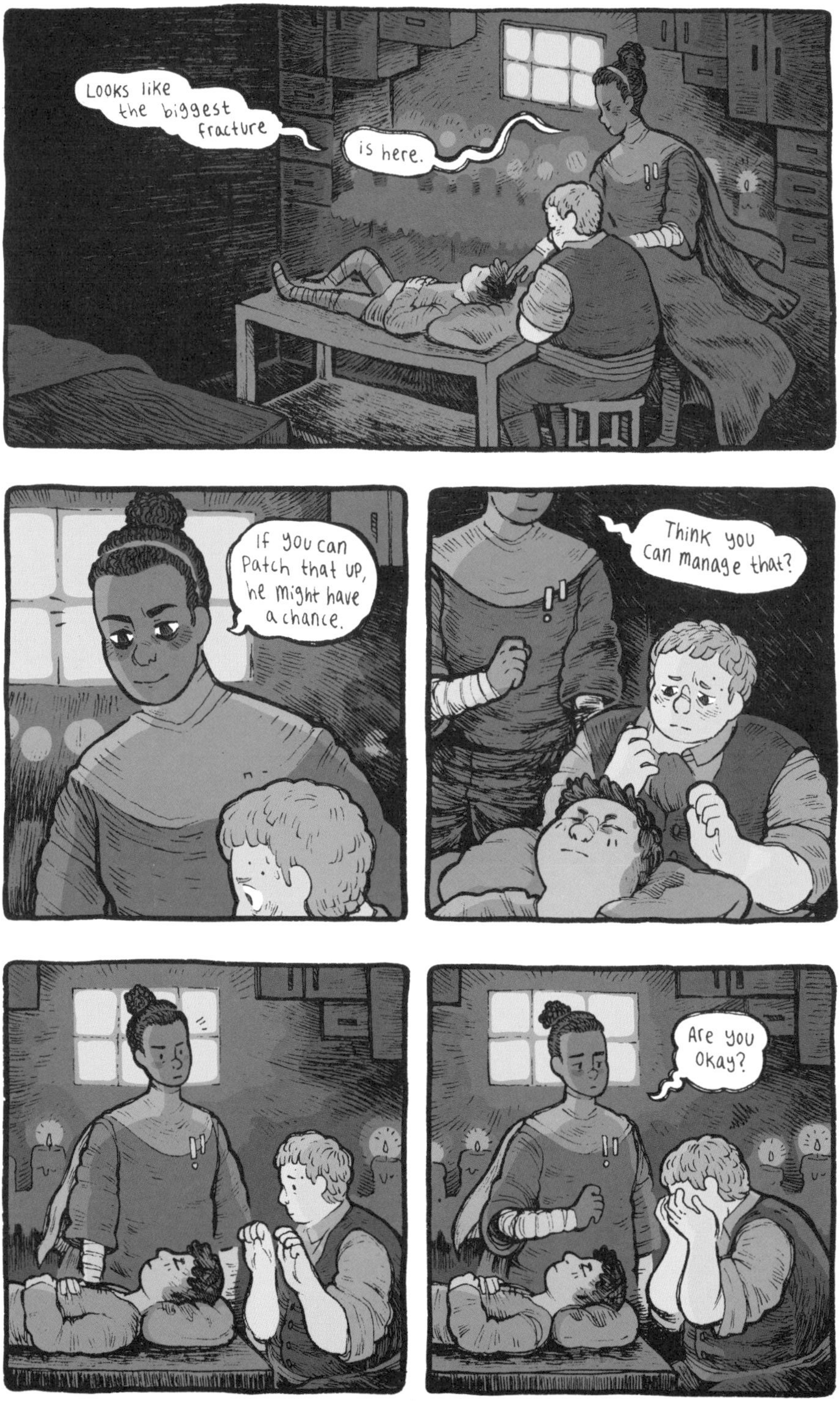
Looks like the biggest fracture
is here.
If you can Patch that up, he might have a chance.
Think you can manage that?
Are you Okay?

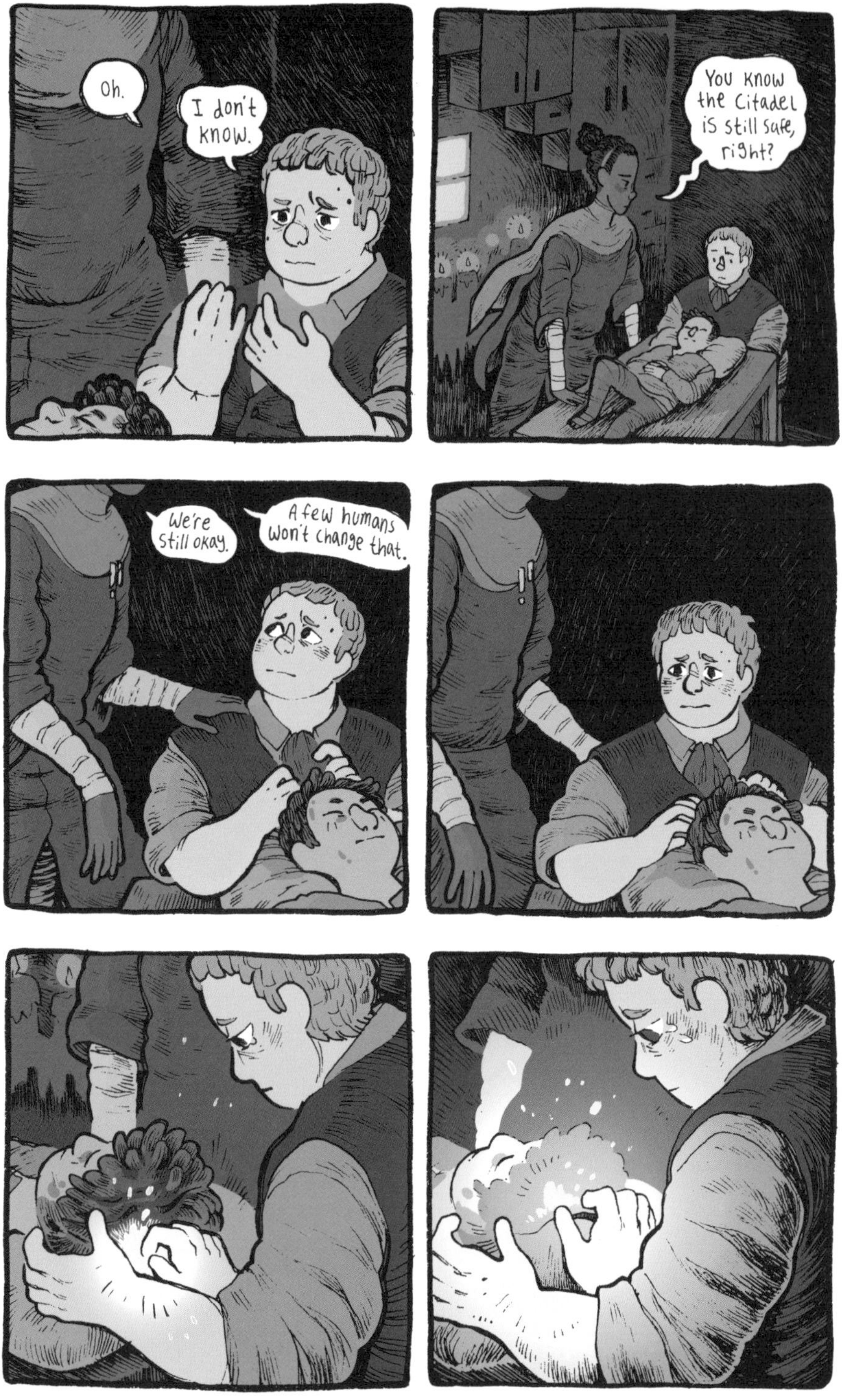
Oh.
I don't know.
You know the Citadel is still safe, right?
We're still okay.
A few humans won't change that.

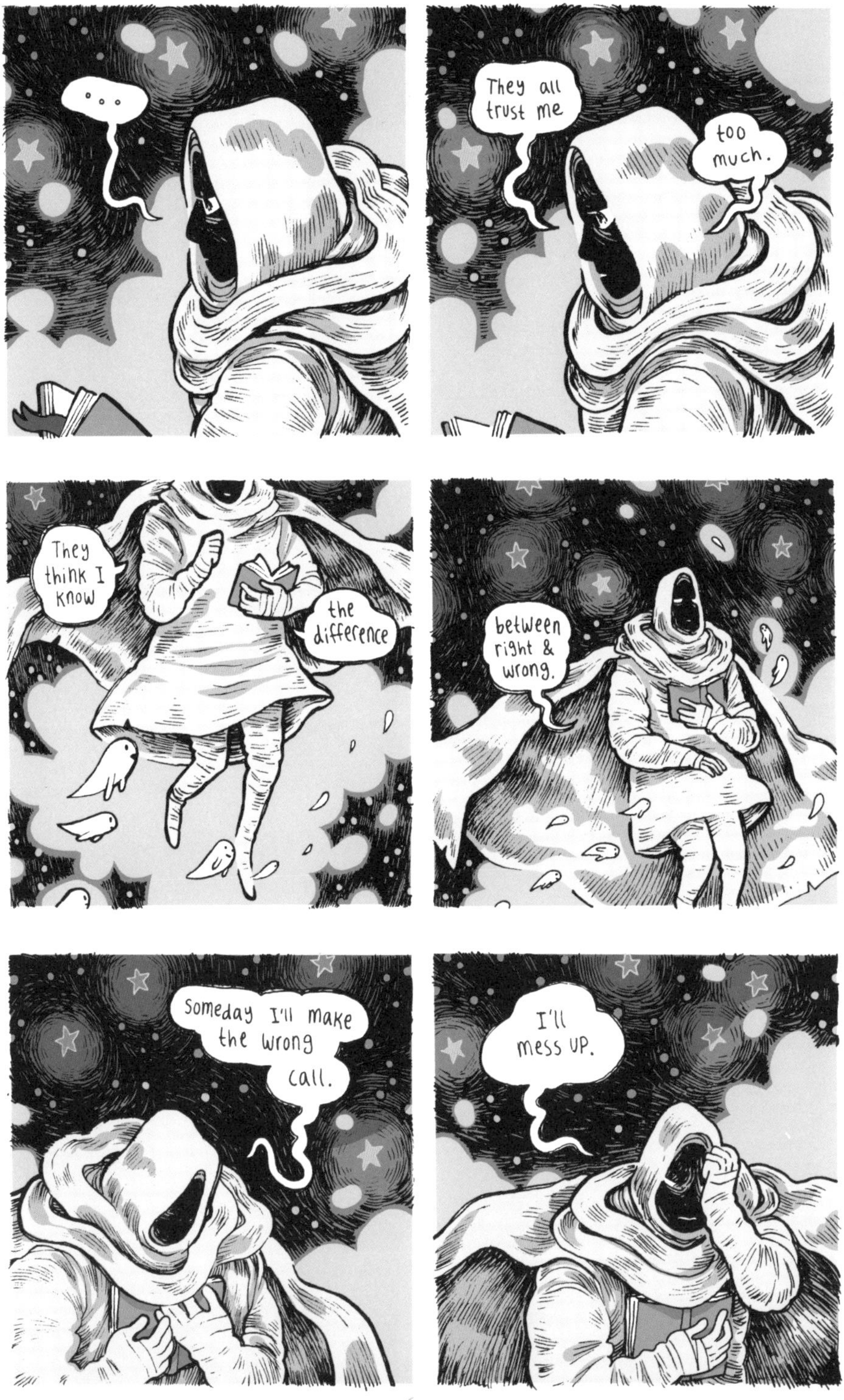
...
They all trust me
too much.
They think I know
the difference
between right & wrong.
Someday I'll make the wrong call.
I'll mess up.

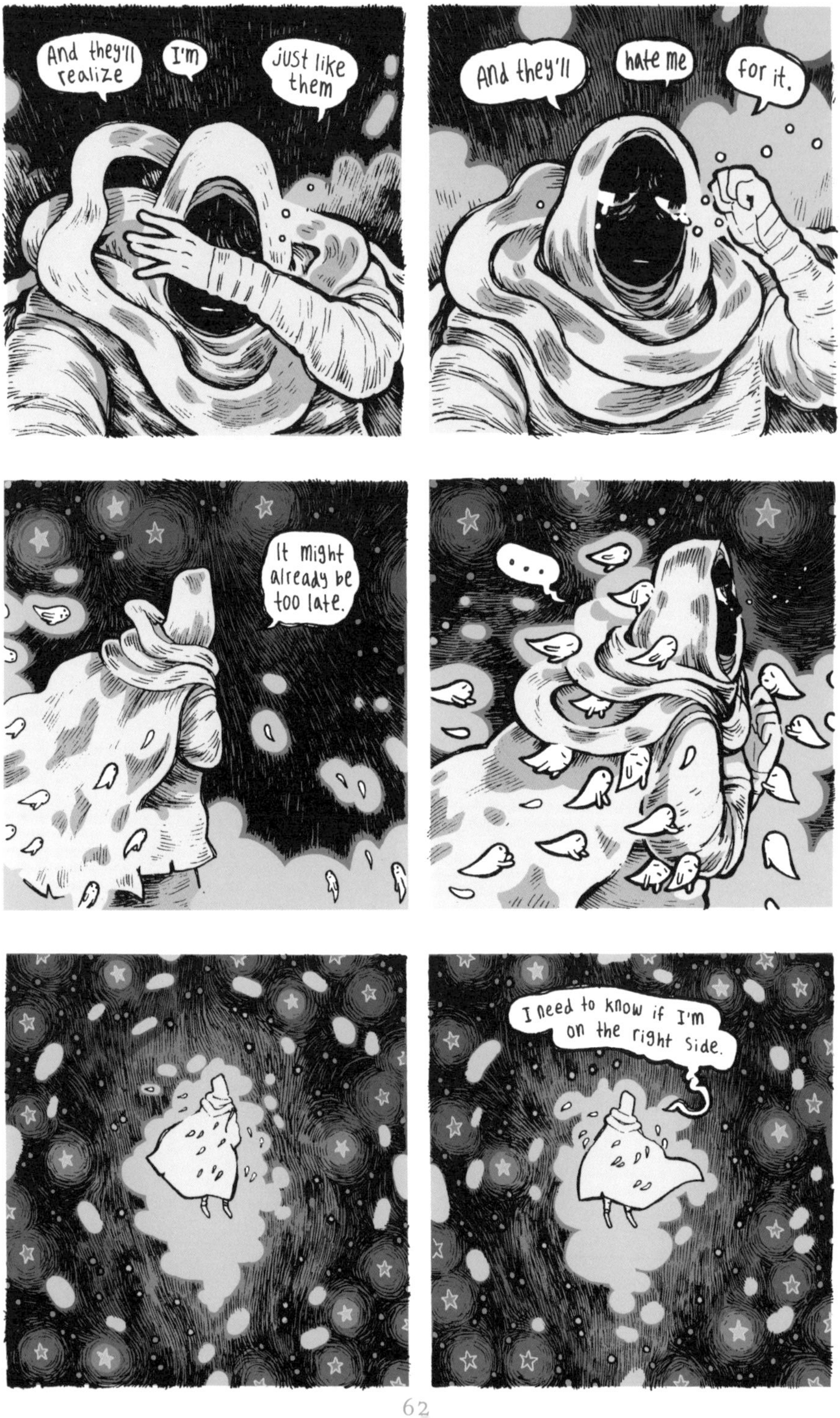
And they'll realize
I'm
just like them
And they'll
hate me
for it.
It might already be too late.
...
I need to know if I'm on the right side.

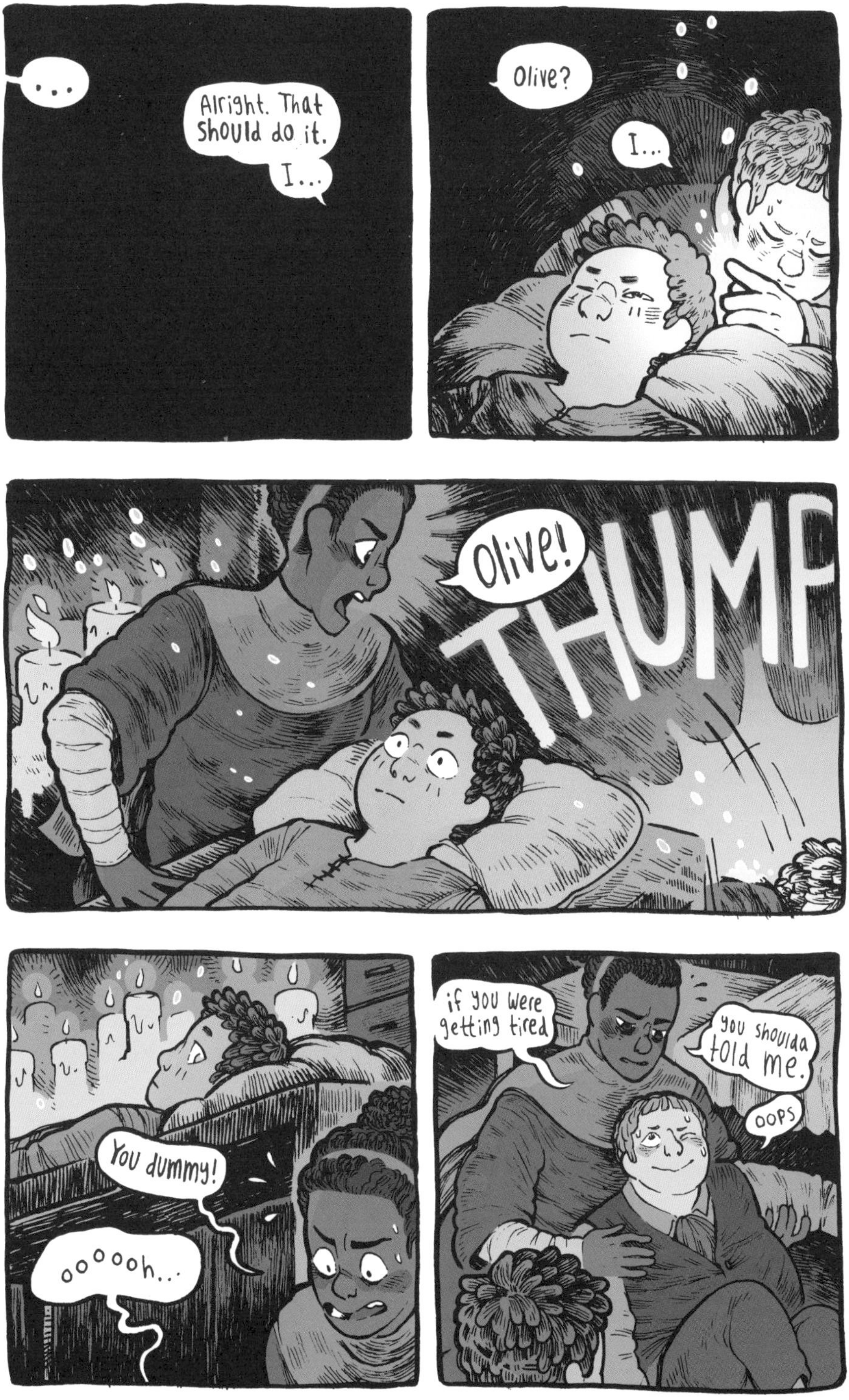
...
Alright. That should do it.
I...
Olive?
I...
Olive!
THUMP
You dummy!
oooooh...
if you were getting tired
you shoulda told me.
OOPS

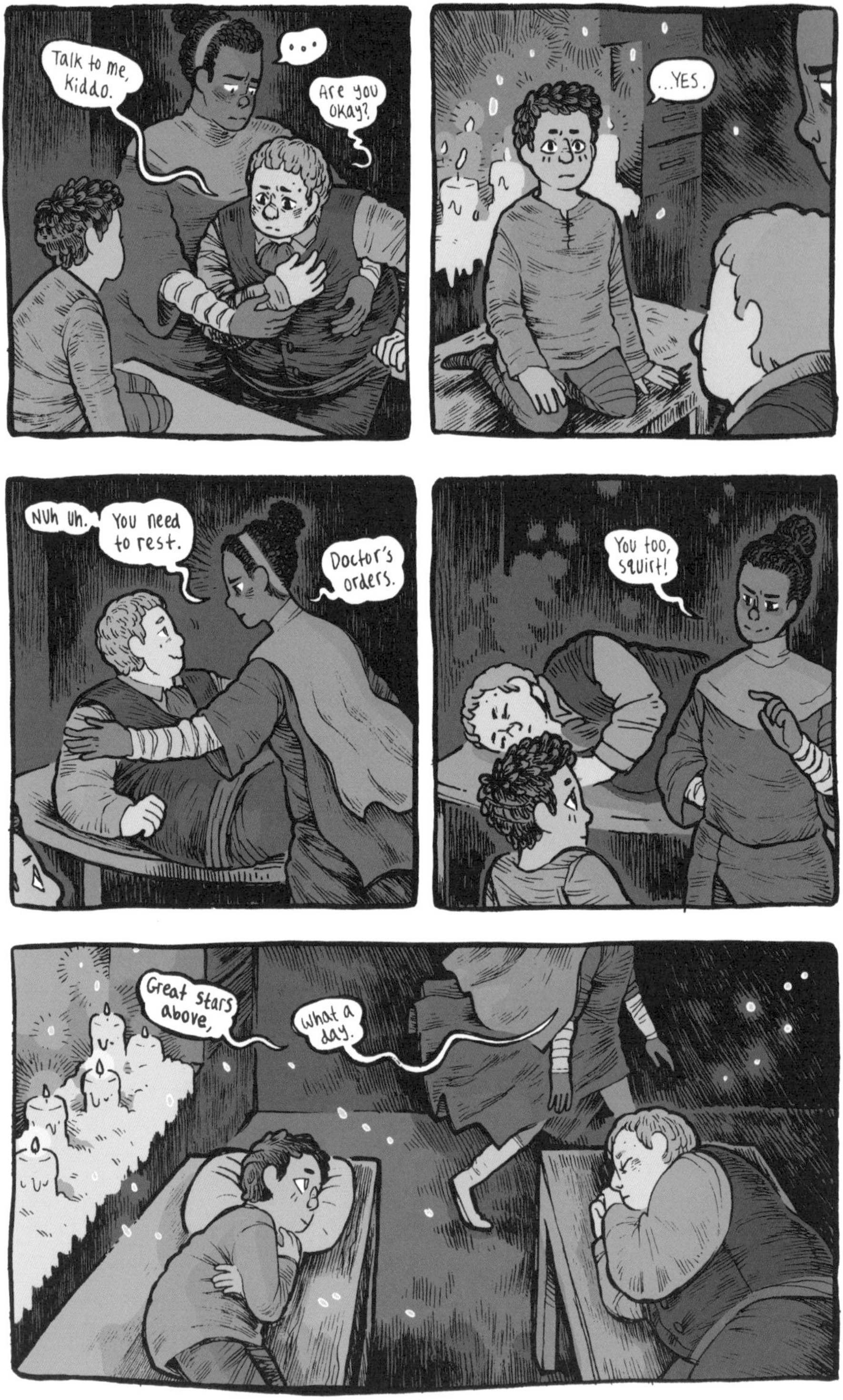
Talk to me, kiddo.
...
Are you okay?
...YES.
Nuh uh.
You need to rest.
Doctor's orders.
You too, squirt!
Great stars above,
what a day.

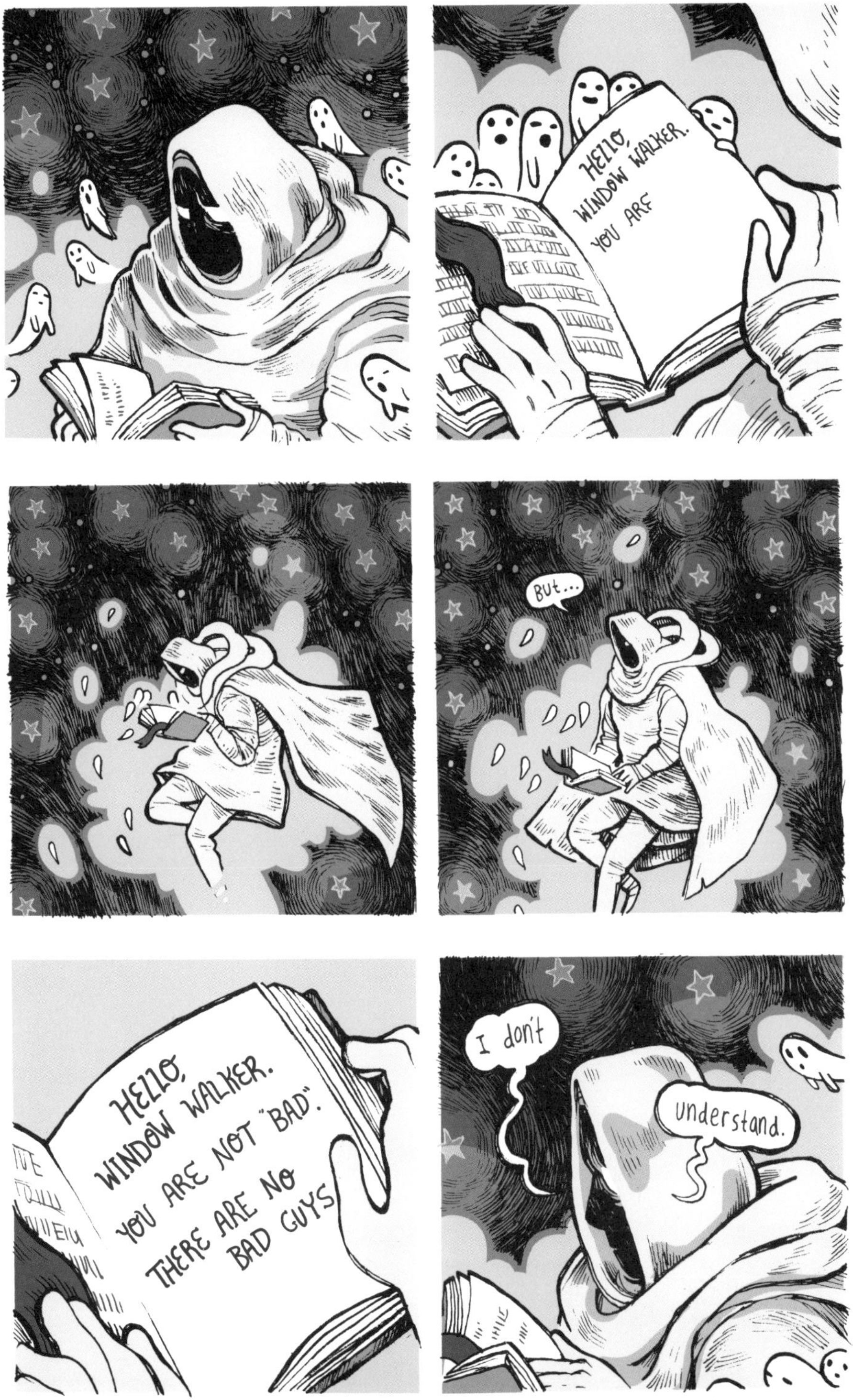
HELLO,
WINDOW WALKER.
YOU ARE
But...
HELLO,
WINDOW WALKER.
YOU ARE NOT "BAD".
THERE ARE NO
BAD GUYS
I don't
understand.

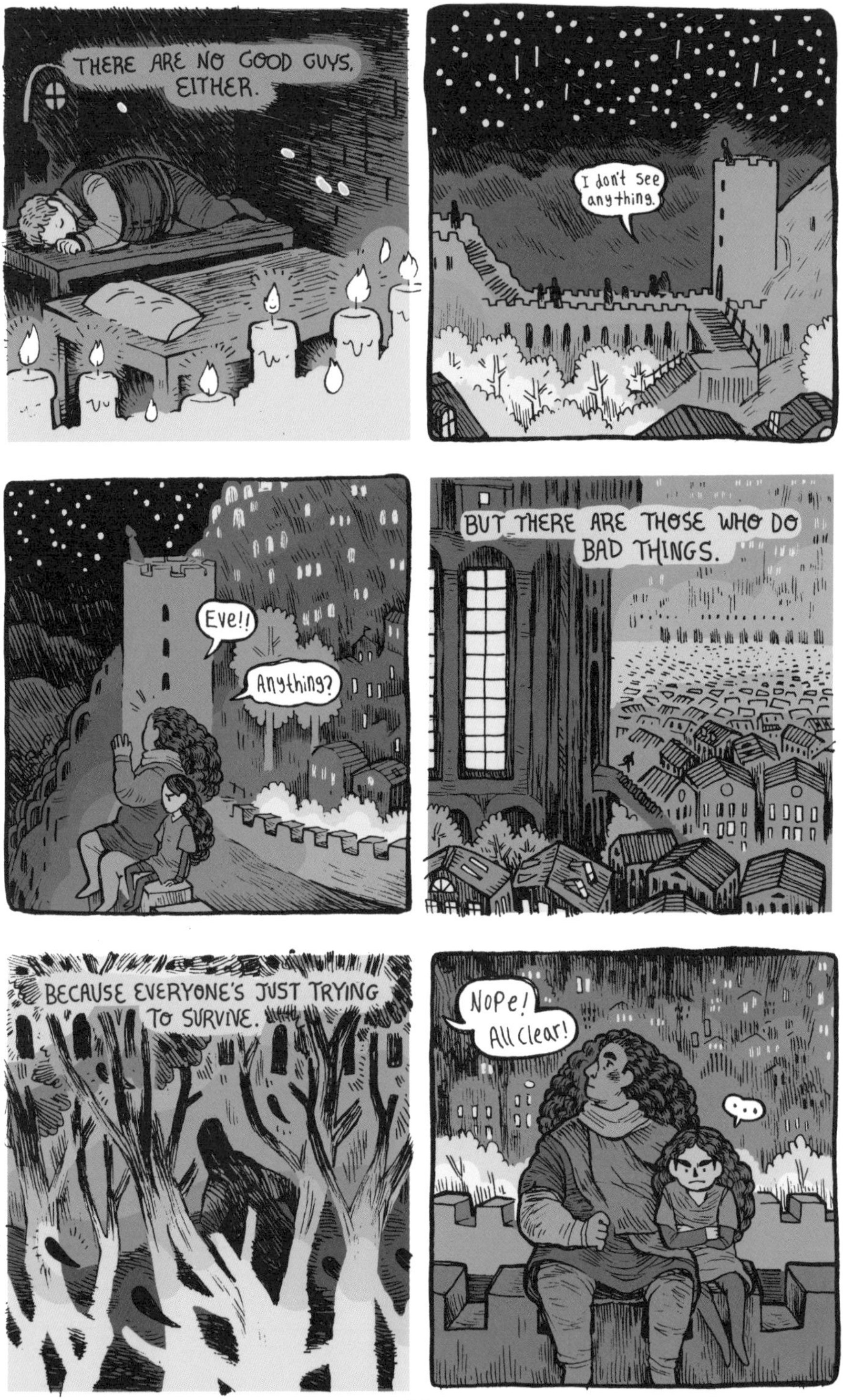
THERE ARE NO GOOD GUYS, EITHER.
I don't see anything.
Eve!!
Anything?
BUT THERE ARE THOSE WHO DO BAD THINGS.
BECAUSE EVERYONE'S JUST TRYING TO SURVIVE.
NoPe! All clear!
...

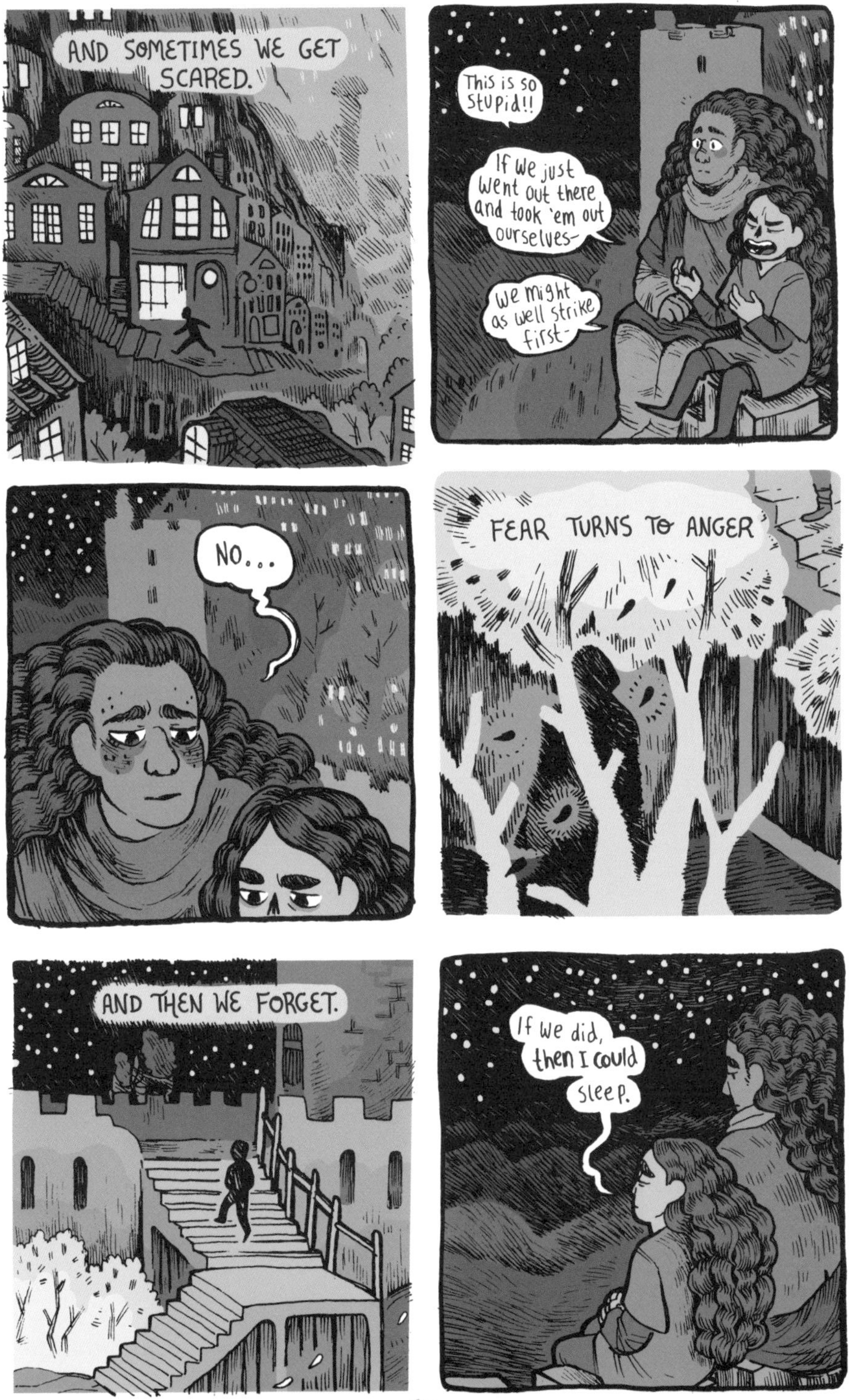
AND SOMETIMES WE GET SCARED.
This is so stupid!!
If we just went out there and took 'em out ourselves-
we might as well strike first-
NO...
FEAR TURNS TO ANGER
AND THEN WE FORGET.
If we did, then I could sleep.

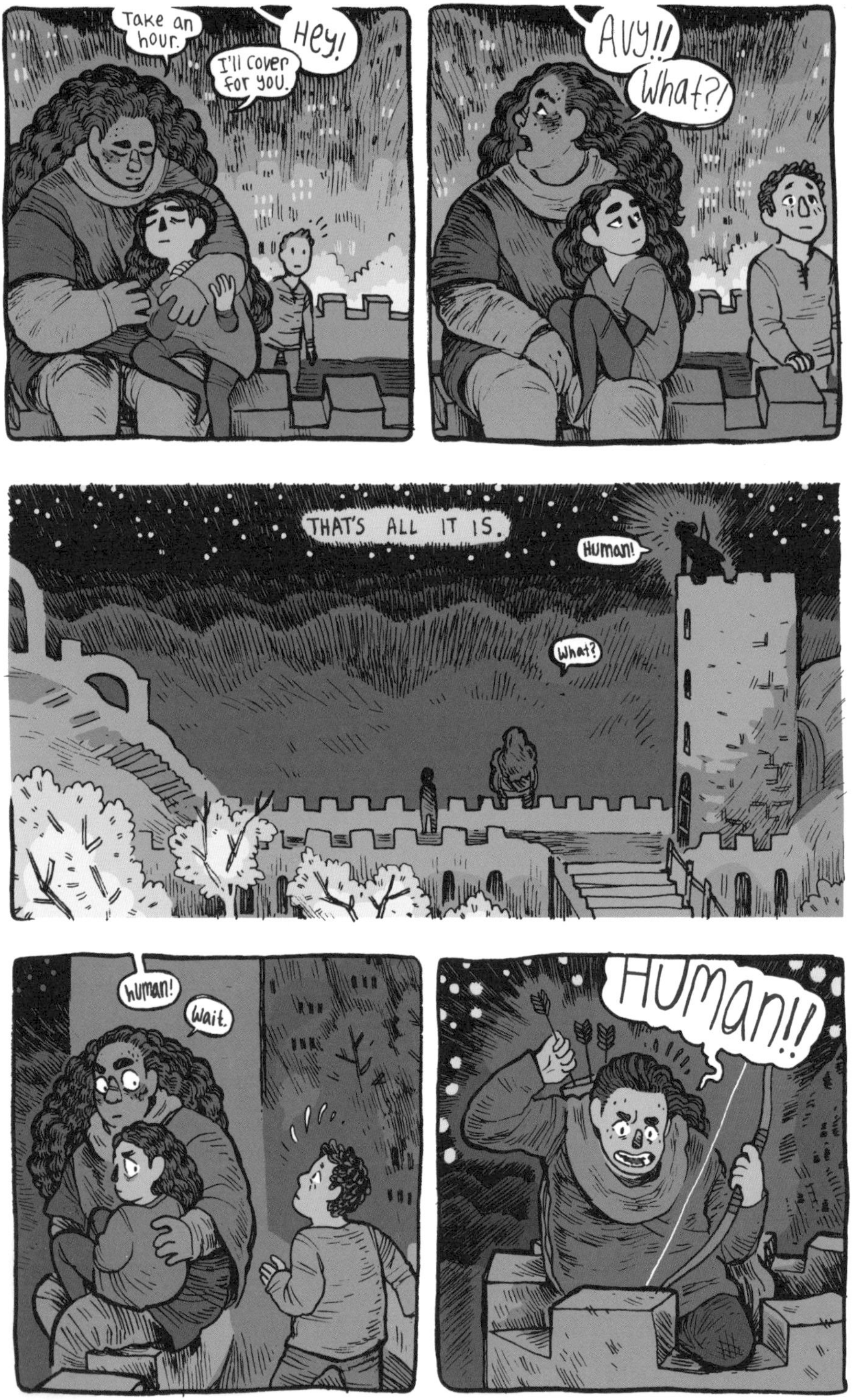
Take an hour.
Hey!
I'll cover for you.
Avy!!
What?!
THAT'S ALL IT IS.
Human!
What?
human!
Wait.
HUMAN!!

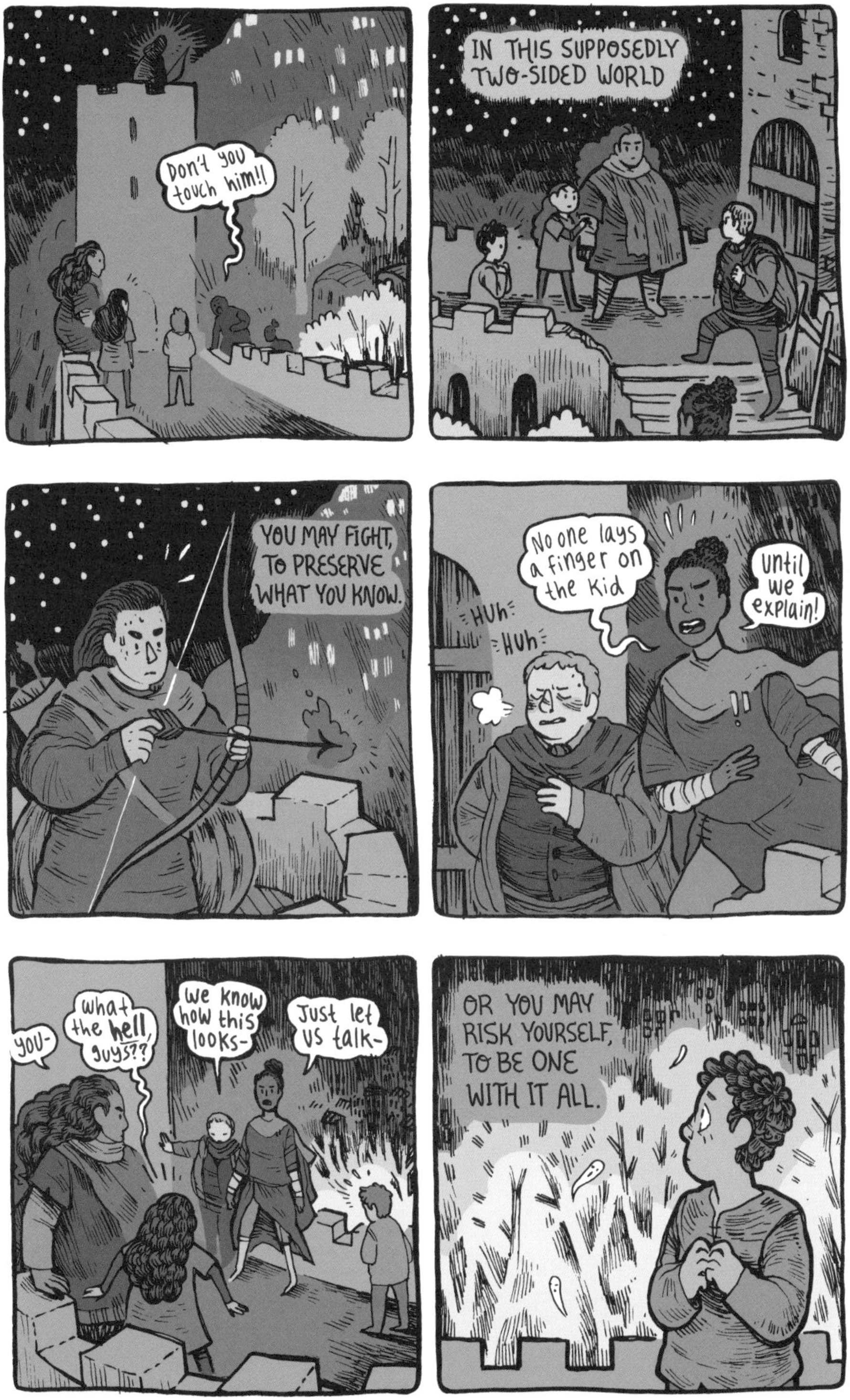
Don't you touch him!!
IN THIS SUPPOSEDLY TWO-SIDED WORLD
YOU MAY FIGHT, TO PRESERVE WHAT YOU KNOW.
No one lays a finger on the kid
HUh HUh
Until we explain!
you-
what the hell, guys?!?
we know how this looks-
Just let us talk-
OR YOU MAY RISK YOURSELF, TO BE ONE WITH IT ALL.

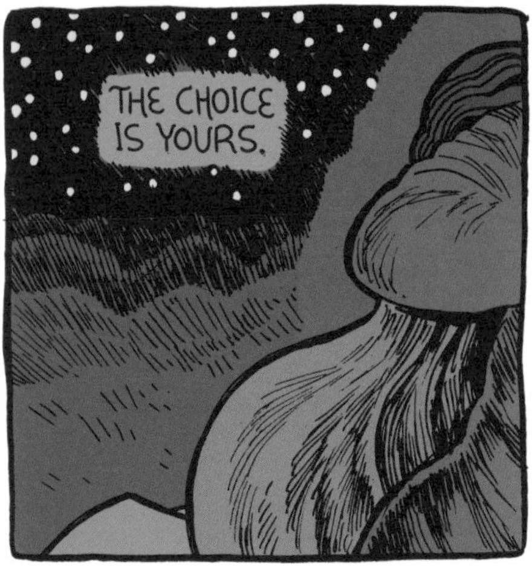
THE CHOICE IS YOURS.

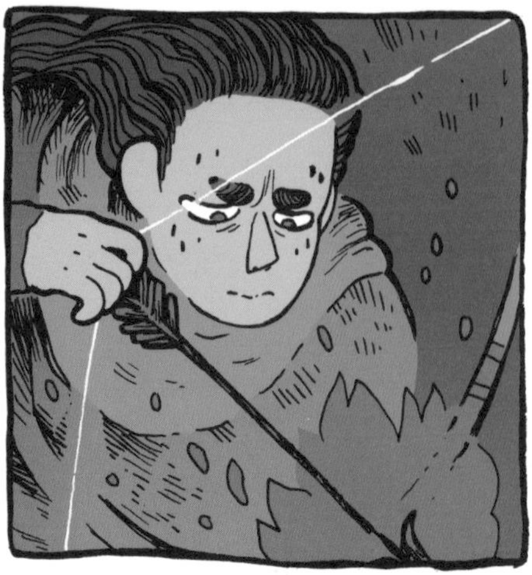

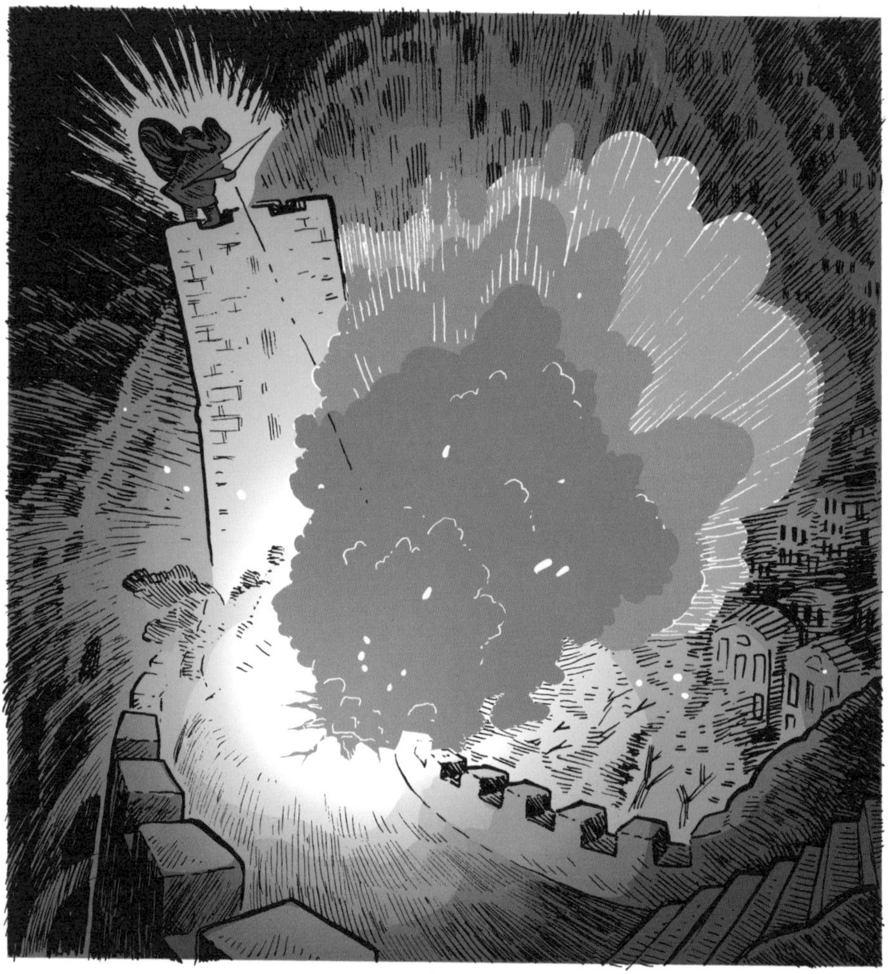

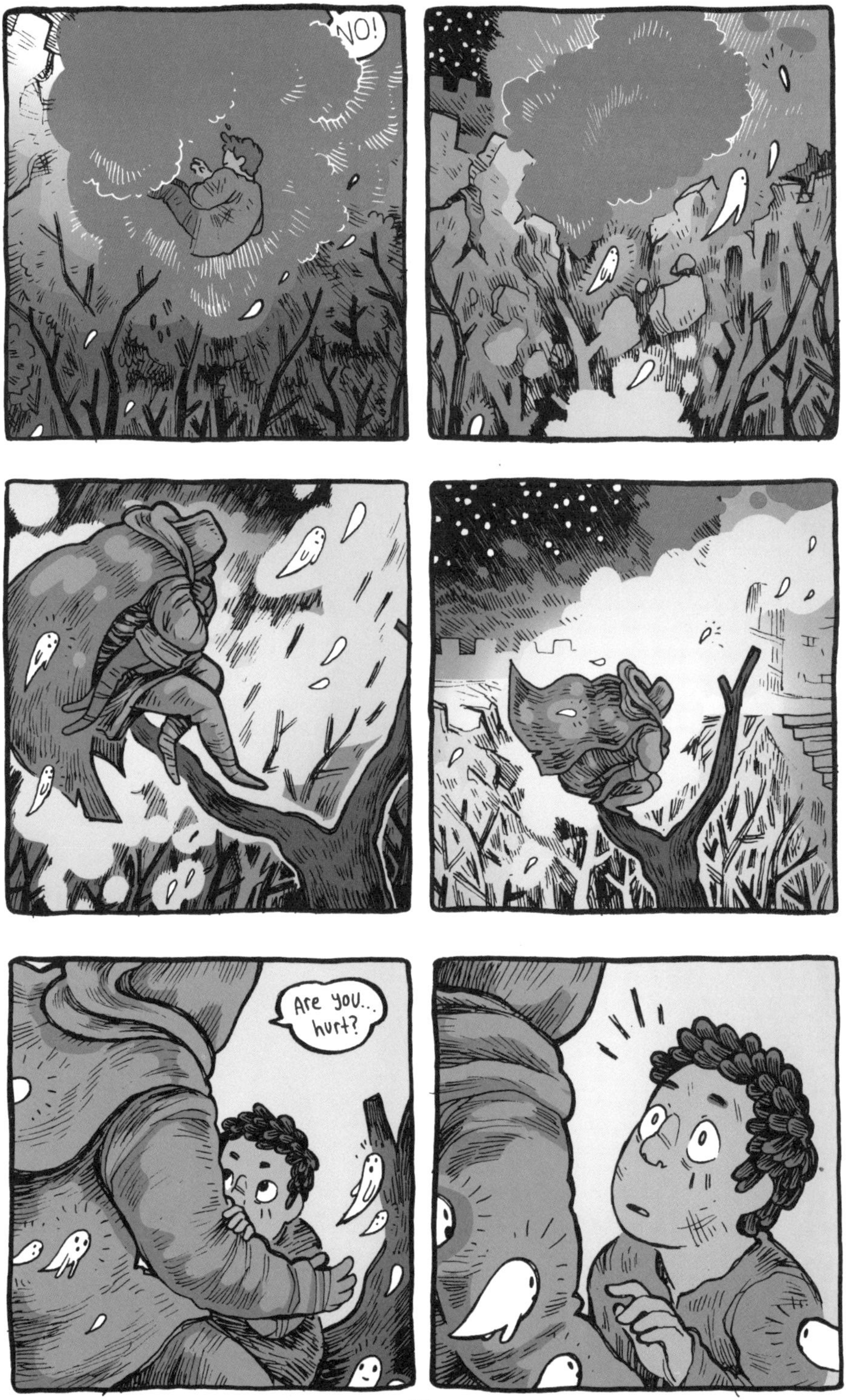
NO!
Are you... hurt?

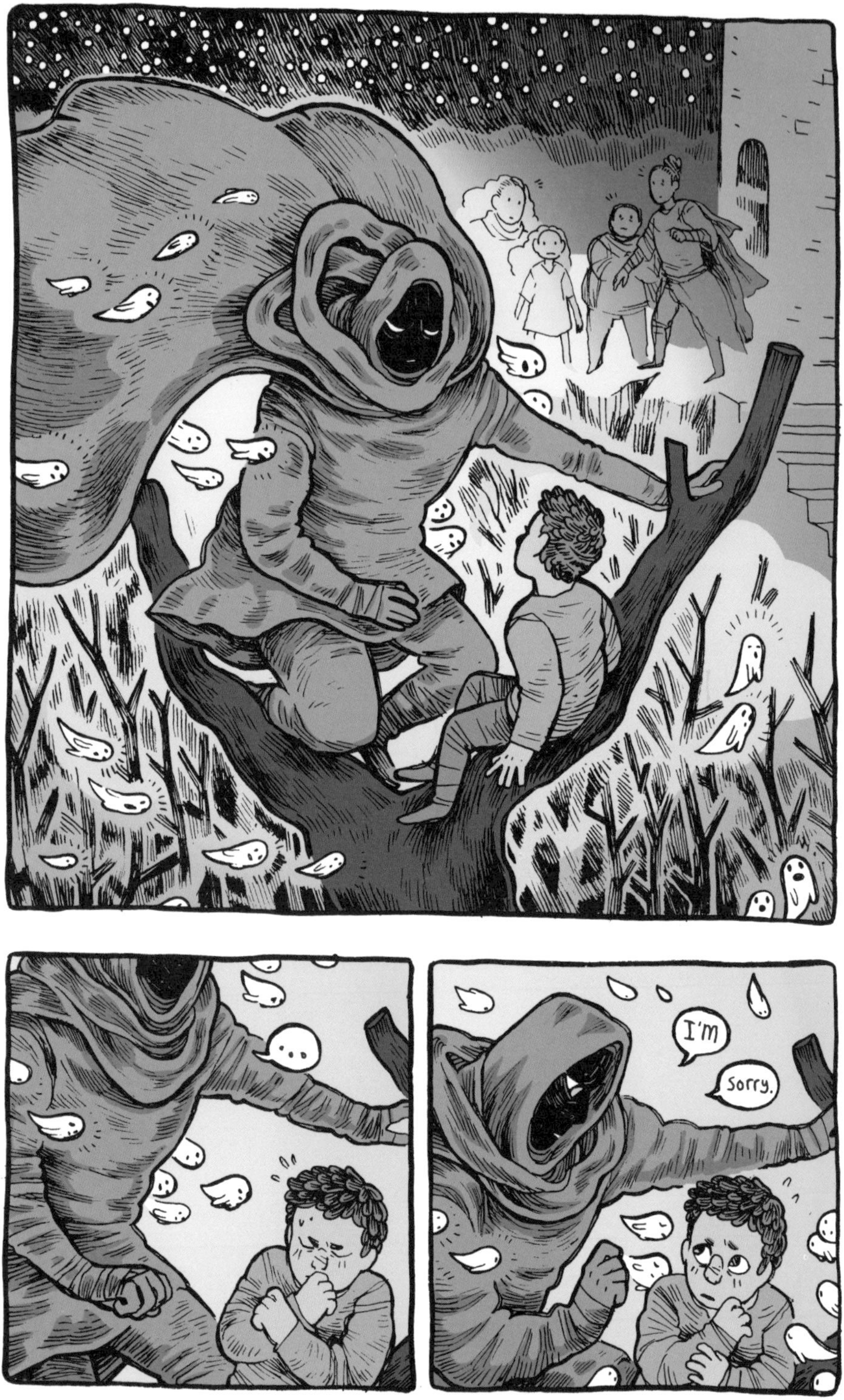
...
I'm
sorry.

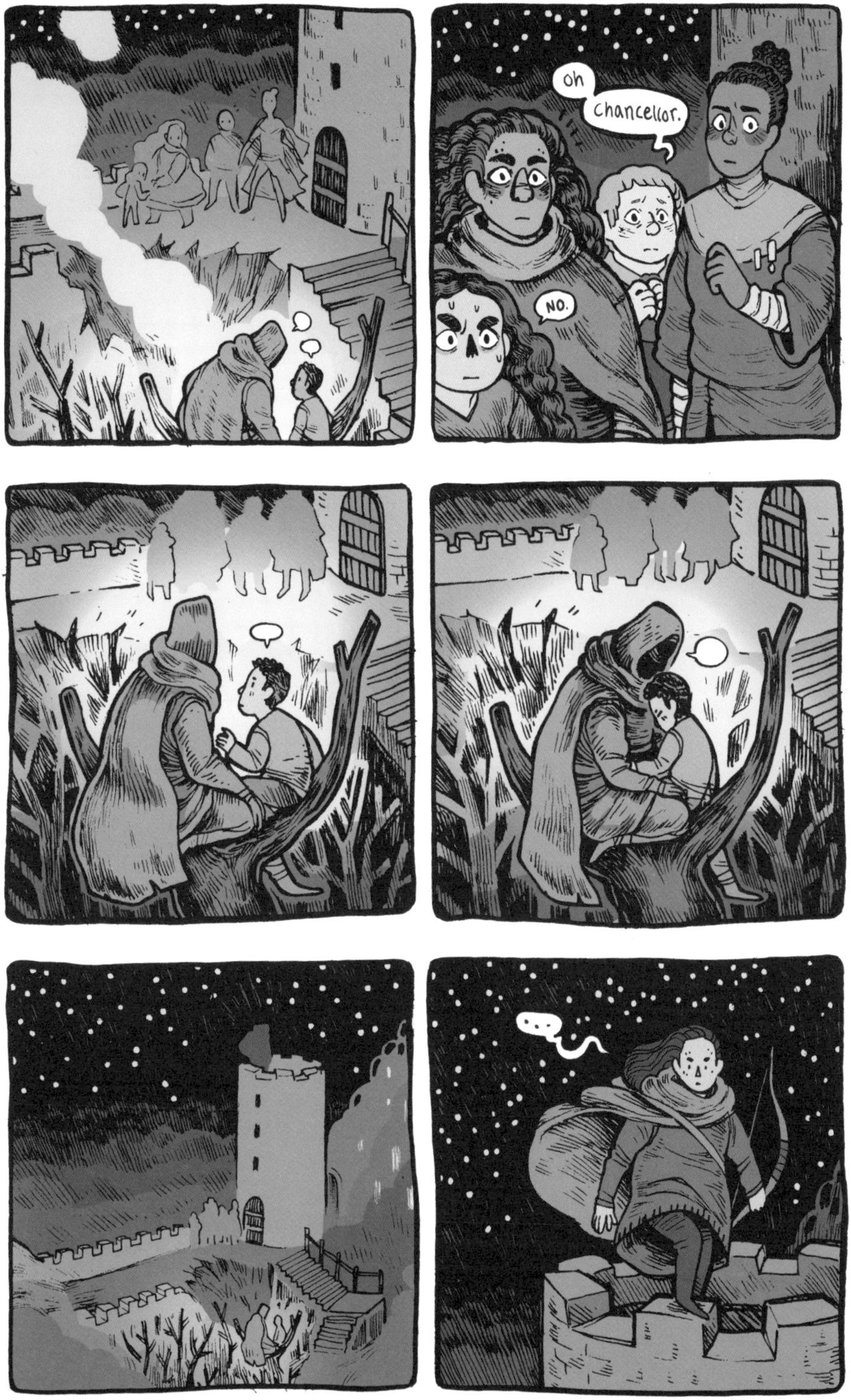
oh
chancellor.
NO.

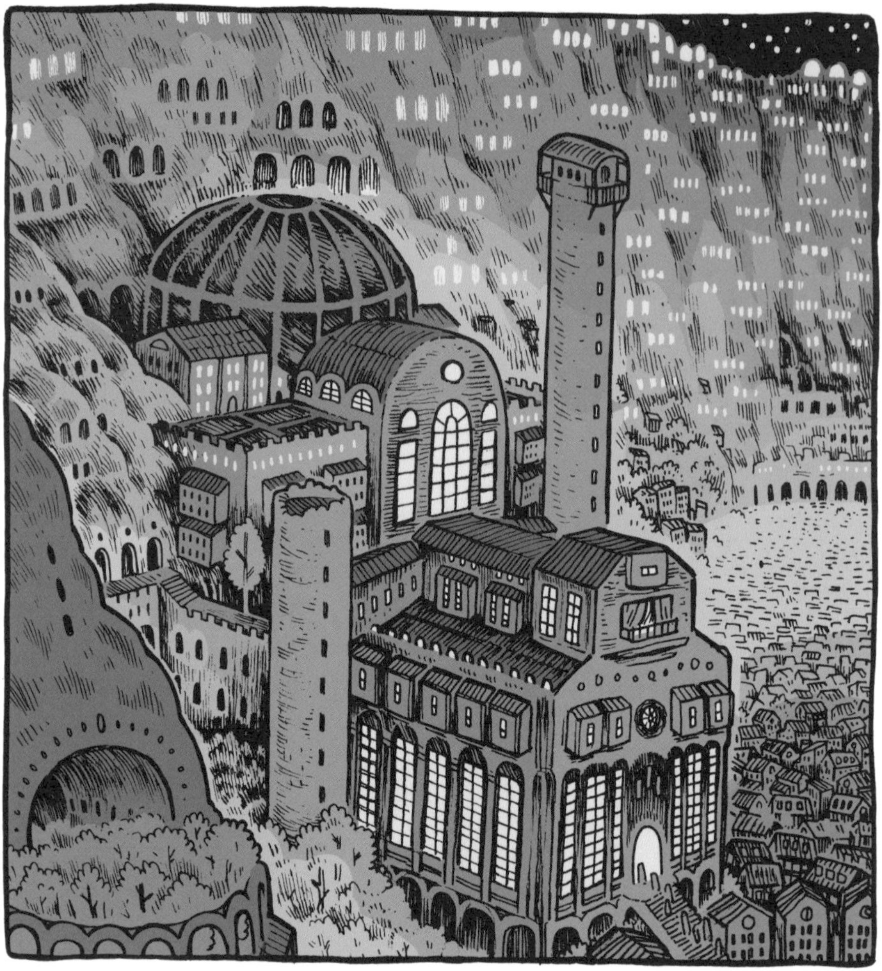

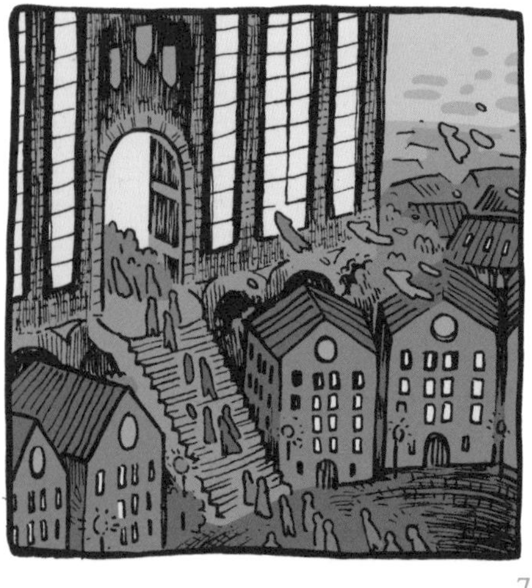

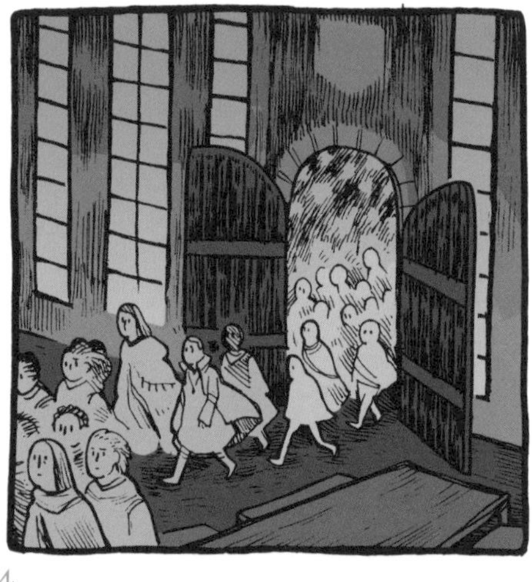

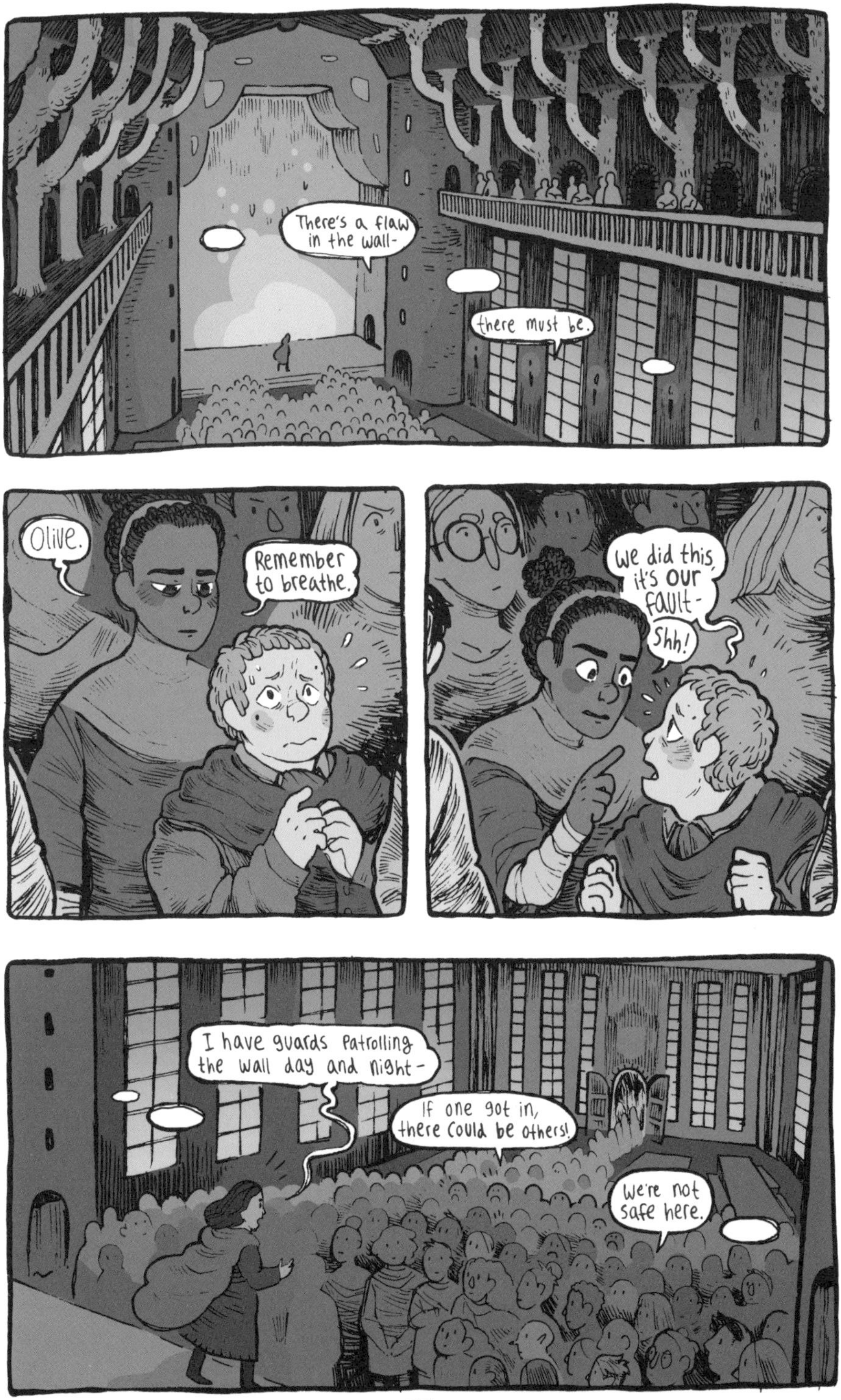
There's a flaw in the wall-
there must be.
Olive.
Remember to breathe.
We did this, it's **our** fault-
Shh!
I have guards patrolling the wall day and night-
If one got in, there could be others!
We're not safe here.

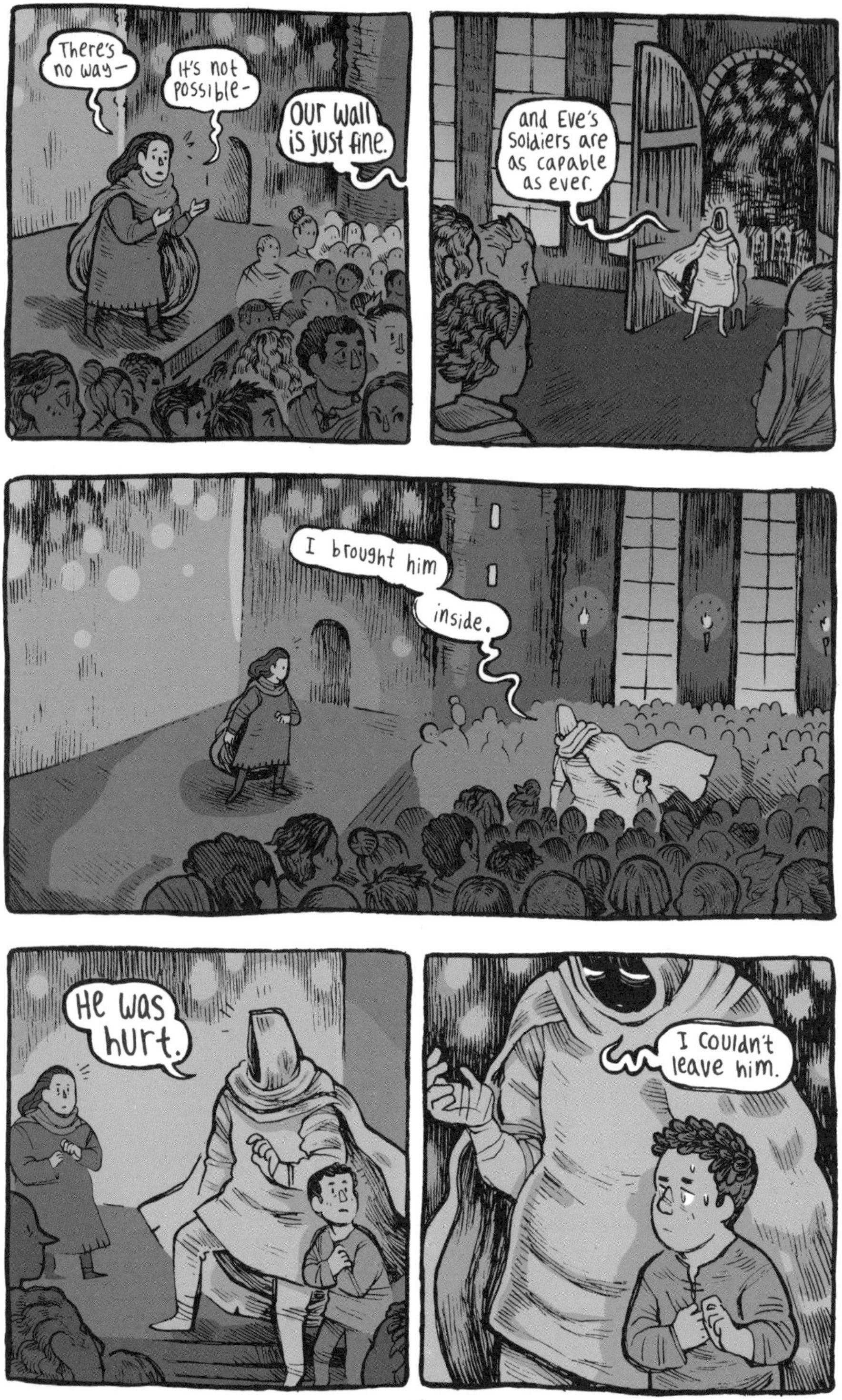
There's no way—
It's not possible—
Our wall is just fine.
and Eve's Soldiers are as capable as ever.
I brought him
inside.
He was hurt.
I couldn't leave him.

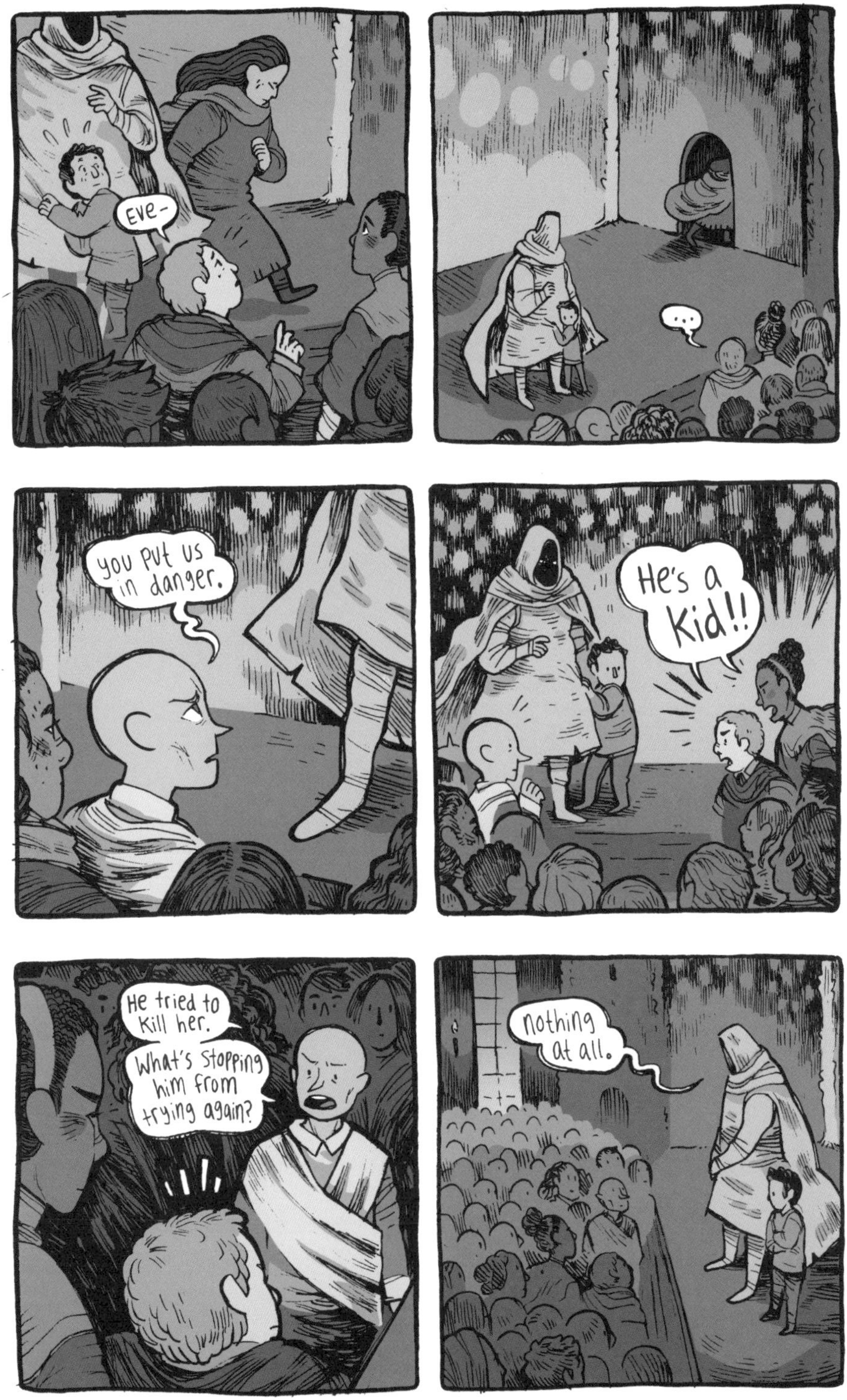
Eve-
...
you put us in danger.
He's a Kid!!
He tried to Kill her.
What's stopping him from trying again?
nothing at all.

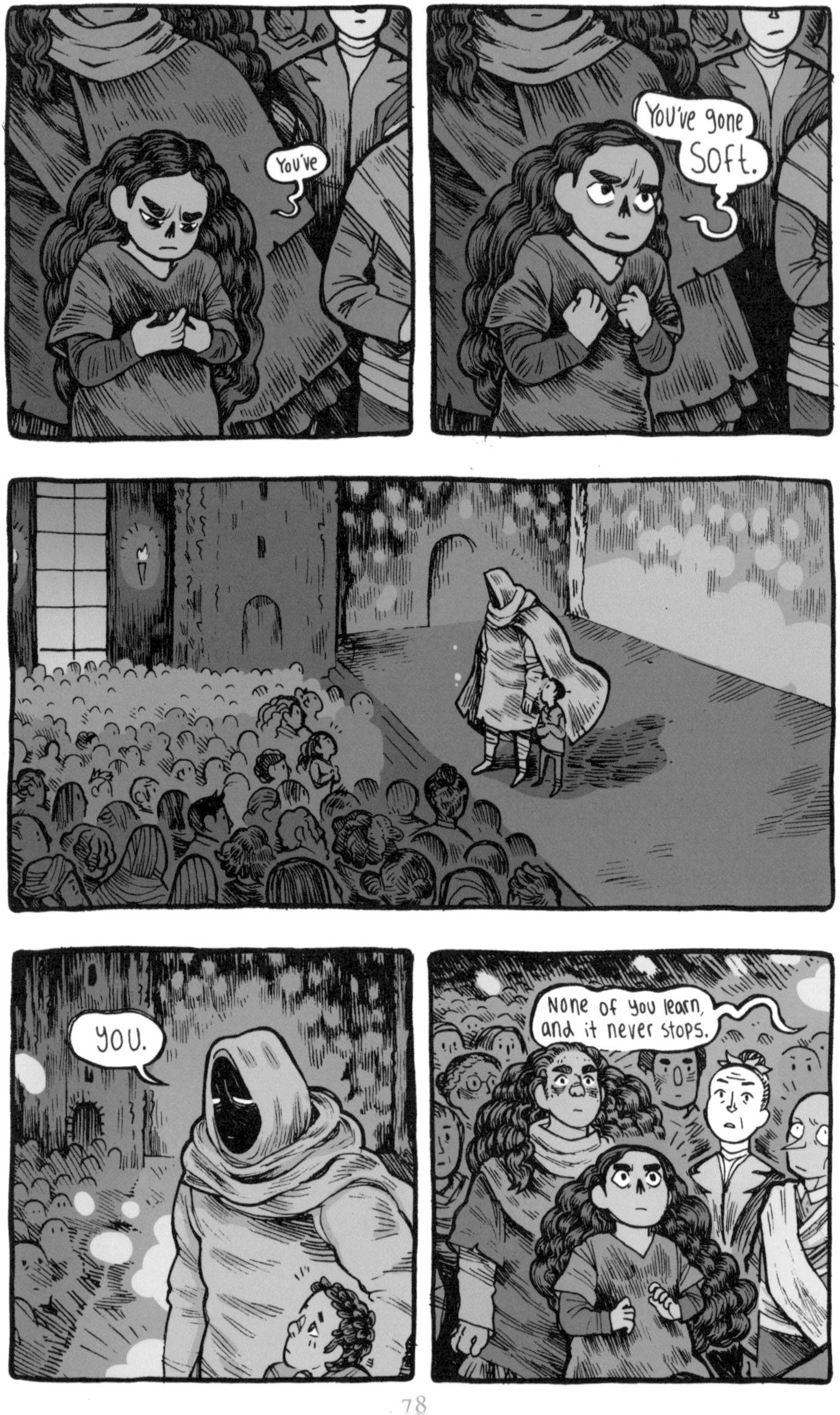
You've
You've gone SOFT.
YOU.
None of you learn, and it never stops.

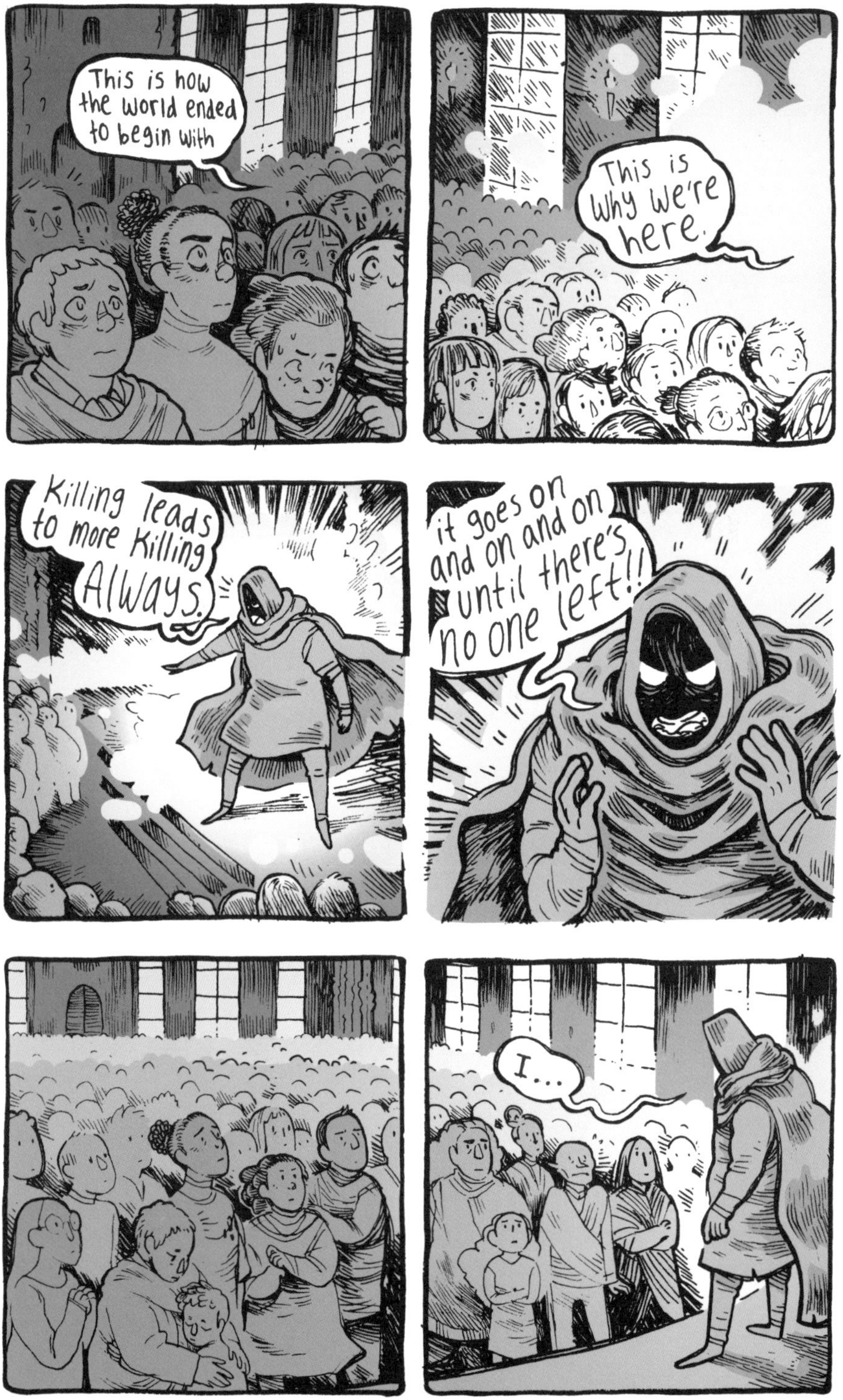
This is how the world ended to begin with
This is why we're here.
Killing leads to more Killing Always.
it goes on and on and on until there's no one left!!
I...

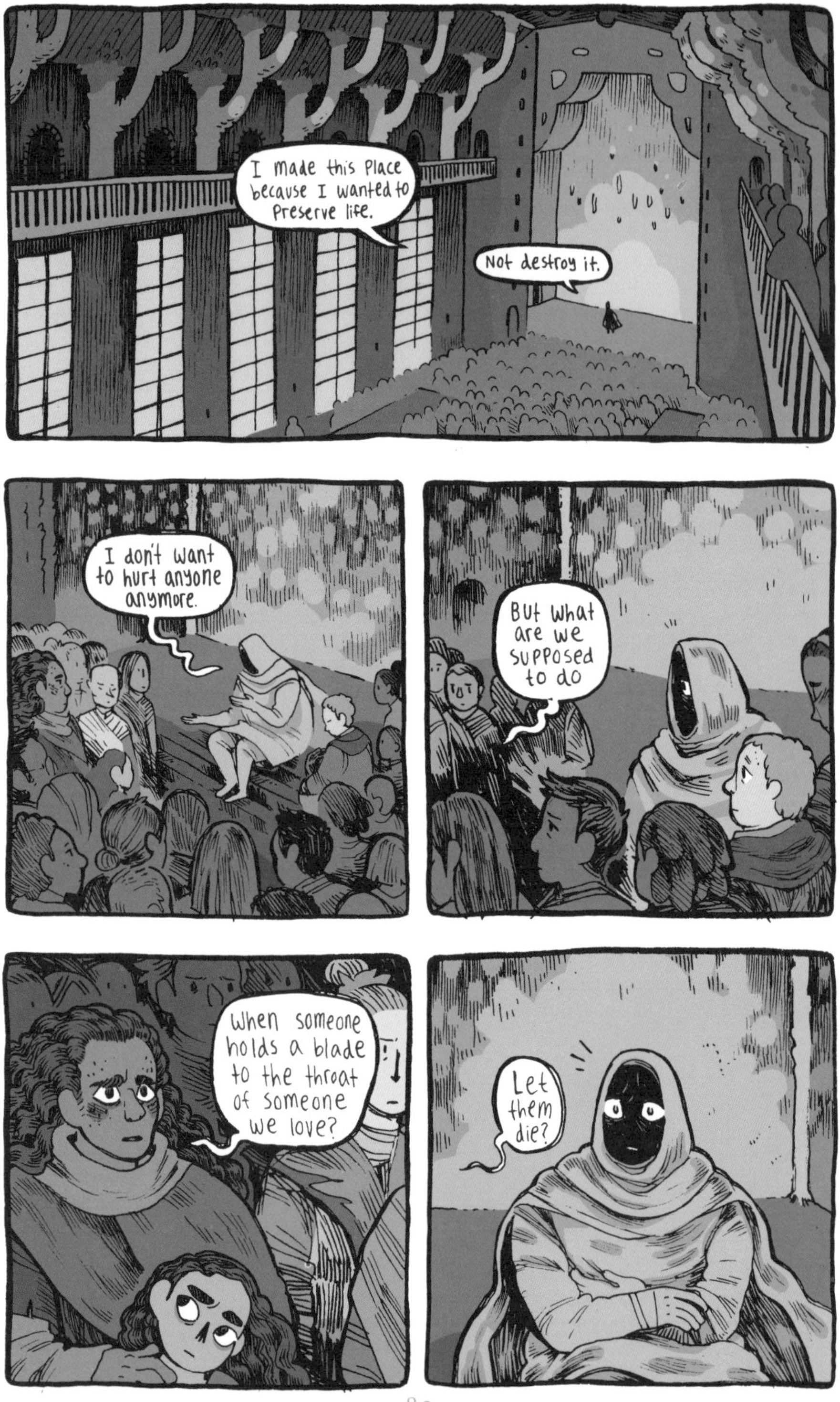
I made this Place because I wanted to Preserve life.
Not destroy it.
I don't want to hurt anyone anymore.
But what are we supposed to do
When someone holds a blade to the throat of someone we love?
Let them die?

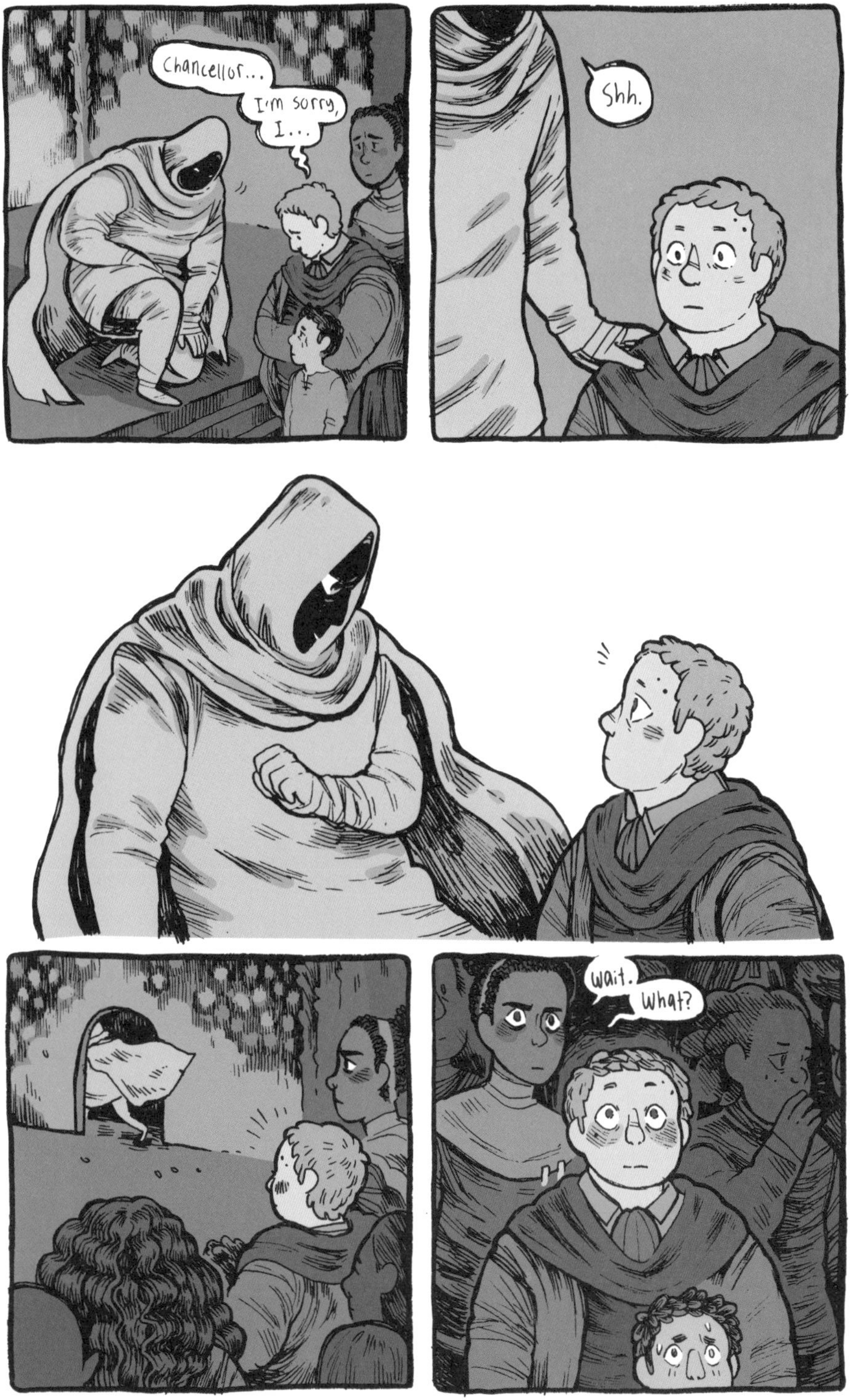
Chancellor...
I'm sorry, I...
Shh.
Wait.
What?

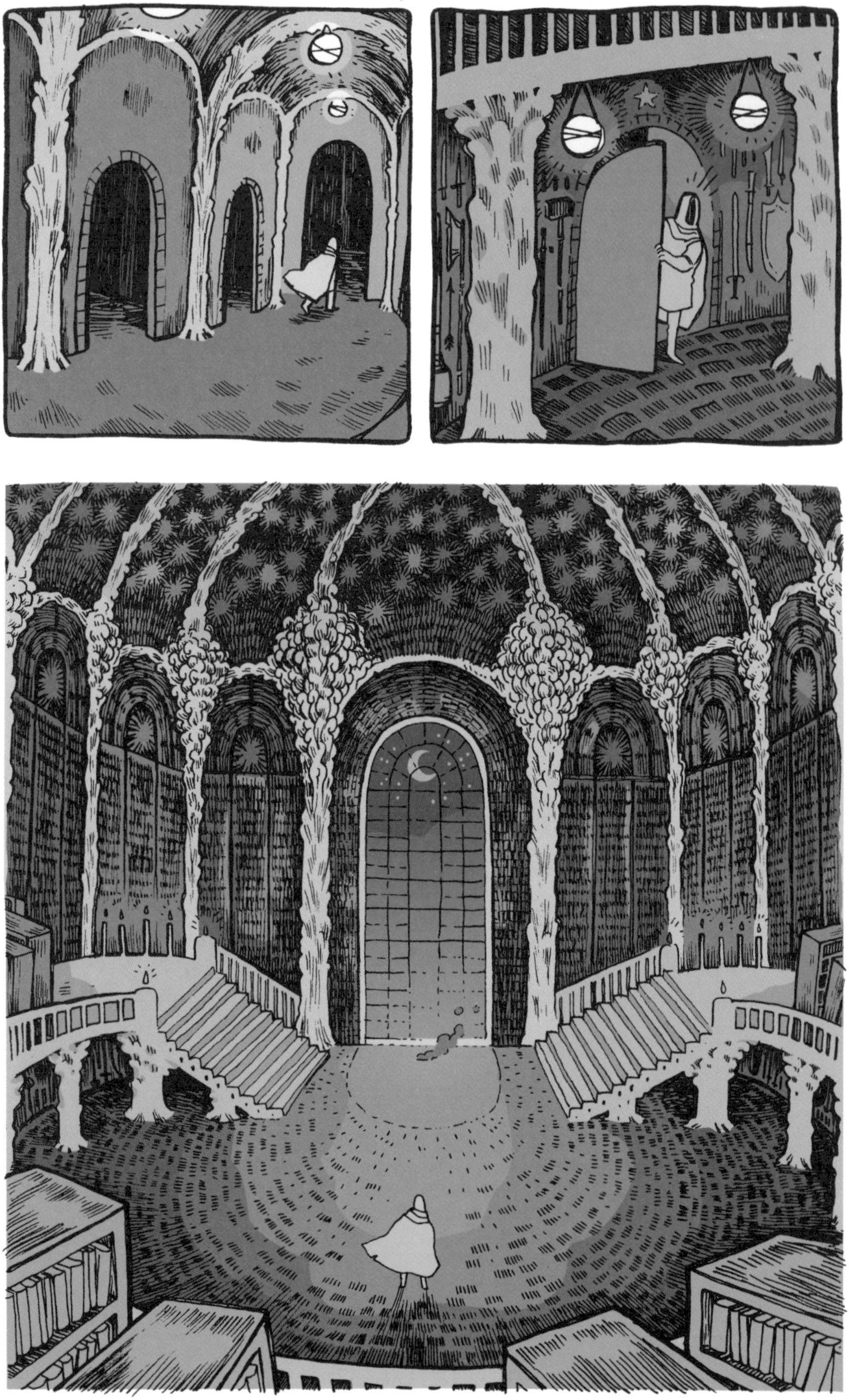

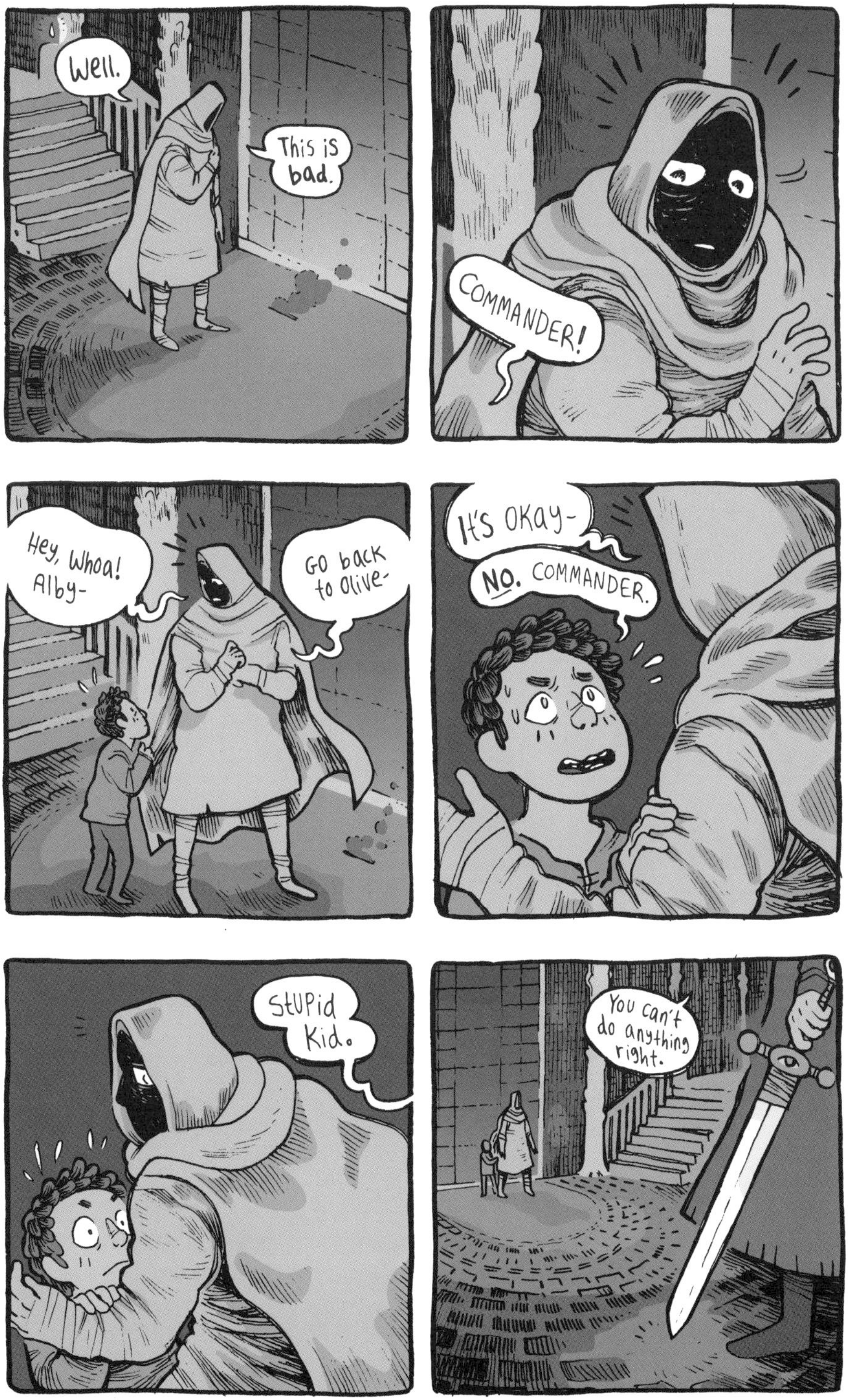

Well.
This is bad.
COMMANDER!
Hey, Whoa! Alby-
GO back to Olive-
It's okay-
NO. COMMANDER.
StUPid Kid.
You can't do anything right.

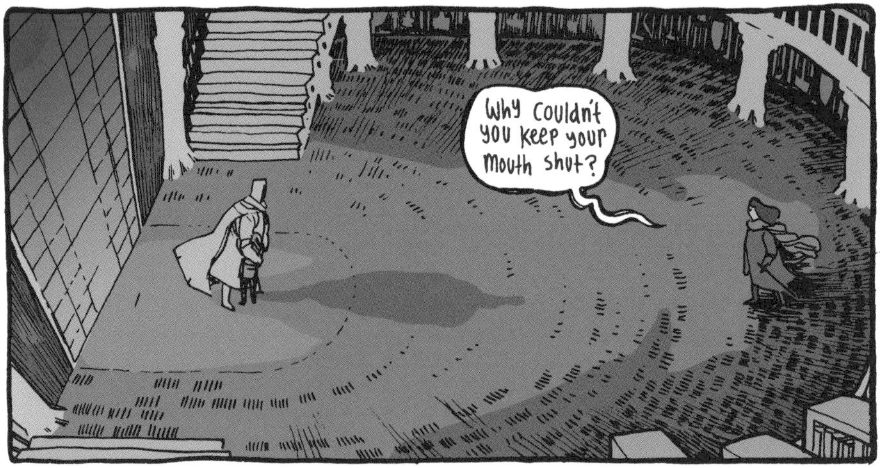
Why couldn't you keep your mouth shut?

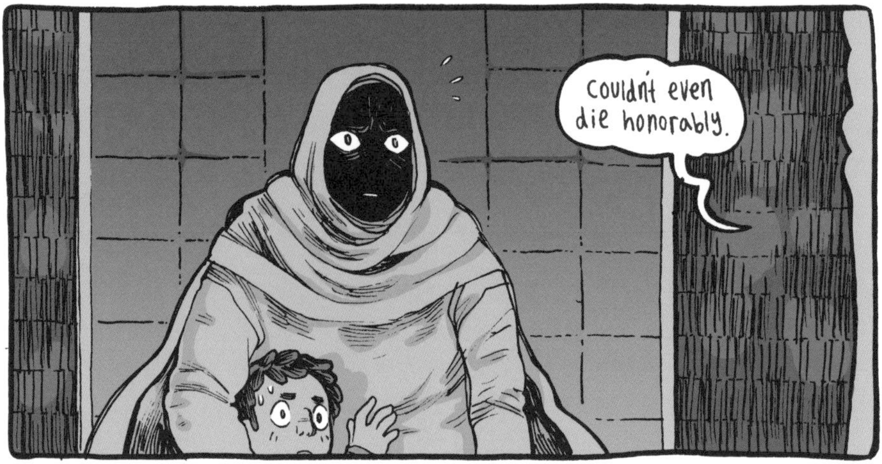
Couldn't even die honorably.

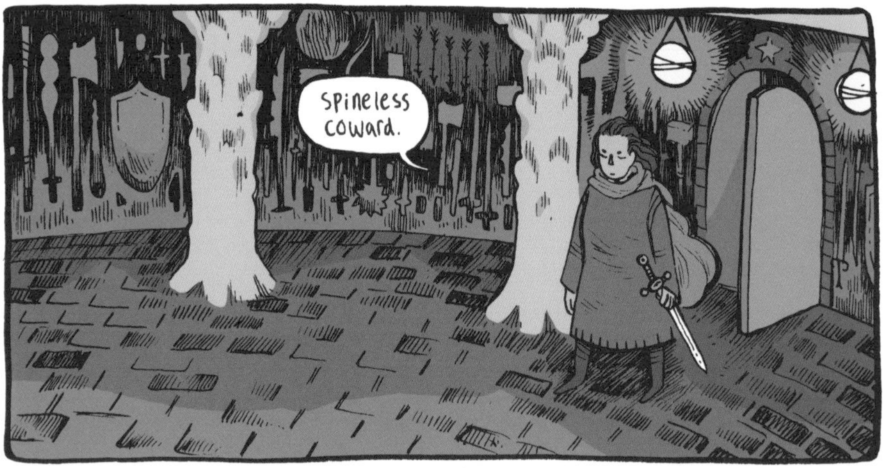
Spineless coward.

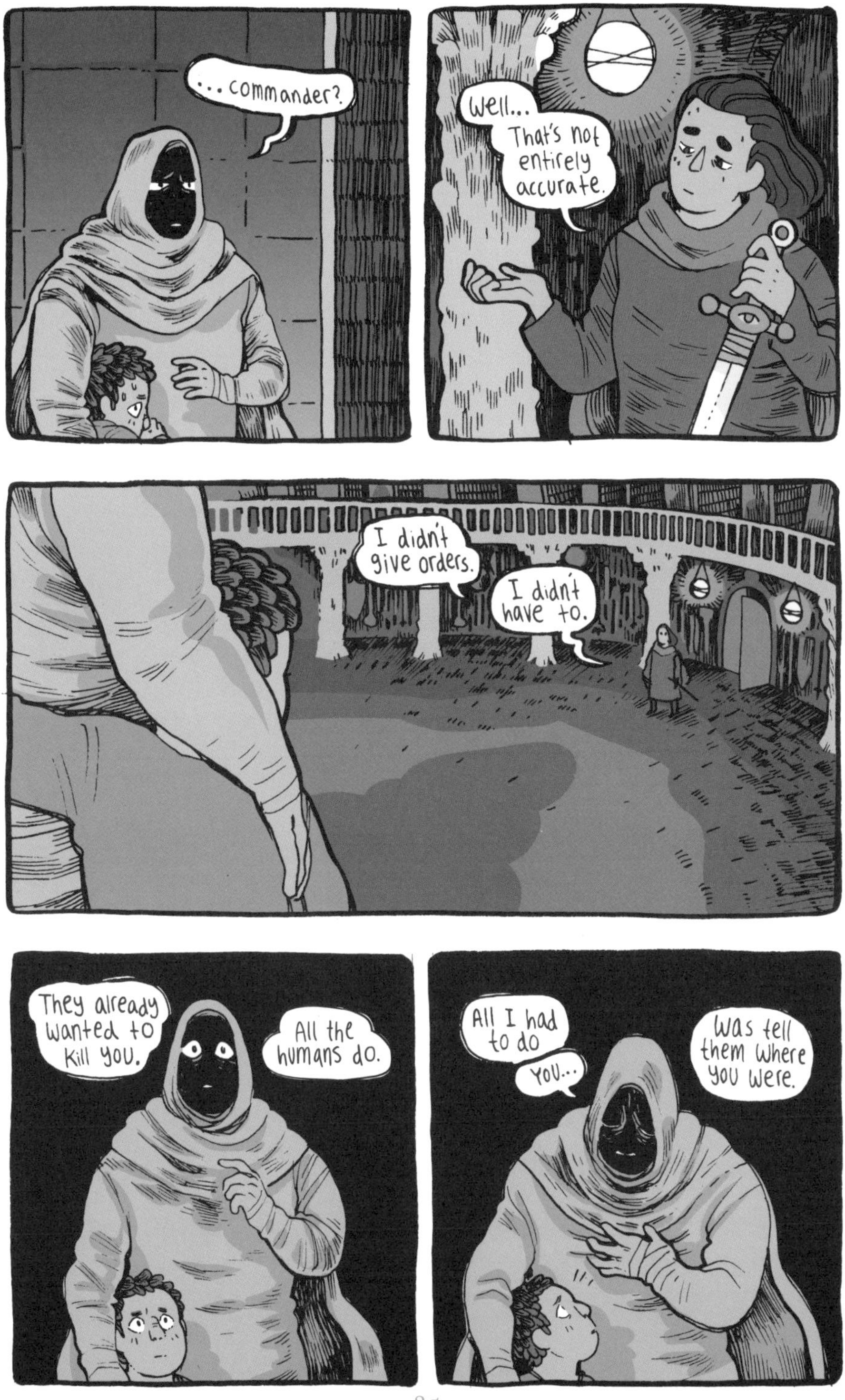
...commander?
Well...
That's not entirely accurate.
I didn't give orders.
I didn't have to.
They already wanted to kill you.
All the humans do.
All I had to do
You...
Was tell them where you were.

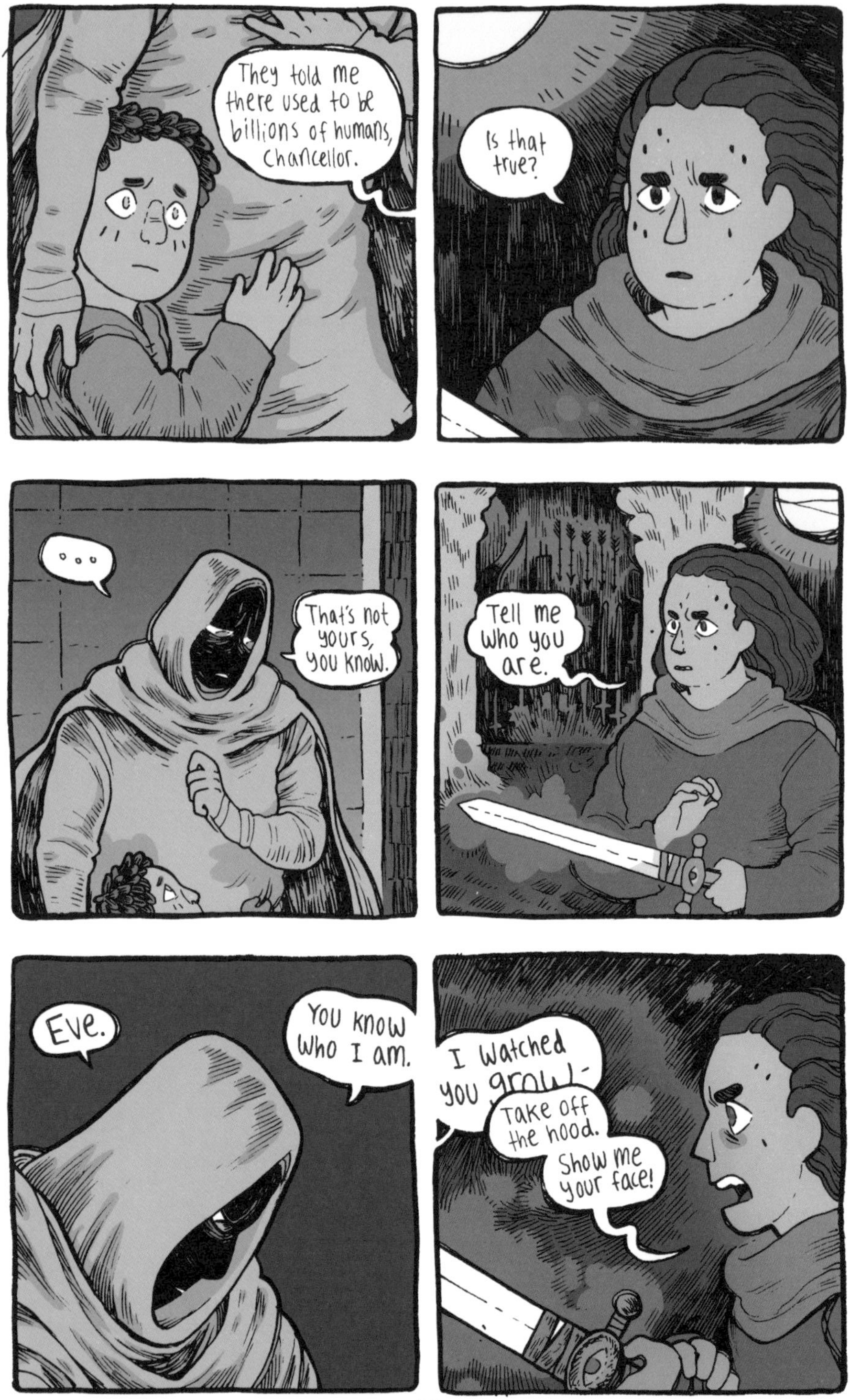
They told me there used to be billions of humans, Chancellor.
Is that true?
...
That's not yours, you know.
Tell me who you are.
Eve.
You know who I am.
I watched you grow-
Take off the hood.
Show me your face!

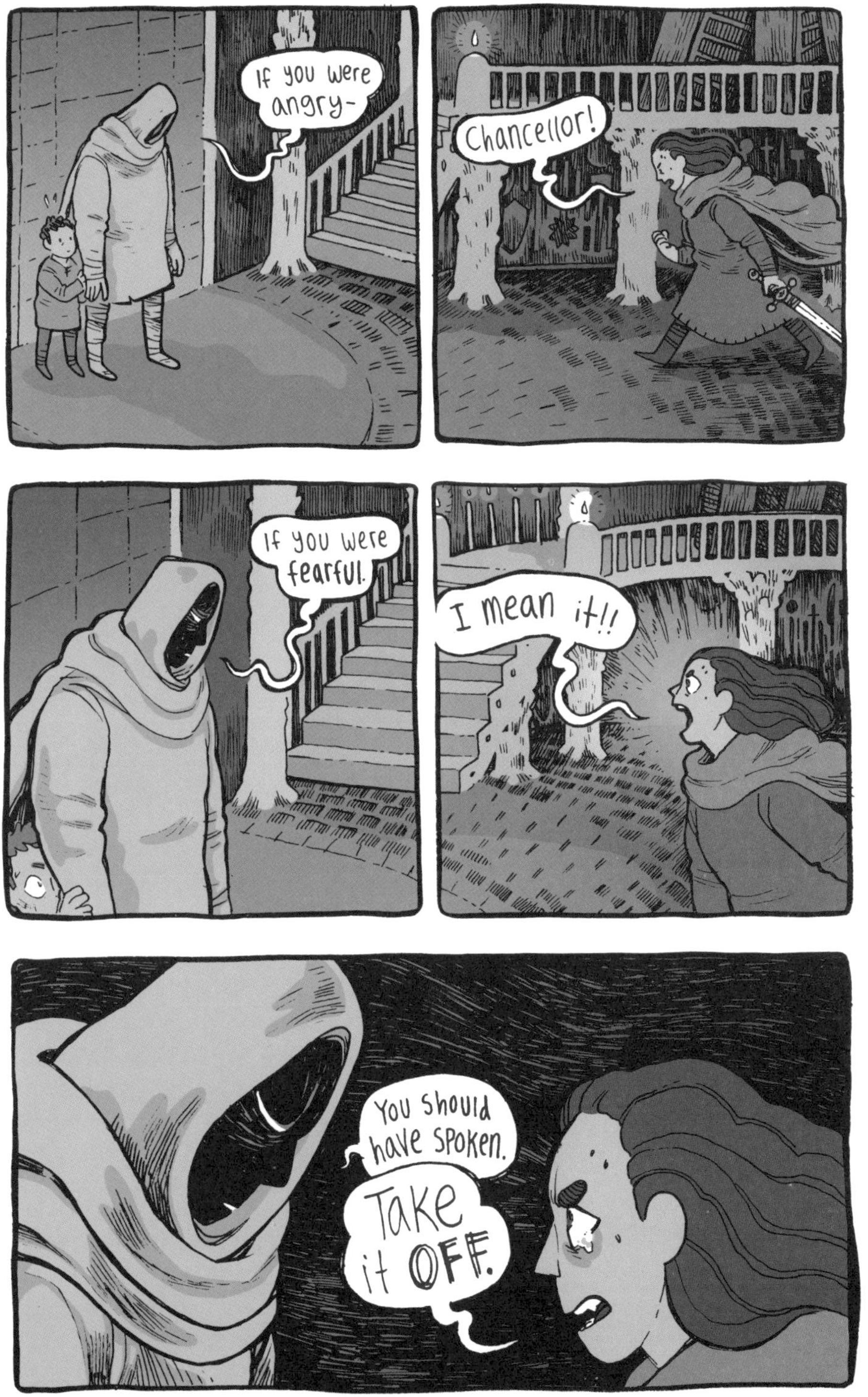
If you were angry-
Chancellor!
If you were fearful.
I mean it!!
You should have spoken.
Take it OFF.

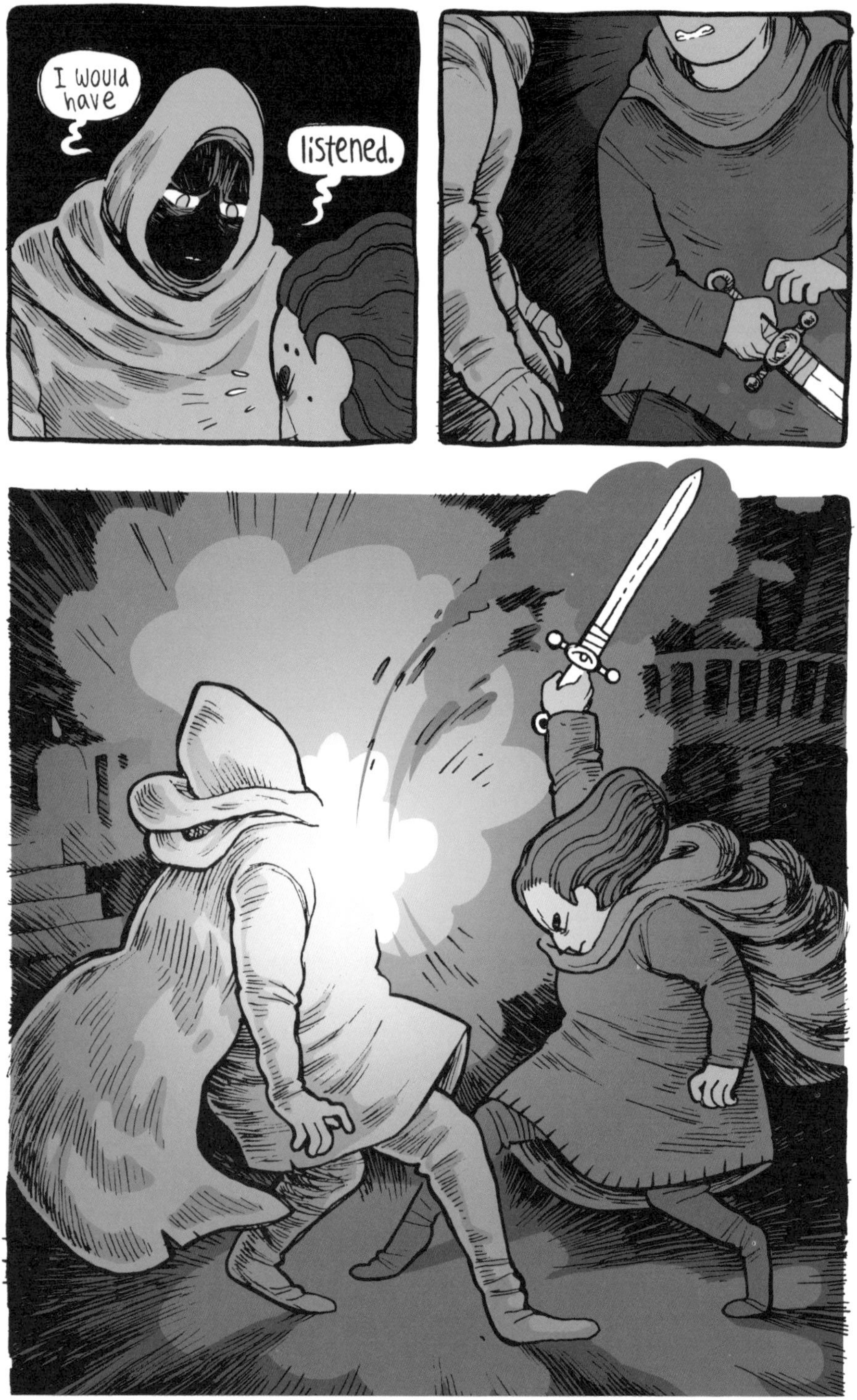
I would have
listened.

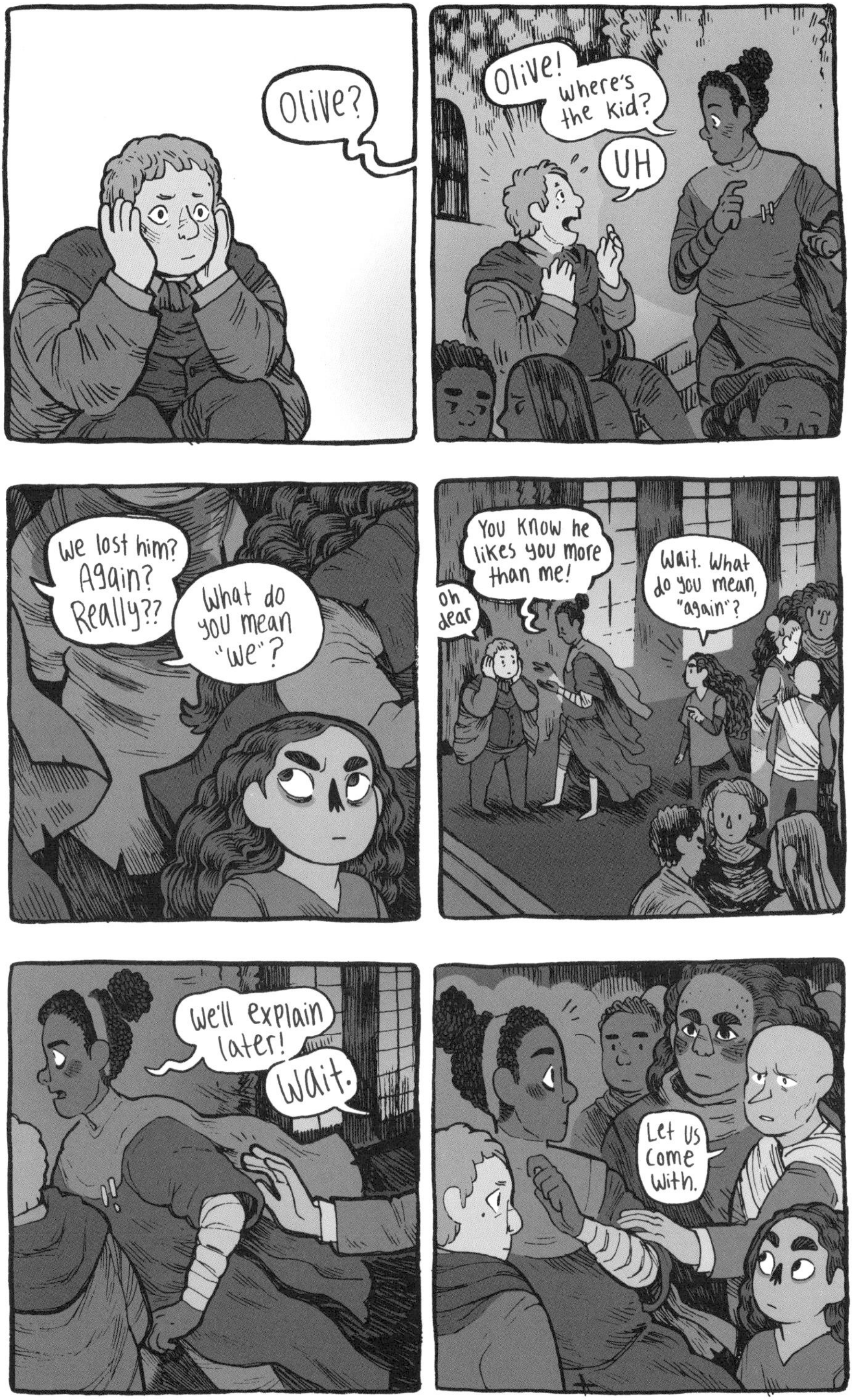

Olive?
Olive! Where's the kid?
UH
We lost him? Again? Really??
What do you mean "we"?
oh dear
You know he likes you more than me!
Wait. What do you mean, "again"?
We'll explain later!
Wait.
Let us come with.

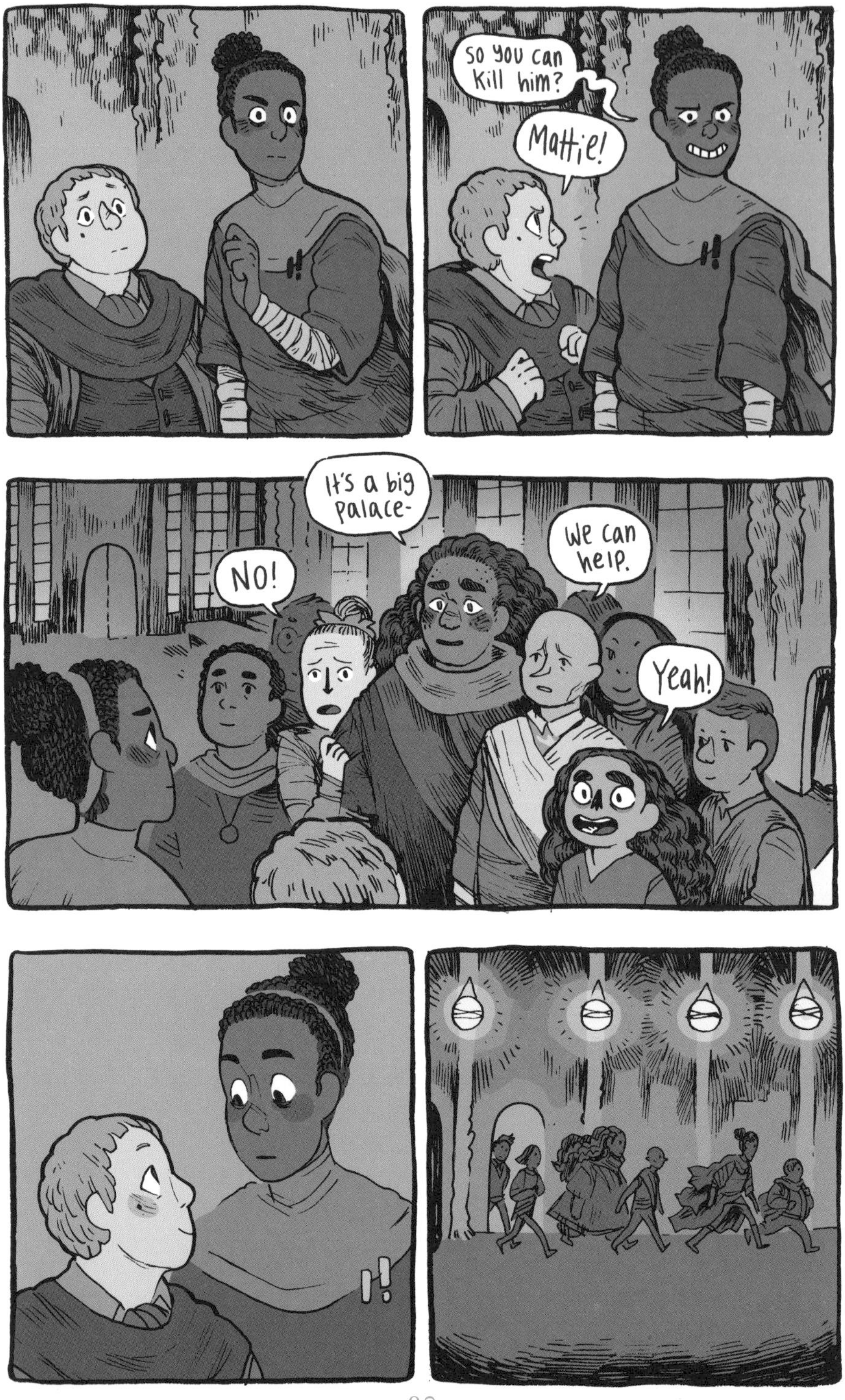
So you can Kill him?
Mattie!
It's a big palace-
No!
We can help.
Yeah!

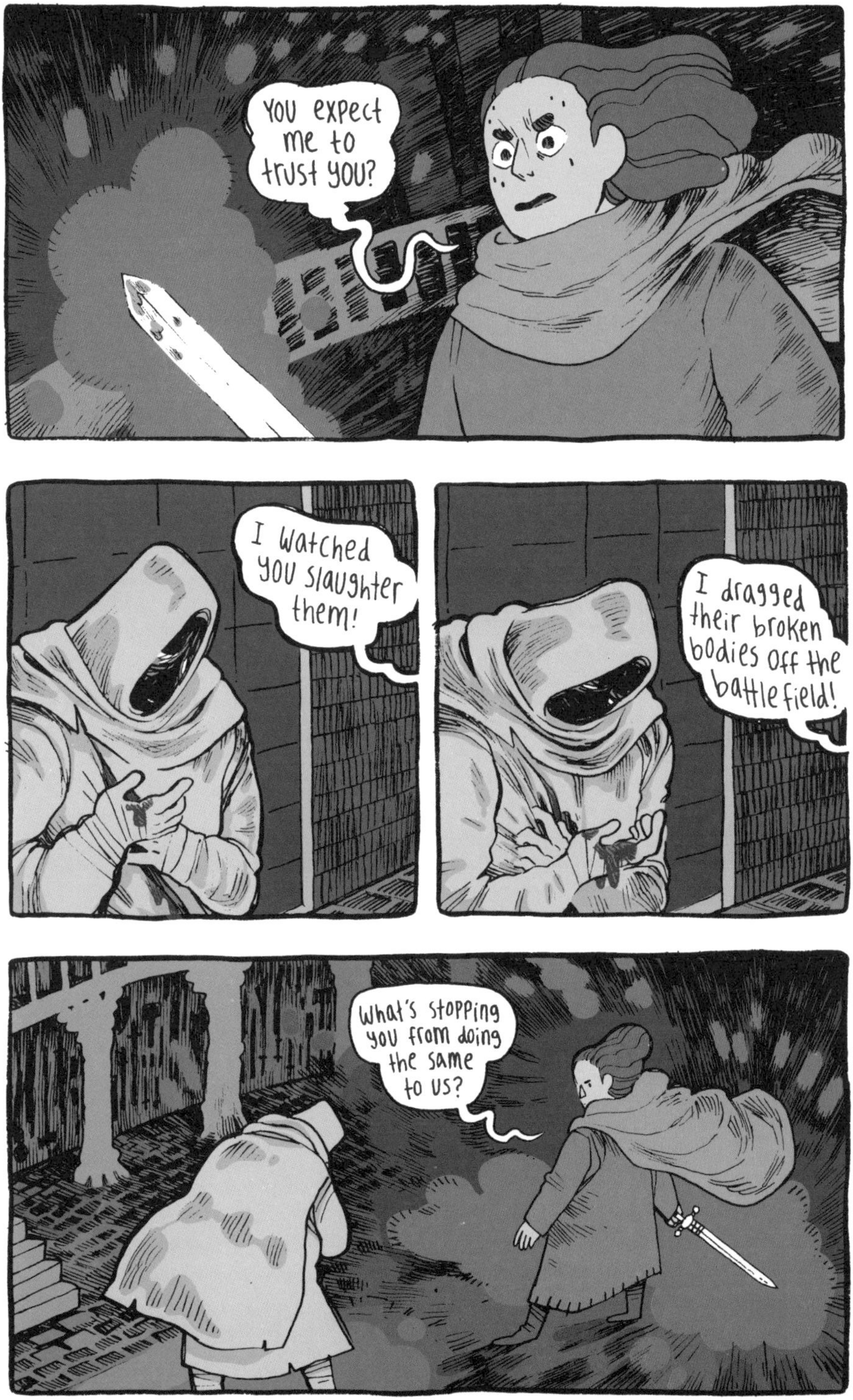
YOU expect me to trust YOU?
I watched YOU slaughter them!
I dragged their broken bodies off the battlefield!
What's stopping you from doing the same to us?

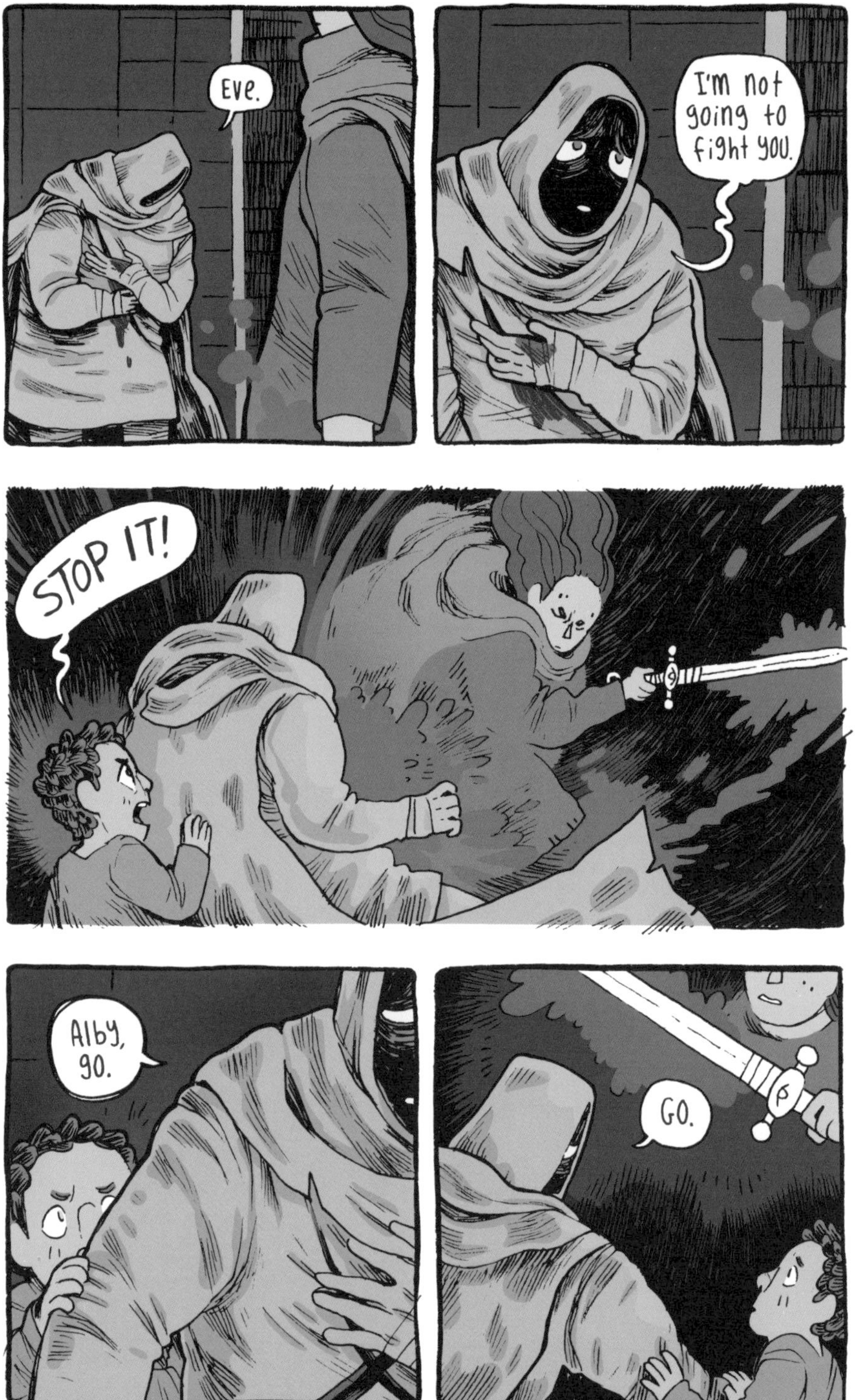
Eve.
I'm not going to fight you.
STOP IT!
Alby, go.
GO.

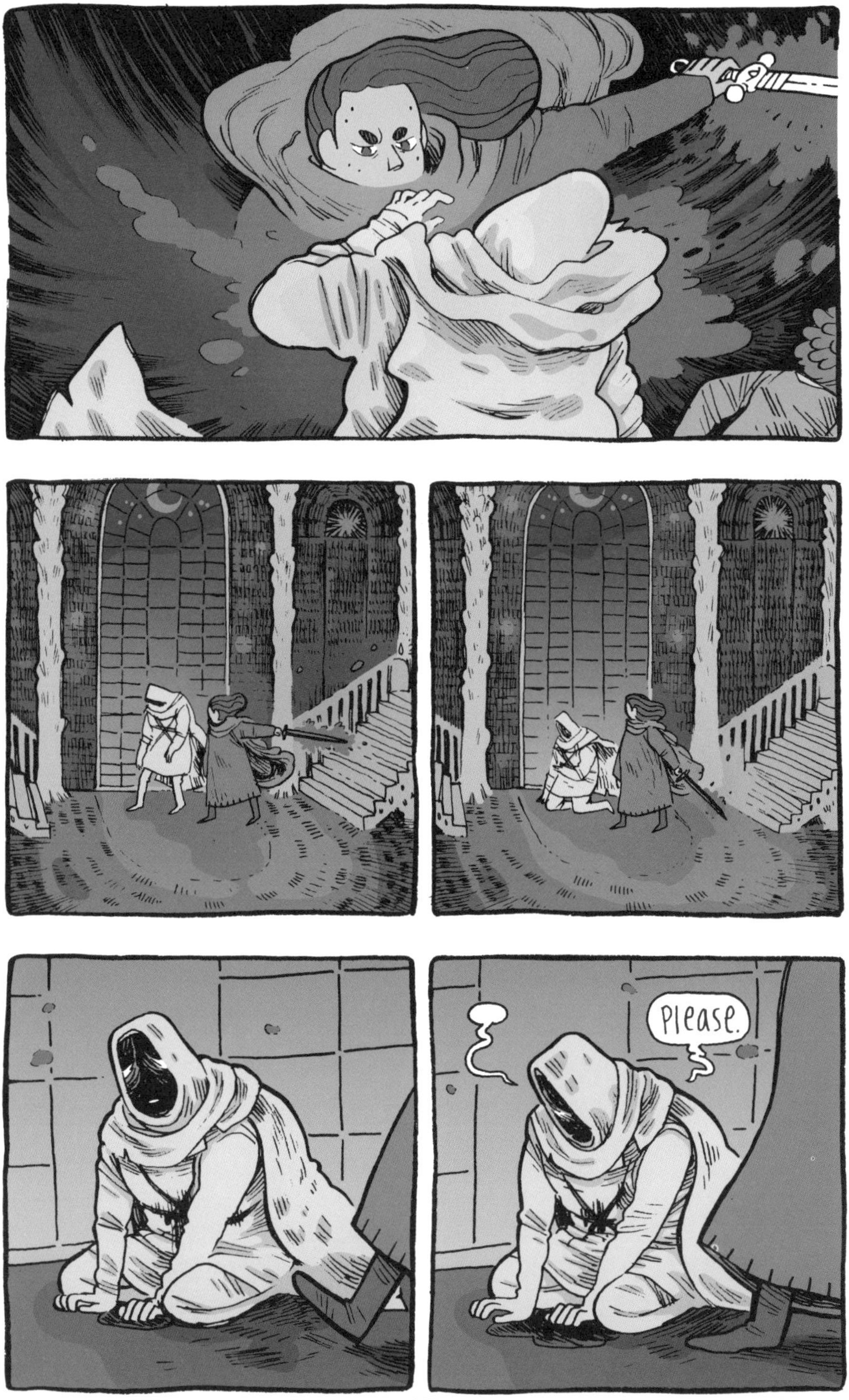
Please.

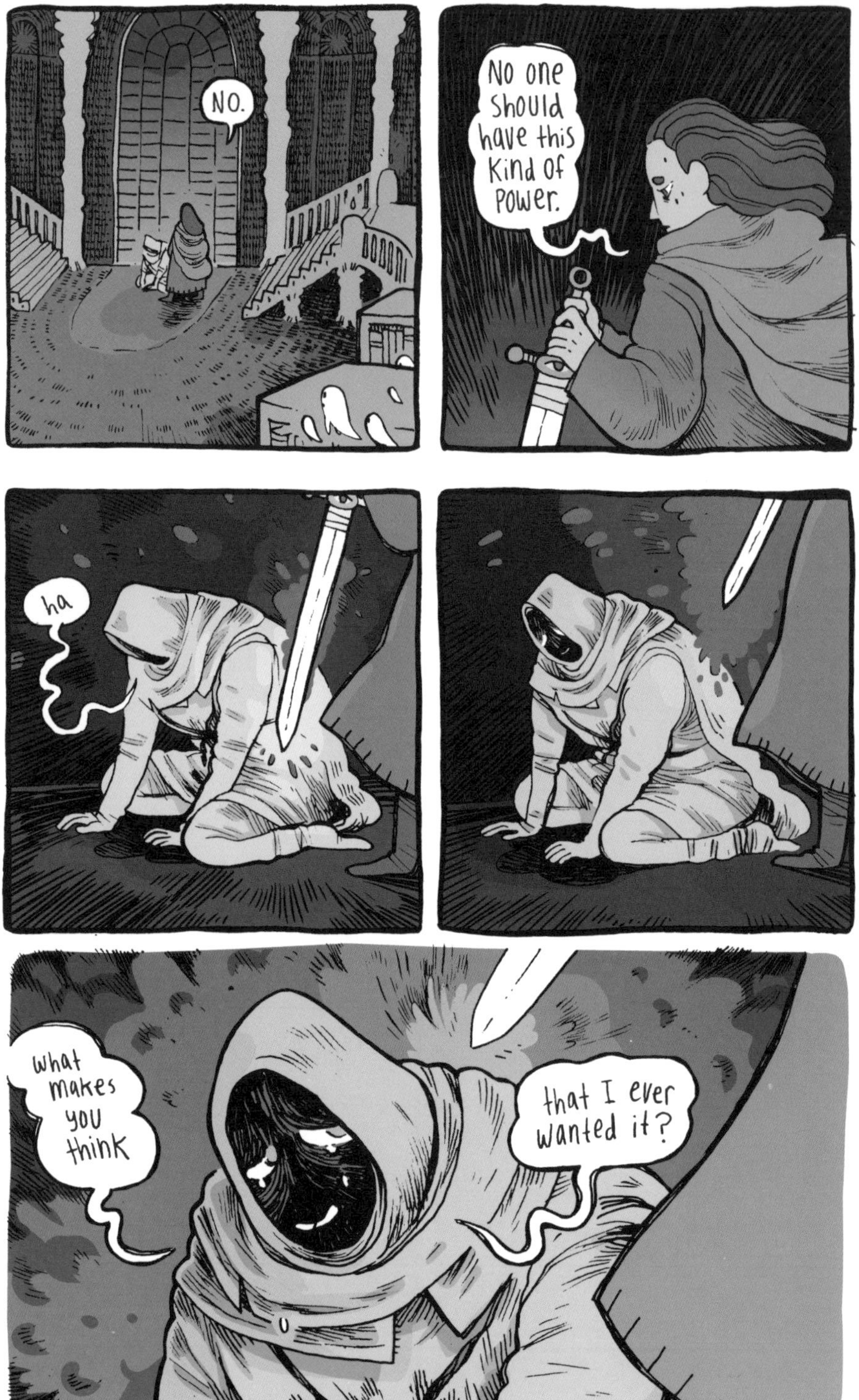
NO.
No one should have this Kind of Power.
ha
what makes you think
that I ever wanted it?

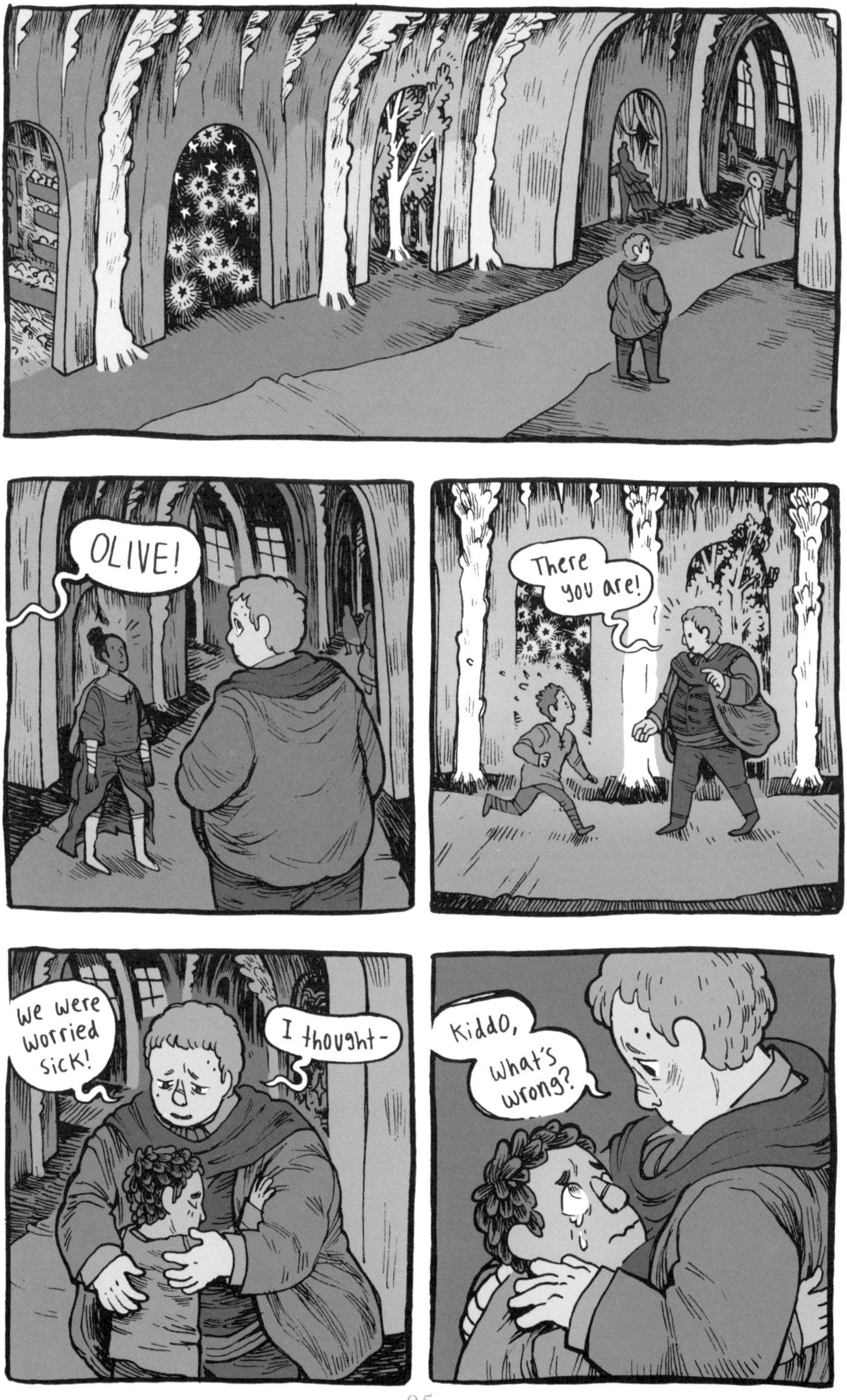
OLIVE!
There you are!
We were worried sick!
I thought-
Kiddo, what's wrong?

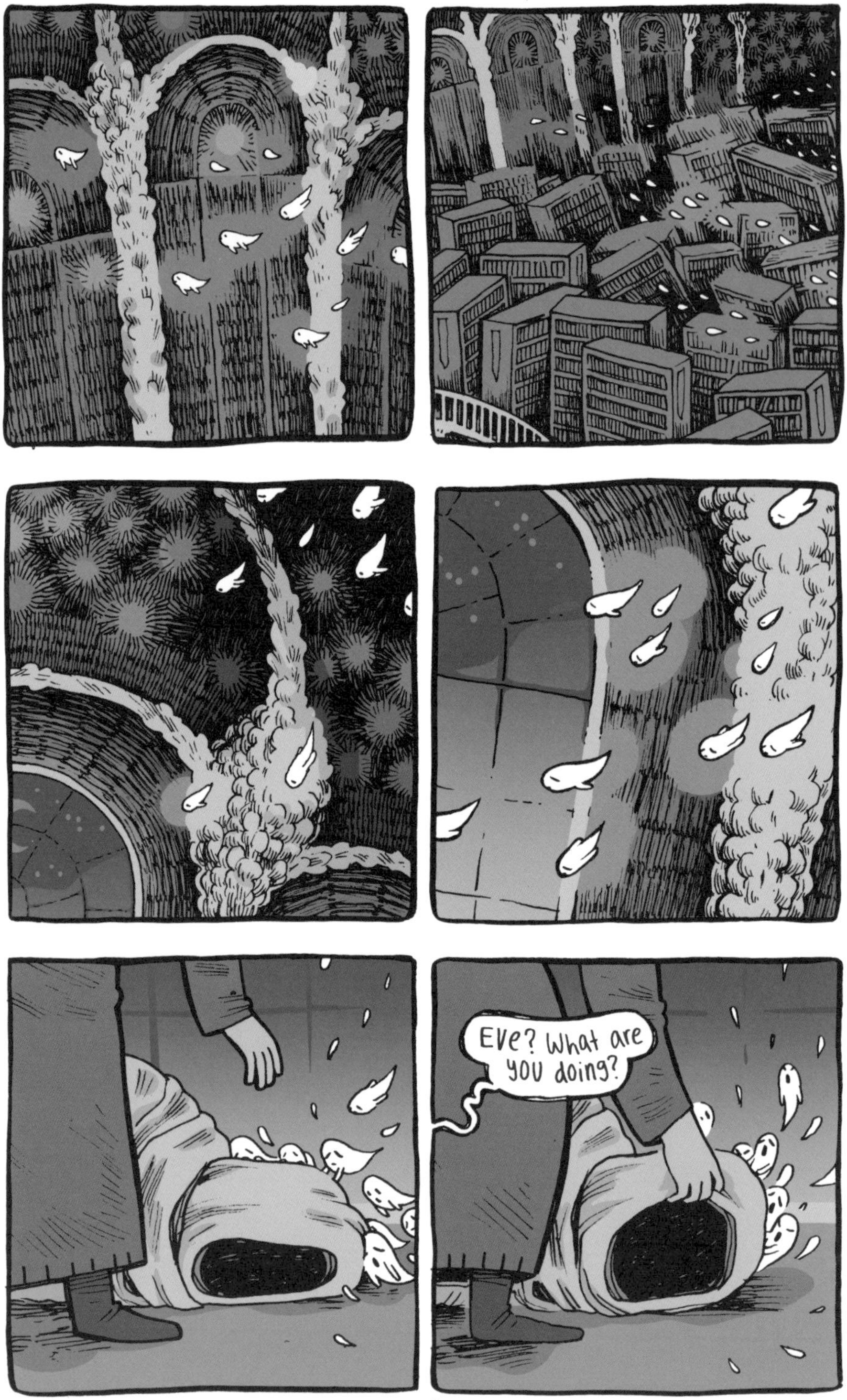
Eve? What are
you doing?

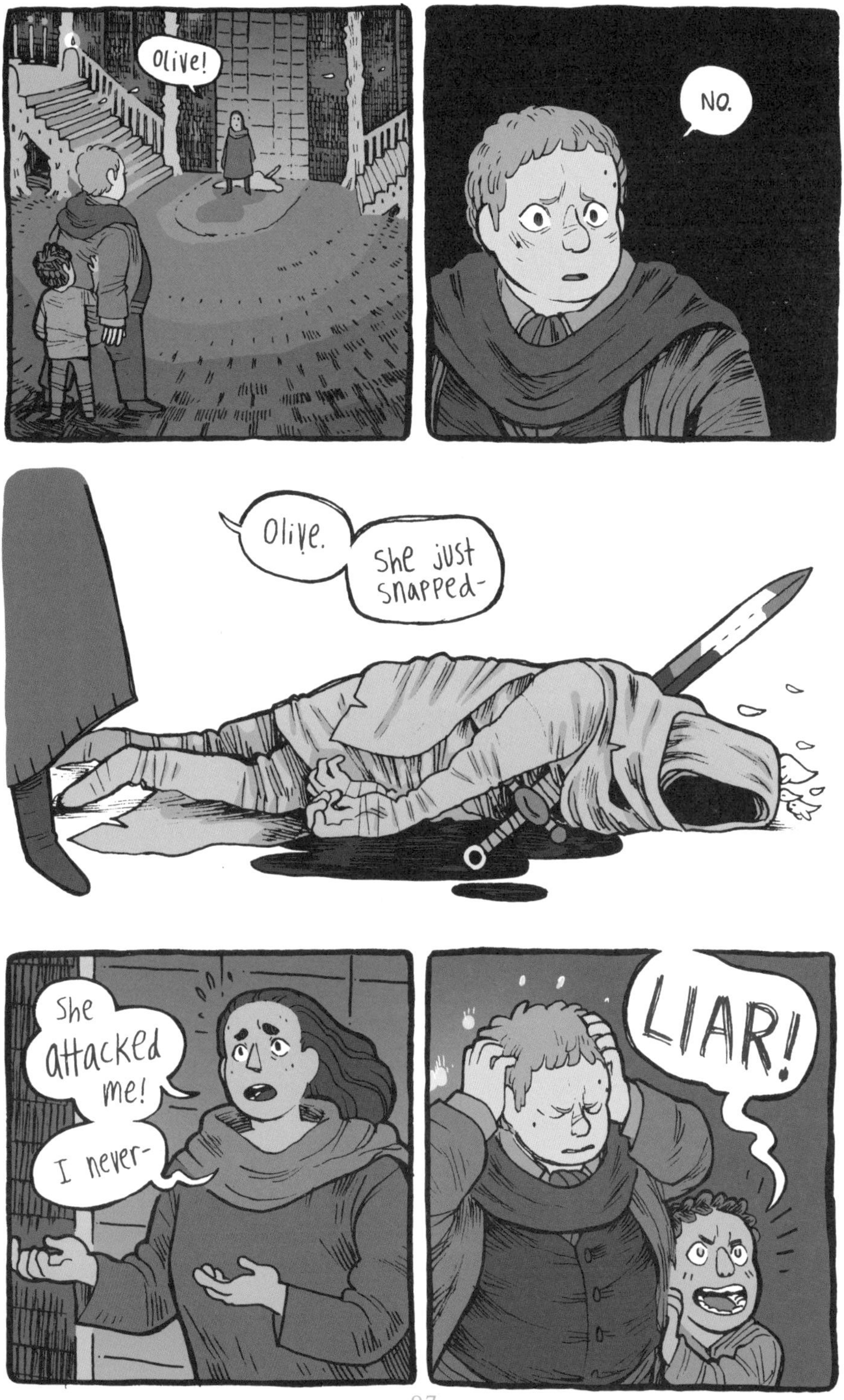

Olive!
NO.
Olive.
She just snapped-
She attacked me!
I never-
LIAR!

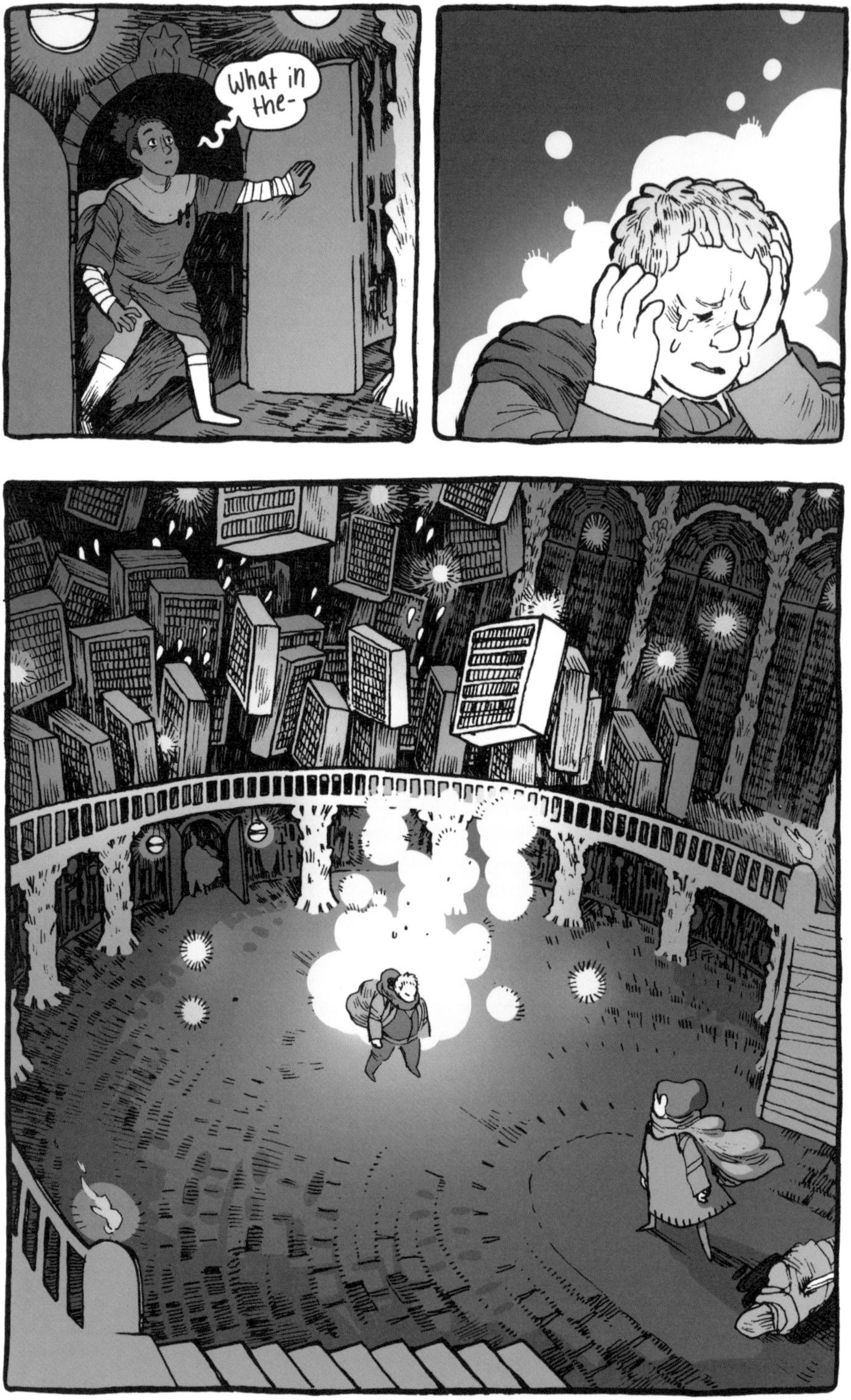
What in the-

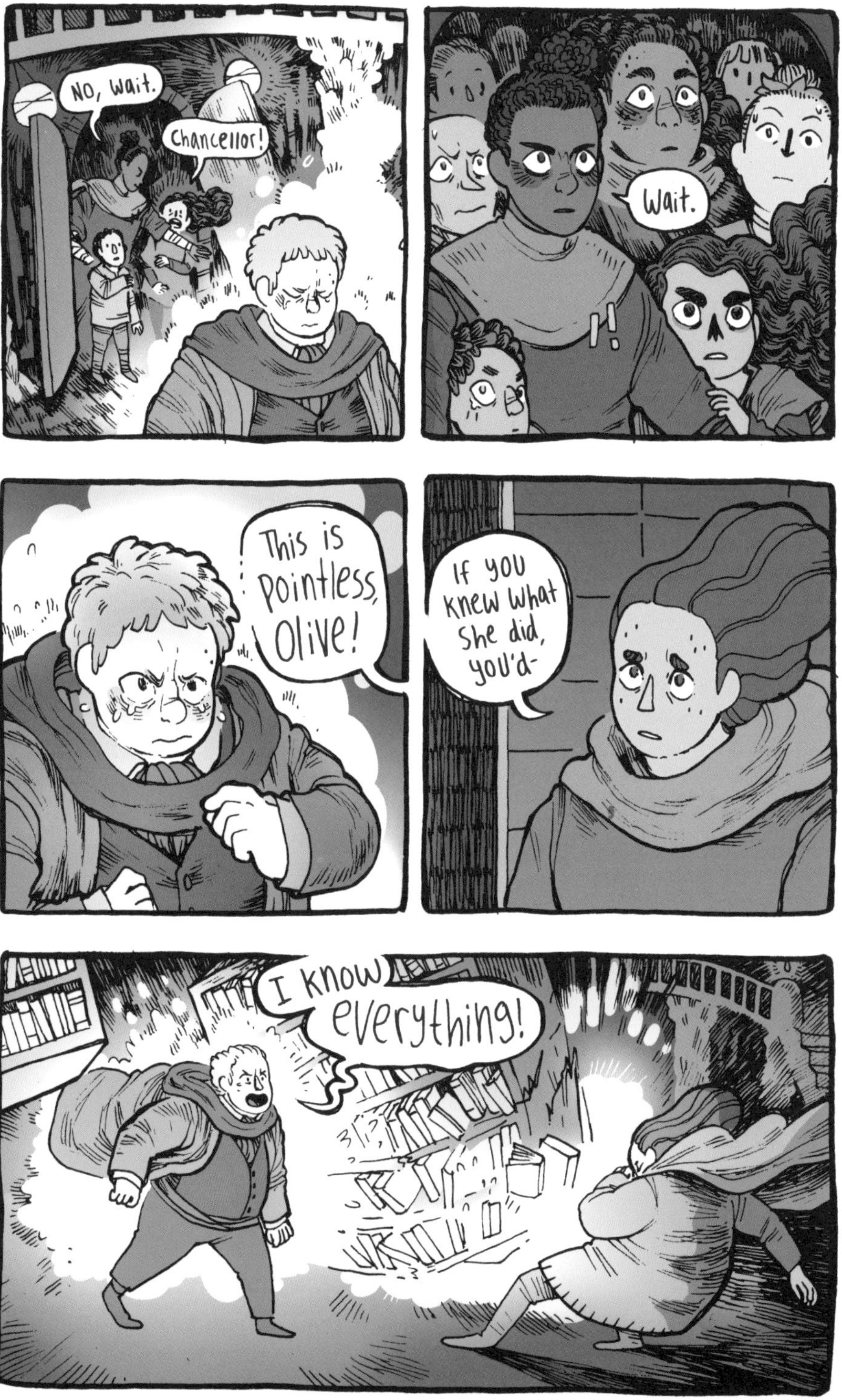
No, wait.
Chancellor!
Wait.
This is pointless, Olive!
If you knew what she did, you'd-
I know everything!

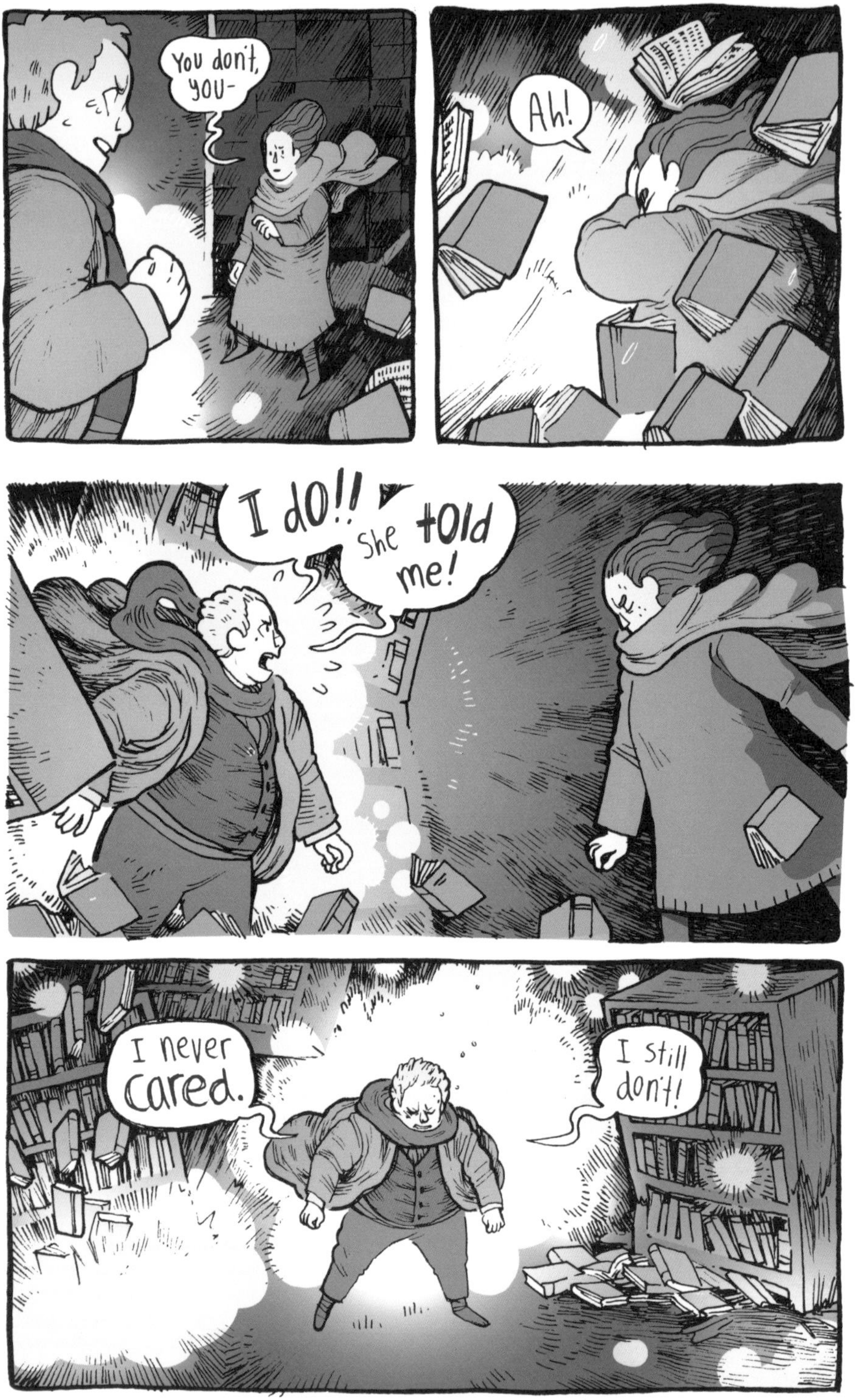
You don't, you-
Ah!
I do!!
She told me!
I never cared.
I still don't!

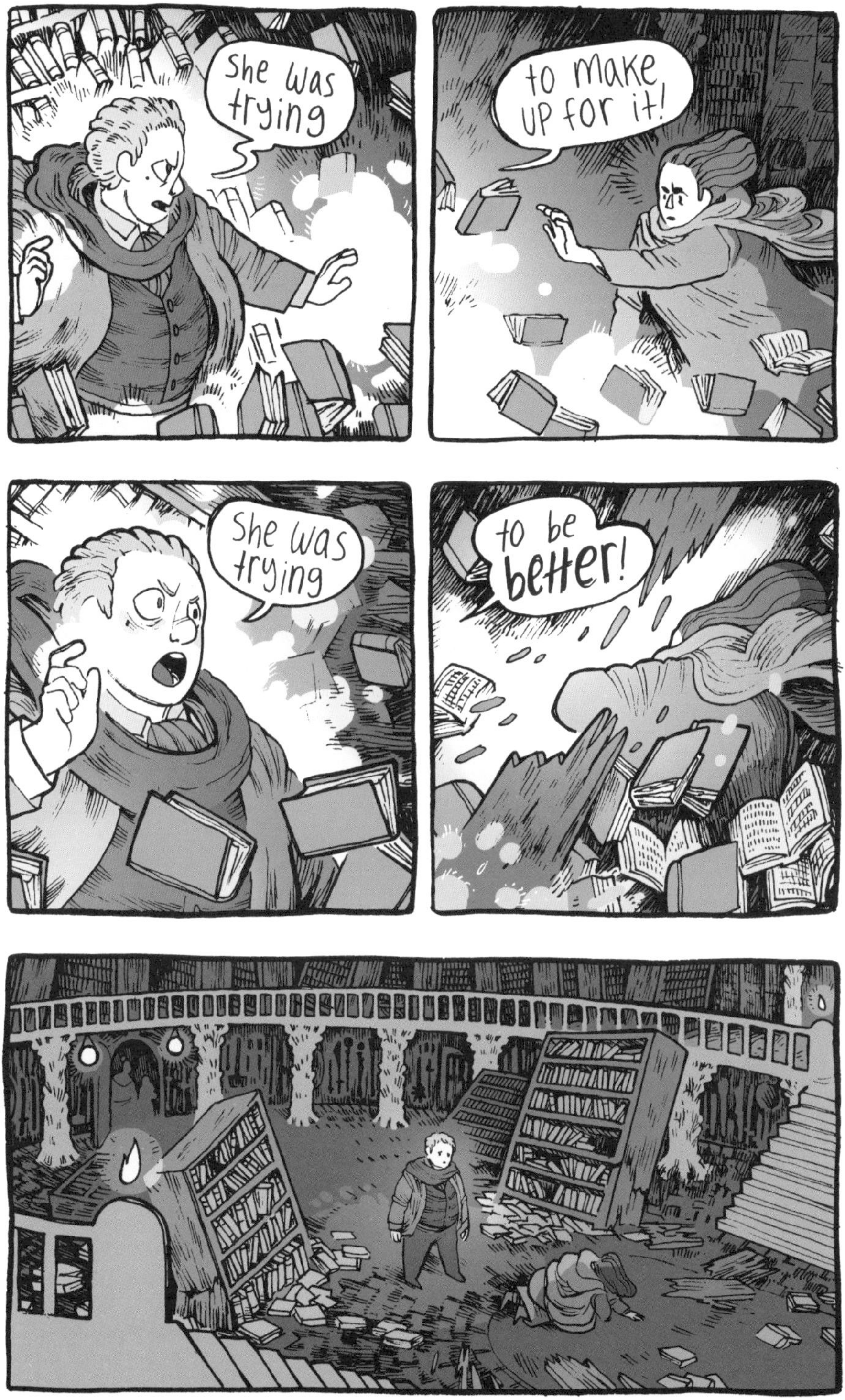
She was trying
to make up for it!
She was trying
to be better!

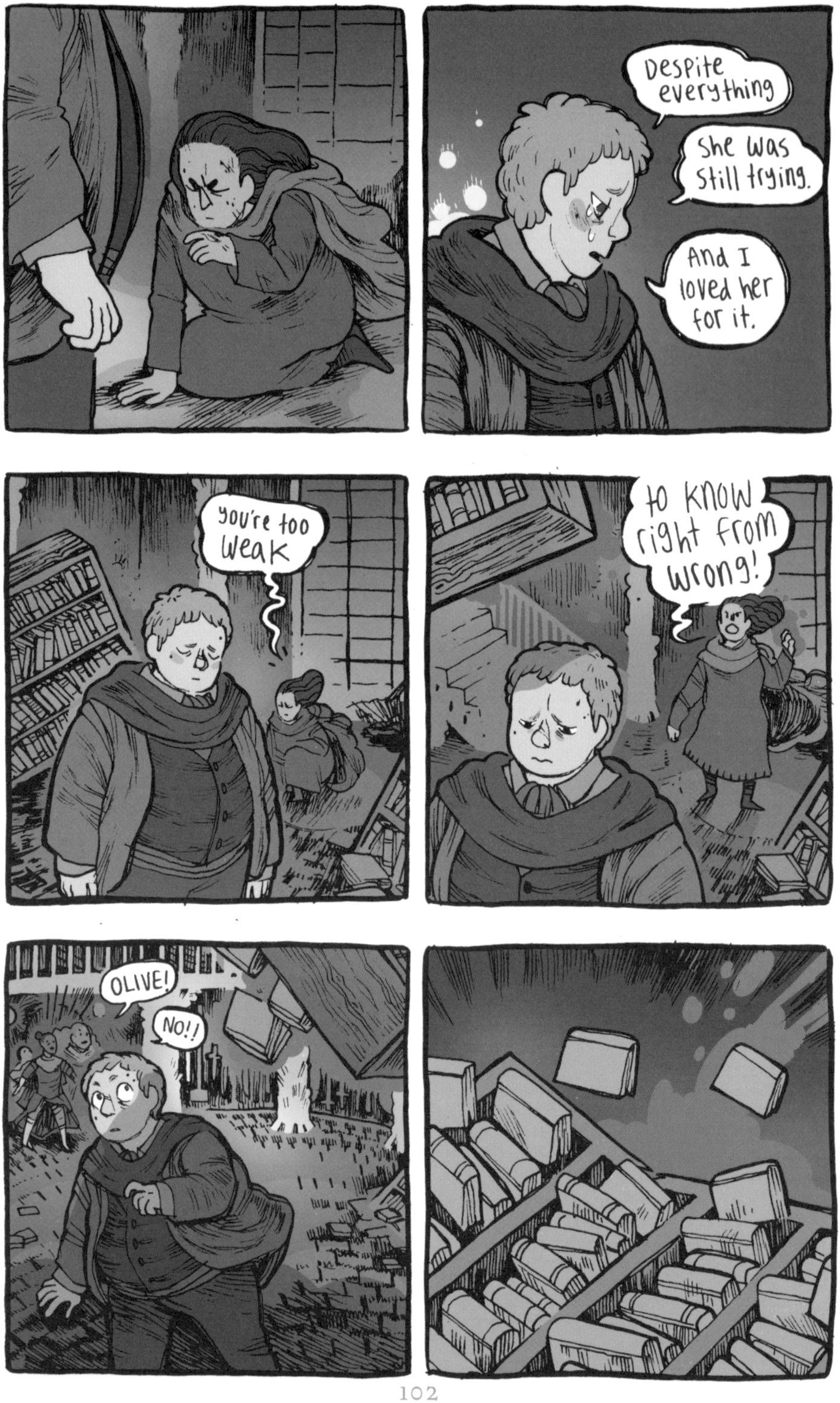
Despite everything
She was still trying.
And I loved her for it.
You're too weak
to know right from wrong!
OLIVE!
NO!!

GET UP.

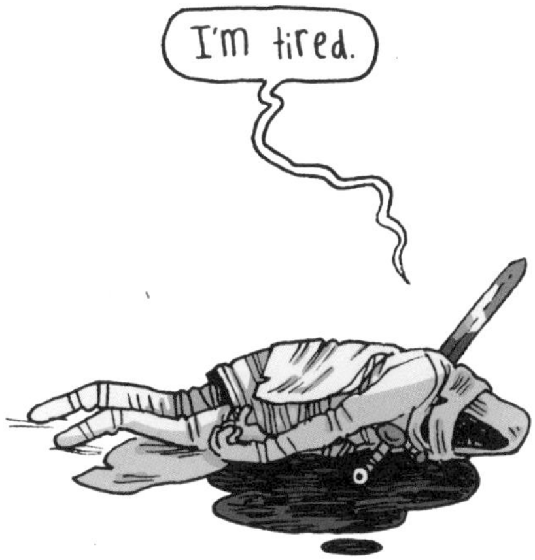
I'm tired.

YOU ARE
STILL NEEDED.

OLIVE!

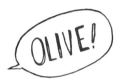

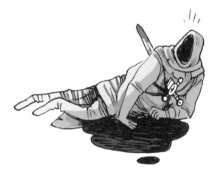

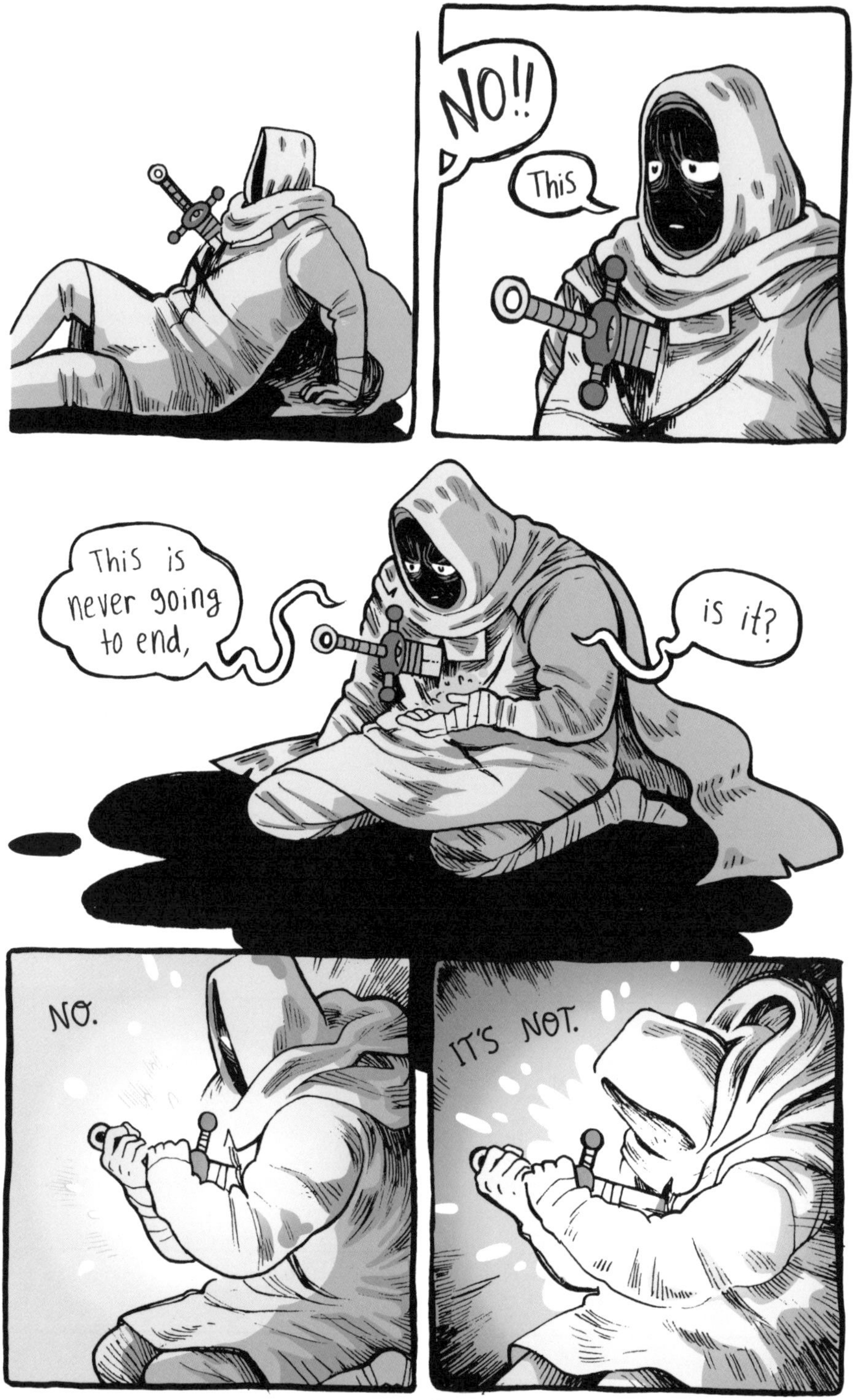
NO!!
This
This is never going to end,
is it?
NO.
IT'S NOT.

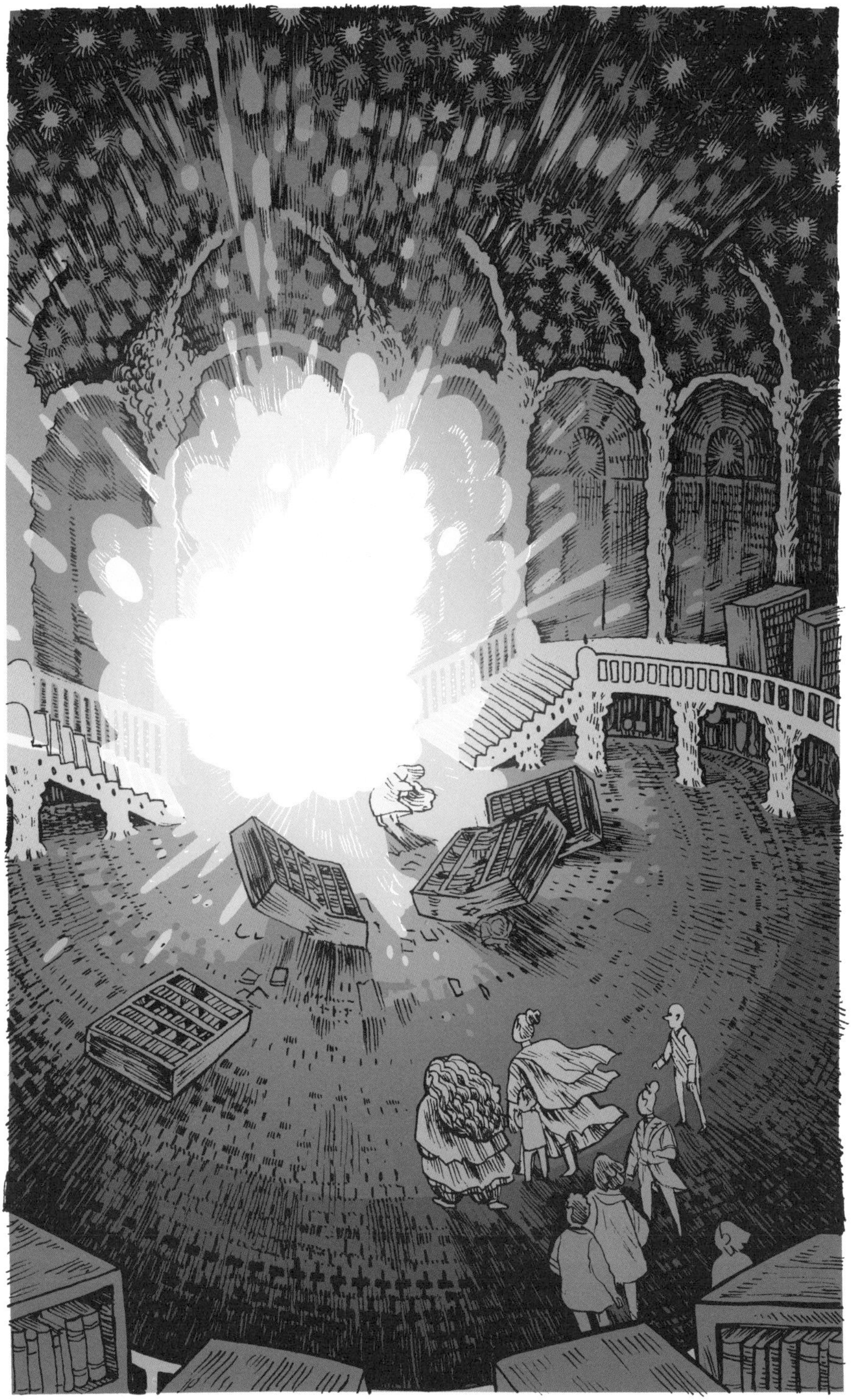

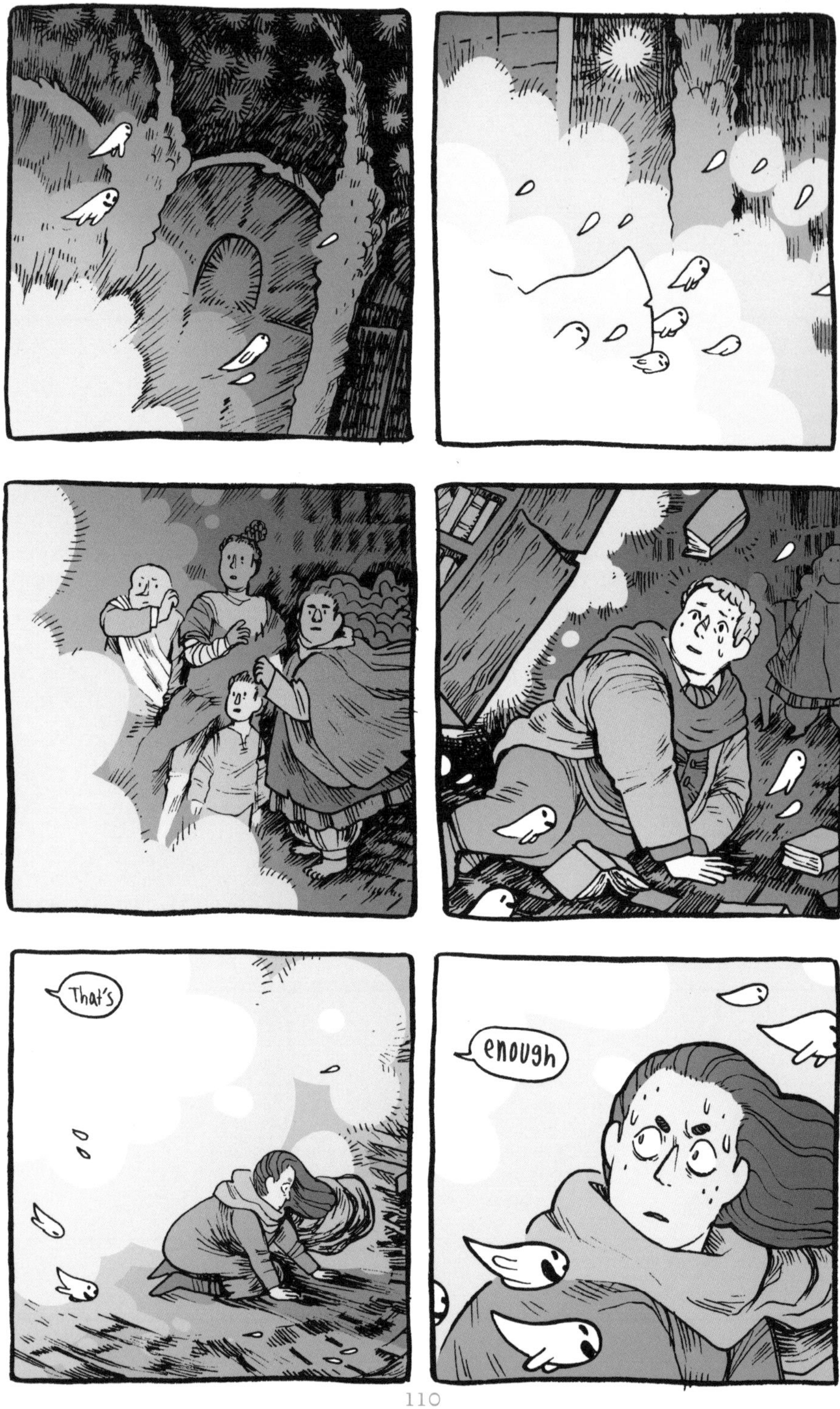

That's
enough

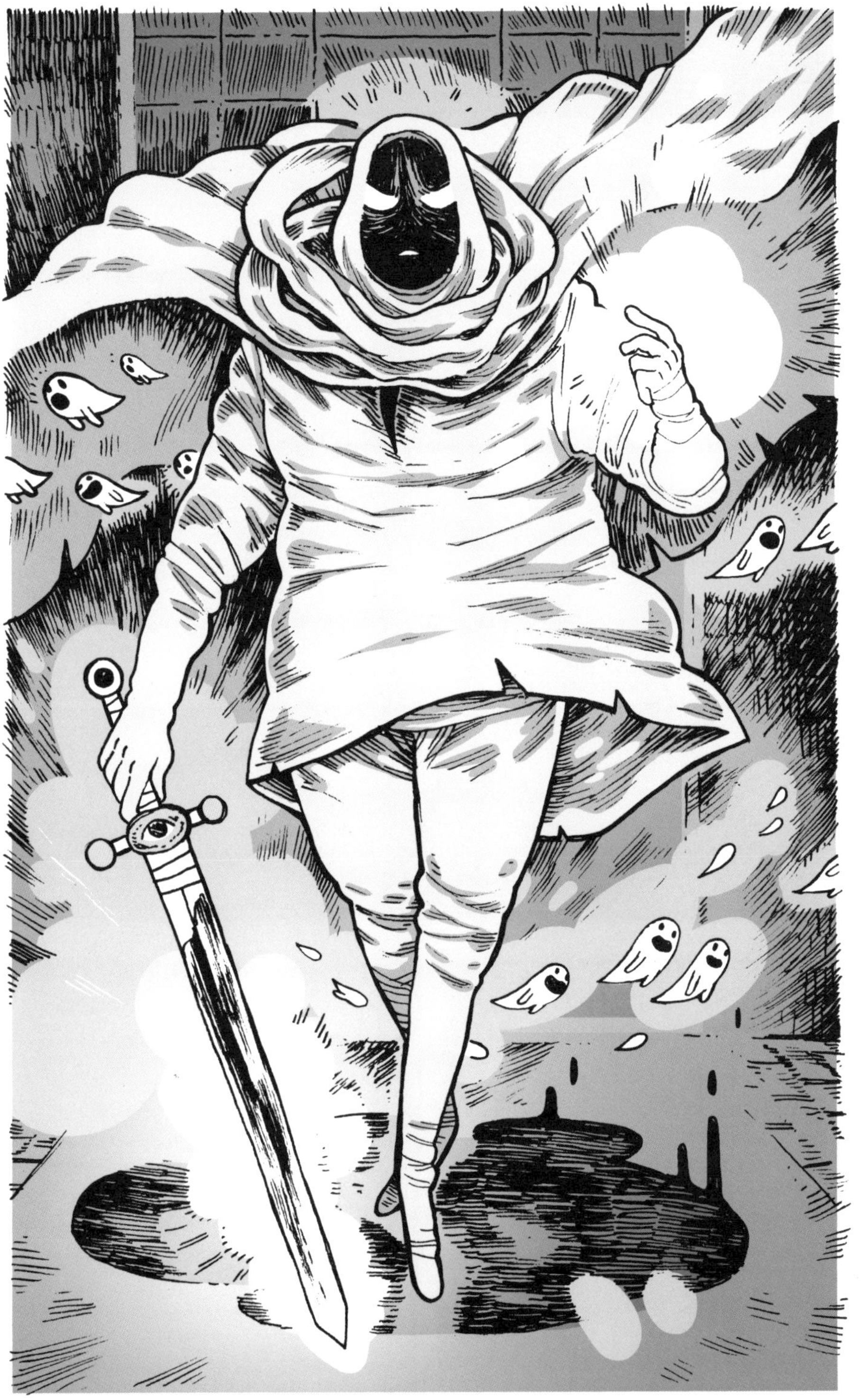

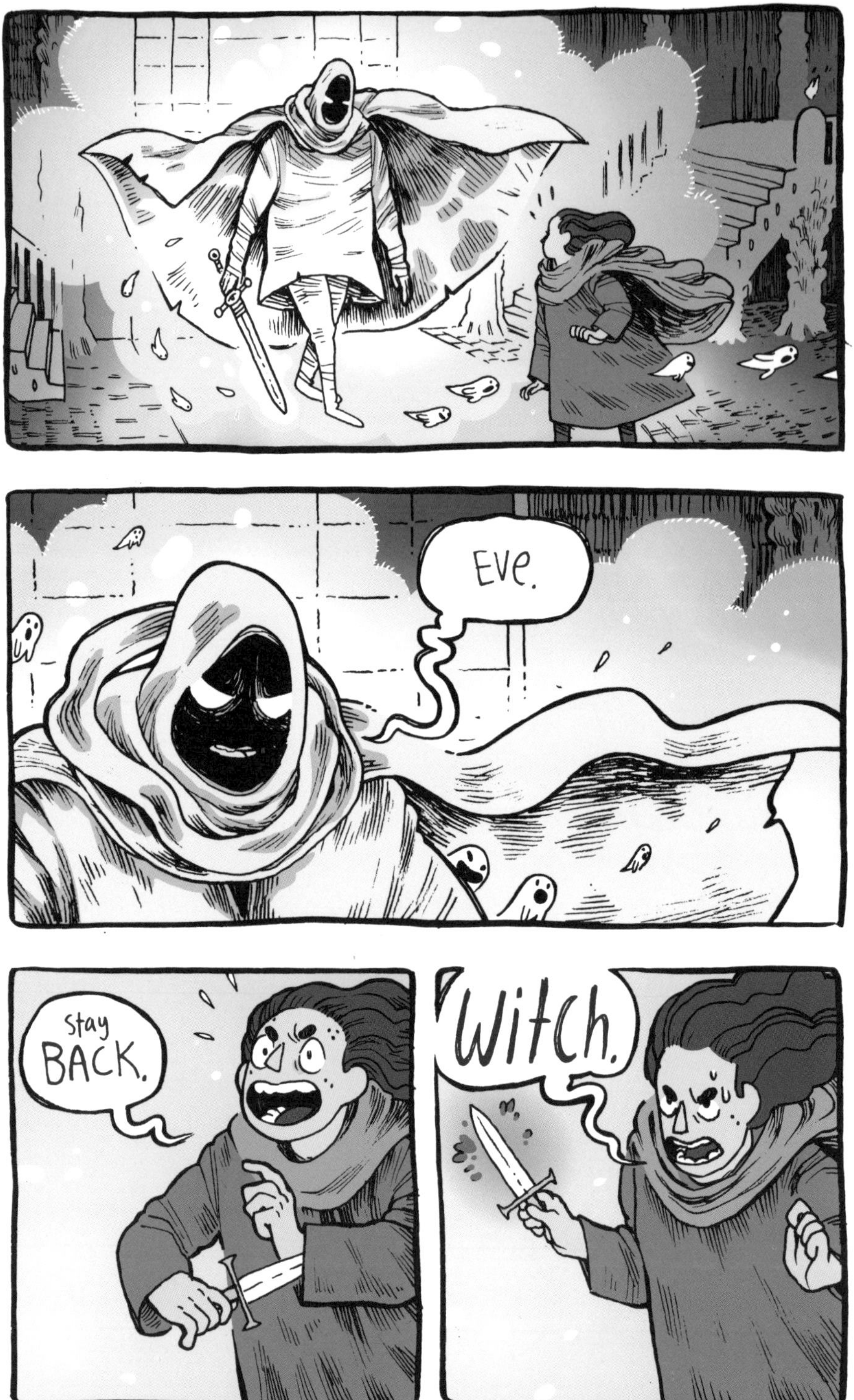
Eve.
stay BACK.
Witch.

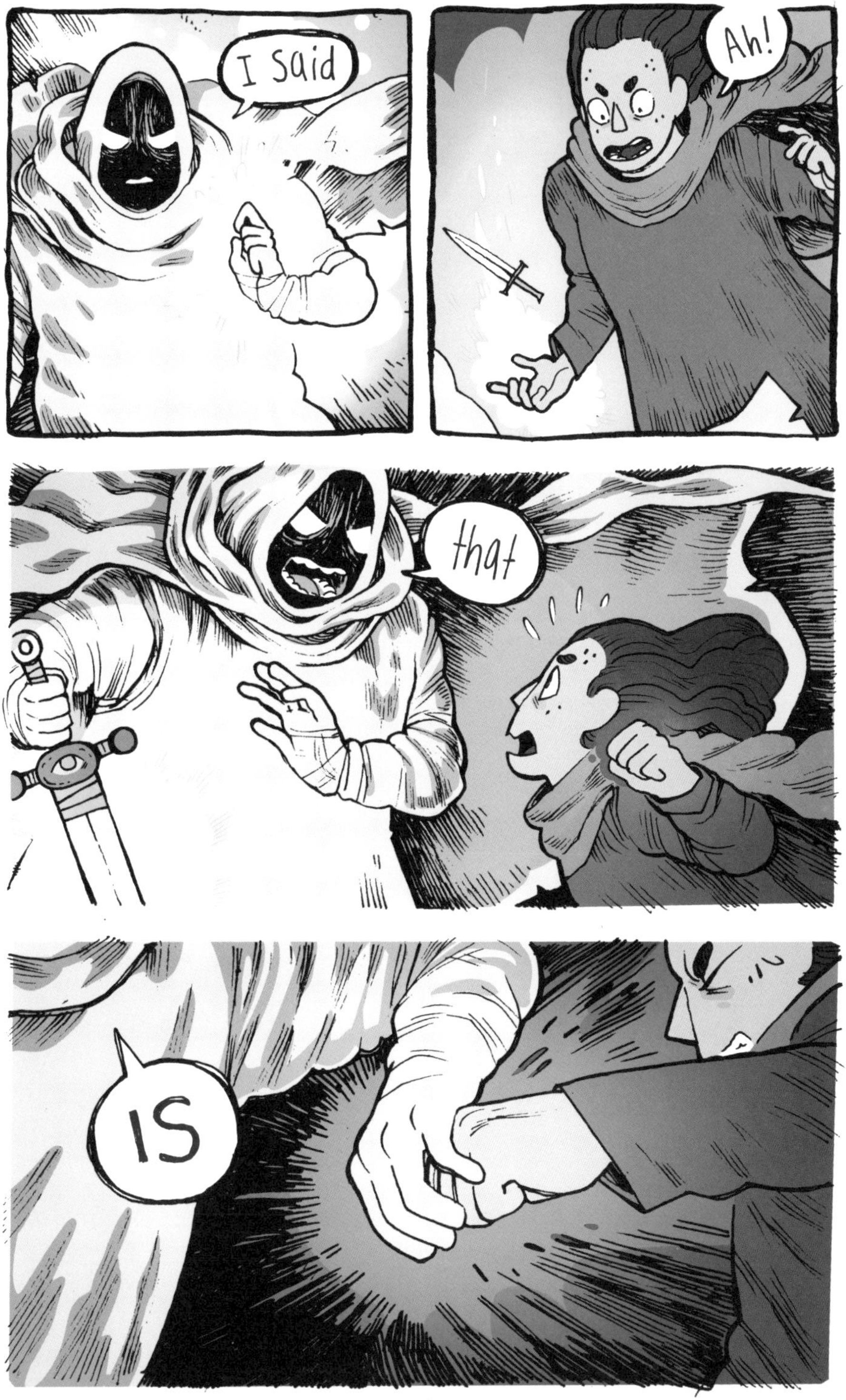
I said
Ah!
that
IS

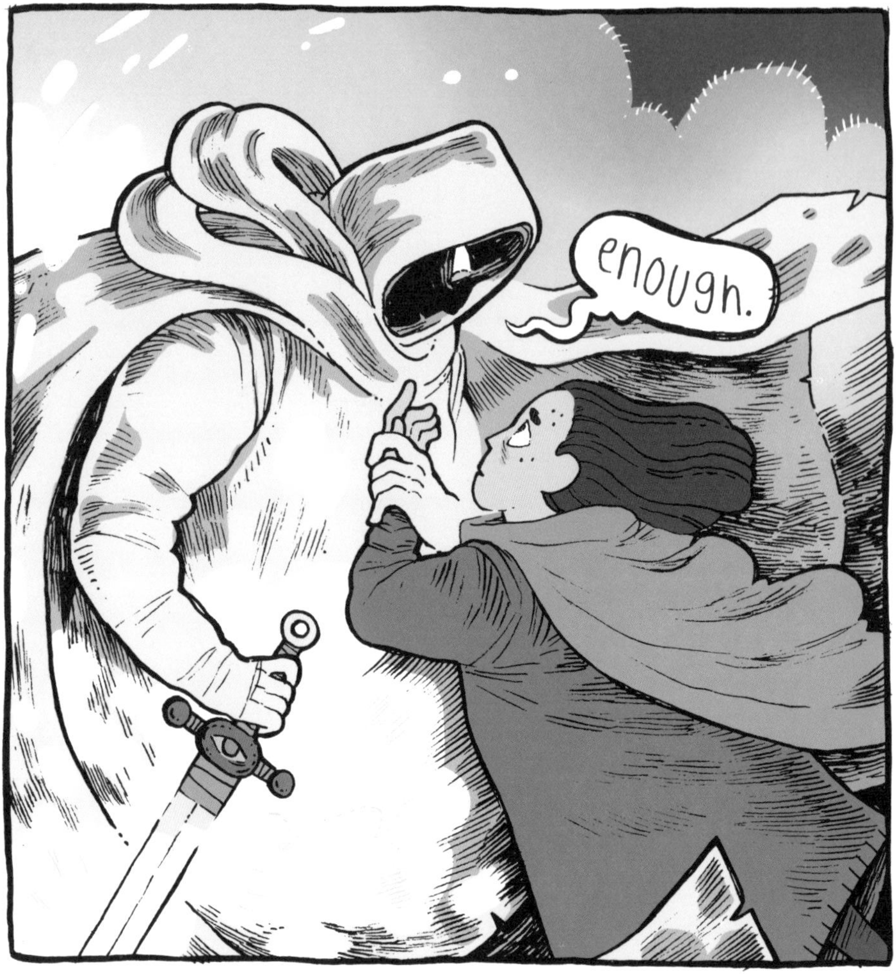
enough.

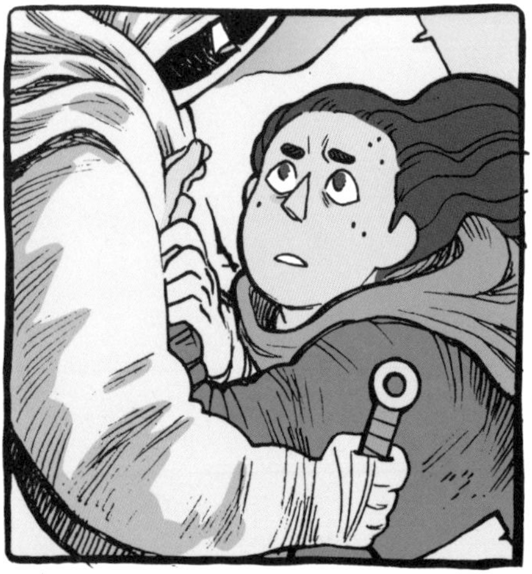

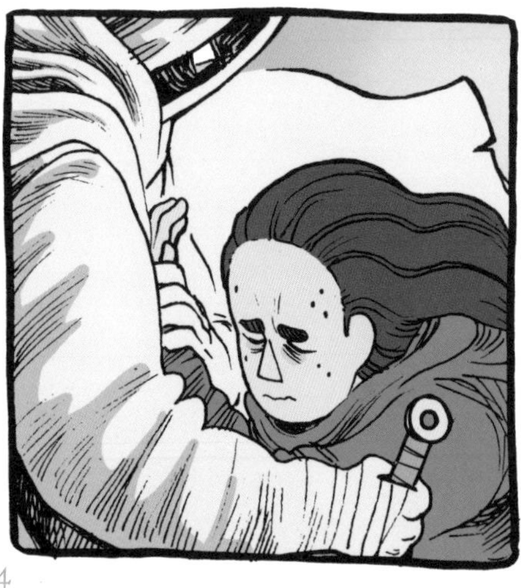

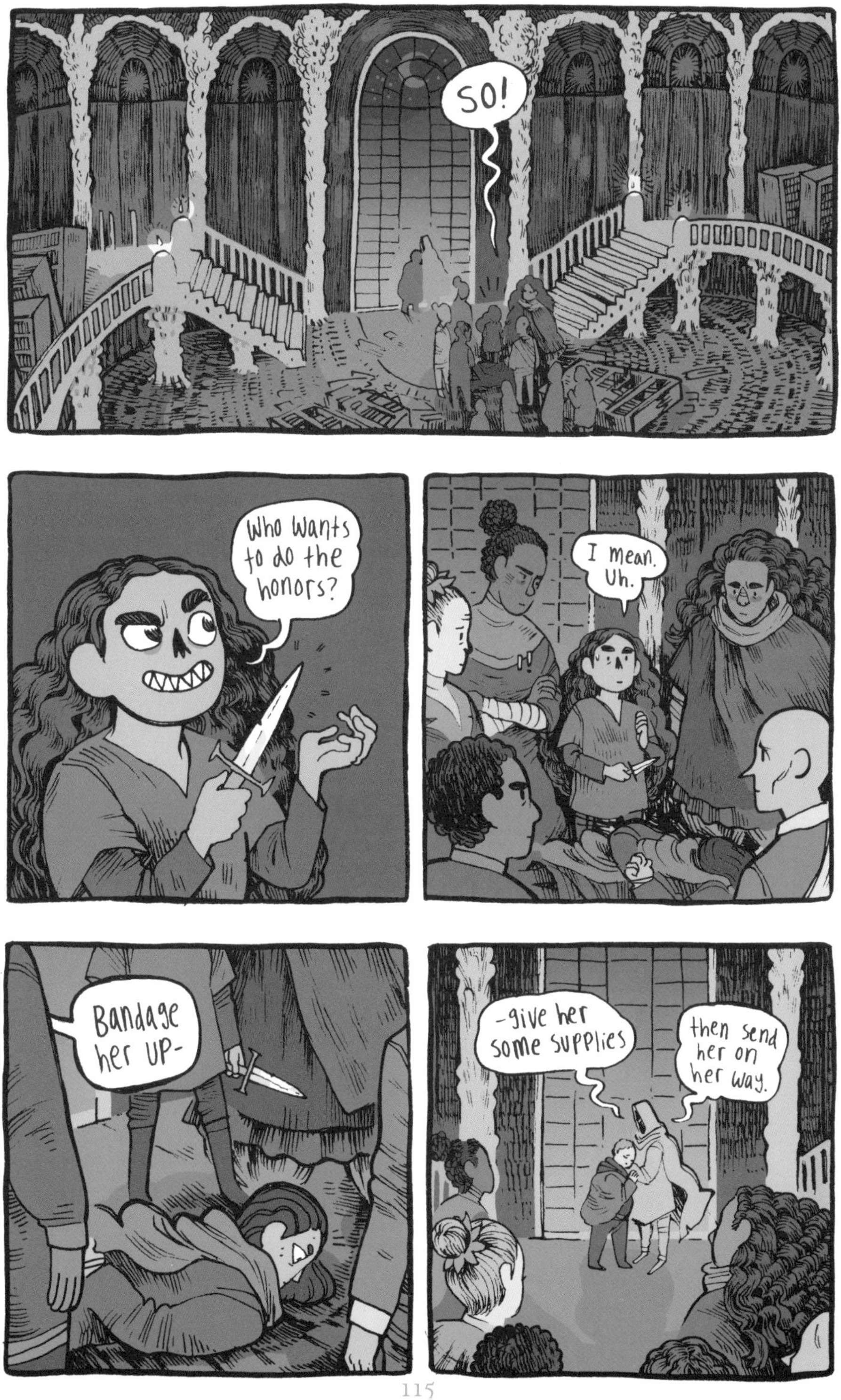
SO!
Who wants to do the honors?
I mean. Uh.
Bandage her up-
-give her some supplies
then send her on her way.

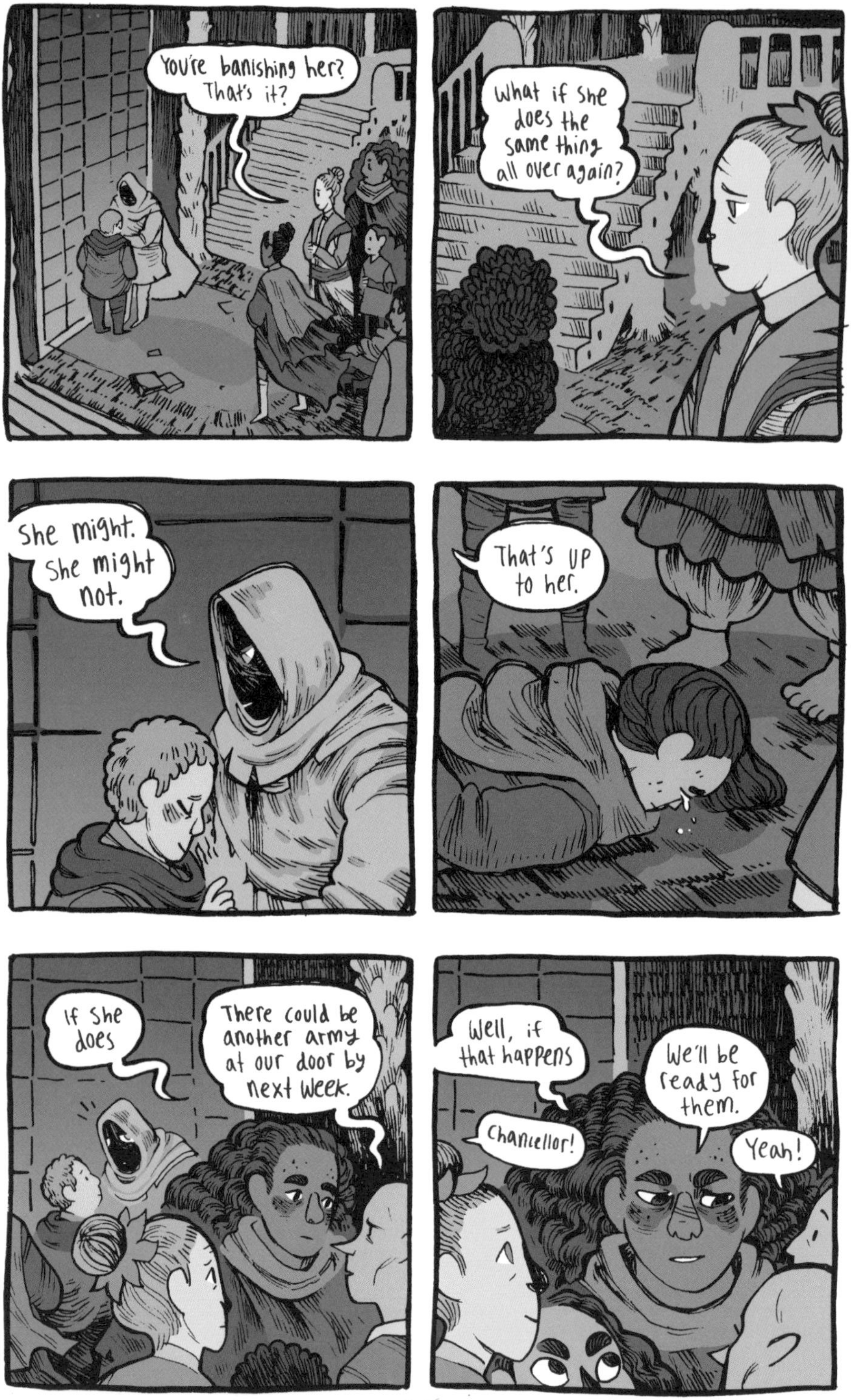
You're banishing her? That's it?
What if she does the same thing all over again?
She might. She might not.
That's up to her.
If she does
There could be another army at our door by next week.
Well, if that happens
We'll be ready for them.
Chancellor!
Yeah!

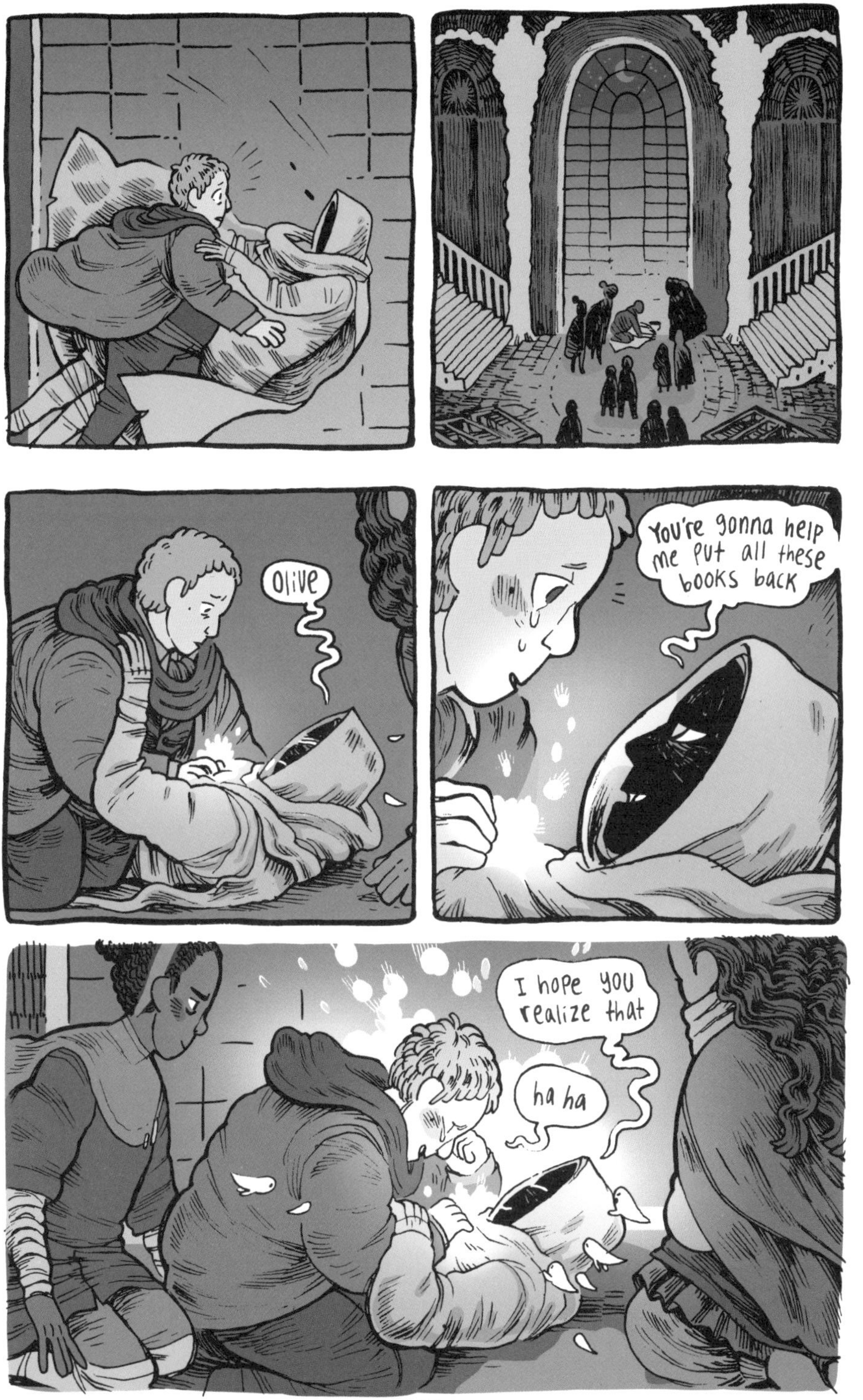
Olive
You're gonna help me put all these books back
I hope you realize that
ha ha

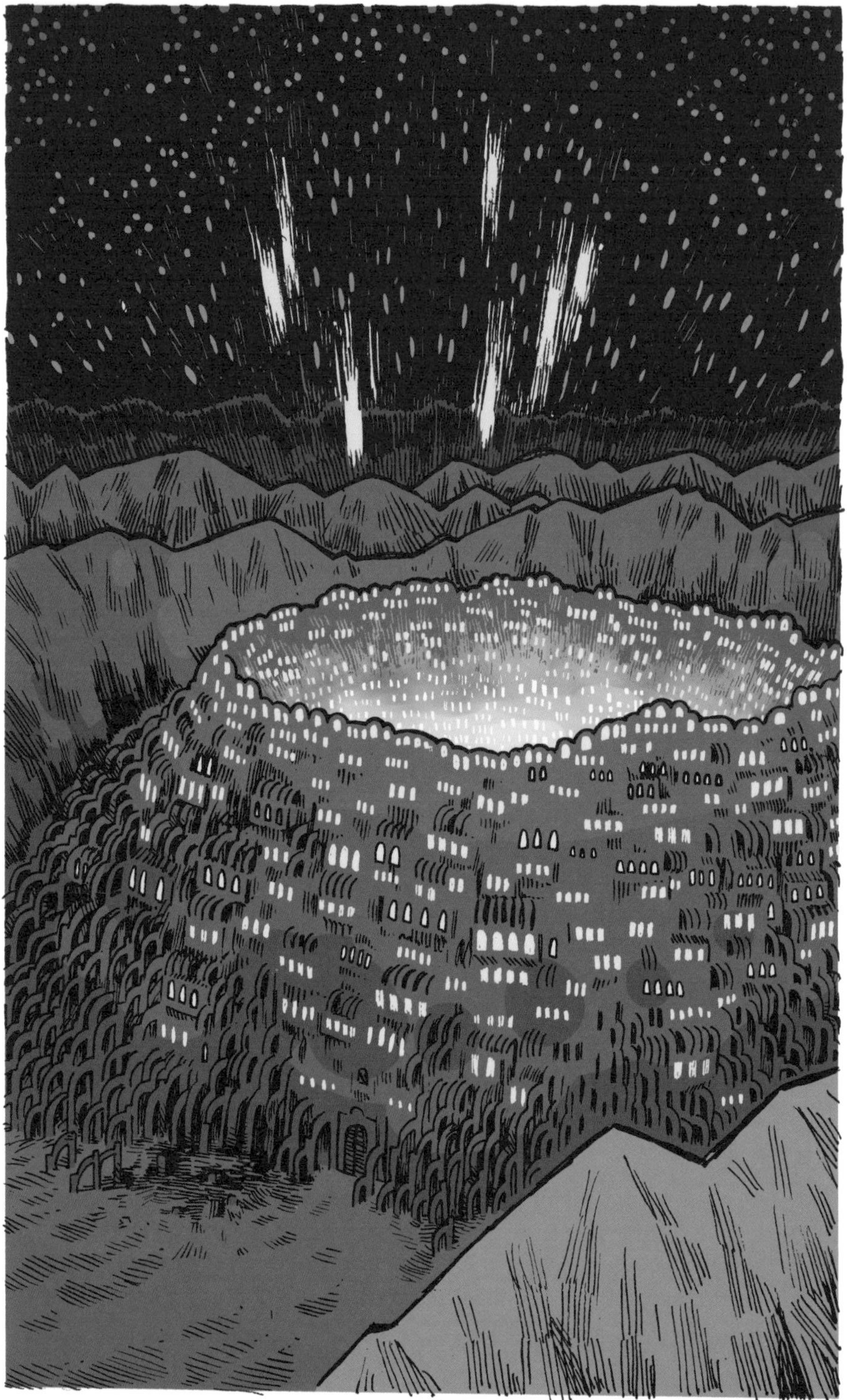

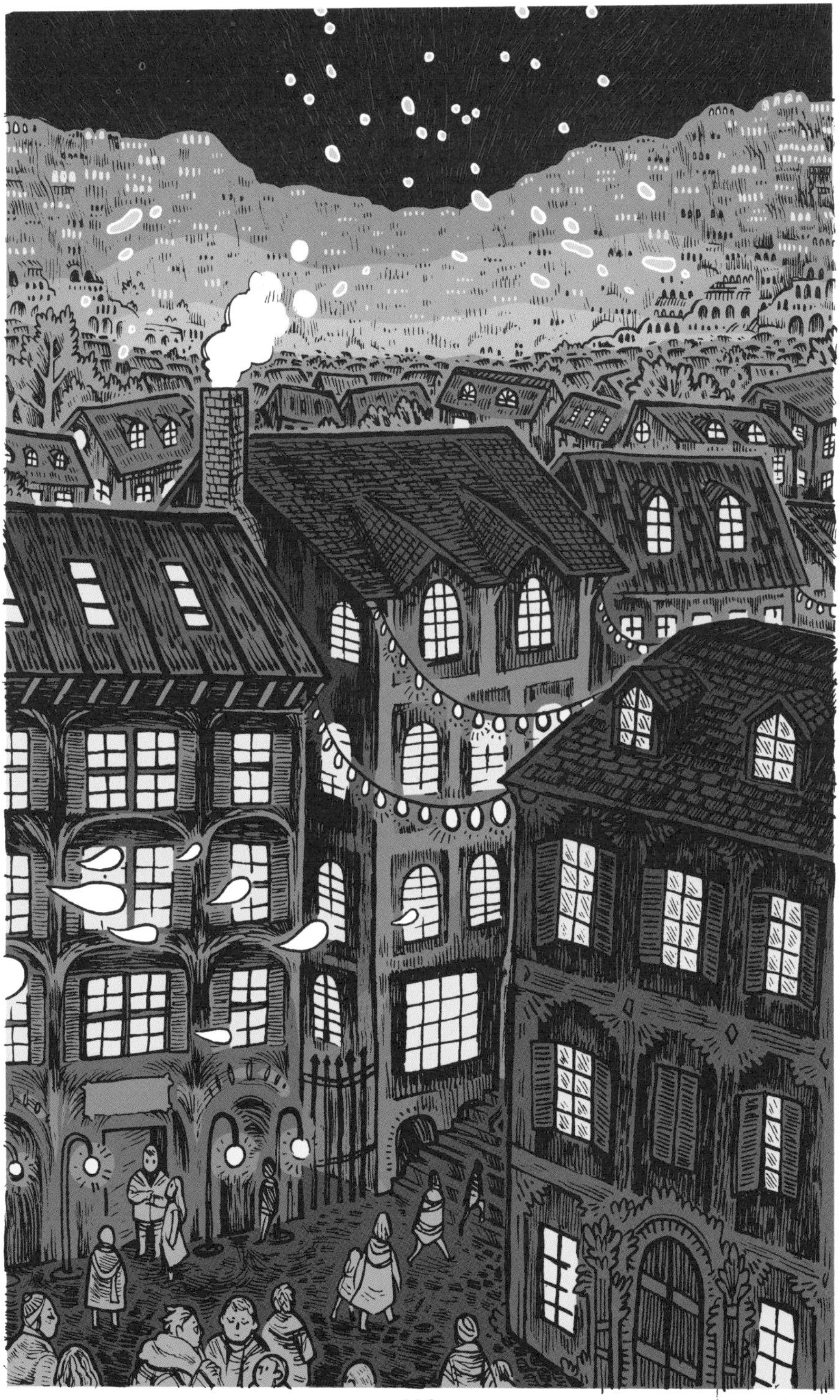

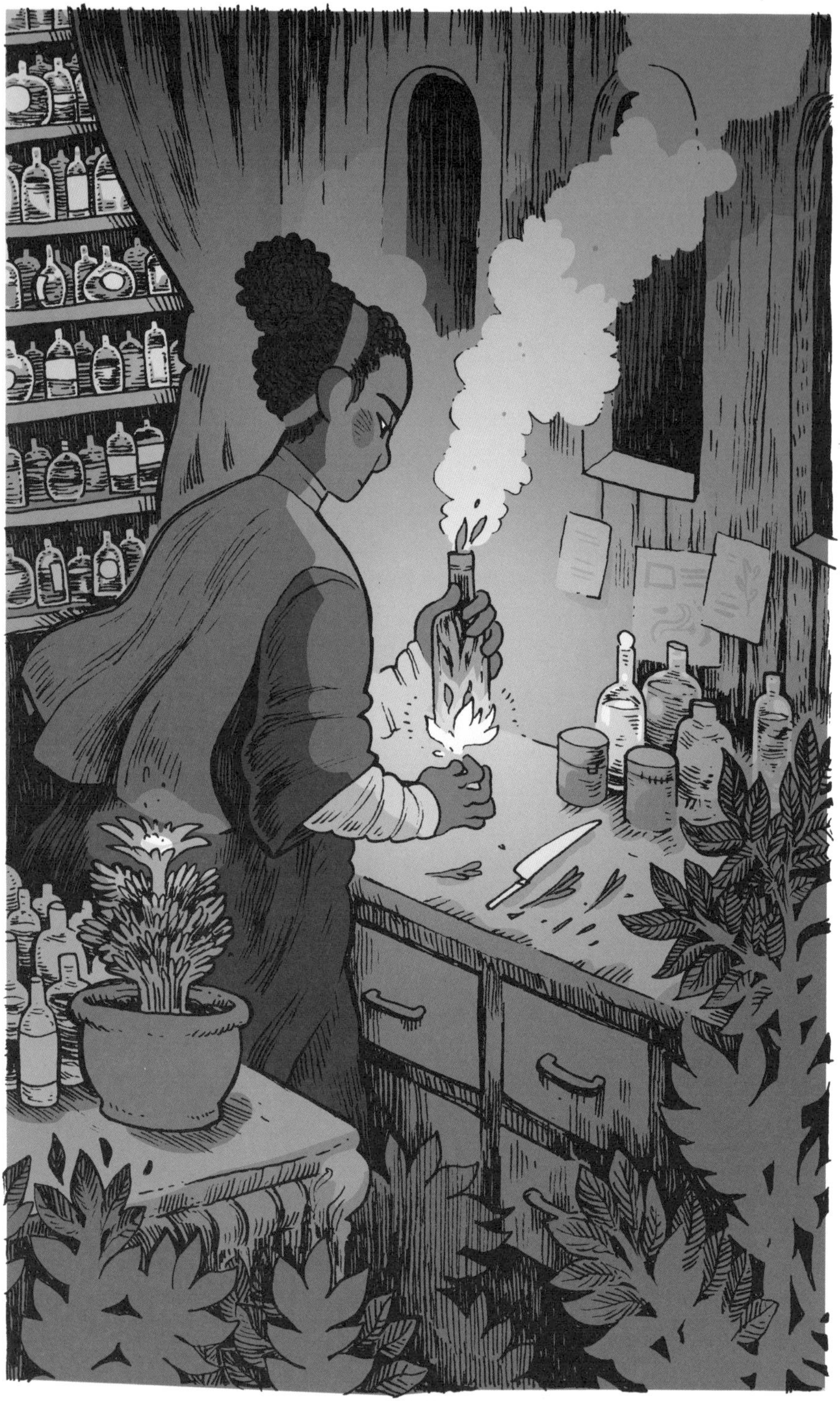

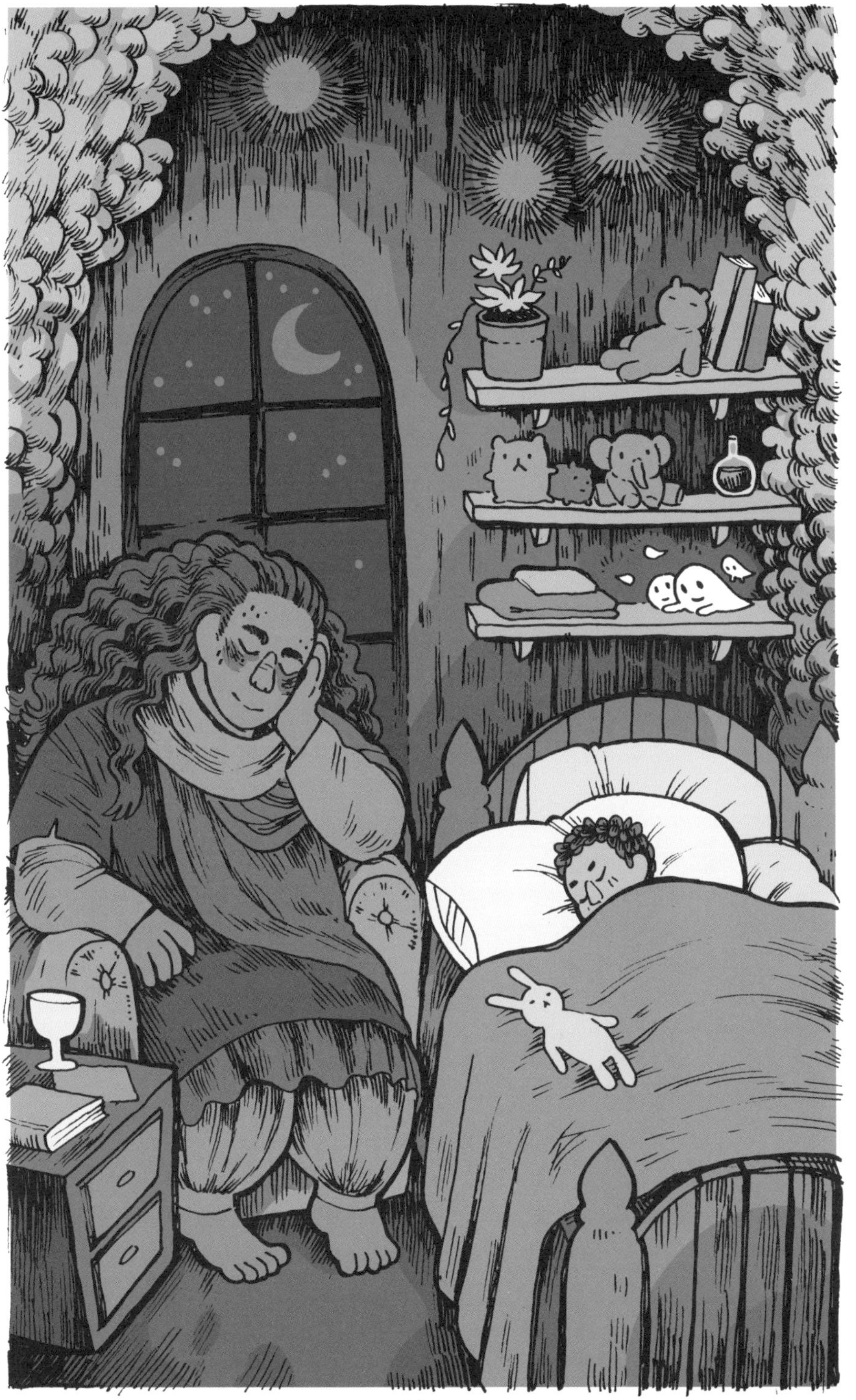

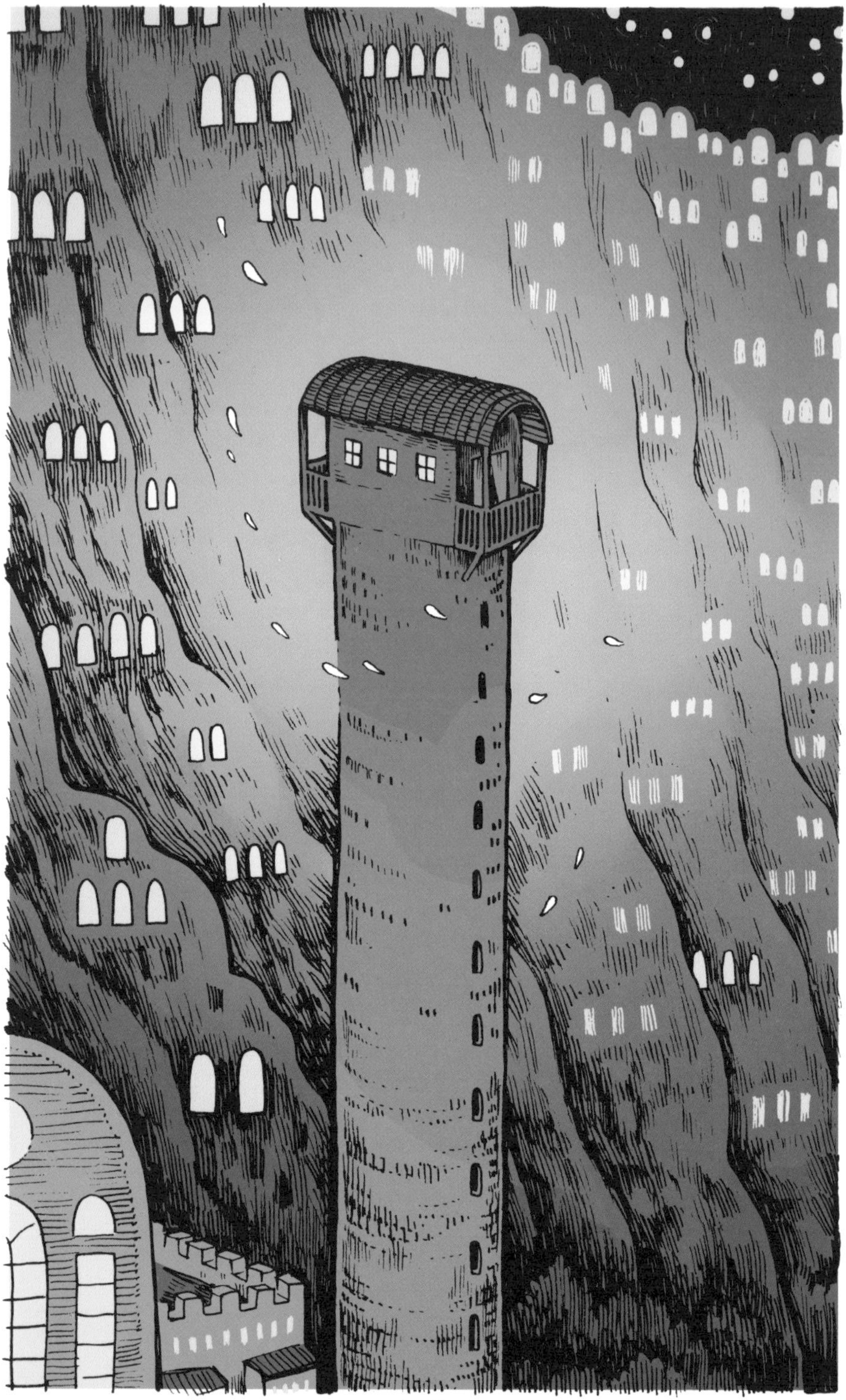

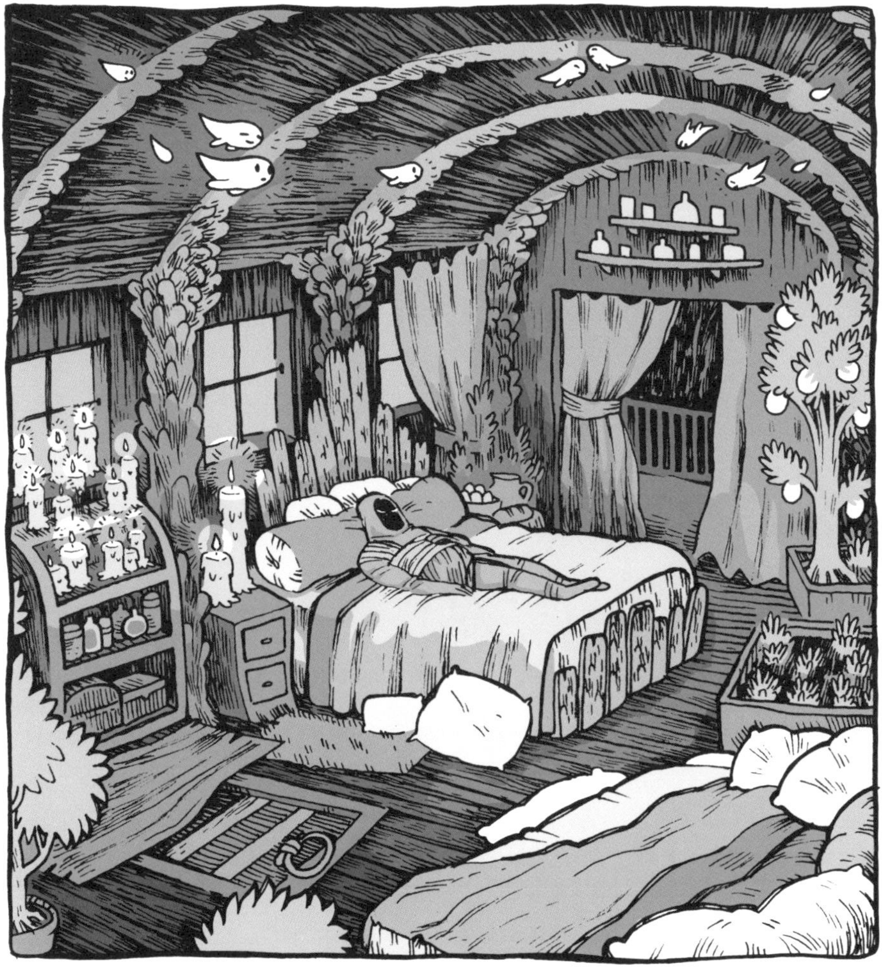

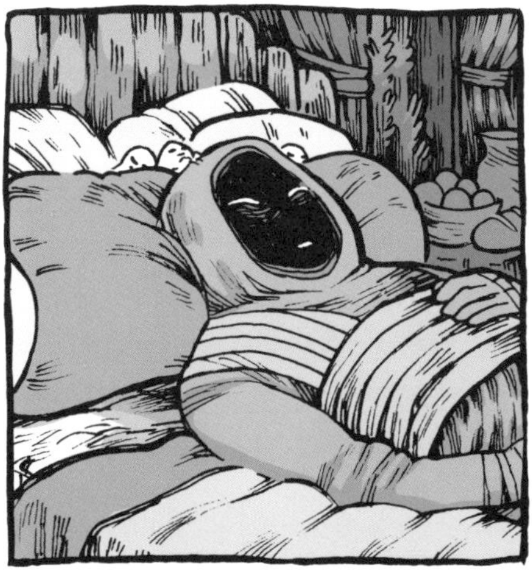

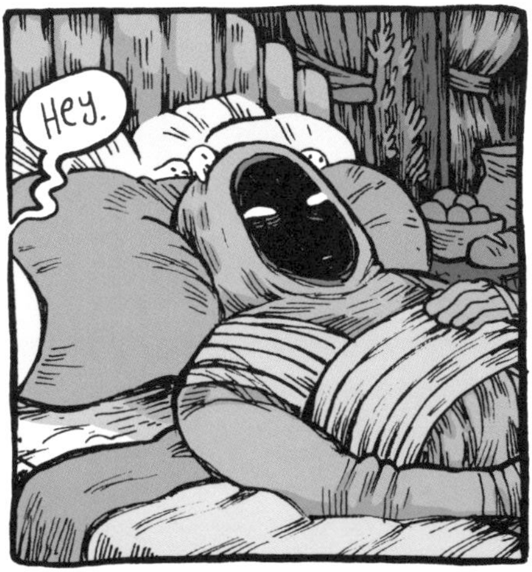
Hey.

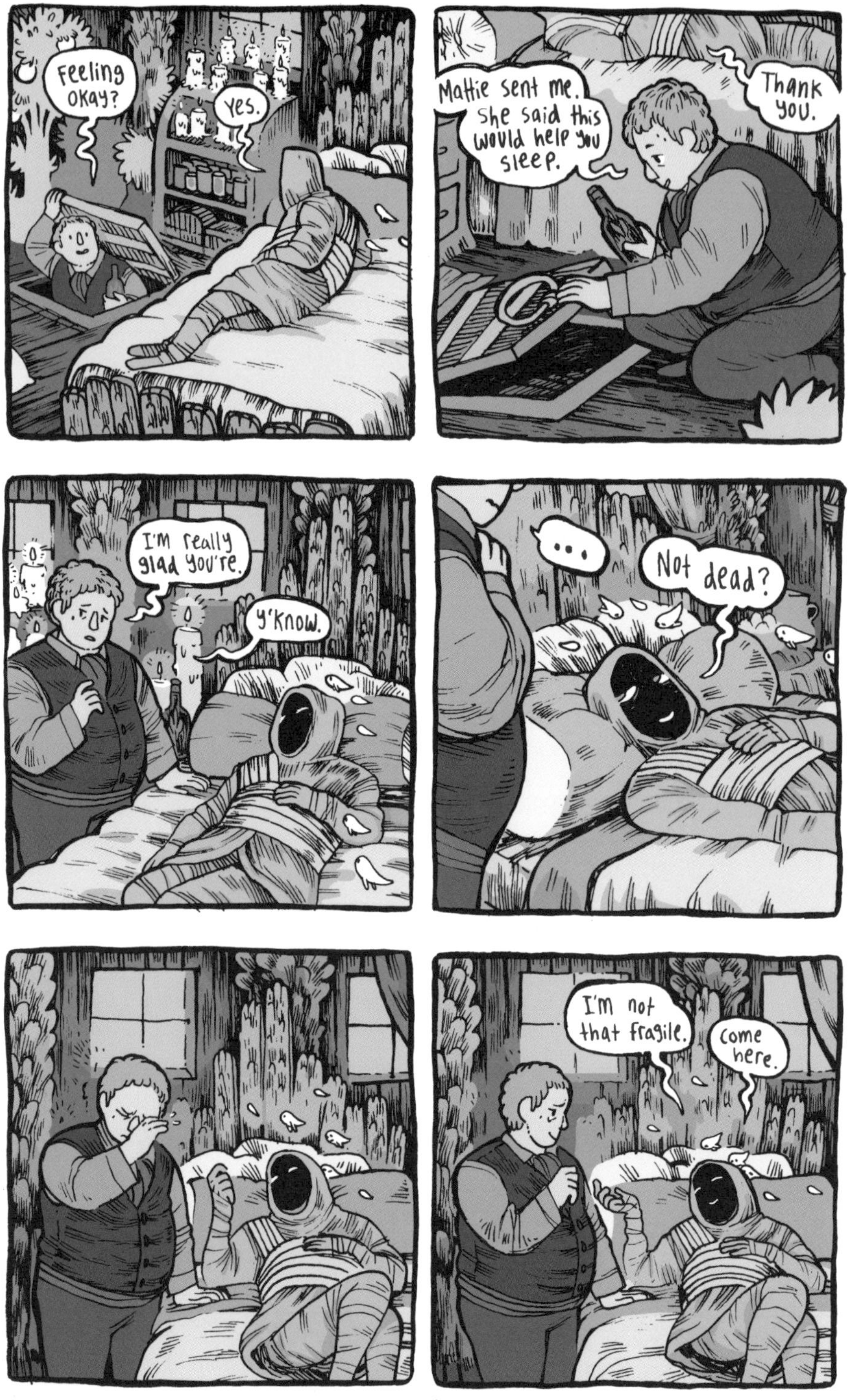
Feeling okay?
Yes.
Mattie sent me. She said this would help you sleep.
Thank you.
I'm really glad you're.
y'know.
...
Not dead?
I'm not that fragile.
Come here.

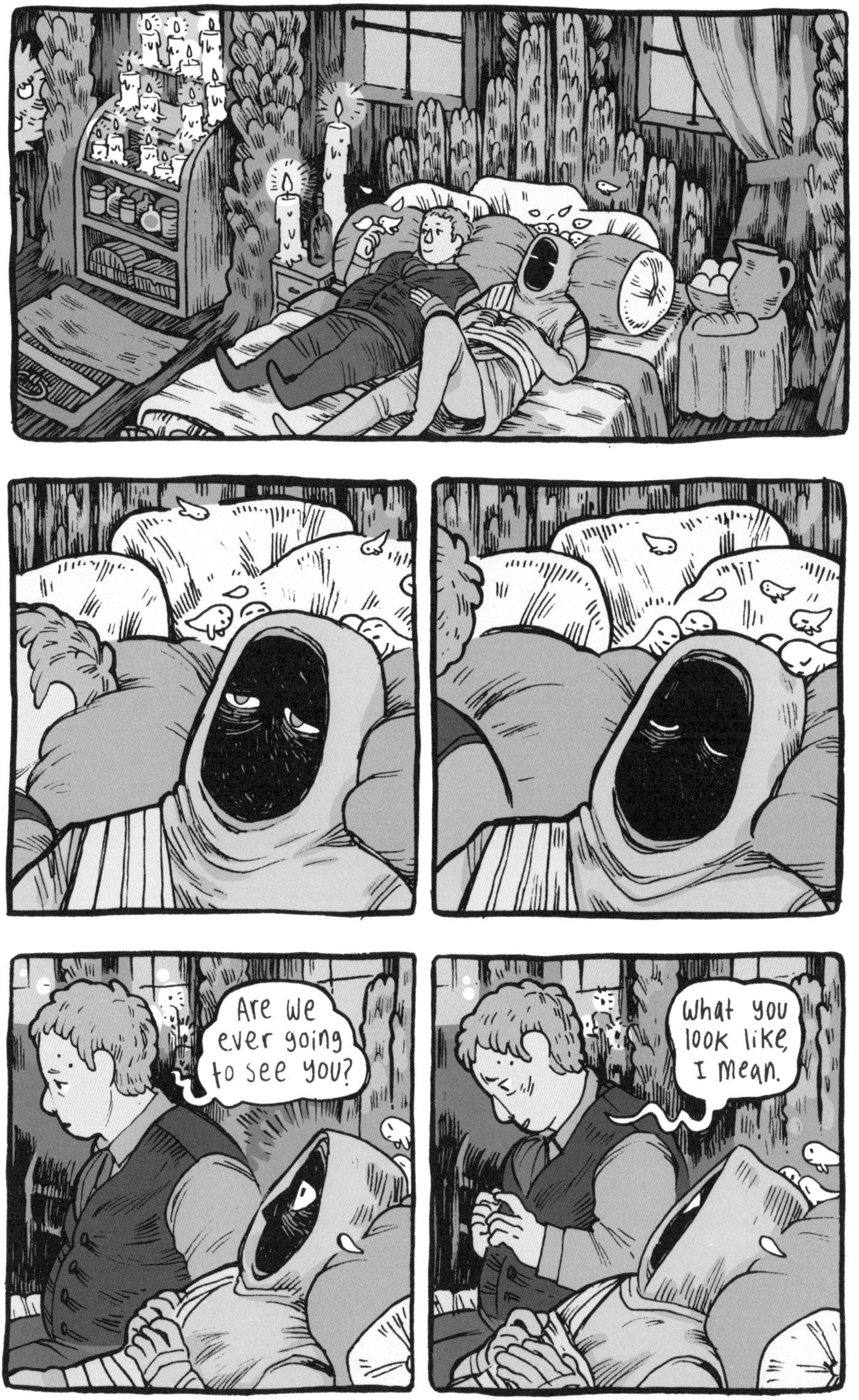
Are we ever going to see you?
What you look like, I mean.

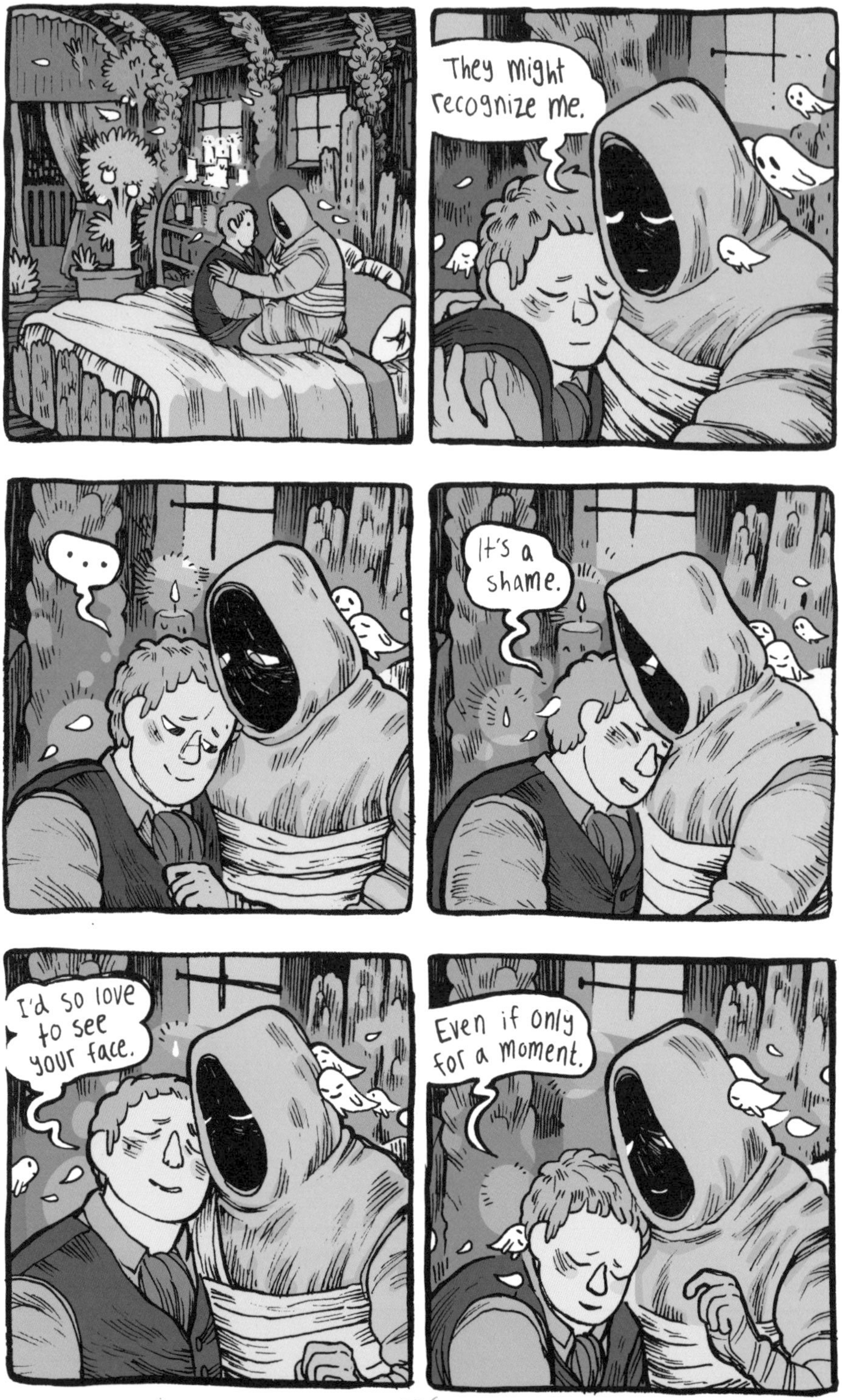
They might recognize me.
...
It's a shame.
I'd so love to see your face.
Even if only for a moment.

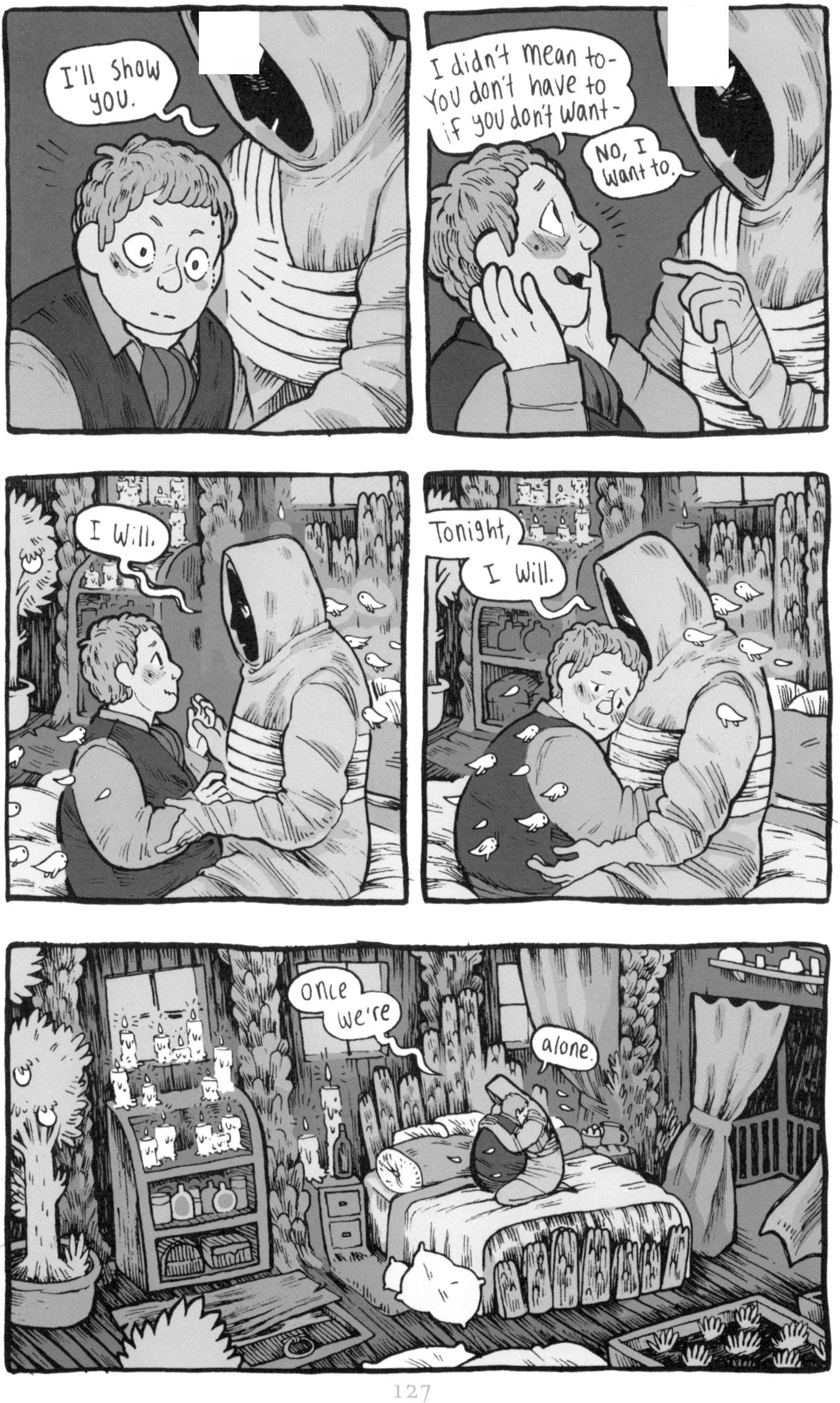
I'll show you.
I didn't mean to- You don't have to if you don't want-
No, I want to.
I Will.
Tonight,
I Will.
Once we're
alone.

Maria Capelle Frantz is a
cartoonist, illustrator and animator
currently living in Portland, Oregon.
She spends her days baking, gardening,
and drawing a ridiculous amount of comics.

@mariacfrantz
mariafrantz.net